✵

# *Frailties*

✳ NANCY GEYER

# *Frailties*

LITTLE, BROWN AND COMPANY
BOSTON      TORONTO

FIRST EDITION

The characters and events portrayed in this book are fictitious.
Any similarities to real persons, living or dead, are purely
coincidental and not intended by the author.

*Library of Congress Cataloging-in-Publication Data*

Geyer, Nancy.
  Frailties.
  I. Title.
PS3557.E9F7  1985      813'.54      85-18050
ISBN 0-316-30892-7

BP

*Published simultaneously in Canada*
*by Little, Brown & Company (Canada) Limited*

PRINTED IN THE UNITED STATES OF AMERICA

To
Bob

# ❉ PROLOGUE

*Monday afternoon, September 12*

IT'S GOING to rain," Zoe Benson thought as she hurried from the grocery store to her car. A folded flyer had been placed under the windshield wiper. She put her sack of groceries on the seat, then reached for the paper. Probably some advertisement, she thought, and opened it.

MRS. BENSON, TELL YOUR HUSBAND YOU WILL BE HARMED
IF HE DOESN'T STOP, FOR "I AM A MAN MORE SINN'D AGAINST
THAN SINNING."

"What kind of joke is this?" she asked herself. "I mean, *really*." Her thoughts braked. "Or is it a joke?" Quickly she looked around the parking lot. The usual ladies were rushing into the store at five o'clock for last-minute dinner items. She peered at cars lined up between the yellow lines. A dog barked from the back seat of a station wagon. The rest were empty. Nervously running her fingers through her hair, she reread the note. Somewhere in the back of her mind, she registered that the type was elite and the paper an expensive bond. She crumpled the note into her pocket then wheeled her car out of the parking lot. Whether the threat was real or a prank, she had to get away. Now. This minute. She had to get home. Why home, she wasn't sure, because she would be alone there. Lance wouldn't be through at the theatre until eight. She tried to concentrate on their evening. Dinner would be late and simple. The artichokes in the sack beside her. Afterward they would have Drambuie and insignificant conversation. She would tell him then, not before. Or maybe she wouldn't tell him. Lately she shared little of her life with her busy, preoccupied husband. Besides, why create an uproar? The note was obviously the work of a prankster.

As she guided her Toyota through traffic, her free hand reached into her pocket. Her fingers closed around the note.

✻ PART I

*Three months earlier:*
*Saturday night, June 11 —*
        *Wednesday afternoon, August 31*

THE EYES were cobalt. The aim dead center. If stares could shatter glass, this one would have sent the full-length mirror flying. Lance Benson stepped back for a better view. And approved. There was not an ounce of excess flesh on his six-foot frame. The cheekbones were still prominent, the olive skin unveined, the straight nose unbroken, the hair thick and blond just as it had been when he was a teenager racing along the edge of Lake Ontario with his old dog Bailey, the long rays of winter sunlight stretching out as if to cast them both in bronze, the moment frozen.

At forty-six, he detected little outward change, unless for the better. (He reasoned that lines only etched mystery and distinction into a man's face.) What was happening inside was another matter. Inwardly he was beginning to scream. He had always done so, yet now the sound seemed primal. Its source could be pinpointed. Unwittingly he had structured that part of his life over which he had control — the adult part — as if it were a box into which he had stepped and the lid been closed.

Tonight would offer a reprieve. The lid would be opened a crack so that he could draw in one long gulp of air. And he was grateful. Grateful to himself. After all, he had done the work to make such relief possible.

The scream inside subsided. But it would start shrilling again. He knew that. Just as soon as the evening's festivities were over. Boredom (the sameness of it all) and responsibility (everybody wanting something, *demanding* something) would slam the lid down again. But maybe not so tightly. The theatre's seventeenth season was drawing to a close. He would have time to sit by his pool and think. Time to conceive a way to climb out of the box and stay out. Since boyhood, he'd been mapping out strategies. Lately, however, he hadn't used that skill to help himself. His expertise had gone into the theatre that he'd founded . . . And into Houston, which he was getting a little sick of, with its tangled freeways and oppressive weather. He smiled, yet his left eyelid twitched as it had done in stressful moments for the past thirty years. He was visualizing himself across an entire ocean. Left behind would be The Arch Theatre, and Houston, trapped in the box. Somehow he would devise a plan to convert that fantasy into reality. And one thing he had already figured out. Money — lots of it — would have to be the focal point of that plan.

He slipped into his dinner jacket and ordered, "Let's go."

The order was rebuffed by part of his problem — a diminutive woman who stood not more than five feet away from him.

"Hey, not so fast!" Her gray eyes widened.

"You want to make a grand entrance, is that it?" He stretched out on the king-size bed, his back against a pillow. Long ago, he'd learned to project a cool detachment in the face of real or potential controversy.

"You know me better than that." She was brushing blush across her cheekbones, high in a face that was smooth and translucent, beautiful only because it seemed to have been sculpted like that of a small china doll — straight nose, narrow lips, deep-set eyes fringed with dark lashes.

"I suppose." Through lowered eyelids, he observed her run a comb through her dark hair, worn short and close against her skull. "Like a cap," he thought. Dressed in the proper garb, she could have passed for a child. Though shaped exquisitely, his thirty-six-year-old wife reminded him at times of a thin, small boy about to enter puberty. Not tonight, however. Tonight she was well on her way to being regal. Zoe could pull off that act whenever she chose.

"Do me, please." She had come to stand close by the bed.

He ran a finger lazily down her bare spine.

"What did you have in mind?"

"What do you think?" She ignored his playful gesture.

He straightened for the tedious task of buttoning twenty-eight —

he counted as he worked — small, round buttons up his wife's back.

"You do good work." She smiled, then glanced around the room.

In search of her purse, he knew.

"At the foot of the bed." He felt he was directing an asinine play.

"Oh!" She stuffed Kleenex into the purse.

In case of hay fever, he knew that too, what with pollen covering Texas.

"Now we can go." She stood before him in her white silk threaded with silver. Shimmering. His wife stood there shimmering.

Suddenly he was in no great hurry. In spite of the bouquets which were about to be strewn in his path, the theatre's end-of-season gala was going to offer him nothing new. It would be more of the same. Same old crap in the same old box.

"Well?"

"I'm moving."

"I should hope so. You're the star."

The accolades had already begun. And in his own house.

As he kissed her, he thought, "What would you think, Zoe Harrington Benson, if I were to announce to you that even intelligent and beautiful women eventually bore?"

So what if he was forty-six and she was only twenty-three? That wasn't any reason for her to admit defeat, was it? History was on her side. Look at Charlie Chaplin and Eugene O'Neill's kid daughter. That had been some marriage. And Arthur Miller and Marilyn Monroe. Sandra Lowrey stepped into her costume and frowned. OK, so that one hadn't worked out. There were others. Which others? She couldn't think. Lately it seemed older women were going after younger men or vice versa. Who recently had it the other way around? . . . Why, of course. Bo and John Derek. And he'd even left his wife! That made it perfect. She brightened. It was not impossible. Lance Benson just might leave Zoe and marry her. Besides, didn't she and Lance have lots of things in common with Bo and John? Wasn't Lance the director and she the actress? And, in the looks department, Lance was every bit as handsome, only in a blond way, as John. And she herself resembled Bo. At least, they both were blonds. "Gorgeous" and "glorious" were adjectives she frequently heard about her hair. Even old Mr. Hook had come up to her after a performance last year and, touching a strand, had remarked, "Rapunzel's tresses." (She guessed so! That had been her most favorite of all the fairy tales Miss Traylor had read to them at The Good Shepherd. For sure, she'd let her hair grow to astounding lengths. Well, maybe not astounding, but certainly to her shoulder blades.)

Her concentration sidetracked, she began stacking her physical assets against those of Bo Derek. The full lips compressed. And then she smiled.

Concerning eyes . . . Bo could give up. Hers were better. The pizza-parlor manager she'd dumped four months ago — because she'd decided it was best to be absolutely pure and free while praying that Lance Benson would come knocking on her door — had given her a bracelet with all these little green stones in it, to match her dynamite eyes, he'd said. So what if the stones weren't real? One day Lance would cover her with emeralds. Suddenly she had this mental image of him sticking an emerald right in the middle of her forehead, like one of those red dots they wore in India. Last week she'd almost knocked down an alien, she guessed it was, in Solomon's department store, and her nose had smacked right into that blood-red spot. She hadn't stared. (That had been The Good Shepherd's training coming through.) "Excuse me, I'm so sorry," she'd said and the woman had been real sweet, like people bumped into her dot every day.

Recalling her own embarrassment, she giggled. There was no one to hear. Betsy had left thirty minutes before to meet her karate instructor for drinks, bitching on her way out the door. "Now, Sandy, don't leave your makeup all over the bathroom, for Christ's sake!" Oh, she hated roommates. She hated this apartment. Well, she wasn't going to let such negativity ruin her night.

She worked black tights up her legs and over her hips.

Now . . . about bodies. Bo came out ahead. There might be a tie if only she could lose five or ten pounds. But she did love to eat all those rich, gooey things they'd never been able to afford at the orphanage. Besides, being tall, she reasoned, allowed her to carry a few extra pounds.

Her scrutiny continued.

. . . Regarding breasts, Bo's were superior. Solely because big boobs weren't currently in vogue. Though she'd never known that to stop any man from staring hard. Except Lance. He was too sophisticated to do anything so obvious. His observations were more general. He'd sweep his eyes down your entire body, then make some genteel remark like, "Sandra, you look ravishing today." It made you feel good, but it didn't mean much. He'd also told his secretary that. She'd overheard him. And, once, he'd even flattered an aging actress who had hair growing out of her chin.

Oh, she wanted more, much more, from him. And she would get exactly what she wanted. All she had to do was pray every night, down on her knees, and, if the Lord didn't mind, help Him figure out a way.

She stuck a fake mole high on her left breast, then lowered her bodice. While Bo preferred a tan, she liked to keep her skin as white as a kitten's paws, as white as cream skimming over strawberries. And, because her skin was like that, she was glad her dumb old costume left her shoulders bare.

It *was* a dumb costume. For a dumb role. Last night they'd taken seventeen curtain calls, holding hands — only thing was, she'd been hidden in the next-to-last row with no room to inch up. Thank God, the run was over. But then so was the season.

That made her sad.

Straight through the summer now she'd be slaving away at Budget Drugs . . . and missing Lance. At least the cast got to attend the gala, even if they did have to wear their *Cyrano* costumes. She'd have been *truly* ravishing in something flowing and elegant. Oh well, who cared? Tonight she would edge her way as close to Lance Benson as she possibly could. Maybe if she got close enough he'd be struck with revelation. Why not? It happened all the time in the Bible. She imagined him awestruck. "Why, here she's been running around my theatre for three whole years," he'd exclaim, "and only now am I realizing this girl is my destiny!"

That was one scene she intended to replay in her mind at least fifty times.

She glanced at her watch then scooped up a shawl. Leaving behind an array of cosmetic jars and tubes across the bathroom counter, she hurried outside to her Volks.

Old age was a pain in the ass. Such was Lowell Hook's assessment as he stood before the glass door and stared out at the city.

Lights were turning on. Nighttime Houston reminded him of a

towering Christmas tree. Or maybe a woman in a fancy dress. He preferred that image. He should get himself downstairs: Jason had already brought the car around. For a few minutes, however, he needed to stand here, looking at his city.

Strange that he felt pensive when he was about to spend an entire evening having champagne corks pop in his face and pretty girls brush up against him. And he would relish every moment, knowing his money had helped put The Arch on the map and kept it there. Others annually wrote their hefty checks — Charles Stanton, for example. But he, Lowell Alfred Hook, consistently contributed the largest amount.

Before he got too inflated, he'd better stick a pin in his own balloon. The real credit, of course, went to Benson. Building a theatre from the ground up took a hell of a lot more than money. The same could be said for any substantial undertaking. He, of all people, should know that. Hadn't he used common sense, guts, and vision to propel himself out of an unpainted wood-framed house in which six people had lived, packed like sardines? Fifty-five years ago, it had been. A whole lifetime since built on common sense, guts, and vision. And heart. A person had to have heart if he was going to be worth more than a hill of beans to himself or anyone else.

Recalling his past, he suddenly longed for one of the fine Havana cigars he had smoked in his youth when he had first begun carving out an empire of land and oil and timber and cattle. But mostly oil.

Now for that, he'd take credit. Not many had started out on an oil rig and ended up wildcatting until they sat on top of some ninety-eight thousand oil- and gas-producing acres spread throughout the state of Texas. Not many woke up in a penthouse centered in one of the world's most impressive cities. Not many had received medals and citations for being the city's most beloved and respected humanitarian. Not many had — what else?

Enough! Who was he kidding? Counting his blessings didn't alter his mood. Tonight he'd rather take off this monkey suit — he hated tuxedos — crawl back into bed, and read a good western.

He slid open the door and stepped out onto his terrace. Traffic sounds from Main Street drifted up thirty-six stories to where he leaned against a railing. Maybe anticipating the gala's high-decibel clamor, all that bursting-at-the-seams vitality, had precipitated his melancholy. He felt old. Often he didn't feel a day over fifty. Of late, however, there were so many "forbiddens." "Doctor's orders," Mrs. Mabry kept saying as she hid his cigars and liquor and pushed strange little pills at him. That was another thing. It was a shame for a man his age to feel closer to his housekeeper than to any other living soul. Where were the wife and children he'd thought he'd have? Nowhere. That was where. Well, it was too late to start complaining. Regretting.

. . . It was a clear night. A little muggy, but that was to be expected this time of year. Masses of stars and a sliver of moon hung over the city. He breathed in the night air. Suddenly he felt better.

Bull and bullshit! He did love this city. It had been good to him. He loved life. It had been a challenging span — moderately tempered with wildness — of more than seven decades. All he had to do now was to hold on to both — life and the city — for as long as he could.

He'd better get moving. Jason would be wondering if he'd had a coronary up here. He needed to do something special for his chauffeur, considering all the poor fellow had to put up with.

Stepping into his elevator, he ran a brown-spotted hand over his silver hair. His stooped shoulders straightened. Tonight would be fine. He'd light up the imported cigar he'd found hidden behind a flower pot, tip his glass toward that champagne fountain he understood Winifred Reese had rigged up, and eye all the pretty young girls. He might be seventy-three years old, but he wasn't blind. Nor was he six feet under!

His packed bags were at the foot of the stairs. Obviously, they would go in separate cars. Afterward, Roselyn would return to their house. Victor Solomon — his jaw jutted in a dark, handsome face that exuded the confidence of the rich and successful — sipped his scotch.

This is one hell of a house, he observed, staring up at the scrolled ceiling in their bedroom. The stately Georgian was solid and spacious enough to last forever, which was how long he had assumed their marriage would last.

He shifted his position on the chaise longue and drank deeply. After the gala, where would he go? Probably to the Remington. That should do him until he found an apartment. What the hell?

Did Roselyn think running a department store, even if it had been handed down to you intact and thriving, allowed time for such nonsense? Was all fun and games? No, she thought worse. Judging from what had spewed from her mouth less than two hours ago.

When he'd come home from taking the Baron up for a circle around Galveston Bay, she'd met him at the door.

"You're late."

"For what?" he'd asked.

"For me!"

She'd walked into the living room and he'd followed.

"So I'm a little late."

"And a little drunk!"

"Look, Roselyn, all I had was a couple of drinks after I got down. Is that a crime?"

"Victor . . . I don't want you to think what I'm about to say is something that's been brought on solely by what you did this afternoon."

"I can't see why you're so ticked off just because I'm a little late."

"Two hours late!"

"All right, two hours!"

"Just let me finish. I'd planned to tell you this tomorrow — after the gala. But I've changed my mind. Now all I want is to get it over with, be done with it."

"You're pregnant." He'd thought a joke would clear the air.

"Hardly."

So, a joke hadn't been in order.

There she had sat, a coffee table between them, her long tanned legs crossed, one sandaled foot pointed as she announced, "Victor, I'm leaving you."

He'd straightened then leaned forward.

He must have misunderstood. This couldn't be the same woman whose strongest objection to his life-style was "Oh, Victor, grow up!" Or, on a really bad day, "Victor, you're disgusting."

"What's gotten into you?" he'd asked.

"I want you to move out."

He'd wanted a drink then, but he'd figured that would really be pushing his luck.

"You're not serious?"

"Dead serious." Her brown eyes had met his head-on.

"If today didn't do it . . . what did?" He'd been unable to think of a single outrageous thing he'd done in the past month that he hadn't been doing for years.

"I took a good, hard look at myself."

He'd stared at his wife. Her black hair was up in a ponytail, her face as striking as when she'd been crowned a University of Texas beauty. That had been nineteen years ago. Christ! Eighteen years of marriage, two children — and now this. He had shaken his head.

"What'd you see?"

"I'm disgusting."

"That's a switch."

"Victor, I can't live like this anymore. I can't live with your drinking, your taking off in that plane — never knowing if you're going to crash if you're drinking —"

That had been unfair.

"I don't drink when I'm flying, you know that!" he'd fired back.

She'd ignored him.

"I can't take your women, your hours — I can't take *myself!* I just can't." She'd begun to cry.

And he had moved in.

"Look, Roselyn, for God's sake, I love you. Come on, *try*."

"I've been trying! And trying and trying." She'd gotten up and walked away from him over to the fireplace. He remembered she'd picked up a figurine and handled it, gently, as if it were one of their children. She was good with the children. But so was he. Maybe he didn't go in for family outings and such, but he was damn good with both of them.

"What about Chad and Rebecca?" he'd asked.

She'd put the tiny china shepherdess back on the mantel and come to kneel beside him, a strained smile on her face.

"Victor, this is for the best. Believe me, everything's going to fall into place. I'll get a job —"

Unthinkingly he'd laughed. It had come out short. Brittle.

"Go ahead! Laugh!" She'd moved quickly away from him again.

". . . Roselyn, I'm sorry. Get a job. But stay here."

"I *am* staying here. You're the one who's leaving. And I'm going to get a job. I'm not sure what, but something fulfilling. I'm going to be part of something other than a messed-up marriage. I'm going to make a difference on my own — as an independent, thinking woman!"

"You sound like Gloria Steinem!"

She'd drawn herself up. Amazing. She'd looked twice her average height.

"I'd like you to leave."

"Just like that?"

"Just like that."

He'd felt a fool, but lamely, as if grasping for a flimsy lifeline, he'd asked, "What about tonight?"

For a moment, she'd hesitated before her chin lifted. "Oh, I'm going. But alone."

"The hell you say!" He'd stalked into the den then, for a drink, yelling over his shoulder, "I'm the board member, remember?"

She'd stood in the doorway, watching the scotch miss his glass and slosh on the carpet.

"Victor, I'm going because I have to. I've worked hard on this gala. And I still have . . . responsibilities."

"As my wife!"

"As entertainment chairman!"

"Which you're certainly providing." He'd dropped an ice cube emphatically into his drink.

That remark had gotten him what she probably considered her sensible adult approach.

". . . I promise to stay on the opposite side of the theatre."

"Well, now, that's exactly what I had in mind." He'd shoved the liquor bottle back into the cabinet.

"All right, so it'll be awkward . . . We both have to go."

He'd lifted his eyebrows. "Have to, Roselyn?"

"Have to!" As if to pacify a child, she'd added, "Who knows? We might even surprise ourselves and have fun."

Again he had raised his eyebrows. Then he'd lifted his glass and toasted air. "To a fun evening."

"Victor, all I meant was . . . maybe it won't be so bad."

"No, it's going to be *fun*."

"All right, fun! You have fun, I'll have fun! Which, quite frankly, is something I haven't had in a *very long time*."

That did it.

He had taken a deep swallow, looked over the glass at his wife and slowly said, "Then, Roselyn, you just go ahead and do that very thing."

At least, she hadn't locked him out of their bedroom.

"You have to pack and dress." She'd stated the obvious.

So, silently, he had done the obvious. And silently, though she was crying, he knew, she had bathed and dressed. And now, he assumed, she was ready to go. She had turned from the mirror toward which she'd leaned for the past fifteen minutes redoing her makeup.

"Well . . ." He placed the empty glass on a table. "I suppose we should walk out together, for appearances' sake. What with the baby-sitter here."

"That won't be necessary. She's seen your bags."

"Good thinking." He flipped off the bedroom lights, bowed low to his wife of eighteen years, then pushed on, roughly, ahead of her.

Martin Fletcher III, his black tie slightly askew, closed the folder he had brought home from the office. This was ridiculous. Caroline would be dressed and downstairs in no time. Why tackle work now? In fact, they would already have been on their way to the gala except that she'd taken a long nap. He could have understood her jogging an extra mile, then hopping late into the shower. But a nap? (To sleep during daytime hours was a rarity for the "Human Dynamo," as Justine had lovingly nicknamed her mother.) And when she'd awakened, she hadn't been her usual effervescent self. On the contrary, she'd been quiet as a tomb. Now that he thought about it, she'd seemed a little down yesterday. He pulled nervously at his moustache, thin like a strip of India ink drawn above his tight lips. Furrows deepened then smoothed across his broad brow. Before the night was over whatever was troubling his wife would surface. Because they were best friends, they were also confidants.

Sometimes he felt they were more friends than lovers. No, that wasn't true. It was just — he tugged at his moustache. Three decades of being faithful to one woman couldn't help but make a man occasionally wonder what it would be like to touch, once again, firm young flesh. And going to bed with his wife didn't offer the excitement that it had in those first spine-tingling years. He should be ashamed! What would the priests of his childhood think? Besides, Caroline — tall and graceful with good, though small, breasts, and long thick hair often dramatically French-braided — was the most attractive fifty-year-old woman he'd ever seen. Well, almost ever seen. One had to rule out movie stars and some of those River Oaks women who yearly had lines eased from their faces. By fifty, a Houston woman who liked the outdoors had usually acquired, along with her suntan, skin like an armadillo's back. He shuddered. At least from their first Texas summer Caroline had taken precautions. A floppy hat was her trademark whenever they went out on their boat or took to the golf course. Still, his fondest dream was that Caroline might have remained physically as she'd been that first time he'd seen her, the blind date he'd been hesitant to accept.

He smiled, remembering how she'd held out her hand and flirtatiously said, "Martin, if you've come all the way from Yale just to take me to dinner, I'm eternally grateful to you for getting me away from broccoli." Always overly serious, he'd become flustered. "Broccoli?" he'd asked. She'd told him her theory that Vassar had been bequeathed land solely for growing broccoli. He'd laughed and decided Caroline Beaufort was unequivocally marvelous. Even so, he'd almost spoiled things by blurting out that he was only in Poughkeepsie to provide moral support for his roommate, who within the next hour would be informing his childhood sweetheart that marriage was out because he'd fallen in love with an Italian from the Bronx.

That first evening with Caroline had brought revelation. Over seafood and a bottle of wine, they'd discovered that not only were they both scholarship students at their respective schools but also they both were Philadelphians, having grown up less than a mile from each other. Fate had outdone itself!

He looked at his watch. His usually punctual wife was acting as if she didn't want to attend an event she'd been talking about for weeks, an event at which they would receive recognition for being the only husband and wife team that sat on The Arch's board. Well, he wouldn't add to her problem, whatever it was, by rushing her.

Meticulously, he worked the thick folder back into his briefcase, which he then zipped with finality, as if sealing his thoughts. He returned the briefcase to its upright position against one side of his recliner and lowered the chair's back. He closed his eyes. The

thoughts obstinately poured out and rolled on. Their course, however, veered, unpleasantly mingling the present with the past.

Perhaps Caroline was right. "You're too conscientious," she
was prone to remark. There might have been some justification
for keeping his nose to the grindstone if he had been an empire-
builder. But he wasn't and never would be. Still, he couldn't complain. At fifty-three he was reconciled. But he was also tired. Sometimes he felt like a roach caught in the fumes of Powell Insecticides.
He was tired of that feeling. He was also tired of being comfortably
well-off rather than wealthy. His financial situation probably
wouldn't have bothered him except that, with all the charity work
they were involved in, they ran in social circles where cars were
frequently chauffeured and boats were more often yachts than
skiffs. He popped his knuckles and tried to relax. Caroline was
definitely right. After all, a man who was only Powell's vice president of personnel shouldn't be bringing home work every night.
At least he rarely broke an iron-clad rule: Home by six-fifteen to
spend the evening with his wife, even if more often than not a
briefcase sat between them. Suppose he were to slow down? What
would he do with himself? Well, for one thing, he would lounge
for hours in this chair, which he loved. Caroline had given it to
him on their last wedding anniversary; before he could open his
mouth, she'd warned, "Now, Martin, don't complain. I know it's
expensive, but you deserve it." His fingers stroked crushed leather,
soft and pale blue like the kidskin gloves his mother had worn.
How often he'd held on to a gloved hand, begging her not to go
as she'd whirled out the door to a luncheon or tea. His twin had
never seemed agitated by her vanishing act. Well, heaven only
knew where those gloves were now. Things had a way of getting
lost, and his parents had been dead for years.

As a child he had known affluence. But he had never benefited
from the vast wealth that had been in his family for four gener-
ations. Several years before his birth, the stock market crash had
sent that empire toppling as if it had been no more than a sand
castle in the path of a tidal wave. But his parents had somehow
managed to hold onto a life-style that kept his brother and him
supplied with nannies and in private schools and themselves on
trips abroad. Later, he and his brother were to pay for that life-
style: there had been left to them only the brownstone in which

they'd grown up and some solid but meager investments. They'd liquidated what there had been to liquidate, and then, hurrying away from Philadelphia, they'd charted separate paths into the unknown to make fortunes which had not been made. On those rare occasions when they were reunited, each twin consoled the other. They and their families were comfortable.

Caroline's inheritance was no more impressive than his. Old money had not converted into new money. Often she laughed ruefully and mourned, "Poor Martin, my dowry was a chest of monogrammed silver. Period." Once he'd replied, "And a fine family name." At that she'd snorted, "Don't be a snob." Well, he was a snob. And he couldn't help it. But, then, so was she. Though they worked hard at charities for the good of the community, they also enjoyed other fruits of such labor, particularly an enviable social position. Wasn't Caroline to be chairman of The Arch's fall gala, by far the more impressive of the two events that the theatre annually held? Long ago his wife had made an astute observation. "Down here galas are the way to go," she'd said, "because Houston society always rallies to a party benefiting a good cause." Yes, Caroline was definitely the brains of their team. In fact, the path southwest had been charted by his wife; he had simply echoed, "Houston it is!"

Again he glanced at his watch. This time he called out, "Are you about ready?"

She hadn't heard.

He let it go. In a few minutes, he would ease out of his chair and climb the stairs to check her progress.

He looked around the sun room in which he sat. Decorated in cool shades of blues and creams with touches of bronze, the room gave him pleasure. Actually, the entire town house did. With Justine and Martin IV both away at college, Caroline and he had had no need for the five-bedroom house in which they'd lived since the children were small. And so they had moved here to this tall, glass town house, set back in exclusive Memorial Woods, where over the past year, surrounded by some thirty or so other fiftyish, graying couples — all of them with children away at college or married or simply somewhere out there experiencing life — he'd felt his days acquiring a mellow cast. If only he could relax about his work, quit jumping at orders from on high, and accept his substantial, if not bulging, bank account. For the hundredth time, he visualized an early retirement. That might fit him comfortably, like a pair of worn bermudas. Already a lot had been purchased near Austin and the plans drawn for a long, low rustic house. Payments were being made on a fine boat to course over a crystalline lake, the same lake they would eventually view from the deck of their retirement home. Their good life would become an exceptional life . . . but that was not yet possible.

"I'm sorry." Caroline stood in the doorway, stately in a gown the exact shade of blue as his recliner. As his mother's kid gloves.

"I was worried about you." Quickly he was out of his chair and beside her. Seldom did he forget that she measured, in her stocking feet, a full inch taller than he. But she had never seemed to mind. And though he knew that, with a paunch and thinning hair, he was no prize, his wife often made him feel — outstanding.

She did that now.

"I just took a little extra time to get ready for my handsome date."

He beamed and kissed her. But then he studied her lovely face. "You're sure there's nothing wrong?" he asked.

"Martin, you worry too much." She straightened his tilted tie.

He sighed, relieved. "What would I do without you?"

"Fortunately," she said, "you don't have to."

As he followed her through their cream-shuttered town house and on into the garage, he began looking forward to the gala. With his elegant wife on his arm, he could still enjoy looking, unobtrusively, at all the pretty young women.

Irene Stanton lifted her gown above her ankles and stepped back onto the curb. She watched the old Mercury, filled with a family of Mexicans, creep slowly past, then on down River Oaks Boulevard. She was reminded of children with their noses pressed against the panes of London shops at Christmas time. The Mexicans had been peering into the lighted homes like that.

She crossed the boulevard and walked slowly up the circular drive to her own tall, pillared house. Lights blazed from every room, because when evening came she did not like it any other way. A dark house reminded her of a tomb . . . and it had been that way for twelve years.

They would be in England for his birthday. What kind of flowers should she take? She didn't know. He had liked daffodils. Perhaps they should have buried him here. But America would always be foreign soil. Yes, daffodils. Or maybe tulips. She didn't know. Charles might have a preference. Together they would decide. And together they would drive to Burnham Cemetery, silently, soberly, fingers entwined, both of them thinking, "Today David would have been twenty-one years old." Unthinkable! Her nine-year-old boy a man. That would have been nice — standing on tiptoe to hug her tall son, handsome and erect like his father. But please, dear God, not another war hero. This was foolish! David had already fought his war — alone — and lost. If only Charles would allow an oil to be painted; if only he could understand that having the boy's portrait, looking at it daily, would close the wound.

She didn't want to go inside just yet. Charles had been stepping into the shower as she'd left. There was still time.

She walked around back to sit on the terrace. The entire garden was illuminated, for nightly the tennis court's floodlights automatically came on at dusk and stayed bright until three. By then she was asleep: the dark made no difference.

She fingered the tiny seed pearls stitched like clusters of stars into the midnight blue lace. It was an exquisite gown. Perhaps she had been vain. Careless, too. She was seldom that, but tonight she had wanted Bonita to see her at her best. Her best was not outstanding. Though for a woman soon to be fifty-six years old, with spreading hips and bright auburn hair graying and wrinkles cutting deep from her nose down beyond her lips — if all that were taken into consideration — she did look exceptional. And she had wanted to stand there, looking exceptional, before Bonita, who at fifty-two was still trim and stylish in spite of her little dowager's hump. But there was another reason she had run across the street to her neighbor. She had wanted to hold on tight to Bonita Graves. Just once more.

"I'll be right back. I have to tell Bonita one last thing," she'd said.

"Can't you ring her?" Charles had asked.

"I could. But I'm ready, and you're not. Besides, this won't take long."

Charles had smiled that slow, engaging smile of his and said teasingly, "What I want to know is how you two are going to get along without each other for the summer?"

"We'll manage," she'd parried lightly and left, thinking: "The

Bobbsey twins, he sometimes calls us, but more than once he has commented, 'Bonita's a jewel. I'm glad you've got such a good friend.' "

She refused to feel any more guilty than she already did. She needed Bonita, didn't she? And Charles had no reason to suspect. Why should he? Her whole life, except for her time with Bonita, was devoted to him. To Sir Charles Stanton. Why couldn't he simply be the Royal Petroleum overseas executive that he was without bringing to his position all the trappings of his valiant past? At times his medals seemed heavy on her own chest. And now, after all these years, there was to be yet another one. Awarded in Taiwan, no less! Well, it would be all right. How could she not be proud of him? Love him? And after the presentation at Taipei, they would go on to the Mainland. Without pomp and circumstance, the two of them would explore that vast country. China! She'd never been there. Truly, when they boarded the plane tomorrow, she would be genuinely excited. After all, ever since she'd read *The Good Earth,* the Chinese had fascinated her. She liked the idea of women giving birth in the rice paddies, then getting right back to work. She felt she, too, would be capable of such a thing. Yes, seeing China would be exhilarating. And after that, England! She would spend hours out in the countryside and at Wimbledon. There would be browsing at Harrods and dining with old friends. Daily she would enjoy tea with her mother. She would have all that . . . but it would not be enough.

"China, Irene. Think, China!" Bonita had coaxed, just now, not seeming nearly as distressed as she by their impending separation.

"I am thinking China! *And* England . . . It doesn't help," she'd argued.

Bonita had stepped back and placed her hands on her hips. "Look, the summer will be over in no time. We'll both keep busy."

She'd nodded.

Only then had Bonita softened and said the right thing. Part of the right thing. "You know, you're going to be one of the loveliest women at the gala."

That had helped.

"It is a pretty dress, isn't it?" she'd asked, seeking reassurances that had nothing to do with her dress.

"Stunning. Now, go!"

Bonita had practically shoved her out the door. But then she'd called her back.

"Irene?"

She'd turned and waited. Her name had been spoken tentatively.

". . . Try to have fun." It was as if Bonita had been pleading. But for what?

The question was unsettling.

"I thought you were going over to Bonita's." Her husband, looking particularly handsome in his tuxedo, she noticed, stepped out onto the terrace.

"I went. Now I'm just looking at my garden . . . and my tennis court." She attempted a smile.

He sat across from her and leaned forward, his fingers interlocked. For a moment, he frowned down at the flagstones. Then up at her.

"Irene, you're not still dreading the trip, are you?"

"Not really. In fact, I've been getting a little excited."

"Oh? Since when?" He settled back in his chair, as if awaiting an extended explanation.

She looked past the court, beyond the roses, on to the pool. She was not a good wife. Her eyes met his.

"Charles, I never tire of people recognizing what you did in the war, *appreciating* you."

"That's what's excited you?"

"Partially."

"Well, I'm pleased you're excited. But you know how I feel about all that. I mean, if it makes people remember what we don't want to have happen again — fine. Otherwise . . . Irene, they could have posted the blasted medal, but I thought you'd enjoy China."

"I'll *love* China."

"And going home?"

"And going home."

Again their eyes met. This time she quickly looked away, their son's grave between them.

"We'd best go," she said.

"If I weren't a board member, we wouldn't bother, you know that."

"Oh, Charles, it'll be great fun." She was remembering Bonita's admonishment.

"Well, I know the theatre's more my thing than yours. We'll make an appearance then leave."

"Charles, I'm not wearing this absolutely stunning gown for just an appearance." She stood. "I don't mind, really."

He studied her face. ". . . No, I don't believe you do." And then he smiled, visibly relieved. "It *is* a stunning gown."

"Thank you, m'lord." She wished he had said that she herself was stunning, but at least he had given her what he'd thought she'd wanted.

Touching the silver at his temples, she observed again that time had been kinder to her husband than to her.

His hand closed over hers.

"Shall we go?" he asked.

As if something undefined between them had been temporarily swept away, he seemed anxious now to leave.

"I'll get my evening bag." Her smile was quick and bright, but strained.

"We'll stay no more than an hour or so. Tomorrow's a full day."

Linking her arm through his, she forced a gaiety she did not feel. "My dear Charles," she said, "what you have just uttered is a remarkable understatement."

Raymond Reese whirled the vault's lock.

"I suppose this is purely woman's vanity." Winifred Adele Reese stood behind him, waiting. Though her sudden whim would make them late for the gala, she was not impatient. Her violet eyes, framed with purple eye shadow and dark mascara, looked out into the deserted shop. It gave her pleasure to be here when phones weren't ringing and clients weren't swirling about.

Her gaze swept over old pewter and brass and silver, polished as if awaiting royalty; fine-grained and lacquered woods; silk-embossed prayer rugs; oils of raging seas and tranquil gardens; porcelains as delicate as moths' wings. For a moment, her gaze rested on a nineteenth-century marquetry armoire. That latest find had cost her a pretty penny, but it would eventually sell to exactly the right person and she would more than recoup her outlay. Sometimes she felt as if she were constantly on treasure hunts. As a child, she'd loved to search for rusty thimbles, scarlet ribbons, and World War One "Keep America Strong" buttons. Then, the rewards of her hunts had been great. Now, they were magnificent. It was as if she were continually scooping up the best of the past and then setting it down gently in her native city where mercifully her efforts did not go unappreciated.

"Mother, it's not vanity."

"What's not?" She was invariably doing that to the boy. She'd make some remark and, before he could respond, her thoughts would hopscotch to other matters. But that was to be expected. Raymond was — bless his heart — boring.

"Wanting to wear the necklace. Besides, the shop's not that much out of the way."

"Raymond, honestly!" Her blue-tinged hair shook. "If you'd lavish half this attention on some nice young girl, like — oh, any number of them will be there tonight. If you'd just do that —"

"Mother, we've been over this before."

"And we will again. Probably before this night is over."

Raymond Reese gulped and tried to concentrate. Sometimes when he failed to please the one person he considered flawless, he became clumsy. But the vault did have a tricky combination. In fact, the entire place was masterfully guarded. Reese Interiors had a wired alarm system, a double-thick steel door on its walk-in vault, and bars on its windows. "If we're going to stock heirlooms, we've got to be prepared," his mother had announced the day she'd decided it was best to keep the West Gray entrance locked and have clients ring a doorbell that chimed "Hark, Hark, the Dogs Do Bark." His mother's reasoning had been sound. The shop was like a fortress. The Mafia could beat on its doors and forget it. Still, such precautions made it hard for everyone, including themselves, to get in.

"Here, let me."

Though she had spoken more gently than impatiently, he stepped back ashamed. Worried.

Raymond Reese, thirty-one, horn-rimmed, thin as the edge of a blade of grass, big-nosed, and rabbit-eyed, was a worrier. He worried that the sky would fall, that his toenails would grow too long if he didn't clip them weekly, that toast would be burned even before he'd put the toaster plug into a socket. He worried about cavities and nuclear power. Most of all he worried about displeasing Winifred Adele Reese.

The massive door swung back. Quickly he followed her inside to bring down from the shelf labeled "PERSONALS" a large steel box. He lifted its lid and asked, "It's in the blue velvet, isn't it?"

"Mauve."

As always his mother was right.

The black jade circled with diamonds lay on mauve velvet. He lifted the necklace out of its case.

"This will be perfect, Mother."

"Well, it completes the outfit."

"Absolutely." His Adam's apple lumped over his black tie as he strained to secure the clasp.

"Maybe I'd better do it."

"No, I've almost got it."

A full minute passed.

Winifred Reese battled exasperation. She could have snapped that necklace around her throat in two seconds flat. She struggled to keep one short, chubby foot from tapping. She zippered her lavender lips. Finally, she twisted the rings on her plump little fingers. Whenever she did that, she was aware that there was a diamond for each of her former husbands.

"It's tricky," Raymond apologized.

"I know," she said and began reviewing, as though they were inventory, the four spouses who had come and gone. There had been Joseph Crawford — the Colonel, she'd called him — who had died young but had remained the true love of her life; then Arnold Beasley, a passing fancy, a plaything, really; William Hamilton, a no-good bastard who had fathered her only child (she'd quickly and legally changed the boy's surname just as soon as she'd landed number four); and finally Clarkson Reese, a consummate gentleman and dear companion until his death from emphysema five years ago.

She sighed. The good ones had to die on her. Well, at sixty-two she was through with husbands. One son, so lacking in manhood, was all she could handle. But he would carry on Reese Interiors in a stellar manner. Of that she was certain. That is, if he could develop the backbone to match his talent.

The necklace fell to the floor.

"Mercy!"

"Raymond, it's not a tragedy."

The ordeal resumed.

Raymond Reese's Adam's apple rose and fell like a yo-yo.

Winifred Reese's eyes rolled heavenward. "Just a little back-bone, Lord," she prayed. "Is that too much to ask?"

"Got it!"

Raymond felt like sounding bugles, clanging cymbals.

The resplendent jade hung just above the crevice between his mother's breasts, which peeped soft and round like overripe melons out of her gown. He felt guilty. They *were* his mother's breasts.

"Thank you, love." She patted his cheek, and they stepped out of the vault.

She spun the combination.

"Done!" Taking off like a jet, the scent of gardenia perfume streaming behind her, she said over her shoulder, "Now, Raymond, I want you to have an absolutely splendid time!"

"I'll try," he answered weakly.

"Try? Do it!"

"Yes ma'am, I'll do it."

Regardless of his Arch board member status, which he knew his mother had secured for him, Raymond Reese predicted disaster. His tongue would become tied, his feet heavy planks. He would want to die. And all the while he would be fabricating his own version of a splendid time. He'd probably have himself doing something fine like dropping frosted grapes, one by one, into the mouth of a dazzling female, then laying bare her long-limbed body — the skin as smooth as the silks he ran his fingers over daily. Ultimately his splendid time would conclude, as all his fabrications did, with his throwing off, once and for all, his own fucking virginity!

Switching on the burglar alarm, he muttered under his breath, "Raymond, no one ever said you didn't have an imagination." Suddenly he visualized horror sweeping across his mother's face if she could but read his mind. That image sent him bolting out into the back alley, where already she sat behind the wheel of her car, its nose pointed forward, its motor idling.

"We're off!" she charged, a smile on her dumpling face.

The Mercedes, like a tanker on the roll, launched into traffic.

As they sped toward the theatre, Raymond Reese focused on the one solace that loomed like a mountain of whipped cream. The Arch galas' buffets were unfailingly superb!

· · ·

Lawrence Harrington placed a chicken thigh and two parsley potatoes, pocketed in aluminum foil, into the oven, then set the temperature. That would be his meal. Food had never unduly excited him. It merely fueled his body. There was, however, one exception: angel food cake with butter-cream frosting, a delicacy his wife had often made from scratch, with Zoe, no higher than her mother's waist, dropping egg whites into the mixing bowl. His daughter, who didn't particularly enjoy baking, still humored him. Occasionally she'd ring his doorbell, cake stand in hand, and formally herald, "Your nemesis, sir." He wished she would magically appear now. He'd assemble another foil packet, while insisting she stay for supper. For dessert they'd have thick slices of the cake she'd brought over just yesterday.

Well, it would take magic to bring her back tonight. At this very moment she was probably standing in the receiving line at The Arch gala.

He hoped she was enjoying herself. "Please come," she always begged. And always — after he'd attended the first five of the lot — he replied, "Thank you, but not this time."

Once she'd pressed him: "They're not really your thing, are they?"

"No." He hadn't elaborated.

And then, solemnly, she'd confessed, "They're not really mine, either. But Lance insists they're necessary."

"I agree with him," he'd said, then mentally added, "for once." His son-in-law's motives, however, remained suspect. Often he visualized Lance Benson clutching adulation as if it were a cloak to keep him warm. This impression — which was highly judgmental, he recognized that — he kept to himself. After all, the man was his daughter's husband. Still, he preferred to stay home rather than watch Benson's show — his hypnotic appeal.

That same charm had bent Zoe subtly into change. He was thankful there had not been a complete metamorphosis. Did his daughter realize, he wondered, that discussing her work as an artist brought a glow to her face, a lilt to her voice, far greater than any mention of her husband? During that brief whirlwind courtship, when Lance Benson had swept into town and swept Zoe off her feet, the reverse had been true.

The marriage was a mistake. He knew it, felt it. Far better had she gone abroad to study art. When she'd broken her engagement to Edwin Landrum, he'd offered a year — "or more" — in Paris. But she'd been hell-bent on Lance.

Throughout the years since their marriage, he had remained silent while encouraging however and whenever he could the re-emergence of the strong, beautiful girl who had once marched on Washington for civil rights, who had always said no to drugs when many were saying yes, who had daily rushed from university classes to teach art where no paintings had ever hung, who had in football seasons waved pompons and in summer months surfed over moun-tain-high waves. That Zoe would come again to the forefront. It was his conviction. Her spark was still there. And he felt his only child to be a more wondrous miracle than any of the definitive books he'd conceived over more decades than she had lived.

He poured a glass of wine then wandered into his study to stand at a book-lined wall, contemplating what he wanted to read while his meal cooked. Last night he'd completed Gurwell's *Aeschylus's Supplices: Feminists' Forerunner*. Perhaps it was time for some-thing light. But he never seemed to tire of reading in his field. Well, he would have all the time in the world now to delve into subjects as close to his heart as Aristotle's *Poetics* or, should a whim arise, as far removed as hot-air ballooning over France's vineyards. And read voraciously was what he intended to do. Until he got his bearings, until he became accustomed to this retirement into which he had been launched last month as if he were off on an extended voyage. He was still reeling from all the hoopla. Crane University's president had hosted a dinner at which pheasant had been served and a heavy gold plaque presented along with a heavier title. Professor Emeritus. He mouthed those two words. They seemed foreign now that they belonged to him.

His eyes skimmed over titles. His mind stayed elsewhere.

Retirement happened to other people, not to those who loved their work. That was the myth he had perpetrated upon himself. But now in his seventieth year, retirement, which he'd staved off by acquiring a few respectable prizes along the path of his career, had arrived. It had come as inevitably as leaves fall from trees. And, just as inevitably, others would soon stand behind his lectern. He recalled that, the week after Kennedy had died, Zoe, a wry twist to her young mouth, had remarked, "Nothing stopped for very long, did it?" He'd answered as best he could. "No, it never does. It can't. Which only points out, in the grand scheme of things, how insignificant is man." Still, he had reminded her that one man could make a difference. "Or one woman," she'd quickly said.

He smiled and decided to offer her the Gurwell book. She would like its feminist premise.

His fingers touched the spine of *Mountain Mystique,* a photography book more suitable for displaying than shelving. He should place it on a coffee table. He'd purchased the book, years back, because between its covers seemed to lie his heritage. He pulled the book from its niche.

Flipping through pages, he walked slowly to his rocker. Then he sat down to search for his favorite photograph. He found it: the Blue Ridge Mountains rising in mist. He felt he was home. For him, it had all begun there. And he had come out of those mountains only because his brain had been swirling with questions. As a child, he'd perhaps questioned too much. But could one ever do that when there were so many answers to be had for the asking? It was all those early questions needing answers which had gotten him a scholarship to Harvard, a school where his hard-working but high-visioned parents, selling their wares to tourists, could never have sent him. Upon graduation, he'd longed to return to those mountains forever, but how could he? No college within miles of his parents' home had wanted a professor of Classics. During stints at lesser schools, he'd written his first book. And with its publication had come enough recognition in academia to bring him here to Crane, where he had remained — only to return to the Blue Ridge Mountains when he needed their strength or when those he loved needed his.

Long before Houston became his city, it had belonged to Leah. And years before her, to her great-grandfather, who had founded Houston's first rice mill, whose wagon wheels had sunk into Main Street's muddy ruts, whose name was immortalized in Texas archives.

Leah Morland Harrington, her lovely gray eyes dominating a small, heart-shaped face, had been the only woman he'd ever loved. And this large old house, to which they'd come soon after Zoe was born, was the only house he'd ever wanted. With its wood-slatted porch and small neat yard, the house sat unabashedly modest amid Sunset Boulevard's more elaborate homes.

He closed the book.

She had died twenty-three years ago this past March. An accident.

He went to check his supper.

"If only she were here now," he thought, "we would travel." She'd encourage him to write. "You haven't retired from *that*," she'd point out. And then she might add, "Larry, life begins at whatever moment you're experiencing." She had been philosophical in that sort of way. Well, he didn't know if he *could* write another book. But travel, perhaps . . . maybe in the fall to the West Coast. He hadn't been there since a convention five years before. He liked the Pacific, waking to its roar, walking along its beaches, staring out across that blue expanse as if expecting the Argo to appear at any moment. And then, when spring came, he would go to his mountains. Perhaps.

The foil packet was steaming. The chicken and potatoes done. For dessert there would be Zoe's cake, made from her mother's recipe.

Cyrano de Bergerac's Paris, 1640. Edmond Rostand's crowd: "Bourgeois, marquises, mousquetaires, pickpockets, pastrycooks, poets, Gascony Cadets, players, fiddlers, pages, children, Spanish soldiers, spectators, précieuses, actresses, bourgeoises, nuns, etc."

The "etc." of Rostand's crowd was The Arch Theatre's "beautiful people." Its patrons, having paid five hundred dollars a couple to attend the end-of-year gala, were celebrating the conclusion of The Arch's most successful season and particularly the triumph of Lance Benson's production of *Cyrano de Bergerac*. The men were perspiring but elegant in their dinner jackets. The women, hair sleekly coiffed, were poured into their designer gowns — fully half from Neiman's, Sakowitz, and Solomon's in Houston, while the other half bore labels from salons in New York and Paris.

The entire theatre — stages, foyer, grand hall, terraces, stairs, dressing rooms — was ablaze with lights and festooned with flowers. Champagne flowed freely and a long buffet, lit by two candelabras, was heaped with delicacies. Dressed in their *Cyrano* costumes, actors and actresses mingled with patrons. Together they danced in the grand hall to the music of the city's leading society orchestra. Old-time favorites were prominent in the orchestra's repertoire that evening, for the patrons were predominantly of the Glenn Miller era.

Each season The Arch held two galas. The opening gala in October was an invitational event for its moneyed supporters. The closing gala in June was different: the people who made the magic happen on stage were included. Although a monetary reward would have been preferred, the actors accepted their gala bonus and were usually among the last to leave the affair, often with hors d' oeuvres and pastries, which Lance had instructed the caterer to box especially for them. Lance Benson understood the struggling artist's nature, and he capitalized on that knowledge. Most Arch performers, and patrons as well, thought him a perplexing but brilliant artistic and managing director. And the closing gala was invariably a salute to him.

This gala was no exception. Lance, appearing to be in high spirits, moved among the crowd. People stopped their conversations to include him in their circle, to congratulate him, to ask his opinions. He fed the egos of his followers as much, if not more, than they fed his. His gaze intent, he would inquire about health, children, and upcoming vacations. He earnestly solicited views on works the theatre should consider.

It was almost biblical — the shepherd tending his flock. But that was not what Lance Benson was thinking as he left one circle of patrons to emerge, as a burst of sunlight, into another.

Zoe Benson watched her husband that evening. She felt little of the pride — almost hurting in its intensity — that she had felt in the early days of the theatre. Then, the two of them had moved together. Now Lance preferred to glide alone, like a sleek fox across the terrain. "You can look out for yourself," was the way he had phrased it when once she had mentioned that she liked the way they had always been beside each other at theatre functions in the old days. "These are not the old days," he had pointed out, a fact of which she was now well aware. "We need to separate. It's better for the theatre that way. Besides, I need to cover the entire scene." And then he had grinned that charming grin which once had the power to melt her.

She turned to the elderly gentleman, a friend of her father's, to continue their lengthy conversation about his grandson, who had broken with the family tradition of law to become a deep-sea diver searching for the lost Atlantis. Suddenly she felt trapped and glanced around the room in the hope that someone would notice her plight. Victor Solomon came to the rescue.

"You are divine," he said close against her ear, stepping on her toes as they danced. "And I am slightly drunk. Do you want to know why?"

She answered lightly, even flirtatiously. "Probably in elation, Victor, because half the women here, including myself, are wearing dresses from your store."

"Wrong. Absolutely wrong." He hiccuped and tripped. "You see that other divine lady across the room talking, as a matter of fact, to your husband?"

"Your wife?" His stare was directed at Roselyn Solomon, exquisite in jade crepe de chine.

"My wife, who is on *my* territory tonight."

"Victor, what on earth —"

"Let me finish. She is stepping all over my territory tonight after having announced to me this afternoon — *only* this afternoon, mind you — that she wants me out of the house. Vamoose. In simple terms, my dear Mrs. Benson, Mrs. Solomon is divorcing Mr. Solomon. Let's go get a drink." He led her off the dance floor.

"Life can get complicated," Zoe Benson suddenly reflected. Tomorrow all of Houston would be talking about the split between Roselyn and Victor Solomon. She sipped champagne and said softly, "I'm sorry." She saw that the man with the sad, heavy-lidded eyes did not really care whether she was sorry or not. He shrugged and watched an actress sway past. Sandy Lowrey, Zoe couldn't help noticing, looked more like a tart than the sweetmeat vendor she had portrayed in *Cyrano*. The mole pasted high on her left breast shone ebony against her white skin. A beautiful girl, but cheap. Victor Solomon tipped his glass. Sandra smiled at him.

Winifred Reese, carrying off in great style a black satin gown she adored but knew was too late for the season, tried to push Raymond away from her side and across the room toward Harriet Hastings, who had recently returned from two years abroad. There, the lovely girl had studied French in depth and gourmet cooking sporadically. But Harriet was home now to teach French at Childress Academy and to whip up poulet cordon bleu and soufflé au chocolat in the family kitchen. Raymond would have none of it. "Please, Mother, let me do my own thing."

"And what is that, Raymond?" She smiled at Barbara Wesley gliding by. How she wanted the Wesley job! To redecorate an entire nineteenth-century mansion would be heaven. She shivered in anticipation. Hadn't one of Barbara's best friends, whose garden room she was changing from yellows to fern greens, hinted yesterday that Reese Interiors was beginning to nudge out Graham Designs?

"Well, er, I'm not sure, Mother."

"Not sure of what, Raymond?" She had forgotten the train of their conversation. Somehow she must subtly work her way over to Barbara's side.

"Not sure what my own thing is, except I would like more pâté. May I bring you some?"

She sighed. "Raymond, darling, you're going to eat your way through this entire evening without dancing once with one of these lovely creatures floating around."

He gulped. If only she knew how much he ached to take one of the fragile young things in his arms and gobble her up. Afterward he would lick his lips as though neatly finishing off a napoleon. He looked around the room. His choice for such a feast would not be Harriet Hastings, upon whom his mother had fixed her attention, but rather . . . his eyes swept over the confections. His choice would be that delectable girl with the long blond hair. She had undoubtedly the most marvelous boobs he'd ever seen, and the mole on the left one was most enticing. He hurried to the buffet. Trembling slightly, he gobbled down the pâté de fois gras and turned to acknowledge the praise a purple-haired lady heaped upon his narrow shoulders.

"How clever," she cooed, the wrinkles in her neck working their way down between her breasts. "To think you wallpapered the dressing area in leopard spots!" She giggled. "My husband says it brings out the wild in me."

Again, he gulped. Sex was rampant tonight, and he didn't know what to do about it. He searched the room for his mother. She was nowhere to be seen. He escaped to the terrace.

Standing outside, breathing in fresh air, Raymond Reese cursed for the millionth time that second-grade year at Childress when he alone had not received a valentine. He supposed it was going to haunt him all his life. Here he was, thirty-one years old with a bulge in his pants and sweat on his palms — neither of which he knew how to remedy. He suspected the same remedy could cure both ailments. He envied a man like Lance Benson, whom he'd noticed the girl with the long blond hair had followed around half the evening.

He walked back inside. Zoe Benson was a pretty woman with whom he felt comfortable. She asked pleasant questions and told witty stories. He would find her and invite her to dance. That should pacify his mother. True, Zoe was married; but at least she was small and graceful and the distaff side of tonight's reigning monarch.

"Shall we have one last dance before leaving?"

"I think that's a splendid idea," Irene Stanton replied to her husband.

She was already praying for a good night's sleep. Their flight tomorrow morning for San Francisco left at an ungodly seven-fifteen. And there was still some last-minute packing to do.

They had always danced well together. "Surprising. You're light as a feather," Charles had remarked that first time, years ago, when they'd danced at the Lord Mayor's Ball. She hadn't known whether to be pleased or insulted. "Surprising?" She'd raised her eyebrows and he, seldom flustered, had blushed beet red. She had found that endearing.

She wished the orchestra would play something from those pre-war years when they had first met. It was not that she was feeling sentimental about her husband. It was just — she felt nostalgic. She looked over his shoulder as they danced. Her eyes were wide, searching. Where was the girl she had noticed earlier? She had seen only her back, but something about the way she stood and her hair reminded her of someone whom she had known a long time ago. If she could see her face . . . but the girl was nowhere to be seen. The dance ended. They would pay their respects to Zoe and Lance Benson, which would take some time, for the two of them were on opposite sides of the hall, and then they could leave.

Their departure became more involved than she'd anticipated. Working their way toward the door, they were stopped countless times by friends eager to wish them a pleasant trip.

"A remarkable couple," she overheard Lowell Hook comment, as they passed, to a pretty young actress dressed as a nun. "*Remarkable*," the little nun echoed.

Suddenly she smiled. On the spur of the moment, she made a decision. She would bring back from China something truly remarkable. And that exquisite gift she would place lovingly at Bonita's feet.

A slight summer breeze swung the Japanese lanterns strung above the theatre's balcony. Flecks of colored lights flashed down upon the guests. Caroline Fletcher's face caught the glitter as she and her husband stood, sipping champagne and talking to Winifred Reese and Barbara Wesley.

Forrest Wesley appeared with a plate of canapés. Winifred began recounting how, in her early struggling days, she had decorated her tiny apartment completely in canvas. ". . . And today, look what's happened to canvas? High fashion itself!" She flung her pudgy, ringed fingers into the air; a bit of champagne spilled on the stone floor.

Barbara Wesley, biting daintily into capers and salmon, agreed. "Canvas," she said, "can be stunning."

Caroline Fletcher leaned over to her husband. "I'll be right back," she whispered. He raised his eyebrows. "Right back," she repeated.

She hurried across the theatre lobby. The distance to her destination seemed interminable. Her peau de soie sandals skimmed over inlaid marble. Tiny beads of perspiration were strung above her upper lip. She felt fine physically. Indeed, she had never felt better. But mentally she was "losing her cool," as her daughter called it whenever one of her parents got the least bit perturbed. Well, her "cool" was going temporarily.

She would be all right after five minutes of sitting quietly in the ladies' lounge. After all, she felt fine. But, no, she was sick. She had been told she was sick. It had begun last week with a routine examination. With the question: "How long has this been here?" The appointment with her gynecologist had been worked in between jogging two miles and shopping for an upcoming dinner party. How long had it been there? She honestly didn't know.

Near the end of the lobby, almost home free, she spied a slight, gray-haired gentleman. She pretended not to notice him. His head thrown back, he was laughing at something an attractive woman had said. As if he didn't have a care in the world. She hurried on. Only yesterday afternoon she had been seated across from him. How different he had looked then. Stern. No, sober. Dr. Levy was a compassionate man. The width of his desk separating them, he had said, "I will not lie to you, Mrs. Fletcher. The mammograms indicate it could be serious. I'm sorry. But let's discuss your options. And then we can get on with it, can't we?"

"Yes, Dr. Levy." She had heard someone else's high, thin voice coming out of her throat. Yes, Dr. Levy. Yes, Dr. Levy. Never, no, Dr. Levy, because getting on with it meant getting on with life. She did not remember a single word he had said after "A mastectomy must not be ruled out."

Home free. The ladies' lounge. She sank onto one of the stiff little boudoir chairs and stared at her reflection. It was a good face. A little pale tonight. Her hair, wound in French braids about her head, emphasized her high cheekbones, inherited from a Huguenot ancestor in whom she took pride. The face would not be marred. But further down . . . She touched the blue silk. Certainly she feared for her life. But what woman would not be vain enough to fear as well for the other? "Dear God," she prayed, "if it has to be, don't let it make a difference to Martin." She had not told him yet. But surely he must suspect that something was troubling her.

She dabbed powder on her nose. Men, she knew — again, according to her daughter, who kept her jargon current — were considered "leg men" or "breast men" or "ass men." Her husband was a "breast man." All these years she had proudly and eagerly met her husband's needs. She playfully used to tell him that he had not been adequately breast-fed as a baby, until one day she had been told that she was correct. His mother, Martin had informed her, had been too busy flitting off to bridge parties, afternoon teas, and trips to the Bahamas to worry about whipping breasts out of blouses to stick into the mouths of twin boys. So the bottle and the nanny had been the brothers' identical fates. He had added that he didn't really know how his twin, Marvin, living in Calgary, Canada, and doing extraordinary work for Can-Am Pipeline, felt about breasts, though he did know that Marvin's wife, Penny, had a chest which extended well beyond the normal range of protrusion. Yes, Penny had been a real sweater girl in college.

Caroline Fletcher retouched her cheekbones with blush. The door to the ladies' room swung open. She jumped slightly. It might not be a bad idea to crumble a bit, let the seams show, to a friend.

The girl who had played Maggie in *Cat on a Hot Tin Roof* entered. Of all the women who might have come to sit beside her, why must it be this gorgeous young creature whose breasts rose into mountains? Caroline Fletcher turned away. She fought back tears. She wished that she were twenty-one again, looking toward all the long bright years that had been hers until this moment.

Smearing crimson across her mouth, the girl spoke. "Gee, this is some party, isn't it?"

"Yes." Smiling stiffly, she picked up her beaded evening bag and left. She would find Zoe Benson and tell her. It was too much to hold inside. Then tomorrow or the next day or the day after she would tell Martin and schedule the operation.

Sweetmeat vendor, my ass! She slammed her lipstick tube down on the marble vanity. And that bitch who had just sailed out of the ladies' room with her nose ten feet in the air was a princess, she supposed. No, queen. Anybody that old couldn't possibly be a princess. An old hag was what she was. She squinted at her reflection in the mirror. Too vain to wear the glasses she kept in a drawer, Sandra Lowrey narrowed her eyelids into slits whenever she wanted to look at anything or anybody closely.

Right now she wanted to take a good long look at herself, because before she marched back into the lions' arena she needed to rebuild her confidence. Maybe, if she squinted hard enough and long enough and saw something really fine coming back at her from the mirror, then she could tell all the old biddies — and the young ones, too, for there were a few of those out there tonight — to go to hell, because nobody, and she did mean nobody, looked half as good or, for that matter, *was* half as good as she, Sandra Lowrey, star product of The Good Shepherd Orphanage, by God, straight out of East Jesus, Texas!

Squinting, she smiled. Inspection passed. As Lance had put it, she was a nice morsel of sweetmeat herself. Suddenly she frowned. Damn him. She couldn't stop being mad about her part in *Cyrano*,

when she had been Maggie, a real star, in *Cat on a Hot Tin Roof.*
Could she help it if the critics had said she had played the role
like she had gum in her mouth? What did they know? Anyway,
they had called her "delectable." So, was that why Lance had cast
her as this sweetmeat thing? Five lines was what she had, five lousy
lines: Oranges . . . macaroons . . . raspberry cordial . . . citron-
wine — shit! She should have been Roxane, and she had told him
so. Lance had laughed. Well, let him laugh. One day he wouldn't.
One day he would sit up and notice her. Really notice her. He
would say, "My God, that gorgeous thing can act! And, besides,
look at her, she is some lovely person. A real person." Then he
would take her in his arms and kiss her and whisk her off to his
castle on a hill. In Hollywood. That was her favorite dream. Mr.
Lance Benson didn't know she went to sleep at night with such
bright ideas shooting off like fireworks in her head. He thought
she was just some two-bit flighty actress who spent most of her
time selling cosmetics behind some tacky drugstore counter. He
didn't know she had dreams. He didn't know that one day it was
all going to be different between the two of them. And as for Miss
Hoity-Toity, his wife, she could just fart on out the door. She
smiled. It was going to be all right. How could it not be? She had
come this far, hadn't she?

She pressed the fake mole on her breast. That had been a clever
idea to stick it there. More than one man tonight had wanted a
feel to see if it was real. Each time she had giggled and sort of
sidestepped like, "Don't touch the merchandise." Yeah, the men
here were all right. It was just the women. She lowered the bodice
of her costume, straightened her shoulders, and, feeling immensely
better, went looking for Lance. Now, if *he* wanted to touch the
mole, that would be different. She would lead him out onto the
balcony where a thousand stars would watch while she slid his
hand down from the mole straight to the tit. If only he knew how
much she loved him. If only, if only . . . well, he would know soon
enough. She just had to figure out how and when she was going
to tell him.

Chin tilted upward, she headed straight for her prince.

"Lance, if *she'd* been Roxane I damn sure wouldn't have gone
to sleep during the second act." Lowell Hook chuckled at his own

joke. He shifted the imported cigar in his mouth. Tomorrow he would pay the piper, but damned if tonight he wasn't going to indulge himself. He puffed expansively, coughed, and eyed the luscious young thing who had marched right up and interrupted their conversation about funding. Hell, he was glad. A party like this was no place to be talking business.

She giggled a high childlike giggle. Benson, he noticed, didn't look too pleased to see her. Well, of course, he was after more money. Weren't they all? It didn't matter whether they were artistic directors or zoo keepers.

"So, young lady, why weren't you Roxane?"

She giggled again. Dumb little creature, but that didn't bother him. It wasn't her brain he was peering down into. God, he'd had enough brainy women to last a lifetime and then some.

"Ask him!" Her incredibly green eyes cut across to Benson, who shrugged his shoulders and nonchalantly spread his hands: "I plead guilty."

That Benson is a cool one, thought Hook. He may be after money, but he doesn't kiss ass.

"I think you're wanted over there, Sandy." Benson's voice was as smooth as molasses.

"Where?" Wide-eyed, she looked around.

"There."

"Oh, er — yeah. Well . . . it was nice talking to you, Mr. Hook."

"Charmed." He bowed and kissed the awkwardly extended hand. Each finger, he noticed, was ringed with cheap costume jewelry. "And next time" — his bushy eyebrows lifted — "I'll expect to see you in the lead."

"Yes, sir!" It was as though she had clicked her heels in attention. Unable to maintain the formality, she giggled. "That is, if *he* won't be a meanie."

The two men watched her move quickly, unconsciously seductive, into the crowd.

For a moment there was silence. Hook reached for a glass of champagne passing on a tray. "Damnit, Benson, why'd you get rid of her?"

"Because," Lance Benson said evenly, "if she'd stayed another five minutes, your blood pressure would have shot up so high I'd have had to call an ambulance."

The tension was broken. Lowell Hook threw back his head and laughed. He slapped the young man on the back. "You're probably right, but I'll tell you something." He stopped.

"What?" Benson leaned slightly forward.

"Sometimes I think I'd give up five good years of the few I've got left to have something like that just one more time. Think about it, Benson, my biggest thrill these days is an occasional glass of champagne and a good cigar when nobody, including myself, is looking. That's not much. But a girl like that. That girl." He sighed. "I can still get it up, you know, but damned if I'd know what to do with it."

"You'd know."

Hook studied the young man. He liked him. Yes sir, he liked him. He had a feeling Benson understood how a man could grow old and still want what he shouldn't want if he knew what was good for him. "Come on," he said, "let's go find that wife of yours. She's always been one of my favorites. Her father once compared me to Zeus, and I've never forgotten it. Though I do think the professor was wrong, because if I'm so God-almighty powerful how come I can't have a good piece of ass every once in a while?"

Smiling a slow steady smile, Benson replied, "You know, Mr. Hook, you do remind me of Zeus."

Lowell Hook straightened his shoulders. Zeus, huh? "You hear that, God?" he silently shouted straight up through the roof. "There may be some thunder in the old guy yet." He mashed out his cigar in a plate half-filled with soggy canapés. Suddenly he felt he should save his strength for pursuits more important than smoking cigars. Just what, he wasn't sure. But Lance Benson, sharp young fellow that he was, had seen the Zeus in him.

There is nothing so quiet, Zoe Benson thought, as an empty theatre after the people have left. Sitting on a step, she held gardenias which she planned to place on a windowsill. She had seen to it that board members had sprays to take home with them. Most had said, "How lovely!" But Charles Stanton, who was leaving the next morning and would be gone for the summer, had suggested that the hospital get his. She'd thought, "That's where the majority of these should go." Tomorrow twelve floral arrangements would be delivered to the city's hospitals. Perhaps it would become a tradition. She lighted a cigarette and looked around.

Why Lance insisted on closing the place up after these events was beyond her. Often he stood on the darkened stage and stared out over emptiness. She wondered what thoughts her husband had as he surveyed his deserted domain. She never knew. But at such times she felt him to be a stranger, peering into an abyss she couldn't fathom.

From the beginning Lawrence Harrington had thought them an unsuitable pair. "Why are you doing this?" he had asked his daughter.

"Because I love him," Zoe had replied. He had accepted her answer because he understood that, although his daughter had given the simplest reason behind her decision to marry Lance Benson, she had also given the most powerful. He had loved her mother, too, but there had been other components which had gone into making their marriage the good, strong union it had been. He could not imagine that such components would ever link his daughter and this man, almost eleven years older than she.

Here was a total stranger, who had appeared one day in Houston with a touring company of *Picnic* and had stayed to build a theatre. Somewhere in the course of his building, he had come home to dinner with Zoe who, looking younger than her twenty years, was playing Hedvig in *The Wild Duck*. The man had smiled and said, "Yes, Dr. Harrington . . . I agree, Dr. Harrington . . . That is so true, Dr. Harrington." But Harrington had peered behind the sleek facade, flawed by a nervous twitch of the left eyelid, and found a hollowness. A lack of profound insights amidst fluent verbalizations; an overzealous concern with his climb over institutions and people in an attempt to make a theatre, struggling in an old abandoned warehouse, great. Or was it himself he was seeking to make great? And what was his conception of greatness? Lawrence Harrington was troubled. And perplexed. Couldn't his daughter see the things he saw? Had he brought her up so carelessly? Perhaps mindlessly? He knew the answer to both questions was no. Romantic excitement had hoodwinked her. Here was someone handsome, different, and charismatic. How could the familiar and ordinary compete?

When the man had come to their door time and again, the father had reminded him, "Zoe has another year at the university."

"I know," the man had said.

"Zoe has a gift. She must paint."

"I know."

And when it became far more serious, he had spoken again: "I don't want her working in a department store to make ends meet, but I also don't want her dissipating the small inheritance which, as you know, she will come into at the time of her marriage."

"I understand."

Finally, sadly thrusting his finger into the dike, the old man — not so old then — had reminded them both, "Before you came here, Zoe was engaged to someone she has known almost since the day of her birth."

"She told me."

"I *told* him, Daddy."

He had continued, "And that fine, bright young man is not taking this lightly."

"He shouldn't," Lance Benson had said, turning his cold, blue stare away from the father toward the daughter, who sat drinking him in as if Apollo himself had descended into their midst. The glow had made her so beautiful that Lawrence Harrington had looked away and given them his blessing.

Sometimes she wondered whether life was a dream in some large universal mind or whether it was real, happening? At times she thought like that. Then, after a while, she would busy herself with life, real or a dream, and forget that the question had been there at all.

Zoe Benson shook her head as she sat there waiting on a marble step of a curved staircase leading up to The Arch's lobby. She mashed out her cigarette neatly in a tiny silent butler that she always carried in her purse. Why had the question come to her, now when the festivities were over, the helium seeping from the balloons? She didn't know, but the question had surfaced and, with it, another more disturbing. Why did she feel suddenly — passionately and painfully — that she would rather leave this theatre and run home to her studio, high up in what had once been a musty attic, to paint wildly — to lose herself in colors she could smear across a canvas — than to sit waiting for a husband who stood on a darkened stage? She was impatiently waiting for a man whom she had once loved enough to block out all else. Her feelings made no sense, except that her blind infatuation — which she supposed had stemmed from a virgin's wild imaginings and strainings toward what had seemed to be the answer to all emptiness — had defused. All that was left was a waning love for a man — handsome, eccentric, egotistical — who demanded extreme loyalty to himself and to his theatre. She poured out all her energy and devotion into both, and only the dregs remained for herself. And for her work. At least Lance often left her alone. There were great chunks of time when she and her work were all there was in the house. She coveted those hours, while dreading the longer ones — loneliness spun out, her day in the studio ended, and Lance still not there while she was expected to wait, always wait, in her proper niche. So what was new about all this? What was troubling her now? Deeply.

. . . The marriage, their union, was in trouble. This absorption into another's life was not the cause she had originally sought. There had been other causes before Lance. But there seemed to be none now at a time when she no longer wanted to espouse only Lance and his reason for being. In this dream life or real life, that espousing was not enough. It wasn't that she was seeking perfection in another human being. It was just that — she shook her head. She honestly didn't know.

But lately, beside her husband, she felt more lonely than when she was alone.

"Admit it," she urged, forcing herself on. She longed for something else. Something as yet nameless. Undefined. But that something would have to be more like her causes had once been. But what had those causes been? Had there ever been a cause independent of Lance?

Better such desires, such questions, swirl in a dream than in reality. Whatever, the hurts and bewilderments were the same. Didn't she run through her nightmares in fear?

She dropped the silent butler with the bent, burnt-out cigarette into her purse, stood, and walked slowly toward the auditorium. Its doors were closed. She opened one a crack so that she could peer inside. He was standing, as she had known he would be, solitary, on a black stage. Seeing that shadowy outline was eerie, unsettling. She quietly closed the door and walked back to the marble step, where she sat, chin cupped in her palm, wishing she were any place but there.

Suddenly she straightened, then twisted, to stare at the clock, centered large and brass-rimmed, on a lobby wall.

In exactly three minutes, she would return to the door and yell out, her words echoing into the chasm, "Lance, I want to go home. Now!" He wouldn't like such assertiveness. Well, she was sorry about that, because to assert herself — while drawing further away from him — was slowly but surely becoming a necessity.

Lance Benson could see only the dim outline of empty theatre seats sloping up into a black infinity. He reflected on the evening. Predictably, the gala had been a success. He reflected on the theatre's seventeenth season. Again, a foreseeable success. He reflected on himself. The shepherd leading his mindless flock.

He was weary of it all.

The excitement of a good production still struck a blow against boredom, but it never quite cracked the hard question: "Is this all there is to life?" That question weighed heavily on his entire being. He would like nothing better than to walk out the stage door with a minimum of one million dollars in his pocket. He would never look back. Instead, he would start over in a metropolis on the other side of an ocean. Start over what? He didn't know. He only knew that he desperately needed a challenge capable of stirring his brain and tingling his nerves. He needed no obligations other than those he imposed on himself. All others, draining his energy, belonged in hell. He was sick to death of how predictable life had become. He was sick of knowing that if you spoke in a charmed manner to a patron you would elicit a favorable response; if you humored your wife occasionally you would keep peace at home; if you brushed your teeth sideways, rather than downward, you would avoid the dreaded cavities; if you budgeted carefully you would manage to get by. He was tired of budgeting. He was tired of being charming. He was tired of his particular slot in life. His rut. Tired of everything about it. There must be a way out of this rut!

The theatre season was over. Now there would be time to think. To plan.

He envied Lowell Hook. Even with his scrawny legs and bent back, Hook was a giant. The zest for life the old bastard had! The life he had lived. No patron or wife ever pulled his strings. He had no strings. He had clawed his way over mountains and bodies to get to the top. The top of what? The top of the money heap. The power heap. The top of the people heap.

If only he could find a viable challenge. The challenge, he suspected, lay somewhere in the recesses of his own mind. He would not trudge through another theatrical season carrying the weak on his back. He would shake himself free. Forge ahead! Surely man had evolved on this earth to survive; indeed, to triumph if he had the stamina and the intelligence to do so. He had both. It was his time to triumph. His turn. And if he had to step over principles and on people, he would do so because if he didn't, he knew that in his boredom — in the predictability and constriction of it all — he would ultimately crush himself.

Sunday after the gala rain came in thin sheets, soaking most of the city. Lance and Zoe Benson slept late through the downpour. When they awoke, he rolled over and made quick love to her. Afterward she padded barefooted downstairs to stand in their yellow kitchen preparing breakfast.

Still wearing her shortie nightgown, she served her preoccupied husband pecan waffles with melted butter, then sat across from him at their glass-top table. She chattered about the gala. Only when she mentioned "poor Caroline Fletcher's condition" did he look up and ask questions.

"Then we're talking about a mastectomy, aren't we?" was the final question.

"Possibly," she said.

"Too bad." His head lowered again to his waffle.

The remainder of the meal they ate in silence. She attributed his mood to an end-of-season letdown.

After breakfast he stood abruptly, kissed her absentmindedly on top of the head, commented, "That was delicious," and returned upstairs.

It was two o'clock. The rain had stopped. An idea was germinating. As if peering through a periscope into the unknown, Lance Benson was beginning to see a way out of the trap.

In her studio Zoe worked on the painting of a bank president which was to hang among portraits of preceding presidents dating back to the year 1890. Lance pulled on his swimming trunks, got a pencil and a legal pad, stuck between the yellow sheets a xeroxed list of Arch board members' names, and headed for his pool. He didn't swim. Instead, he stretched out on a chaise longue, its plastic still damp from the rain. Motionless, he lay squinting at the sun, which had begun to shine.

Some time later Zoe looked out the window of her third-floor studio and saw her husband below. He was scribbling furiously on a pad that rested upon his drawn-up knees. She wondered how long he had been there and what he was writing but decided not to disturb him. Quickly she showered, left him a note, and drove to the university area to visit her father, who would be pleased to hear that last night's gala had been a success and that Lowell Hook had spoken so favorably of him.

At six o'clock Lance Benson stretched his cramped muscles. He dived into the pool, swam twelve laps, then got out of the water, and returned to the house. Relieved that he was alone, he poured a drink and smiled.

Lance Benson had learned early in life two truths about sex. He learned both from the same girl, Hilary Evans.

That sex is a powerful drive he suspected from his first plunge into masturbation. The suspicion became fact in Hilary Evans's parents' bed. "Are you crazy?" he'd asked, feeling as though they would be doing "it" on top of some sacred altar. But Hilary, a few months older than he and, he realized now, vastly more experienced, had assured him that her parents would not return from the Rochester Philharmonic concert until much later and that it was silly not to do "it" in a big deep feather bed when all she had in her room was a narrow and lumpy twin. So he'd had his first screw in feather down and thought he'd surely died and gone to heaven. He couldn't wait to do it again. To get between her wide hips and bury his head in her firm, round sixteen-year-old breasts. The next time they did it was quick and messy in the swing on her front porch. Embarrassed by the stains spotting his underwear, he'd furtively washed the garment himself rather than have his mother *know*. The third time was out near Lake Ontario in broad daylight, behind a large rock with cars whizzing close by but out of sight.

There was not a fourth time with Hilary Evans, because before that could occur she taught him the second truth about sex: Sex can be used as a powerful weapon. "I don't feel good," she'd said.

"Besides, I'm not in the mood." He'd taken his engorged extremity home and burned out his hot humiliation and rage by hitting a basketball against the side of their gray, slanting garage. He'd show her. He hated her fat ass, her too-small breasts. But, only three days later, he'd gone back to try to obtain more of the nectar — to suck from her body the greatest joy he had ever known. The only thing coming close to giving him that kind of satisfaction was sitting in the movie house watching all those beautiful people doing fine things. He knew now for a fact what went on, what ecstasy was being felt by the hero and heroine when the fade-outs came. When Clark Gable and Lana Turner closed a door in *Honky Tonk,* and the next scene showed everyone acting as if nothing had happened, hell, he *knew* now what had happened. So he went back to Hilary Evans for his own piece of ecstasy. But she had not been at home.

The following afternoon she'd appeared unexpectedly in his father's hardware store. She'd looked a little green. The way she'd stared at him was as though any minute she might whip out a butcher knife and cut off, if not his head, then certainly his penis. "I've missed my period," she'd said. And terror struck his heart. Terror like he had never known. "If you'd worn one of those rubbers like I told you to get, but no, you bastard, you had to go on and stick it in!" Never mind that she had practically ripped off his pants on the way to her parents' bed; never mind that she'd kept insisting, "I'll show you how. I know all about it"; never mind . . . shit. "Are you sure?" he'd asked, the corner of an eyelid beginning to twitch like he was some old man with palsy. "Of course I'm sure," she'd snarled, her mouth twisting down into an ugly line. "We'll just have to get married." She'd tried then to smile, touching the sleeve of his shirt, like maybe that wouldn't be the worst thing in the world . . . two sixteen-year-old kids getting married and setting up house. But at that moment something snapped hard and final in his brain. No slut, no woman alive, was going to trap him into something like that. The twitch had gone from his eyelid. He'd straightened his shoulders and told her to go home. What in the hell was she doing anyway, coming up to his daddy's store while he was trying to work, sweep out the place, and his daddy not more than ten feet away? What in the hell was she thinking of? So she had just better go on home and let him think. Did she hear, did she understand? He still remembered the look on her face, like she'd dropped her pants right in the middle of the floor and didn't know what to do — whether to pick up the bit of silk there about her ankles or just step out of them and run.

He'd called her two days later and told her that the entire mess was her problem and if she ever again came near him he would, so help him God, shove her up alongside his garage and throw basketballs, hard, right into her gut. A couple of weeks after that she missed a few days of school. When she returned, she looked pale. She told people that she had eaten something — "this sword-fish" — that had made her want to die.

For a time he worried that he'd been too hard on her. He'd always feel better, however, when he remembered that if he'd gone along with the whole thing he'd have been a father and a working man at sixteen, slaving away as a delivery boy until he was an ancient twenty-five or something like that.

He continued to satisfy his powerful sex drive. Mary Sue, Helen, Elizabeth, Belinda, Mona, and some few dozens of others were vessels into which he had poured his throbbing need. But he never trusted words like "I'm wearing a diaphragm" or "It's not the time when I could get — you know, *that* way." He always kept hidden in his wallet a thin sheath of protective rubber, ready to pull out at a moment's notice. No, if sex were going to be used as a powerful weapon, then he would be the one wielding it. Never again would that club be held over his head.

But sex was not what pushed his ultimate button. It was power, derived from sex or otherwise, which did that.

Lance Benson had always been a loner. Because he preferred it that way. Though people placed him in leadership positions, sel-dom did they like him. Unless he decided they would do so. Then they became charmed, mesmerized. Still, beginning in grade school and continuing through the State University at Buffalo (which he'd attended because his parents could afford no better), he was never without a sidekick. That he tolerated. For convenience's sake. "I need this or that," he would say and then order, "See what you can do about it." Invariably the sidekick would bend over double to do his bidding. Such devotion came in handy. For example, whenever he edged up too close to exams and found he didn't want to bother with cramming, there was always the sidekick, who would slant his paper in such a way that the correct answers could be copied with a minimum of devious effort. He unfailingly selected someone who was bright, scrawny, overanxious, and pathetically outside the inner circle of things. As for himself, he was unequivocally within but above those social events which whirled, throughout his school years, like vanes on a pinwheel.

Each September would herald the time to replace one sidekick with another. Constancy was not his nature. Usually the castoff — whimpering, pimple-faced, and disgusting — would curve back into his shell. The tenth-grade discard, however, had reacted in the extreme. That one had suffered a mild nervous breakdown. But then Fritz Delmar had had other problems (the boy wheezed asthmatically since the day he was born).

Still, he couldn't help feeling guilty. And he'd worried about the kid, who had ended up spending six months in the hospital after he'd started huddling in corners and imagining spiders were after him. When news had finally circulated that his ex-sidekick was home, he'd gotten on his bicycle and pedaled as fast as he could, with Bailey racing along behind the spinning wheels. Strapped to his bike was a half gallon of banana ice cream, because Fritz could eat a ton of the stuff. He'd stood there ringing the Delmars' doorbell, while Bailey, his tongue hanging out after the chase, had nuzzled against his leg. He'd reached down and patted the dog's head. "I'll bet old Fritz is going to be glad to see us," he'd said. But the two of them never got past Mrs. Claude Delmar, who kept the storm door tightly shut. Through lips pursed, like she'd eaten a dead buzzard, she'd spat, "Lance, my boy doesn't want to see you — now or ever."

He had kept his composure. "Sure thing, Mrs. Delmar," he'd said, then motioned to Bailey. After dumping the ice cream behind some bushes, he'd pedaled, long and hard, until he'd reached Lake Ontario. For thirty minutes he'd sat out on a jetty and stared into water. Bailey kept licking his cheek. Finally, he'd knocked the dog away. He had to think. As he sifted through memories, he thought mostly bad thoughts about himself. Gradually, however, his perspective veered from incrimination toward justification. Soon after that he'd flung his arms against wind, shouted, "What the hell!," and charged headfirst into the icy water. Bailey, crouched on the jetty's edge, howled. The poor mutt couldn't understand. Plunging into that lake, where he'd stayed until he'd counted to a hundred, was something he had to do, because doing that proved he was larger than life. Gary Cooper in a pea jacket. Imaginative. Indestructible.

His former sidekick had lost his marbles for one reason and one reason only: the frail Fritz Delmar was about as enduring as a butterfly's wing.

The moment he'd reached home he'd called his current sidekick, so that they could laugh their heads off about the loon who was still as crazy as ever. "And I want everybody," he'd ordered, "I mean, the whole school, to be aware of that fact by noon tomorrow."

Peeling off his frozen clothes, he'd suddenly remembered something and cursed. That banana ice cream, melting by now into snow, had cost him a fortune.

His sidekicks were never selected from those who possessed wealth as well as brains. He preferred instead to make off with such elitists' girlfriends. (Even if doing so rarely presented a challenge.) All he usually had to do was murmur a few words of flattery, stare through lowered eyelids as if he were removing the girl's clothing piece by piece, and then leisurely, as if he didn't give a damn, walk off. A cardinal rule was never to look back. That would have been a sign of weakness. Nine times out of ten, the girl followed. Occasionally he asked himself why. The only answer he ever came up with was that was just the way it was. Always had been. Without even trying, he was voted Most Handsome straight through his high-school years. And it was his looks, more than his considerable talent, that slid him past crew work into leading roles on amateur stages. Along the way he also managed to wangle a few honors that were not contingent upon appearance: class president in his sophomore year; the debate team in his junior year; and in his senior year Most Likely to Succeed. With the help of sidekicks and a little studying, he'd even ended up salutatorian.

College was virtually the same. So much so that he came to think of glory as his destiny.

From the beginning, however, he was aware of a stumbling block: he had been born of poor and blundering parents. With a silver spoon in his mouth, he'd have been able to glide through life like a kite above trees. Such was his reasoning from the moment he found out that somebody else's daddy owned the building —

dilapidated though it was — in which his own father sold nuts and bolts. Michael Barnett, who had gone the summer before to an expensive boys' camp in the Adirondacks rather than the YMCA day camp, had flashed that explosive bulletin during fourth-grade recess.

As the years went by, he came to view his meager beginnings not as a stumbling block but as a boulder. He was convinced that, had wealth and refinement undergirded him, there would have been none of this never letting up, none of this horrendous effort to charm at all times, to scheme at all times, which was what he'd had to do ever since he'd cast his lot with legitimate theatre. At first he'd relished the challenge. And he'd had great expectations. But quickly he'd realized the theatre was no place to slide by on looks alone, to reel in a lone sidekick, to steal a few girlfriends. This was a place where one had to win over a hefty slice of upper-crust society. The miracle was that he always managed to hold sway over a strategic few.

The most obvious person he bent to his will was the woman he'd married. Intrigued by her breeding, her intelligence, and a thin core of iron beneath a fragile appearance, he could have taken her to bed and been done with it. But in her he saw more.

From the first evening Zoe Harrington had taken him home, he'd realized she possessed all the qualities a wife must have to help her husband succeed. Born into a fine old Houston family, she hadn't grown up watching her father peddle screws and nails. Pinafored and scrubbed-faced, she'd listened to the professor's rhetoric. And later, in her white debutante satin, she'd become engaged to her childhood sweetheart, Edwin, the son of a leading architect. Bearing considerable weight on his decision to take her away from Eddie, as she'd called her fiancé, had been her small but comfortable inheritance from her mother's grandfather, the founder of Bayou Rice Mills. (It was an inheritance which was to stand them in good stead. They'd been able to buy a large old house in what was now a residential section second only to River Oaks.)

Swiftly yet painstakingly, he had wooed and then married her. He had no regrets. Having a career of her own as a portrait painter kept her out of his hair, and, except when he chose to include her, out of his business. Pretty enough, she was also a gracious hostess who knew when to open her mouth and when to keep it shut. In return, he tried to be attentive. At least, attentive enough so that she never threatened to bolt out the door. Whenever he felt boredom or irritation setting in, he held himself in check, opened up partially to her, and took her to bed. That last was no chore.

The virginal Zoe had surprised him. Had fidelity been his nature, he would have been content. He considered most intellectuals to be lousy lays. But, almost from the beginning, his wife had spread her legs passionately, brought his head down to her breasts, and gripped him with an intensity that left him breathless. That had been the surprise. The rest had played out as he had anticipated. Only now was the scenario changing. He found himself bored and irritated nine-tenths, instead of half, of the time. With her as well as with the theatre.

And she never let up about wanting children. Those he would not have.

He'd been nine years old that afternoon he'd scrambled up to the attic to search for buried treasure. Well, he had found it, all right. But not the sort he'd expected. Hidden in a trunk of old clothes were newspaper articles, yellowed and crinkled with age. "WALCOT, N.Y., WOMAN GIVES BIRTH TO SIAMESE TWINS" was the first headline he'd seen. Reading on, he'd discovered that the twins, born eleven months after Norma Benson had given birth to a normal boy, had lived three hours and twenty-one minutes.

When he'd confronted his mother with the clippings, she'd yanked them out of his hand and yelled, "That's private!"

"Private?" he'd questioned. "But I just *read* about it."

"All that proves is you can read," she'd retorted, slamming a wooden spoon down on the kitchen table. Her only other comment — and it had sealed the subject forever — was, "Now you mention this just once to your father and he'll beat the shit out of you, you hear, the living shit!"

From the day he read of the births, his mother had taken on grotesque proportions. And his father, as well. What kind of people were they who could produce some hulking monster like that? And only eleven months after he himself had been born? Where was his other head? Often he woke up at night, sweating, seeing the two sisters, joined at their skulls, moving into his house, sleeping beside him.

The fears were irrational. The twins were dead. As for sprouting another head — that was absurd! And the odds of conceiving such monstrosities were no greater for him than for anybody else. But fear of the ones already born and of remote possibilities stayed with him, submerged — to resurface in dark hours.

He never voiced these fears to his wife. And he never took her home to Walcot. She knew nothing about his parents, the freaks who had produced freaks. She only knew he wanted no children. He'd explained countless times that in his life there was no room for such an emotional and financial burden. For clutter. And though that was the only explanation she would ever get from him, it was at least part of the truth.

His wife may have been the one most securely under his thumb, but there were others as well. Many had become faceless, nameless. And there were still those in his present and future who would eventually sink into that same anonymity. People, he felt, were to be used. To help meet transitory needs, attain long-term goals. For instance, years back there had been a director's wife. With her help, he'd landed his first starring role. She'd been a good twenty years older than he, but that hadn't stopped him. He'd seduced her solely because he'd heard she wore the pants in the family. As it had turned out, they'd enjoyed each other's company. So much so that one day they'd started out in her heart-shaped bed at ten in the morning and stayed there until fifteen minutes before her husband was due home asking, "What's for dinner?"

Here in Houston he'd pretty much stuck to seducing low-profile admirers and the occasional model. He strictly avoided those sacred cows — his board members' wives. Quite a few of them, however, cornered and practically straddled him weekly. He always refused without offending. After all, he wasn't dumb. Once, and only once, he'd made an exception. He'd taken an obsessive fancy to a senator's wife and they'd had to work something out. That had been a mistake. She'd repeatedly called the theatre. When she began calling him at home, he'd told her to get lost or he'd send her husband's career down the Buffalo Bayou in a tin cup. A few months later the senator's career began careening anyway. Rumor had it that the old gentleman had become consumed with keeping his child bride away from the bottle.

After that, he renewed his vow never to be led off course by passion.

Two years out of college and into his chosen profession, he'd realized that the greater power lay neither in bedrooms nor behind footlights, but rather somewhere in the depths of an auditorium where a voice boomed commands and the sidekicks on stage jumped. That became crystal clear. And it would be in those authoritative aisles, he determined, that he would plant himself as soon as he could devise and implement a plan to get there. It had taken a few years more before he came to fully realize that true power lay beyond a darkened auditorium. With that realization, he'd revised his plan. He had yet to extricate himself from the debonair-moustachioed and undershirt roles (he could play either equally well); but now his goal became to move quickly on to what he deemed his rightful place behind a massive desk. To do this he would have to found and build a theatre.

It was in Houston that he shot his plan, like a cannon ball, up in the air and down to the ground. When the touring company of *Picnic* had been ready to move on to Tulsa, he had not packed his bags. Ignoring the manager's threat of a lawsuit, he calmly stepped out of the leading role and into an abandoned warehouse, where he felt his life was just beginning.

That had been eighteen years ago.

A stage was constructed where storage bins had been. Church pews were hauled in (he'd scattered pillows, filled with goose feathers, across their hard surfaces). Walls that stretched up into rafters were painted a soft cream. Working fourteen hours a day, he did most of the renovation himself. Exhaustion became his middle name. He didn't care. He went into debt. He wasn't fazed. He had a goal.

Finally, came the advertisement: "Amateur Actors Needed." Three months later, the leading daily papers announced: "CURTAIN GOING UP." . . . Lance Benson was in business.

From the beginning, the pews were filled. Houston indeed had been fertile ground. Another theatre — the Alley — had already done the spadework. He was grateful. Undaunted. His vision was great: *his* theatre — The Arch — would surpass its predecessor.

As he had ordained, the old warehouse gradually became the artistic arena to which the rich and the prominent thronged. Sitting in pillowed pews watching Chekhov or O'Neill had become the chic thing to do.

He observed it all. Elated. But also amused. It gave him a kick to throw Shakespeare's name up on the marquee, which hung by ropes from the warehouse's portals. He himself, however, would always prefer plain simple movies, with sprawling mansions and Rolls Royces parked in curved driveways and some man in a velvet smoking jacket reaching over for a lady who was halfway out of her dress before the big fade-out. In that sense, he was most definitely a product of his heritage.

The Pix in Walcot, New York, had early on sealed his fate. As he sat in that darkened movie house, forgetting to eat his popcorn, watching Charles Boyer bigger than life up there on the screen, something had clicked in his ten-year-old brain. He, Lance Benson, could do that, be that, just as easily as anybody with a foreign accent and a balding head. He, too, could wear a velvet smoking jacket with quilted lapels. He could do that and more.

The more was to be in Houston.

As his theatre prospered, the elite became patrons. And that meant money. He shook himself free of debt. No longer had his father shouted orders down the phone. "Boy, get on back where you belong!" No longer did the old man dole out guilt. "Look I'm not so young anymore, I need you to take over the hardware business." (The nerve of somebody who never so much as took his son fishing, who never so much as had more than a five-sentence conversation with his son. And the "hardware business" that same son was expected to take over was little more than a narrow stretch of rented building thrown up between two other equally unpretentious and struggling enterprises — a gift shop with items guaranteed to be under ten dollars and a two-pump gas station — all three slung with the rest of the slanting, little town against the edge of Lake Ontario.)

Well, suddenly there had been no more directives from his father or, for that matter, from his mother. ("This theatre business's a bunch of foolishness," had been her supportive comment.) At last the freaks had shut up. And that suited him fine. Let Emmett Benson go on sweeping out somebody else's store only to come home at dusk to sit, stooped and sour, on a slanting front porch. Let Norma Benson, the vaccination as round and poxed as an old quarter on one of her fleshy arms, continue slamming down wooden spoons, brewing pots of beans. Let them both go on . . . with nothing. And while they were doing that, they could only imagine his glory. Because they weren't welcome in Houston, Texas, where he had raised a sign on which blazed three words — THE ARCH THEATRE!

Success spiraled. "Phenomenal," old-time Houstonians commented while making their tax-deductible checks payable to The Arch. Amateur actors (Zoe had once been among those) were replaced with experienced professionals, many of them Yale drama graduates. And the old warehouse, positioned against the Bayou, gave way to a modern, white edifice rising up in the heart of the city. There loomed the Esperson Buildings, Pennzoil, Exxon, Houston Center, the Hyatt, First City Tower, Texas Commerce Bank, One Allen Center, Jones Hall, and, one fine October day, The Arch. *His* theatre.

Pride stretched him tall as he watched his monument take its place in a skyline sculptured by moguls.

On move-in day, a mahogany desk, eight feet long and five feet deep, was centered on an Oriental rug in his office. Lance Benson had arrived.

But he hadn't counted on four things. First, there would always be others to make him jump. Others more important, freer agents. Those same early patrons, now squared around a boardroom table, believed their contributions gave them the prerogative to dip in and out of his theatrical business as whimsically and dictatorially as children at play. Second, the massive desk behind which he finally sat would never be cleared of paperwork piling up and up in ragged mounds. Third, frustration and tedium were slowly but inevitably to come and stay. And fourth, the theatre would never make him a wealthy man. These four things Lance Benson hadn't foreseen. But now these realities were here, beside him. Closing in. They were as sidekicks, only ironically, controlling him more than he controlled them. And there was no way he could ever view that situation as his just deserts.

The plan Lance Benson had conceived during those long hours out by his pool was both intricate and simple. The intricacy was to be the challenge, the simplicity the end result. Together they would enable him to escape from the trap. The plan itself was a blueprint for blackmail.

.    .    .    .

During the night he dreamed of two blond-haired infants, flailing, twisting to free themselves of a single skull which bulged, large and round. The tiny creatures opened their toothless mouths and screamed soundlessly. A small boy, with a dog that whined and yapped at fleas, stood close to one side. Staring. The infant girls kicked, writhed, until finally they lay still. The boy took his thumb out of his mouth, smiled, and beckoned to the dog. Together they ran outside toward the lake.

Benson awoke at three o'clock and stared at the clock. The dream had seemed not so much a nightmare as a grotesque little tale with a happy ending. That was a switch! Usually he awoke panic-striken from one of those subliminal surfacings. Tonight his breathing was even, his pulse rate normal. He decided to view the dream as a portent of good fortune.


"Eighty-five, ninety, ninety-five, four, and five dollars is your change." She counted the money into the outstretched palm. Disdainfully she dropped the eye shadow into a sack. Dumb lady. She had tried to steer the fortyish matron toward bronze. Blue was definitely out, yet try to tell somebody that when they had clung to the same fashion for twenty years. "But my eyes are blue, and my best asset," the woman had argued. Well, let her stick with her old blue eye shadow. Trying to help a fading, spreading wife in an important matter like looking her best for a husband who was probably screwing every office girl who handed him a memo was a pain in the ass. She folded a fresh stick of gum into her mouth and glanced at the clock. Five-twenty. Ten more minutes in this stupid place and she could leave.

To do what? Betsy usually got to the apartment first, so she'd probably be there scrubbing everything with Lysol. She hated, *hated* roommates. The Good Shepherd had been filled with them, and now here she was stuck with one who had an obsession about cleanliness. A person couldn't even leave a wad of bubble gum in an ashtray. What she really wanted was a place of her own. But who could afford that? With the theatre season ended, she was going to be both broke and bored. Ugh! Right now, if she were Zoe Benson, she'd be languishing out by that pool Lance said they had. She'd be sipping a Tom Collins while a husband any woman would kill for rubbed suntan oil on her back. That's what she'd be doing if she were Zoe Benson.

She reached under the counter for her purse. Might as well get everything in order for a quick getaway. She tallied up. Maybe she'd stop by Kroger's for some hominy grits. She loved those things. She'd stir up the hominy and open a can of little Vienna sausages, watch television, and spit out the window all the way to snotty Memorial where Zoe Benson lived with a man who didn't know half of what he was missing.

"Buy you a drink?"

Christ Almighty! If she'd been Catholic, rather than a good Baptist, she'd have crossed herself.

"Speaking of the devil, I was just thinking about you." Sandra Lowrey blinked her long lashes and giggled. She wished she'd combed her hair or something, but it was too late now.

"Oh?"

The way Lance Benson said something simple like "Oh?" demanded that you tell all — that you turn your brain inside out for him as if it was no more than a sewing bag filled with old bits and pieces you just had to get rid of, and you knew he'd take all the scraps of faded cloth out to the garbage can for you. She guessed that was why he was such a good director.

"I was thinking . . . I'd like to be stretched out by your pool right now." She smiled so that the dimple to the left of her mouth deepened.

"That wouldn't be such a bad idea. Except . . ." He paused. "It would be crowded there, don't you think?"

Shit, she thought, all those prayers I prayed down on my knees till I got red spots where my heels were digging into my ass are paying off. Dear God, she promised, just give me this man and I'll never commit another sin. Not big sins, that is. Just little ones.

She closed the cash register with a flourish. "I'll bet it would be as crowded as all get-out."

"Then we agree."

His stare drew her out from behind the counter. She'd be damned if they weren't going to get it on tonight even if she had to pay for the movie ticket herself to get Betsy Cleanup out of the apartment.

·    ·    ·

There was no screwing that first evening with Sandra Lowrey. Lance Benson saw to that. He chose instead a circuitous route: drinks and an elegant dinner at a little French restaurant, where dim lights and a corner booth wrapped them in anonymity.

As she sat awkwardly in her denim skirt and white blouse stained with the blush she had recently rubbed onto a customer's cheeks, he placed his hand on her knee. Staring intently into her eyes, he confessed that for a long time now — yes, a very long time — he had watched her, admittedly wanted her, and finally today had said to himself, "Lance, the only way to get what you want is to go after it."

"Oh, you are *so* right." She spoke softly. Her green eyes glowed.

Crap, Benson thought, all crap, and she's buying it. Though Sandra Lowrey was no Phi Beta Kappa, she was certainly smart enough to be in The Arch's company. But her schoolgirl crush was drawing her into his plot. That was what he had counted on. Perhaps he wouldn't even have to pay her. He'd just fill her up with fairy tales. After all, like a bitch in heat, she had followed him about the theatre these past few months. He thought of his old dog. His accomplice — this new sidekick — would become his Bailey. Zoe had been that long enough.

"What're you thinking about?" There was coquetry, yet shyness, in her voice.

"You, me."

"Then — to us!" She raised her glass. Wine sloshed over its rim. "Oh no!"

"It's all right, Sandra."

"But it isn't!"

"I assure you it is."

"It's not, it's not." Her blond hair swung back and forth.

He watched the hair swing.

Clumsy peasant, he thought as he realized that Zoe had never once spilled wine; and, if on the off chance she ever should, she wouldn't act like she'd killed your next of kin. But, unfortunately, his wife was an extra piece of a puzzle. In time he would leave Zoe Harrington Benson painting her austere faces, stirring mint tea for a father who was an old fool not even worthy of disdain.

"Lance? I'm not going to do that again." The girl spoke meekly. Sipped her wine sedately.

"It would be all right, Sandra, even if you did. Now, let's see if we can fix this." He began rubbing the crimson spots on her skirt.

She sat, scarcely breathing, until he lifted his hand.

"You're blushing." He had no idea whether she was or not.

"Well, I — I always blush when I'm happy. And I'm happy."

"Why?"

"You sitting next to me and all."

"Actually, I'm happy, too . . . Tell me, do you think your roommate could be away tomorrow night?"

"Oh, she will be. She always is on Tuesdays. Just about every Tuesday." She was babbling now. "I mean, you can count on it. Betsy Cleanup —" She put her hand to her mouth like a naughty child. "That's what I call her. Betsy Cleanup has these karate lessons on Tuesday nights and afterwards they all keep on their belts and go out dancing. So she'll be gone. Yes sir, right at six-forty-five, zoom." Her hand shot into air. "Betsy Cleanup is *gone!*" She gulped the remaining wine in her glass.

"Well then, that makes it perfect, doesn't it?"

"Perfect!" Timidly, yet as if he belonged to her now, she reached over and felt his leg. He stiffened, then relaxed. Why not allow himself to be tantalized? He could always go home to Zoe, because he was not, *not,* he told himself, going to touch Sandra Lowrey until tomorrow night. Sweet Jesus! The girl was closing in. He removed her hand and signaled for the check. This had gone far enough. After all, he, not Sandra Lowrey, was the one in command.

By four o'clock the next afternoon Lance Benson had concluded that locating a ground-floor corner apartment with one large bedroom and an enclosed front patio available for immediate occupancy was about as easy as unearthing a Neanderthal skull.

He had elected to find the unit on his own. An apartment locator would have driven him around, but all the while she would have been peering over her sunglasses, asking nosey questions. He couldn't afford the risk.

He'd arrived at the theatre before eight that morning and begun phoning around only to discover that apartment complexes still had their recorded messages plugged in: "Thank you for calling. The office is open from nine until six."

He'd sat waiting, thinking, drumming his fingers on his desk.

At nine he made his first contact. By twelve he had listed in his yellow pad seven possibilities resulting from thirty-six inquiries. Not one was available for immediate occupancy. July the first was the best move-in date offered. "It's the beginning of summer, sir, and college graduates are pouring, just pouring, into Houston," one of the more helpful managers had explained.

At four o'clock he swung his Continental into the sixth complex on his list. There had been something wrong with each of the others: a bedroom not large enough for a king-size bed; a back door which made him nervous; a complex too small for privacy; a location too far from his own home or those of his victims; a location too close for comfort.

Mrs. Reba Barker, a fleshy, lavender-haired lady, unlocked the door of Apartment 88. "It hasn't been vacated, but the tenant has granted permission for showing." She stepped back for him to enter.

He surveyed the wreckage.

"These young people!" She tossed her lavender head.

Empty beer cans, overflowing ashtrays, and *Playboy* magazines were strewn about the living room. A mangy dog, mud-caked and wide-eyed, stared suspiciously from behind an oversized television set.

Without saying a word, he walked over the eight hundred square feet. Once the garbage was hauled out, the place would have a bit of class. Only two years old, Carrousel Square, with its 438 units, had a bright, modern exterior, and its interior was more than acceptable. "Not bad," he noted. "In fact, nice." The large bedroom was tastefully wallpapered, and the bathroom had a marble vanity. The kitchen counters were butcher-block. A miniature chandelier hung in the dining alcove. Throughout there was beige carpeting. The single front-door entrance was shielded by a high redwood fence that surrounded the patio. Just off Westheimer, the complex was in a central location. Unfortunately, the rent was more than he had expected to pay, but the stakes were too high to let fifty extra dollars a month stop him.

"You'll clean it up?" he asked.

"Oh yes." Brightening, the manager moved deeper into her sales pitch. "It's all singles here and, of course, mostly young people, but there are a few your age and we do encourage mature adults, you understand. There's an Olympic-size swimming pool and lighted tennis courts, and —"

"Occupancy July first?"

"Definitely."

"I'll think about it." He was ready to leave. The dog had taken a liking to him. Something about the look in the mutt's eyes reminded him of Bailey. He felt uneasy.

"Mr. Harris, I wouldn't think too long if I were you. An apartment like this can be snapped up in the next thirty minutes."

"I understand," he said. "Thank you."

He would have to take his chances. It would be Sandra, not he, who tomorrow morning would walk in off the street, look at the apartment, put down the deposit money he would give her, and lease at Carrousel Square. There would be no connection between the new lessee and Mr. Harris who, never once having taken off his tinted glasses, had scrutinized the tiny apartment.

Driving out of the complex, he flicked on the radio and glanced at his watch. Damn, too late to shop for a bed. Besides, there were the inevitable responsibilities awaiting him at the theatre. It was imperative that he close up one season and launch into the next. At least only old movies were shown in the auditorium during the summer months. The actors wouldn't be there, crawling all over the place — on top of his desk, between his shoulder blades, into his brain. Well, soon it would all end. He had found the buried treasure — the setting where the evidence was to accumulate.

After last night's prolonged lovemaking, during which he had fantasized that he was doing exotic things not to his wife but to Sandy, he was hardly eager to crawl into the real Sandra's bed; yet only ninety-five minutes from now he was due to arrive on her doorstep. All he really wanted was a cool drink, a swim in his pool, and a few hours sunk in his recliner watching television. An old Humphrey Bogart movie would be heaven.

A radio commercial began advertising fun in your own Jacuzzi. "Invest today in a tomorrow of pleasure." He flicked off the announcer's syrupy voice and abruptly turned his car around. The theatre be damned. He was going home. There was just time enough for a quick dip in his pool before he set out again to further his investment in a brighter tomorrow.

This is foolish, Zoe told herself as she reached for *The Secret Garden,* a favorite book from her childhood. Foolish or not, reading the book for perhaps the sixth or seventh time was what she intended to do. Whenever things were not going right in her life, she turned to those warm, safe certainties which brought her comfort: eating a bowl of cereal; reading a familiar book; browsing through art galleries and museums; visiting her father; walking in wooded areas; swimming; and, of course, painting. Tonight she would seek the fictitious friends from her past.

She pulled her terry-cloth robe tighter about her and leaned back in Lance's recliner. Sipping iced tea, she tried to read. The usual remedy didn't work. Finally, she closed the book.

Staring across the room at her portrait of *Lance, the Director,* she asked herself, "What are you going to do about this marriage?" She remembered the night before. Surely her husband still loved her. But how did she feel about him? And why had she been left alone tonight?

"Stand on your own two feet," she ordered herself. But she did do that, didn't she? Hadn't she carved out a career in a city where traditionally artists became known if they were adept at painting large canvasses of Texas oil derricks? And didn't she form opinions independent of Lance? Lately she even staunchly defended those opinions. Wasn't she beginning to search for the person she had suppressed? Surely that schoolgirl and the thirty-six-year-old woman she had become were still one and the same. Independence was being fought for and regained. But that wasn't enough. Tonight — at nine-seventeen specifically — she wanted her husband with her. He could even be upstairs in his darkroom where intermittently he closeted himself. She would then march into that sacrosanct garret to ask that they examine what had gone wrong in their marriage. Had they ever been right as a couple, she wondered. Of course they had. She had to believe that.

Well, for the time being there would be no shared dissection of a screwed-up relationship. During the past forty-eight hours Lance had gone in and out of the house as if he were in the throes of mounting a new play. Long ago she had ceased asking for his exact whereabouts and the time he would return. And now — though more often than not he volunteered the information — she frequently didn't care. Tonight, however, when she needed him here, it was frustrating to feel he was inaccessible. It was as if he had stepped behind a secret door and, though she might run her fingers over the smooth paneling, the door would never be found, never be opened to her.

She stirred the mint in her tea. Her eyelids lowered until the portrait across the room blurred. She groped for comfort.

While growing up, she had often heeded her father's advice: "Zoe, if you're down, do something nice for yourself . . . or, if not for yourself, for someone else." She would give Caroline Fletcher a call and ask when she would be going into the hospital. She would say warm, bright, understanding things. Poor Caroline was the one with the new problem. Hers was an old one. And, unlike Caroline, nothing traumatic was causing her pain. Nothing threatening. Or sinister.

She straightened. Sinister. A strange word to think of suddenly. Why did she feel as she did? Not just isolated, but uneasy. Fog closing in. She turned up the lamp, with its three-way bulb, to its brightest glow.

"Enough!" she told herself.

Still, she prayed that tomorrow would come soon. The sun would surely shine. It would be a good day. Wouldn't she be completing her portrait of Willis Young, a man who had become a bank president before he was forty? And tonight would be tolerable just as soon as she reached out, like her father himself so often did, to someone else.

She picked up the phone and dialed.

After three rings, Caroline Fletcher answered and told her how glad she was to hear from a friend and that, yes, a date had been set, though — foolishly perhaps — she was procrastinating so that Martin — and herself, too, she guessed — could get used to the idea. But, yes, the operation was scheduled for Friday, July first.

"I'll come to see you as soon as you feel like company," Zoe promised.

"Thanks," said Caroline. "I'm sure I'll be needing a friend."

"Stop, stop, I can't take it — I can't take any —" She let out a long, high scream, then a moan, and silence. She was crying softly. "Lance, I never — never — ever — oh, I love you so much." He touched one of her nipples. "No, don't — *don't,* I can't take any more, please." He pulled her close and stroked her hair. She snuggled against him. Her fingertip traced the hair on his chest as she asked, "Was it . . . good for you?"

"Very," he said. It was true. The girl had natural talent. She would make an excellent pawn. Right now he felt a tenderness for this strange girl-woman. He knew it would pass, but for the moment he gave in to the feeling. He kissed her forehead. Later he would tell her to sit up in bed and listen carefully. But not now. For a time they would sleep. He kissed her fingertips, then bit them gently. "Sleep a little, OK?" he said.

"OK." She burrowed closer. "Anything . . . anything . . . you ask . . . I'll do."

"Is that a promise?"

"Cross my heart," she murmured, already half asleep.

"Fuck you!" Her huge breasts trembled in righteous indignation.

"Slap me."

"What?"

"Slap me. Come on, Sandra, slap me hard!"

"No!"

"Yes! Hard, get it all out, all the anger." He was the director at work. "Come on, hit me, hit me!"

Her small, pink fists doubled up, and she began pounding his chest hard, then harder and harder. He grabbed her arms and threw her back on the bed.

"Now," he said, still panting after it was over, "get your clothes on so we can talk about this sensibly."

Subdued, she pulled on her robe. He made a mental note: Replace chenille with black lace.

"Bring me some wine," he ordered.

"All I've got is beer."

"That'll do." Something else to change around here. Inwardly he groaned. His expenses were mounting.

He pulled on his pants and went into the bathroom. Splashing water on his face, he thought suddenly of the legal pad which detailed his scheme. As he had sat out by his pool, he had printed and centered at the top of page one a single word: "PROJECT." That heading seemed fitting. For wasn't a project an organized and goal-oriented undertaking? And wasn't he, Lance Benson, systematically about to bring men down, like duckpins, in order to set himself up as the maker of his own destiny? Once he had succeeded, he would never again be struck in the gut by either pressures from others or imposed boredom.

He straightened, dried his face, then studied his reflection in the mirror. For a moment, he didn't like what he saw. Sandra shattered that moment.

Coming up behind him, she held out a beer.

He took a long swig and felt better.

"I'm sorry I hit you," she said meekly.

"I told you to."

"I know, but Lance" — she padded behind him into the living room — "when you asked if I would fuck other men for you, I just — Lance, that *hurt* me. I mean . . . what kind of love is that, for Pete's sakes?" She was getting mad again.

He sprawled on the sofa. "Sit down." He patted the cushion beside him. "I'm going to tell you a bedtime story."

"Bullshit!"

"Sit *down*."

She sat.

"I'm going to tell you about a little girl who grew up in an orphanage."

"Hey, that's me!"

Her naïveté was coming through again. It would be hard to recapture the tenderness he had felt for her a short while ago. He supposed it didn't matter. It was just a feeling he'd liked having. But having or not having that feeling was in no way vital to the success of his project.

"That's correct. The little girl is Sandra Christine Lowrey. And this, Sandra, is a Cinderella story."

"Does she get the prince?" she asked eagerly.

She *is* still a kid, he thought, half expecting her, any minute, to begin sucking her thumb.

"You're jumping ahead . . . but, yes, she gets the prince, the castle, the whole bit."

She bounced happily on the sofa.

"But first, she has to undergo some experiences she may not like. So the important thing to keep in mind is the end result. You understand — *end result?*"

"Which is?" She eyed him suspiciously.

By rote he repeated, "The prince, the castle, the whole bit."

"Translate that, please."

"To begin with, you quit your drugstore job and move into a new apartment."

Her eyes widened appreciably. "That's heavy."

"Absolutely."

"When do I get the prince?"

"Actually, you've got him now."

"You know what I mean."

"No."

Coyly, she held up her left hand and began rubbing the wedding-ring finger.

Damn, the girl was moving fast! He protested, "For Christ's sake, Sandra."

"You got it. For Christ's sake. If I'm going to do something nasty like fuck a whole bunch of men —"

"Five," he corrected.

"All right, five. That's a bunch. Look, I'm religious. I grew up going to church half my life, remember? So if I'm going to fuck one man or twenty, it doesn't matter, I want to be" — she took a deep breath — "legal. I want to be Mrs. Lance Benson."

"Sounds nice," he said dryly.

"Meaning?"

He sighed. Suspicious creature that she was, he would have to stuff the biggest lie of all down her throat. He was reminded of a hungry baby sparrow.

"You'll get your wish. After — *after,* Sandra — our project is completed.

"Which is when?"

"Soon."

"How soon?"

"Look, give me time! There's a logic, a timing, to all this. If I leave Zoe —"

"*If* you leave Zoe?"

He began again. "When I leave Zoe — and I am going to leave her — she'll take me to the cleaners. Every cent."

"Every cent? Come on, Lance."

"Because I'll be leaving her for another woman." He spaced each word carefully; the lie, like radium, aimed into her brain.

"Oh." Radiation beamed. And then she spoke softly, awed. The baby sparrow nesting down deep into a nest. "Yeah . . . yeah, she would, wouldn't she?

"She would. So you and I, Sandra" — he cupped her hand in his — "will need money. To pave the way, to make it all possible."

"I guess we have to think like that, don't we?"

"Yes, yes, we do." She had used the word "we." Excellent. His finger outlined the curve of her breasts. "Believe me, I've given this a lot of thought and this is what I've come up with."

"You can't think of something else?" She shifted on the sofa.

"Can you?"

"Well . . . we could just be poor."

"Hardly." His voice purposefully hardened.

There was a long pause.

". . . Tell me what you want me to do."

Scrupulously he explained as much as she needed to know. He even threw in that the experience of acting like she'd never acted before — feeling revulsion while faking ecstasy — would enhance her career. "God, you'll become one of the world's greatest actresses!" He spread his hands wide. For a moment, marquee lights glowed in her emerald eyes. Her head began nodding. But then came the questions — some dumb, some not so dumb — that he answered with half-truths which seemed to satisfy her.

Finally, the task was completed. But it had been a more difficult one than he had anticipated. Her Good Shepherd training had come through far too many times.

"Above all," he cautioned, near exhaustion from his own performance that was not yet over, "this is between you and me, nobody else."

"Between Cinderella and Prince Charming, right?" she asked solemnly.

"Right." He gave her the reinforcement — the fairy tale — she apparently needed.

At the door, he handed her money. "Leave work, say you're sick, anything, but get this deposit over to Carrousel Square at nine o'clock sharp tomorrow." He'd punched the right button. Her enthusiasm spiraled.

"My own apartment, my very own, my very, very own!"

"But no swimming, no tennis, no speaking to anyone."

"My very own prison." Now she was pouting.

"You'll like it." He grinned.

"Only if you're there. *Lots*."

"As often as I can be, Sandra."

She snuggled against him. "And that better be lots."

He stiffened, suspecting she was ready to go off again like a firecracker. It was time to recap a few pertinent details then leave.

"Remember, you'll quit your job June twenty-ninth; June thirtieth, pack; then July first, you'll be moved in. And the operation can get launched."

"You make it sound like a rocket." Again she was pouting.

"It is a rocket." He glanced at his watch. Eleven-fifteen. Any minute Betsy whatever-her-name-was could come crashing through the door, her black belt flying.

"I'll see you tomorrow?" Her whole heart was pulsing up into her face.

"More than likely. But I suppose with Betsy Karate —"

"Cleanup."

"Yes. Well, I suppose we'll have to go someplace else. There are things, Sandra — magnificent lover that you are —"

"I am?" The eyes widened. They had a way of doing that.

"You are. But there are techniques I want to teach you."

"Such as?" Her suspicions had resurfaced.

He answered lightly. "Simple enticements. To use on the others."

"Well, only if it means . . . what you promised."

"I gave you my word, didn't I?"

"Then, OK . . . I guess I'll do it."

"You guess?"

"I know. Lance, I *know!*" She threw her arms around his neck.

"Bravo!" Suddenly weary of it all, he disentangled himself.

Halfway out the door, he remembered a strategic instruction. "Oh, Sandra, if you have any boyfriends around, get rid of them."

"I already did." The green eyes unblinking, she stated as if on holy ground, " 'Cause I was waiting for you."

The warm feeling returned. Waves rushing over him. He would drown.

"How astute." Coolness measured out into his voice.

"Yeah. Well . . ."

His response had thrown her off balance. That was where he should keep her. He stood, silent, observing her.

"Lance, I just want to tell you . . . I want you to know I'll do anything — anything at all — for you."

"Keep repeating that," he said and left.

Walking to his car, he tasted her name. "Sandra Lowrey. Sandra Christine Lowrey." He smiled to himself. The girl was going to do fine. Just fine, indeed.

. . .

"I got it," she whispered into a Budget Drugs phone at ten-twenty-five the next morning. "I got it, I got it, I got it!"

"You got it? That's my girl!"

"You got it, I got it! I got the apartment." She popped her gum.

"And this conversation is crazy!" He laughed, then hung up the phone and hurriedly left The Arch.


"So who needs a king-size bed?" he reasoned, unable to find one with a canopy. He circled the four-poster double. Debating. Actually, the double might better serve his purposes. There would be less of an area for the camera to focus on and a smaller mirror could be cut and hung beneath its canopy. He squinted at the swoops of purple moiré.

"Custom-ordering would take at least ninety days," the sales-clerk said after he had selected a pattern of plum peacocks strutting on pink chintz.

"Then I'll take the floor model."

"Oh, we can't sell *that!* It was just set up yesterday and the interior designer would be furious."

Cash and charm can buy anything, he concluded as he wrote the address where the canopied bed was to be delivered the morning of July first.

"I'm purchasing this for a friend." He neatly printed Sandra Lowrey's name on the ticket.

The lady smiled knowingly. "That's nice, Mr. — er —"

"Grayson." He looked, unblinking, into her eyes.


"This is what I want." He handed a drawing to the barrel-chested stump of a man.

Guy Luden scratched his balding head. "I've cut a lot of mirrors, but this one sure is interesting." He turned the drawing sideways and squinted. "You want squares of mirrors, you say, glued to a heavy board?"

"Adhered tightly. It will be, you understand, hanging over a bed."

"Yeah." Guy Luden grinned. He bowed his head again to the drawing. "And up in one of these corners a hole . . ." He circled his thumb and one of his work-thickened fingers. "Like so?"

"Like so. Near" — Lance pointed to the drawing — "where two of the squares meet. Unobtrusively."

"I got you."

"Since the board will hang beneath a canopy, it needs to be secure. That's why I want steel hooks to latch the board to the canopy frame."

"Gotcha. I'll pad the hooks with felt so the wood won't get scratched. Even though they'll be out of sight — under a canopy, you say?"

"That's right."

"I got a thing for wood. Can't stand to see a fine piece of wood scarred up."

"I feel exactly the same way. Felt will be fine."

"It'll take a couple of weeks. I'm pretty busy, and this is a real tricky thing what you're asking, I mean kind of different, you understand, from most of what I do around here." The stubby man glanced about the lofty old barn he had converted into his place of business.

"What I do is a lot of church windows," he added as he watched his customer walk around the workshop.

"I can see."

"So I reckon this'll be a right interesting switch."

"I would imagine so." Lance turned from the sheets of colored glass stacked against the walls. "If you can deliver the finished product to this address" — he handed him a slip of paper — "the afternoon of July first at four o'clock, I'll meet you there and we'll see how it fits."

"July first." Guy Luden rubbed the auburn hair, fading gray, which sprung out of his open shirt. He looked up at the beamed ceiling, then down at the hard-packed dirt floor. "July first. That should work. Ought to, Mr. Black."

At nine o'clock that morning Lance Benson had withdrawn five thousand dollars from his only source of available money — Zoe and his joint savings account. Two thousand ninety-eight dollars and seventy-six cents had gone for the four-poster canopy, equipped with a firm mattress. By five-forty-five that afternoon the remainder of the money was tied up in an investment residing in the trunk of his Continental: one Port-a-Pak color camera, with automatic exposure control; two portable videocassette recorders; one eight-inch color television set; and one remote-control center, containing one On and one Off button.

"Two VCRs!" the young man waiting on him had exclaimed. "You've got to be going into this in a big way."

"I am." He'd placed cash on the counter.

Two VCRs were essential to his project. He would position one, plus the small television set, in his darkroom. The second VCR would go, along with the camera, on the board suspended from the frame of the canopy. From its underside, the board would be camouflaged by mirrored squares. Anyone sprawled in the bed looking up at his mirrored reflection would never suspect that approximately fifteen and a half pounds of video-recording apparatus resided over his head. The remote control would be fastened to the back of the headboard so that Sandra, casually stretching, could switch the equipment on or off.

After the camera had recorded a session, it would be a simple matter to lift the canopy cover, eject the cassette from the VCR, take the cassette home, and slip it into the VCR waiting on a shelf in his darkroom. He'd plug the VCR into the small television set and, whamo, instant replay. Should the footage be the dynamite he expected, the cassette would then go into his pocket to be dangled later in front of his victim. And, if the confronted wished to see himself in living color, that could be arranged.

Before viewing the footage himself, he would make sure that Zoe was either downstairs or out of the house. He'd develop a few photographs of one thing or another as evidence of the work he'd been doing up in what she called his "garret."

Until July he would keep the equipment designated for the apartment in the trunk of his car. The rest could be moved to the darkroom at some time when Zoe was away. He was glad he had initially installed a lock on that door. Intuitively he had known that one day he would want his room barricaded against everyone except himself. Indeed, within the next few days his garret was to become his sanctum sanctorum.

He yawned behind the wheel of his car. It had been an exhausting day. He'd stop at a pay phone and inform Sandra that this evening was out. There remained more than enough time to train her. Tonight he was taking his wife to a movie. A comedy would be a diversion from the drama which was about to draw him into a vortex he welcomed but could not hasten. July the first was still sixteen days away. He had better relax — "cool his heels" as his father used to admonish whenever he'd been about to explode from wanting to be done with his chores and on his way, racing with Bailey, toward Lake Ontario, where somehow a whole other world seemed to be waiting.

High above the city, Irene Stanton lay awake at two in the morning. She listened to the faint noises drifting up from the street below. The sound of the small hours was the same whether in Beijing or Houston. Careful not to wake her husband, she eased out of bed and groped her way to an open suitcase. For a time she held the hapi coat she was taking to Bonita. Its silk was shocking pink. An embroidered dragon streamed fire across its back. The hapi coat was hardly Bonita's style, but she would love it. For some inexplicable reason, Irene thought of the slogan "Put a tiger in your tank." She missed Bonita. And still to come were the long weeks in England. She refolded the hapi coat into its tissue. She missed her son. He would not be waiting for her in Houston, as Bonita would. He would not be waiting for her in England, as her crinkling eighty-six-year-old mother would. David would not be waiting anywhere. She could visit his grave, place flowers there, but it would change nothing. She bit her lip and wished the noises of the city were loud enough to drown her thoughts. Why had she used that word? Why couldn't the word — the guilt — be obliterated? She had turned her back for only a moment — and he had been an excellent swimmer. Everyone had remarked, "Look how that child swims!" She would ask Charles in the morning to please, please, let them hang a portrait of David in their home. Though she didn't understand her own feelings, she knew that seeing his solemn little face would help. It would not rip out her heart as Charles insisted it would. Instead, she would promise over and over to the portrait, "I will never, never, never turn my back on you again." That would make it better somehow.

She slipped back into bed. Her husband didn't stir. Often he slept, smiling, as if one long, bright dream were engulfing him. Sometimes she hated him, sleeping so peacefully like that, denying her their son's portrait, gliding through life plastered with hero's ribbons and badges. She touched his cheek. "Forgive me," she whispered. And then she prayed, "I love China . . . and England. But, please, dear God, let the summer end soon."

. . .

"Because I couldn't find a girl who was as pretty as my first-grade teacher, as smart as my tax consultant, as exciting as one of my oil gushers, and as spiritual as the beads on a rosary," Lowell Hook replied to Amanda Stebbins's question: "Lowell, why have you never married?"

Biting into a petit four, Hook surmised that if he didn't miss his guess Amanda Stebbins, with her little widow's hump and deaf left ear, was angling for a proposal. Well, it was a little late for that, he thought. Fifty years ago, maybe, when she was peaches and cream rather than pancake.

"Amanda, you and I are as old as Indian burial sites."

The pancake crumbled.

He quickly added, "So it's remarkable to me how you've remained so beautiful."

"Oh, Lowell, how sweet." She smiled, a bit sadly. He knew she was not completely fooled.

Gallantly he extended his arm and escorted her back into the chamber hall where the string quartet was tuning up for the second half of the program.

The musicale to which she had invited him was a pleasant way to pass a Sunday afternoon. In his declining years, he had discovered that the purity of classical music pleased him. He studied the program and remarked to his companion that the Wesley mansion was a perfect setting for the Debussy. He could look out onto the lawn where peacocks strolled.

As the music began, he eyed the peacocks and fancied himself the most arrogant of the lot, spreading his brilliant plumage for the little peahen edging toward him. The peahen would be, he fantasized, that lovely young girl, spilling out of her costume, with whom he had spoken briefly at The Arch gala. Ah, how he wished! . . . At least next season he would be able to sit in his aisle seat and watch her on stage. Though he never interfered in artistic matters, he hoped Benson would cast her in a role that kept her in full view for most of the evening.

He closed his eyes. The music filled his being. He trembled slightly. He'd never give up his love for country and western. "Up Against the Wall, Redneck," his all-time favorite, sent him into a rhapsodic reverie. But this afternoon Debussy's Quartet in G Minor was definitely coming in a close second.

"Raymond, you've got a real thing about desserts."

"It completes the meal for me, Scruffy," Raymond Reese explained apologetically as he took the first bite of his cheesecake and felt absolutely orgasmic.

"Maybe I'm jealous." Scruffy Dawson looked down at the beginnings of a pot belly. He sipped black coffee and watched the orgy going on between Raymond and the cheesecake.

"Scruffy," Raymond rhetorically asked between bites, "you and I have known each other a long time, right?"

"Since kindergarten."

"And that's a long time. By anybody's standards, agreed?"

"Agreed," echoed Scruffy, a bit bored with the conversation.

"So, tell me something. Do you think I am . . . uh, what is it about me? I mean, you have a wife and three kids and all the normal things — what's wrong with me? I mean, women don't like me."

"Raymond," Scruffy reminded him wearily, "we've had this conversation before."

"Yeah, I know." Raymond shifted the horn-rimmed glasses on his nose and dug deeper into the cheesecake. He was thinking. If your best friend, dating back practically to B.C., wouldn't tell you what the matter was, then maybe there was something horribly wrong. Maybe he should avoid the subject of himself entirely and concentrate on keeping the conversation light with Scruffy at their monthly luncheons.

The luncheons had been going on since he had graduated from Parsons School of Design and Scruffy from Harvard Law School. As though preordained, they'd both returned to Houston and their friendship had continued. Being friends with Scruffy was the closest he would ever come to being "in." Scruffy — so named because of the tennis shoes he insisted on wearing straight into his high-school graduation exercises — had always been "in." The link between Scruffy and himself was that they had grown up in big stucco houses side by side in West University, shared stray dogs and cats, and moaned out on the curb about homework and stepfathers. At Childress, whenever jibes had been poked at skinny, arms-tangled-in-legs Raymond Reese, big likable Scruffy had thrown his arm around his buddy's shoulders — stretching them both up ten feet — and declared, "This is my best friend."

Well, if a friend like that wouldn't help you out, who would? Maybe he ought to concentrate on business. There was certainly enough of it, what with his mother running around the studio this morning hugging everybody and everything, proclaiming that the Wesley job was theirs. "Raymond, *we got it!* We honestly got that nineteenth-century mansion!" You would have thought any day now they'd be moving in. Well, for all practical purposes they would. The contract specified that the entire place was to be re-decorated. Starting in August. Right now visions of fabrics and wallpaper should be spinning in his head. Instead, all he could see was long blond hair and fantastic boobs. He'd run into the Bensons at a movie, and that had started him thinking all over again about the actress he'd admired at the gala. After the movie, he'd gone straight home to masturbate in his Thomas Jefferson alcove bed and pretend. Pretend what? Hell, he was still a fucking virgin! He had been pretending in unknown territory.

"So, Scruffy, what's wrong with me?"

"Raymond, you're about the horniest bastard I know. My advice to you is to just get yourself a piece of ass, *any* ass. Then we'll take up this discussion over next month's lunch."

"But how?"

Scruffy signaled for the check. As it was, Raymond and his blasted cheesecake had already made him late for an appointment with a client whose divorce would involve a considerable settle-ment. His mind had gone beyond Raymond's screwing problem and on to how he could tactfully advise Roselyn Solomon to quit getting her name linked with those of eligible bachelors in the society columns.

"Scruffy," Raymond persisted, "just how am I going to get myself *that?*"

"Hell, Raymond, I don't know. Go to one of the night spots . . . Cody's . . . anyplace. I'd take you myself, but Missy wouldn't appreciate it."

"Yeah, I guess you're right." He envied Scruffy Dawson for having his pretty little wife Missy and their straight-teethed chil-dren. All he had was a mother — the best in the world, to be sure — and the Wesley contract. Well, things could be worse. And Scruffy had given him good advice: Just go get yourself screwed.

"Thanks, Scruffy," he said as they parted in the parking lot outside Rudi's.

"Anytime," said Scruffy, not completely sure why he was being thanked. Mentally he had already joined Roselyn Solomon and was reading her a tasteful riot act.

The monthly luncheon was adjourned. Once again that slender ritual, which bound the two of them together in their adulthood, had been performed. Dawson breathed a sigh of relief. Raymond slumped in sadness. Tenaciously he clung to the friend of his youth, though he was beginning to suspect that in return the "in" Scruffy Dawson merely tolerated his old buddy Raymond.

Walking slowly to his car, Raymond Reese wondered if anyone felt more than a mild tolerance for him. He guessed only his mother, and sometimes he wasn't so sure about her. What she adored was her son Raymond as he appeared. Maybe she would feel differently about the hidden Raymond who desperately needed to get himself fucked . . . and soon. Hell, he'd even considered men. But he wasn't so sure about that. He only knew he ached for bodily contact with another human being. He was lonely. And in his loneliness a mother's adoration was simply not enough.

"Bitch!" He threw the paper across his narrow living room. What a way to start the day! Plopped down in a lousy but exorbitantly expensive apartment, drinking coffee warmed over from yesterday, and reading in some shitty society column that your wife was seen at the Zoological Benefit chatting with Cramer Jordan. So what if Cramer Jordan had been a friend of the family for years? So what if Cramer Jordan, three stools down from him in a bar the other night, had said sympathetically, "Sorry to hear about you and Roselyn"? So what? So what? He was pissed, that was "so what." Cramer Jordan, recently divorced, disgustingly rich, and damn good-looking, had no right to be "chatting" with his wife. Roselyn Solomon was Victor Solomon's wife. That was what she was. She might be a lot of other things he hadn't figured out yet, but she was first and foremost his wife and the mother of his children.

Well, he would show her. They had screamed more than once at each other over the phone in the past two weeks. He guessed they could scream again. He didn't give a damn what his lawyer told him. He wanted to talk with his wife.

Bleary-eyed from rage and a hangover, he dialed the wrong number. "West Belt U-Totem." Shit! He put his head in his hands and groaned. She could u-totem her ass on back where she belonged was what she could do. But she wouldn't. He knew that. Not yet. Maybe never.

He'd better pull himself together. Shave, shower, and get to work.

He looked out the window. It was a gray, drizzly day. He closed the curtains.

Shaving, he began wishing he were at Reins Airport. He'd climb into the Baron and cut through darkness, slicing clouds, going up and up where sunlight hit against his plane. He'd have Roselyn beside him. Damn! A bright red dot formed on his chin. He dabbed at blood and winced. Hell no, he wouldn't take Roselyn. He'd leave her crawling in dirt with Cramer Jordan. He'd swoop up past clouds with some sweet young thing who thought him the wonderful, devastating creature that he was. He'd done that before, and he'd do it again. The only difference would be that Roselyn wouldn't be waiting at home to ask if he'd had a good trip.

Well, sitting around hoping she'd want him back was no good. Not anymore. If she could get her name plastered all over the paper like that, who knew what tomorrow might bring? Probably an enlarged photograph showing her glued to the side of the next susceptible man. She seemed to be doing just fine in that department. But he could fuck around, too, couldn't he? Bradshaw would croak, "You want to hang on to your money? For God's sake, keep a low profile." His lawyer, of course, would be right. If he intended to drown his misery in beds as well as in bars, the drowning had better be discreet.

Besides, if Roselyn continued thinking of him as "the solitary sufferer," she just might change her mind about this whole ludicrous business. Meanwhile, it was time to resume a familiar sport. The profile would be low. As far as Roselyn was concerned, it would be nonexistent.

Dressed in a gray pin-striped suit with a mauve shirt and gray silk tie, he viewed himself in the full-length mirror on his closet door. He looked a lot better than Cramer Jordan had ever looked a day in his life. As for money, he could almost — not quite, but almost — buy and sell the bastard anytime he chose. In spite of his own shining superiority, however, it looked like Cramer Jordan was making time with his wife. Such an implication clearly necessitated his picking up the phone later in the day and giving Roselyn hell. That way he could at least hear her voice.

She did not awaken when he reached over and cupped her left breast. It fit nicely in the palm of his hand. His thumb searched for the small hard lump then quickly moved away from what it had found. She stirred. Martin Fletcher inched over to his side of the bed. Across the room was the open suitcase. Tucked among new silk nightgowns was a bottle of Christian Dior he had brought home yesterday, knowing that Caroline wore perfume whether in high moments of crisis or in routine hours of drudgery. "It makes me feel feminine — and alive," she'd explained once as she'd dashed back into the house to dab fragrance onto her wrists before heading for work at an Arch garage sale.

Well, his wife would need more than perfume to keep her feeling alive and feminine. But perhaps the Dior, her favorite, would help. Help Caroline. It would not help him. He was afraid. Unsuccessfully he fought the familiar images. For the past several days it was as if a huge machine rolled incessantly over his brain, flattening it out, then stamping into the flatness pictures of lush, full breasts. The machine invariably would back up and roll over the erotic imprints only to come down hard again on his brain, leaving stark charcoal etchings of scooped-out, lopsided chests, angry scars seared jagged into their hollowness. At night he dreamed. His arms flailed out; his hands reached beyond Caroline's deformity — for that was what it would be — to mounds of flesh, gleaming tan and ripe with the firmness and litheness of youth. Awakening, he would feel old and depraved.

"What am I? Some kind of monster?" he asked himself. It was as if he did not fear for his wife's life. But the possibility of Caroline's dying was even more remote to him than the acceptance of his own eventual death. Caroline was the stronger of the two. From the beginning he had known that. Rather than resentment, he felt gratitude that her strength was linked to his weakness. Caroline would refuse to die on the operating table. She was incapable of dying. But she was capable of letting him down. He knew that now. One of her small, reliable breasts was about to be removed from his grasp. That was his fear. That the breast would be amputated.

Tomorrow they would walk with false cheerfulness into the

hospital. And the day after that, they would see. Until then, they would wait. The seeing would come soon enough.

"These are possibilities." She handed the librarian a stack of prints.

"Then they're as good as ordered." Mavis Horlock flipped through the prints. Stopping at van Gogh's *The Starry Night,* she trilled, "Such colors!" She peered over glasses, which had slid to the end of her patrician nose. "Zoe, you're wonderful to take the time."

"I like doing it," she said. And it was true. She liked researching and recommending prints for purchase by the library's lending department. She liked being a part of the program "Art in Your Environment."

Leaving the librarian, whose head was bowed low over a Matisse, Zoe Benson retreated among shelves to select a book to read during those evening hours when she was alone.

She reached for something light, but her hand moved on, her fingers touching titles. She stopped at Styron's *Sophie's Choice.* Again she thought of advice given by her father: "You must examine the agony of other people — particularly the victims of war — so that you will feel . . . *hurt* for them and never forget that there are those who have undergone far more pain than you or I will experience in our lifetimes. The odds are that it will be that way."

She felt ashamed. Her distress was disproportionate to her problem. She checked out the book and left.

Still . . . as she drove home, her thoughts returned to her own pain, to the incongruities in her marriage, in her husband's behavior. Lance was more attentive now than he had been immediately following the season's close; but often after dinner he would push back his chair and say, "I work better at the theatre when nobody's there."

"Is it too noisy around here?" she'd asked once.

"No, no," he had assured her, mistaking her sarcasm for concern. "It's just my artistic temperament."

"Bull!" she'd said so he couldn't miss her point.

At that he'd slammed out the door.

Admittedly Lance had not been gone long these past evenings. But always when he returned it was as if in the short time he had been away the theatre had become his mistress. He would sink into his recliner to watch the ten o'clock news or, if it were later, an old movie. Usually she left him alone. Once she'd tried to talk to him, but he'd retreated deeper into *Stolen Life*. Finally, she'd thrown up her hands and said, "Forget it."

But she was not yet ready to write off their marriage.

"We circle one another," she thought, still analyzing. "Our minds and our bodies rarely touch." She would suggest that they take a vacation. Perhaps, far from Houston, the circle around which they moved would become smaller until there would be no escaping the contact she needed. Yes, she would insist they go away. Before the Fall. Before the new theatre season devoured her husband. That season, she determined, would not do the same to her. And neither would the marriage. Their vacation would have to offer hope. Promise change. Of that she was certain.

Lance Benson knew, with great authenticity, about the male's sexual turn-ons. For, after all, he himself was a male with those appetites that maleness implies. It was from this point of view that he carefully trained his devoted pupil. "You are to please the men, and I shall show you how. Do you understand?" She'd nodded. "If you like it — fine. If you don't — fake it. They'll want to think you're turned on. As for coming yourself, that's not to be a concern. I will take care of all your needs. I will take care of you. You take care of the clients."

"I thought they were called customers," she'd said.

"Clients, Sandra, clients. But you'll call them nothing at all to their faces. This is a classy, short-lived operation. Five men at most. Five. I promise."

By June twenty-ninth, Lance Benson was just about fucked out. He took pride, however, in the results of his tutorage. He could now sit back and relax while Sandra Lowrey earned five gleaming As on her report card.

"I quit," Sandra Lowrey announced on the same day that Lance Benson had concluded he was close to being fucked out.

"I quit — starting right now!" She stared down the manager's dirty glare before taking a deep breath and sailing out the door of Budget Drugs. From now on she would buy all her cosmetics, thank you, at Solomon's. After all, Lance had assured her that from here on in it would be first-class all the way.

If only the people at The Good Shepherd could see her now! Next Christmas she was going to send gold, shining pins to each and every one of the kids. "If I can do it, you can," she'd write on the cards. And she'd mail a big sack of bubble gum for Miss Traylor to pass out in Hut 21, which was where she'd climbed into her bunk at night and looked out the window to wish long and hard on the Big Dipper and the Little Dipper and on the tail of the Dragon, just to cover all bases.

She'd better hurry home now and begin packing. There were a few things other than herself to move into her lovely new apartment.

It was gone. Forever. The lump. With it had gone the breast. "What do they do with such a thing?" Martin wondered. Did they throw the bloodied flesh into the garbage? Certainly the filbert lump, the pit of the cherry, was saved. But the breast? What was there to analyze about that part of her which once had given him such pleasure?

"The auxiliary lymph nodes, nearest to the breast, were removed, but the pectoral muscles were saved," Dr. Levy explained. "It was a modified radical mastectomy."

"And you got it all?"

The surgeon hesitated. "Yes."

Martin sank into a chair. Let others in the waiting room stare at him. He buried his head in his hands. His son touched his shoulder. Had his daughter not been studying art history in Rome, she would have been here, too. He wished his son weren't here. He wished for the priest of his youth. He would tell the black-frocked confessor that he had never doubted Caroline would live and that of course, yes, he was grateful to have his assurance substantiated, but could the priest explain why — why she couldn't have lived *intact*? "You know what I mean, Father? Intact." He raised his eyes.

"Son, you'll be able to see her this evening. Then maybe you'd better get on back to UT. She would want that." Martin IV protested, but they both knew that tomorrow he would leave. He was struggling through summer school in a second attempt to pass trigonometry.

"She'll be all right?" the boy asked, then repeated, "She'll be all right?"

"Yes." He wondered about himself. He would go for milk and crackers in the hospital cafeteria. So what if that was his bedtime snack and it was only two thirty-five in the afternoon? He needed his stomach lined, padded with what his nanny had prepared for him those many nights after he and his twin had bathed and had had pillow fights and were ready for sleep. He needed the familiar. The reassuring. Caroline would not be at home to fix him his evening martini. She would not be seated in her favorite chair, across from him in the sun room, chattering brightly about her day. And, finally, in the late evening hours, she would not be in his bed, curled close against his back. She would be lying in a hospital room, drugged, unaware of the anguish that was raging through his brain. The machine had begun rolling down the images again.

"Are you OK, Dad?" Martin IV was peering closely into his face.

"I'm fine. I've just been worried, son, that's all."

"Whew! For a minute there, you scared me."

The two of them went to the cafeteria. Caroline wouldn't be awake for hours. He was glad he had given her the perfume. When he saw her, he would dab some behind her ears and assure her that nothing was changed. That everything was the same. Perhaps the fragrance would hide the odor of the lie he would be perpetuating.

"Isn't it the nuts!"

"Indubitably."

Her legs were spread as she arched and moved her hips. He lifted his hand. "That's enough."

She frowned.

"Come on, Sandra, now me."

"Then I can't see!"

"But *I* can. If you don't block my view."

Over their heads the reflection of her lips moving down his body was strong and clear.

"Deeper!" he commanded.

The cock went in and out. Over and over. Faster. Deeper. Harder. He watched and thought of a rooster crowing and came.

"Close to You" drowned the soft whirr of the camera. He rolled over on his side and grinned at the pouting Sandra.

He guessed she deserved to pout occasionally. She'd been an exemplary student, balking at only one of their sessions.

"Ugh!" she'd said, shaking her head vehemently. "I don't want to do that."

Armed for the expected protest, he had clasped a gold chain, a tiny diamond centered in its links, around her neck.

"Well . . . I guess I can," she'd said.

He had kissed her and cheered her on. "Sure you can. I know you can."

She'd looked down at the diamond, then up at him and repeated softly, "Sure I can."

She sat up. "Where're you going?"

"Where am I going?" He was pulling on his pants. "I'm climbing on top of your bed, darling, and taking the cassette home to see what we've got."

"I want to see, too."

"Sure. Let's invite Zoe to join us."

He kicked himself. There was a look of clear unadulterated murder in Sandra's eyes. He slipped the cartridge out of the VCR.

"You could have hooked that up to my TV."

"And have wires running all over the place? No, thank you. Anyway, some of the greatest performers avoid seeing themselves on film. They're afraid it'd make them self-conscious. And that, sweetheart, is what I'm afraid would happen to you."

"But you and me. That's not *acting,* Lance. Besides, it's the premiere — the christening, you said, of the bed."

"Look, I'm going home."

"Fuck you!"

"You did. I did. We did. And it was beautiful!"

"Hey! . . . Wait."

He stopped.

"What now, Lance?"

"Stay put. I'll be in touch."

"I'll get bored. I can't swim, I can't play tennis, I can't talk to anybody, I quit my job, I —"

"Are you complaining?" The threat was frozen in his voice.

"No, but —"

"Yes?"

". . . I'll miss you." Defeated, she whimpered.

"Sandy, just remember the end result, please. In the meantime, read plays, eat celery, watch television, write your mother —"

"I don't have a mother."

"All I'm saying is, for God's sake, let me run the show. OK?"

"OK."

"Now I'm leaving." And he meant it.

He was headed for his darkroom to see just what amount of voltage was packed into the thin little cassette he held in his hand.

That was the trouble. Part of the trouble, anyway. She didn't know whether or not she had a mother roaming around out there in the world. The same could be said for a father. Were her parents dead and buried underground or were they raising a houseful of kids that had never included her?

The rest of her trouble? Sure, it gave her goose bumps just looking at her fine new apartment. But sometimes when she was alone, she started thinking horrible thoughts — like how one of those men with the shadowy faces might stick his thing up her ass or push it all the way down her throat to her lungs. She wouldn't be able to breathe then. She'd suffocate . . . Maybe she shouldn't send the kids at the orphanage those little gold pins with the cards about becoming like her. Not yet. Like Lance said, she was just going to have to wait for the end result before everything got completely right.

Opening a cold beer, she plopped down on her canopy bed and concentrated on the end result. Who would have dreamed after all those months of following Lance Benson through the theatre that one day he would turn around and start following *her?* "It just goes to show you," she thought, "if you pray and believe, really *believe,* then anything is possible."

For a long time she lay on her back, staring up at her reflection. She forgot about the camera, hovering behind the mirror, over her head.

The flame struck the videotape and flickered angrily until only a black sludge remained in the tin container used for the burning. No one could ever blackmail him with the explicit pornography he had just witnessed. The evidence of Sandra and his liaison had been destroyed.

Once Zoe had knocked on the darkroom door to ask if he smelled "something funny." He'd suggested, "It's your hay fever acting up. You know your nose does strange things." She had argued, "But I don't have hay fever tonight." Impatiently he'd replied, "I'll look around in a minute, but there's nothing wrong here." She had gone away from the door, and he had scooped the charred residue into his handkerchief.

Ceremoniously he buried the knotted cloth beneath the azaleas in back of his house. He felt as though he were performing some ancient fertility rite. From the dark earth, he reasoned, would rise the fruits of his labor.

"How nice! Zoe came by this afternoon, now you tonight. And the flowers are lovely." Caroline Fletcher rose slightly from the hospital pillow, then sank again into its softness as though talking exhausted her.

"I won't stay long. Sit down, Martin." Lance gestured to her short, stocky husband, who had risen quickly as if greeting royalty.

Ten minutes of pleasantries and he would be gone. Unobtrusively he timed his visit, then stood.

"What I'm going to suggest is that I take this devoted husband of yours out for a drink, and let you get some rest."

Martin brightened, then declined. "No, I don't think so, Lance."

"You don't think so!" Caroline straightened. "Martin, *I* think so. And the patient should be humored. Besides, in thirty minutes I'll be gloriously sedated for the night. Lance, take this dear man with you. I'm tired of looking at his face." She smiled lovingly at her husband as her hand shooed him away.

"Well —"

"No well, Martin."

Lance observed the exchange. Zoe was right. Caroline made the decisions in the Fletcher family. Tonight, however, she would have been wise to have remained silent. Her husband's name headed the list of those persons whom he considered, regardless of their moral or social encumbrances, to be prime targets for Sandra Lowrey's charms. Only a month ago he had run into Fletcher standing at a newsstand, staring at a photograph of a huge tit thrust into a man's mouth, the lips puckered as though clamped around a bottle. Martin had slammed the magazine shut and reached for *Time*. Too late. He was a weak man who had become weaker now that one of his wife's breasts had been removed. And, while not wealthy, he was affluent enough to satisfy the monetary requirement.

Martin was still stammering; Caroline was still shooing.

It was time to step in.

"Well, shall we please your wife?"

Martin's head bobbed; Caroline's hand relaxed on the sheet.

"Good! We're on our way." He leaned down and kissed the patient, whom he thought of as "the pale, fine lady."

Then calmly he ushered her husband out the door.

"Does God punish a man for his adulterous thoughts by seeming to reward him?" he asked himself through a haze of four martinis. He was going under, staring all the while up into the murky reflection of the drowning. The sinking. He rolled over, straining to suck the elusive milk from her breasts. She reached for him. For so long he had been terrified that one day he might have to be the strong one; and now here, miraculously, just when that demand was upon him, someone had appeared to take care of him. Stroking, squeezing. Bolstering! The provocative words she intoned like a litany were suffused with strength. Oh, it felt good! Was good. Unable to wait any longer, he plunged into her. Silently he cried out: "God, forgive me; Caroline, forgive me. Damn you, Lance; thank you, Lance — you went home to Zoe. But there was no one waiting for me. No one. Her breasts are bigger and better than Caroline's ever were, ever could be. Her cunt, tighter. More alive! Faithful for thirty years and now this. Thank you, God; forgive me, God. Thank you." He plunged deeper. His body stiffened and erupted.

Drained of his semen and of his desire, he lay on his back. He closed his eyes against his nakedness. The past paradoxical hour had been among the most glorious and debasing of his entire fifty-three years.

She stretched. Her hands went all the way up and behind the headboard, then she reached over him for a wad of bubble gum stuck to the nightstand. She popped the hardened mass into her mouth and chewed. Suddenly he felt revulsion. How could he have thought her beautiful? Her breasts were ugly, hulking monstrosities. Streaks from his biting striped the skin.

"Honey, you do that good." She yawned. "But you got to go home now."

Stumbling, he got out of the strange bed. He needed a priest. If only he were still a Catholic! Standing at the toilet, he imagined he was spewing out his shame. He sought absolution. Didn't most men have base, animal desires? Fantasies? Hadn't he simply lived out his fantasy? He would not go near the girl again. An expensive black dress had not hidden the cheapness to which he had been drawn. No, the cheapness had not been the lure. It had been the smooth, firm skin, the health and vitality of youth, that he had sought for himself. He looked down at his own pale sagging flesh.

Robed in black lace, she stood in the doorway. "Are you all right?"

"I feel a little nauseated." He was afraid again. But this was a new and unfamiliar fear. "You won't tell Benson, will you? He's a close friend of mine — and of my wife."

She smiled knowingly and popped her gum. "Martin, this was strictly between us."

He wanted to slap his name off her lips. Instead, he nodded gratefully. ". . . Thank you. Do you want, er . . . money?"

A horrified look crossed her face. "I don't do it for *that*. I was helping you out, what with your wife being — sick and all. Face it" — her voice hardened triumphantly — "you wanted me."

What she said was true. He had wanted her. The wanting had begun even before there had been a name and a body connected to the wanting. The wanting had been strong before she ambled over to their table, tossed her long, blond hair at him, and ex-claimed to Benson, "Fancy meeting you here!" The wanting had been strong before she slid into the booth, edged close, and her hand reached under the table to stroke his leg. For days and nights his head had throbbed. He had been afraid. And then suddenly, incredibly, what he had ached for and thought unattainable was placed before him. He had wanted her and taken her. Though in actuality, she had taken him. Except for reaching out for her breasts. Once, biting and sucking, he'd felt her hands push his head away. "Hey, leave something there!" He had slowed down, only to begin again.

Exhausted now, he pulled on his wrinkled clothes. He looked at his watch. Twelve-fifteen. What if the hospital had tried to reach him? Caroline could be in shock. They wouldn't know where to find him. She could be dead! Panic-stricken, he headed for the door.

"Want a good-night kiss?" Her full lips were pursed.

"No!... No, thank you." He ran his hand over his thinning hair. Her startled face was imprinted on his brain. At least he had let her know there was not to be another degrading, incredible evening. Not with him. Not ever again. She could do what she liked. As for him, he planned to be at the hospital by six o'clock tomorrow morning to take his wife's hand and thank God she was alive. There were worse things than losing a breast. He would tell her that. A breast was only a pound of flesh, give or take a few ounces. From now on, he would hold tightly to the not-quite-whole but still beautiful person.

Driving away from the girl's apartment, he could breathe again. Living out one's fantasy was all right, he rationalized. Provided there was only one such indulgence. "And now," he spoke aloud, "it will be like it never happened."

Absolved, he unlocked the door of his empty town house. As if entering a cathedral, he knelt in the dark and prayed.

"I did not like it, I did not like it, I did not like it!" Sandra Lowrey closed her eyes tightly. She didn't want to cry, damnit. The Fourth of July was a time for fireworks. A time when bright streaks of color flashed into the air. Bullshit! The Fourth of July was the pits. For her, anyway. On this day of celebrating independence, she was bound to a man whom she loved, to be sure; but, in her captivity she was forced to perform acts which, if they only knew, would turn Miss Traylor's and Brother Stevens's hair chalk white. Hell, if they even *suspected* what one of their star children was doing over here in Houston, a mere 182 miles away, their hair would fall straight out of their heads and hit the ground!

She shuddered. Martin Fletcher's flesh had been clammy, like mud and slime and seaweed you stepped on accidentally when you were out splashing around in the Gulf, which was probably where Lance and Zoe Benson were right this very minute. All she could think of doing on this Fourth of July was roast two dozen marshmallows over her new gas range. Then she would eat every single one of the sticky little things. And cry. She guessed, after all, she would do that, too.

"And Caroline's all settled at home now?" Lance Benson asked, noting the lobster bisque was exceptionally good today.

"Two days at home and she's already talking about chairing the Fall gala." Martin smiled proudly. "She's strong, that one."

"You're a lucky man."

"I know." Martin Fletcher bent his head to French onion soup.

Unobtrusively Lance reached in his pocket and placed on the peach linen, among the crystal and china at Maxim's, a small innocuous-looking box.

"In exchange for this, Martin," he pointed downward, "I expect one hundred thousand dollars."

"Mr. Benson is here, sir," Hazel Mabry, a tall stout woman in her late fifties, announced.

"Thank you, Mrs. Mabry."

From the beginning, Hazel Mabry had requested that her employer address her formally. She had hastily explained that she hated her given name. "Hell, that's no problem." The fiery gentleman had waved his arms expansively. "Pick a name. Any name! You like Victoria . . . Diana? You choose, and that's what you'll be from now on."

"No sir, it's too late," the new housekeeper had solemnly stated. "My people were good people; and they named me after my father's sister, who raised him. So if you don't mind, sir, call me Mrs. Mabry. My husband was the best man who ever lived, and I'm proud to have his name."

"My dear lady" — Lowell Hook had bowed and kissed her hand — "Mrs. Mabry is what you shall be called in this household." That had been twenty-eight years ago, and an amicable formality, belying a stronger bond, had existed between the two of them ever since.

Hook glanced at the Dresden clock on the mantel in his bedroom. Two-thirty. The young man was punctual.

"Tell Mr. Benson I'll be out in a minute and to make himself at home."

"Yes, sir."

"Oh, and, Mrs. Mabry, you might offer him a cigar."

"I'll do that, sir."

Tucking a linen handkerchief into his pocket, he wondered what

was on the director's mind. "I've got a present for you," Benson
had said, "but I have to take you to it."

"If it's a new theatre you want me to buy, forget it," Hook had
chuckled.

"That's not a bad idea," Benson had replied, going along with
the joke. "But that's not it. It's something you told me you wanted."

Lowell Hook couldn't think of much he wanted except to be
twenty-five again, knowing what he knew now, and enjoying a
robust night in the sack with a good woman. Suddenly he laughed
out loud. He had remembered something. That enterprising young
man! No, he wouldn't have the nerve. "Hook," he told himself,
"Benson probably wants you to admire his wine cellar, and then
he'll present you with some rare old bottle of cough syrup." Still,
he exchanged the gray tie he was wearing for a bright blue one
and recombed his silver hair. The hair persisted thick and alive
atop what, in referring to his aging body, he ruefully called "the
ruins."

"I'm dropping you off to have tea with Miss Sandra Lowrey,"
Lance Benson stated with much the same formality that Hazel
Mabry draped about her person.

"Now that's a patron I don't recall," said Hook, excitement
and apprehension stirring in the pit of his stomach. Both of them
knew full well there was not an Arch patron alive whom he couldn't
immediately call by name or nickname as he inquired how the
spouse, children, and great-aunts were faring.

"Oh, it's not a patron." Lance steered his Continental toward
the freeway.

"I know damn well it's not a patron. It's that girl."

"Yes."

"That's my gift?"

"*She's* your gift."

"What am I supposed to do with her?"

"She'll take care of that."

"Now just a minute, Benson."

"No, you wait just a minute. Mr. Hook, you are beyond a doubt
the most magnificent man I've ever known. You *are* Zeus. And
after what you said at the gala the other evening, I've been thinking.
There's no need for you not to occasionally enjoy something you
were no doubt superior at doing not too long ago."

"And that's just where I'd like to leave it."

"Would you?"

The old man was silent.

"Look, she considers this an honor. She admires you."

"Like I admire Whistler's mother!"

"You underestimate yourself."

"What's in this for you?" The old man studied the younger man.

"Let's just say it's repayment for all you've done for The Arch."

"Benson, that's a lot of bullshit!"

". . . Do you want me to turn around?"

Sunk in his corner of the car, the old man again was silent. Finally, he asked, "What if I can't?"

"You can."

Proud peacocks strolled on a mirrored lawn; the brilliant purples of the fanned plumage blinded his eyes; the taped Tchaikovsky was close against his eardrums. She bent to lick and suck and gently bite until a firmness swelled between her lips. Finally, he lifted her head and said, "Not that way, Roxane." He was twenty-five again. Mounting her, he placed the firmness she had brought to him between her thighs. Twice the erectness faltered, but returned as she tightened and moved and whispered, "You are such a lover." He believed her. A small bright burst of strength flickered then roared until there was no longer any need for strength. Spent, he closed his eyes. The pounding of his heart against his frail chest frightened him. He was reminded of a small bird flailing its wings at the bars of a narrow cage. Still, Benson had been right. Lowell Hook was grateful. Indeed, he felt indebted more to the man than to the woman beside him. She was not a Roxane, after all, but a Sandy, because, was it — what was she doing? God forbid, she was chewing bubble gum. They should have done their thrashing to the strains of "Up Against the Wall, Redneck" and left Tchaikovsky alone.

"You are dumb, Sandra. Dumb, dumb, dumb!"

"You just try getting in bed with somebody as important as Mr. Hook."

"I seriously doubt that I'll ever have that distinction."

"Shit, Lance, it'd make you nervous, too!"

"Maybe. But not so nervous that I wouldn't even *think* to turn on the VCR until I was halfway through the act. And then, goddamn it, Sandra, nobody seeing it could be sure — I mean, *absolutely* sure it's the old man you're doing it with!"

He scowled.

"I'm sorry." She sat on the floor, twisting her fingers together. "Lance, I hate to mention this now, but I'm broke. Flat broke."

"Christ!" He threw up his hands. "You're out of wine. You're bored. And now you need money . . . As soon as Fletcher pays. No sooner."

Her lips trembled. In two seconds she would be bawling. He threw fifty dollars at her.

Glaring, he watched her tuck the bills into her out-of-season, fake suede purse and blow her nose loudly.

He sighed. "Look, Sandra, it's OK. Everything'll be all right. We'll tape the others and get back to Hook. He liked it. He said he wasn't up to that too often, but it's given him a new lease on life."

"He said that?"

"Yeah. So later on. A couple of months, I guess."

"You mean, I have to do it again?"

"Christ, you blew it!"

Suddenly she giggled. "I blew him."

Her wit threw him off balance. In spite of himself, he laughed. "Come here." The little puppy dog, his faithful Bailey, bounded from the floor into his arms.

"I hate it, Lance. I mean, *hate* it, when you fuss at me. I'm sorry I messed up. I really am. And he is a sweet old man. I'll do it. I'll do it again. Whenever you say."

"That's my girl." So occasionally she gets flustered, he rationalized. Still, because of that shortcoming she had ruined the tape which — above all others — was to have made his project worthwhile. One cool million collected from Hook would launch him straight out of this country and into a new life where, by investing prudently, he could amass millions more. But, first, he must have a hefty capital. Only two men targeted for his project were able to provide him with that.

To initiate another session between Sandra and Hook would be tricky. But possible. At the gala, hadn't the old man gazed at the girl and lamented, ". . . I'd give up five good years of the few

I've got left to have something like that"? Actually, it had been that remark which had prompted the ideas to begin ricocheting around in his head. Well, the king fish would be reeled in yet. Again he thought of his father towering over him, ordering, "Simmer down, son." He would have to do that.

"Let's go eat Italian food," he suggested.

And the bored, caged Sandra Lowrey, whom he had forbidden so much as a listed phone number in her new, plush prison, rushed to pile hair on top of her head, to put on something fancy.

He smiled. Even if he was only taking her around the corner to greasy Luigi's, she was appreciative. He liked that in a woman.

"Half of it?" his stockbroker asked.

"Well — what would a fourth bring?" Fletcher's hand was clammy as he gripped the phone.

The stockbroker did some figuring. "Let's see, under the SEC rules, it'd have to be a 144 sale. A fourth would bring about thirty thousand dollars."

"How long would it take?"

"Oh, I'd say — after you deliver the certificates — seven or eight days at most." The stockbroker wondered if his client were in some kind of trouble. He dismissed the possibility. Martin Fletcher was among his more conservative customers. The man probably wanted to remodel a beach house or plow additional funds into his kids' educations. He would not ask questions. Still, he felt compelled to comment, "Martin, I hate to see you sell any of your company stock."

Martin Fletcher debated. Then he made his decision. "I'll sell one-fourth." He thanked his broker and hung up the phone.

Immobilized, he sat at his desk. He felt as though he were playing Flying Statues, a childhood game he had hated. The victim was flung into the air by his classmates. Once landed, he remained in position until someone guessed what, according to the stance, the person had become — Pluto, Jupiter, a Model T, a can opener, Benjamin Franklin. The imagination knew no bounds. But the thrown person must remain as stone while the others chiseled away with conjecture. Often, Martin had cried out to an incorrect guess "That's it!" simply because his arms and his legs had begun to ache. He detested even mild physical discomfort.

What statue was he now? He didn't know. Perhaps an insect

rigid in insecticide. A fool. If he could only pick up a pencil, he would feel better. If he could only talk his problem over with Caroline, he would turn ecstatic cartwheels. "Look, Caroline," he'd say, "I'm slicing into our retirement cushion because Benson is blackmailing me with an . . . episode that never really happened."

"Lance? Blackmail? What *episode?*" she'd ask, her eyes widening incredulously.

This morning her eyes had darkened as she'd looked down to the bandage, then up at him. "It hurts a little," she'd mildly complained.

No, the problem was his alone. Besides, his blackest fear was that Caroline would discover "the episode." And to realize that she could see the particulars in living color! God forbid. A slow rage began churning inside him. A rage swirling and burning his guts. Suddenly, he could move. He picked up a pencil and struck long, jagged marks down a scratch pad. Benson would not wipe out Caroline and his retirement reserves. They would still travel to Scotland and Wales, and even India. They would still build their rustic house in the hill country. They would do everything they'd planned because he, Martin Fletcher, without the help of Caroline's insight, would outwit the bastard. He would pay Benson thirty thousand dollars then stall for time. Perhaps an additional payment would have to be made. He could borrow against his life insurance. Then the payments would cease. He would demand return of all his money. "With a receipt, please," he would add, "and, of course, the evidence." He would, somehow, devise a scheme to accomplish the impossible. It would be Benson, not he, who would ultimately pay.

Leaving his twentieth floor office at Royal Petroleum, Sir Charles Stanton took the lift down twelve flights to the London headquarters' postal-service room. He wanted personally to mail the slim envelope, addressed in his tall, firm script to Mrs. Lance Benson. He estimated the letter would take about a week to reach its destination, more than four thousand miles away.

Five bars later and less sober himself than he'd planned, Lance Benson directed his companion into The Arch Theatre. "It's all right, Henry," Benson said to the night watchman. "Just keep an eye on the upper levels. We'll be down below for a while, then we'll leave by the lower exit."

"Sure thing, Mr. Benson."

"Oh, and Henry?"

"Yes, sir?"

"Don't think you're crazy when you hear music. It's just we've got some talented nut who insists on auditioning at this ungodly hour."

Mistaking the rumpled Mr. Solomon for the "talented nut," the night watchman was unfazed. Hadn't he seen the likes of God-knows-what ever since he'd been in show business? "Don't worry about a thing, Mr. Benson," he assured his boss. "I'll just keep doing my rounds right here over you."

"Good. Give us about thirty minutes."

Benson guided his board member through the lower corridors. Unlocking double doors which led into a small arena theatre, he cautioned, "Watch your step."

"Jees! It's pitch black," muttered an inebriated Victor Solomon as the two of them descended a sloping aisle.

"The best seats in the house." Lance gestured to the front row, section A. "I'll be back as soon as I let our performer in the door and turn on the spotlight."

"First time I've ever been in an audience of two," Solomon said, slurring.

"You'll like it," Lance commented and walked away.

Unbolting the lower-level stage door, he dreaded the greeting he was about to receive. He couldn't blame her. "Be outside at eleven o'clock sharp," he'd instructed, and here it was past mid-night. He'd miscalculated the number of drinks it would take for Solomon to reach his present malleable state.

"Well, I've heard of the star holding up the show, but never the audience." She stood legs apart, hands on hips. Her long black cape fanned out from her body.

"You look like a bat ready to draw blood."

"Funny. Funny." Sandra Lowrey swooped past him. "Let's get this over with."

"At your service." He bowed low.

"Cut it out, Lance. I'm nervous." She hugged the cape tightly about her.

"If you do exactly what we rehearsed, you'll be sensational." He went to turn on the spot and start the music, which was hardly original but apt.

Victor Solomon straightened in his seat as the strains of "Let Me Entertain You" came out over the sound system. Squinting, he focused his blurred vision on a figure kneeling in a pool of light. A dark blanket covered her. His head was clearing. No, it wasn't a blanket. She was wearing a cape. Slowly she moved. Her arms spread outward. The cape flared open. Son of a bitch, it was the girl he had admired at the gala! She took the combs out of her hair and tossed them into his lap. He jumped slightly. Benson, who had slid wordlessly into the seat beside him, laughed. "Calm down," he whispered. "That's just the beginning."

Victor Solomon had witnessed strip performances from coast to coast. And he had also enjoyed some few in other parts of the world. He thought he had seen it all. But this girl was the best! Mesmerized, he watched. He leaned over to Benson. "I want that girl!"

"I don't blame you. Let's turn off the music and see what we can arrange."

"No, let her finish."

"Oh, I think she has." Again, Benson laughed. He stood. "Sandra, darling, get your clothes on. You're taking my friend home with you."

"Why not here? . . . Right in the middle of the goddamn stage!"

"Because she's got a mirrored bed you won't believe."

"Christ, you think of everything!" Awe was in his voice.

"I try."

Lance Benson guided a stumbling Solomon out the stage door. "I'll drive you over," he said, "sleep on the living-room sofa while you partake, then bring you back to your car."

Abruptly Solomon stopped and experienced his one lucid moment in the past few hours.

"Why?"

"Because, Victor, as drunk as you are you might not get there."

"Good thinking." The liquid blanket descended again.

As they sped toward the girl's apartment, Victor Solomon closed his eyes and made a decision. He would take her in the ass. He had especially liked the way she had moved her hips. That would show Roselyn. Just what it would show her, since she would never know, he wasn't sure. But it would show her. He felt in his pocket for the girl's combs. He must remember to give them back to her.

An expression of horror crossed the girl's face as he rolled her over and spread her legs. The image was unmistakably clear. Slumped in his leather chair, Victor Solomon watched and sipped scotch. The screen went blank. The performance was over. He pressed the remote control of his VCR.

"You're a bastard, Benson," he said to the man who had stretched out on the sofa to watch what he had obviously seen before.

"A bastard," Solomon repeated into silence.

Benson sat up. "Since you insisted on seeing what you were buying, it was convenient, wasn't it, that Roselyn gave you VCR equipment for your birthday last year?"

"Who said I was buying?"

"You know, Vic, I don't think Sandra enjoyed that very much. 'What kind of friends do you have?' she wanted to know. She swore she'd march straight into a divorce court to testify against somebody who'd tear her up like that."

"Bastard!"

"I believe you've said that." Benson walked over to the VCR and ejected the cassette. "If you don't mind, I've got things to do at the theatre."

"Wait!"

"Not long."

"You'll wait! When we're talking about one hundred thousand dollars, you'll damn sure wait."

"Five seconds."

Solomon went into his bedroom and unlocked the lower drawer of his desk. The money withdrawn from the bank only that morning lay in neat green stacks. He stuffed the bills into a large manila envelope. All along he had known he would pay.

Wordlessly they made the exchange.

Victor Solomon stared down at the cassette he held in his hand. He looked up. ". . . How can I be sure you'll destroy the duplicate?"

"I'm a man of my word."

"You'd better be!"

"Look, as I explained to you, I'm not a greedy man. One hundred thousand dollars covers my needs. Besides, I'm no fool, Solomon. You could bring me down, too. We'd both go down. And neither of us wants that. Agreed?"

He nodded curtly.

"So . . ." The smooth, unwinding ribbon of logic continued. "I'll destroy the duplicate and consider our negotiations closed."

"You're damn right! Now get out of here. You're a no-good —"

"I know — bastard." Benson paused at the door. "Victor, your imagination boggles the mind."

His hands were shaking as he reinserted the cassette into the machine. He'd be damned if he wasn't going to watch it all again before he punched the erase button and blotted out the evidence of what had been, he had to admit, one hell of an evening. Besides, he had just paid one hundred thousand dollars in cold cash for a performance he frankly admired. If it weren't for Roselyn and the kids, he'd have told the bastard to do whatever he wanted with the thing. He was goddamn proud of himself ramming, like some wild dark bull, into the girl. Even drunk he had been magnificent. No doubt about it, he was a super stud; and Benson, the bastard, couldn't take that away from him.

Lance Benson did not drive directly to the theatre. Instead, he headed for Memorial Drive Bank where he deposited five thousand dollars into Zoe and his joint savings account. He did not record the deposit in their savings book. Nor had he recorded his earlier withdrawal of five thousand dollars needed to finance the VCR equipment and the mirrored bed. Rarely did Zoe examine bank statements, and in these past six weeks she had had no reason to deposit into or withdraw from the account. Using the pretext that he had theatre business that day at the bank, he himself had deposited her commission check for the portrait of Willis Young, another one of her pompous bank presidents. With the odds in his favor, he had gambled that Zoe would remain ignorant of his borrowing the money, and he had won.

His second stop after leaving Solomon's apartment was far up in the northwest section of Houston. There he placed the remaining ninety-five thousand in a lockbox. The amount irritated him. Clearly, the mogul could have paid more. (As an infant, Solomon — born to haute-couture wealth — had probably worn satin diapers.) But he'd reasoned that to extract a larger sum would have entailed too great a risk. A smart divorce lawyer — and Roselyn would surely have that — might then have gone snooping for scandal. This way Solomon could explain away a mere one hundred thousand dollars as a company expenditure. Such was life. With his penchant for drink and good-looking women, the silver-spooned playboy had been too logical a choice to pass up.

He walked out of the vault to return to The Arch.

Though his secretary had gone for the day, she had left a note on his desk: "*Please* don't be out of pocket for so long again. We needed you!"

"If you only knew, dear sweet little Suzanne," he thought, already savoring the independence which was soon to be his, "as far as this theatre is concerned, I plan eventually to be out of pocket forever."

She examined the cream-colored envelope with its English postmark. Such elegant masculine script. Why, she wondered, looking at the return address, would Sir Charles Stanton be writing to her? She slid her letter opener beneath the waxed seal.

For some time after reading his request, she sat motionless. Once a fly lighted on her arm. She didn't brush it away. Finally, she refolded the letter and put it back into its envelope.

She went to the window as she often did when she needed to think. Staring out at the pool, she thought, "I have never done it, and I can't now." To paint from a photograph was impossible. Besides, she had never even seen his son. How could she capture the essence of the child? The person? She was sorry that his wife's birthday could not be "immeasurably blessed," as he had written, "by a Zoe Benson portrait of David." But she was not the artist he thought she was. The eyes would escape her, the cheekbones, the smile.

Why, then, did she want to try? The finished product could only disappoint her. And, more important, disappoint Charles Stanton, a man who for years had intrigued her. Often she had wondered what lay behind that handsome exterior. That formality. And yet, whenever they spoke at theatre functions or dinner parties, she became somewhat restrained herself. How strange that this man, about whom she had wondered, had approached her to do that which must surely come from the core of his being. And that he had expressed confidence in her work! Certainly he had the means to choose from among the world's greatest portraitists. She wanted to accept. To try. But she was afraid.

She ran her fingers through her hair, then turned from the window. The task exceeded her talent. Sir Charles would have to commission another artist, or Irene Stanton would simply have to rely on that image of a little boy, age nine, which no doubt existed in her head.

"Of course you'll do it."

"Lance, I have never painted from a photograph. And a little boy who's dead? I just can't."

"You can and you will."

"*Why?*"

"It's obvious."

"Not to me."

"Zoe, you can because you have the ability, and you will because Stanton's one of my most influential board members."

"Your theatre has nothing to do with my work as an artist!"

"In this case it does."

"You're wrong!"

"Zoe, listen to me, this is the chance to get to know him better. For him to become indebted —"

"To *whom,* Lance?"

"Indirectly to me! Every time he looks at that portrait he'll know who brought his son back to life!"

"A portrait doesn't — that's sick!" She turned to leave.

He had misjudged, pushed too far.

"Zoe, *please,* don't go!"

Wordlessly she waited.

He went to her. His arms encircled her waist. But she remained stiff, her back to him. "Like rigor mortis setting in," he thought, and began rubbing her neck.

She shook free of him.

"Don't do that! And stop acting as if my accepting this commission was a matter of life or death."

"OK, I was wrong! I'm sorry." He went to a window and stood staring out at fireflies. Waiting for her response. Thinking. He had been a fool to use pressure tactics. Better to lead his wife gently. Once she accepted — and that he must make her do — he would be linked more securely to this man who was to be his fifth and most formidable victim. This man who had been selected not only because he was wealthy enough to come up with five hundred thousand dollars but also because the challenge of corrupting the incorruptible intrigued him. Though Sir Charles Stanton did not appear to possess a psychological makeup that would be susceptible to Sandra Lowrey's charms, one could never be sure. To tackle that upright, uptight gentleman would be to match wits, to prove or disprove theories. If he could lure such obvious purity into his lair, then he, Lance Benson, could stand on the mountaintop and proclaim, "It is just as I suspected. No man is invincible." That would be the ultimate victory. And it was one he intended to have.

He turned again to his wife, who had begun flipping through the pages of *The Atlantic*. Amazing. This was her response? Withdrawal into her cocoon? He felt like ripping the magazine from her hands.

"Zoe . . . I said I was sorry."

"It's all right." She closed the magazine. "Look, I'm going to bed."

"May I say one more thing?"

"If it's not on this subject."

"It's precisely on this subject."

"Then forget it."

"No! Now you listen to me. Zoe, you are an artist, I think a great one. But about this portrait — I want you to do whatever you like. I mean that."

She studied his face.

"You mean that?"

"Scout's honor."

Unexpectedly she smiled. It was barely a smile. But then she said softly, "I haven't heard you use that expression in years."

She left the room. He leaned back in his recliner and counted slowly, gambling that before he reached ten she would return.

On the count of nine she stood in the doorway.

"Lance? . . . I want to do it. It's just — what if I fail?"

"I thought that was it."

He pulled her into his chair, onto his lap, where she stayed, close against him. He stroked her hair. And she didn't pull away.

"Zoe, I can understand how you feel."

"Can you?"

"You think I wasn't scared walking out on a stage that first time? Directing my first play? You think it wasn't scary starting this theatre?" He kissed the top of her head. "I believe the word is 'empathize.' "

She shifted to face him. To stare into his eyes. And then she touched his cheek.

"Such a strange, difficult man."

He took her hand from his face and entwined his fingers with hers.

"Such a strange, difficult woman."

She laughed. They sat, quiet for a time. Each thinking.

". . . You know, my father told me once if you fear something laugh at it, or, if you can't do that, just stare it down. But, best of all, he said, if you can, tackle the fear head-on."

"I agree. You see, even I can admit that occasionally your father makes sense." He leaned to kiss her lips.

But quickly she was out of his lap.

"So what are you going to do?"

"Think about it."

"Well, I repeat, do what you want."

"I appreciate that. But, Lance, regardless, that is exactly what I intend to do."

At eleven-thirty-five that evening Zoe Benson sealed the envelope which held her reply: "I am deeply honored that you would trust me to paint a portrait of your son. I think you should know that I am apprehensive; but, I promise you, I will do my best."

Three weeks to the day after the operation, Caroline Fletcher's final bandage was removed and Martin Fletcher delivered thirty thousand dollars to Lance Benson, explaining that there would be three, possibly four, additional installments: "Take it or leave it." Disgruntled, Benson had taken it and deposited the mass of bills in the lockbox which held Victor Solomon's payment.

That same day Benson turned his thoughts to his next victim: Raymond Reese. Though the mother rather than the son was the wealthy one, Raymond was still a perfect candidate. Sliding up against Winifred's shadow, he was a mama's boy whose natural inclination was to look up to the figure in command. Whoever that figure might be. Well, he, Lance Benson, was going to be that figure. In spite of rumors to the contrary, he suspected that Raymond ached for some good heterosexual sex. Perhaps it would be his first. He laughed out loud. That boy's Adam's apple lumped up too hard whenever a good-looking girl crossed his path. How simple it would be to cram Sandra Lowrey down Raymond's throat and relieve his discomfort. After that, it would be up to Raymond to figure out a way to get into his mother's purse.

Before tackling that manipulation, however, he needed a rest. Zoe had been pressing for a vacation. He would make the lady happy. Besides, a brief departure from the scene would fit in nicely with his entrapment of the vulnerable Mr. Reese.

They flipped a coin to determine their vacation site. It was to be either North Carolina, where Zoe's paternal grandparents had lived against the side of a Blue Ridge mountain, selling honey and antiques to tourists, or California, where the Monterey peninsula jutted into the Pacific. California won. Zoe and Lance Benson flew over the Grand Canyon, then on to the western edge of the country, where they rented a cottage close to the ocean.

At night they lay in their bed and listened to waves rushing in to the land, then out again. "It's like life. Birth, death. Birth, death. Over and over. Repeating itself. Every second . . . somewhere," she murmured once into the darkness.

"Poor little Zoe. Trying so hard to be profound. When actually there's nothing in the world that merits profundity. Unless it's a single man's tenacity to hold on, triumphantly, for as long as he can."

"Do you really believe that?" she asked, dismay and disagreement spreading throughout her being.

"Probably not." He patted her shoulder, then edged away from her to sleep.

During the day, they stretched out on sand dunes and walked, barefooted and aimlessly, along the beach. Occasionally they bent to gather shells or examine a deserted sand castle.

Once they drove into Monterey, where she mailed her father a postcard from Steinbeck's Cannery Row. Often they browsed in Carmel's bright little shops. Zoe bought beads and paints and a purple shawl with long, thin fringes. Lance purchased a fine-grained leather jacket for Houston's brisk winters and a matador's cape simply because it reminded him of Tyrone Power in *Blood and*

*Sand.* His most extravagant purchase, however, was an antique letter opener with a jewel-encrusted handle in the shape of a serpent. Zoe recoiled. "We have a letter opener," she argued, hating the ruby eye, the coiled tail flecked with emerald chips. She thought of the records, the books they could buy with the money he had placed on the counter in order to own that one small, sinister item. And she protested further. But Lance was not dissuaded.

They spent four days in San Francisco. One evening after choosing lobsters from a tank and dancing somewhat drunkenly to no music on a pier, they went to bed and made love.

As they lay damp and exhausted from the intensity that had been between them, she urged, "We've got to talk about our marriage."

"Not now, Zoe."

"Please, now."

And he listened while she rambled on for thirty minutes — listing, objecting, voicing her needs.

Finally, she was silent.

". . . I'll do better," he promised, kissing the tips of her fingers, lowering his head to her breasts.

Encouraged, she pressed on.

"I'd like a child."

"Zoe, don't spoil it!" The voice became familiar. The steel beam on which she balanced.

A child, she decided, would have to come later. Perhaps it was best that way. "I'll do better," he had said. She must wait and see. But, here, with the ocean air blowing cool into their room, over them, his words seemed to offer the hope she had prayed their time together, away from the theatre, would bring.

When finally they were packing to return home, she sensed, already, their closeness dissolving.

"I wish we didn't have to go back. Ever," she remarked.

"That's an absurd thing to say." Lance continued packing. She watched him wrap the letter opener in tissue, then carefully, as though tucking a child into bed, place it among his shirts. She felt angry and sad. Betrayed.

"August is almost over," he reminded her. "And, as it is, I'll be buried in work."

It was true. Rehearsals for the new season were less than a month away. But she had the feeling that if they stayed here, or some place far from Houston, their marriage might have a chance.

"It was only a wish," she said. And closed her suitcase.

Ten minutes later, after taking one final look around the cottage, she hurried outside to Lance, who was calling, "Zoe, come on! We'll miss our plane." Glancing at her watch, she noted that in exactly five hours they would be home. They would arrive just as the city was turning on its lights.

"Let's have dinner this evening, and you can fill me in."

"Sure. Sure thing, Lance!" Raymond Reese, knee-deep in embossed velvet, gulped nervously but with pleasure.

When Benson had asked him to keep an eye on The Arch while he and Zoe were away, Raymond had been astounded. Why him? His narrow chest swelling with pride, he had assured the director that not a day would pass without his dropping by the theatre to make sure everything was running as well-oiled machinery should.

"Oh, I think a couple of times a week will be fine, Raymond," Benson had said. "I just believe it's psychologically sound to have a board member somewhat visible while I'm away."

"Well, you'll certainly have that. And, Lance —" He had never before felt free to call The Arch director anything other than Mr. Benson. "Thank you."

In the days that followed, Raymond Reese poked into managerial and clerical cubbyholes, driving the entire Arch staff to distraction. Finally Beatrice Thorpe, the box-office manager, heaved a thunderous sigh that shook her 210-pound frame and declared, "If that little creep comes around one more time, I'm going to swat him like a mosquito."

Fortunately Benson had returned just in time.

His selection was a downtown restaurant, close to the theatre and noted for business luncheons and dinners. It was not unusual for two men, papers spread between them, to be seen enjoying the Epic's hearty but elegant cuisine.

"And that's about it." Raymond Reese slammed shut the thin little pad he had whipped from his pocket.

His list had ranged from promotional expansion to dust in the corners. The crowning suggestion had been: "A three-tiered chandelier would enhance the ladies' lounge."

"You went in *there*?" Benson asked in amazement.

"Of course," Raymond replied matter-of-factly.

Damn, thought Benson. Maybe what I need is a two-man operation. Reese and myself. Forget the janitor, the scenic designer, the assistant director, and even the stalwart Beatrice Thorpe, whom Reese had described as "deeply aroused over constructive suggestions."

The dissertation had carried them through oysters bourguignon, cream of asparagus, hearts of palm, and tournedos Rossini. Benson felt he had a tiger by the tail. The passion locked up in this weed of a man must be volcanic.

Early in the evening Reese had flatly stated that dinner without dessert was like "champagne without the bubbles." Amused, Benson watched his companion's level of concentration peak as he studied the dessert menu until finally, as though announcing the Kentucky Derby winner, he proclaimed, "It's baked Alaska!"

"Good. I'll have the same."

Raymond Reese beamed while Lance wondered how in the hell either of them was going to swallow another bite. He decided the kid's culinary baggage went immediately to space in his oversized feet.

"Excuse me, Mr. Benson, there's a call for you." The waiter bent low and spoke softly.

Pushing back his chair, Lance Benson creased his forehead. "Excuse me. I always leave word with Zoe where I'll be."

"Right on schedule," he complimented Sandra. "Give us about thirty or forty minutes." He hung up the phone and went into the men's room to stall for time before returning to the table.

"Is everything all right?" Raymond asked, nervously dropping his napkin.

"Not exactly."

"Zoe isn't —"

"No, no, she's fine. One of the actresses called, looking for me. It seems a burglar broke into her apartment."

"Gracious!"

Lance observed that Raymond's response was the kind a maiden aunt would make. "Look, Raymond" — he leaned across the table — "the police just left, but she's crying. Still scared half to death. Obviously she needs a friend."

"Of course. You'll have to go." Raymond rose from his chair.

"Unfortunately, I can't . . . But you can."

"Me?" Raymond Reese sat back down.

"I told her someone I was close to and I felt she'd be comfortable with would be over."

"Lance, I wouldn't know what to say. I mean, if I *knew* her."

"You'll do fine. All she needs is somebody to hold her hand for a couple of hours."

"Oh." Raymond Reese suddenly imagined himself placing a strong right arm about the shoulders of the beautiful girl he'd seen at the gala. His Adam's apple lumped. Perhaps it was she who was pacing the floor of her apartment at this very moment. Waiting for him! In the past few weeks he had followed Scruffy Dawson's advice and had frequented Splash, Cody's, and Texas Rose. After sauntering into each establishment, he'd leaned against the bar and plastered what he considered to be a highly sensual look across his face — only to score a flat zero. Nothing. Scruffy would have laughed. But here was his chance! He would be magnificent rescuing some gorgeous creature in distress. She would be eternally grateful. Dear God, he prayed, don't let her be one of those elderly actresses who generally played grandmothers or witches.

Mistaking his hesitation for refusal, Lance played his trump card. "Raymond" — he lowered his voice — "what I'm about to tell you is confidential. You understand?"

"Absolutely." His little rabbit eyes widened. He couldn't believe his good fortune. Here was this incredible man, who had already called him a close friend, taking him into his deepest confidence.

"Zoe and I have a good marriage." Benson appeared pained as he spoke. "But she's jealous. Insanely jealous. I don't dare go to Sandra's."

"Christ!" Raymond's Adam's apple triple-lumped. Until this moment he had considered Zoe Benson the epitome of all that was fine and noble in womankind. His heart ached for his new, dear friend. And that poor girl! She must be threateningly beautiful. Lance didn't dare go to her himself. The raging Zoe might carve him up with a butcher knife.

Raymond cleared his throat. "Lance?"

Benson raised his head. Raymond fancied he saw tears. If only he could be half as strong as this man seated across from him.

"Lance," he repeated. ". . . Of course I'll do it."

Ten minutes later Raymond Reese, his Adam's apple by now bulldozing in his throat, was headed for Carrousel Square.

Remaining at the table, Lance Benson stared at two untouched baked Alaskas, sipped a solitary Benedictine, and smiled.

"You have a magnificent thing," she told him as she stroked his quivering penis and noted that it was no more than a pathetic tidbit. She felt repulsed yet strangely protective of Raymond Reese. She also felt grateful. Earlier he had come to her, mourned with her the broken lamp, the missing television set (which she had hidden in her closet), the empty jewelry case (which had never held more than crystal beads and fake rubies). He had wrapped his long, thin arms about her trembling shoulders. "I'm here," he'd said nervously, yet solidly, as she'd sobbed and pressed against him. Over strong black coffee, which he'd made, she had apologized. "I should have gotten dressed."

"It's fine. You look just fine." He'd gulped, turning his stare from the pink negligee that Lance had selected for the virginal encounter.

On schedule she had begun crying again, easing from one end of the sofa to the other, where he sat, his legs crossed primly, his glasses high and tight on his nose. She'd asked, "Would you mind holding me again?"

Listening to her little girl's voice, Raymond Reese had pinched himself. "Goddamn! She's the girl of my dreams," he'd thought. "And I'm the one here protecting her from dragons and demons and black-masked men."

"Sure," he'd said quickly. "Sure. I'll hold you, Sandy. As long as you'd like." He'd wanted to say, "Forever," but he'd decided that was a bit extravagant. She'd clung to him while he awkwardly patted her shoulder. His nostrils filled with the scent of her perfume. He thought of wildflowers sunk deep in woods. She lifted her face to his. He bent to kiss her. Then it had happened.

She'd led him away from the sofa into a room where darkness burst into light and a mirror over their heads shot off quicksilver images that glittered and blazed until he'd closed his eyes as though blinded. "You have a magnificent thing . . . you have a magnificent thing," the girl of his dreams intoned, bubble gum rotating in her mouth as they writhed on pink satin sheets.

"Trust me. It's your first time, isn't it?" she was asking now as if leading a small child into water over his head.

He ran his tongue nervously across his lower lip and whispered, "You won't tell Lance, will you?"

"I won't tell anybody," she promised, as she guided him inside her.

The girl of his dreams was wiser, more experienced, than she'd ever been in his wildest fantasies. The girl of his dreams was a whore! But, Christ, virgin that he was, he knew nonetheless that she had to be the best whore there was. He didn't understand everything that was happening, but what did it matter? She was taking over. One thing he did know: they were going to screw as long as his magnificent thing held out. He prayed that his mother had taken one of her little yellow sleeping pills and gone to bed early.

As he sank into his reverie, Sandra Lowrey was thinking: "He does all right in spite of his teeny prick and knowing from nothing. Of the four, he's the one it's been easiest with." Though she felt numb, she decided to let him fuck her as many times as he wished.

After a while, she stretched and turned off the VCR equipment. She lay on her side, away from him. "Fuck you, Lance Benson!" she thought. "This is a kind, decent man; and you and I — *you and I,* Lance — ought to be ashamed. I hate you, Lance, hate, hate, hate, love you, Lance. Don't be mad at me. But I owe this man *something.*" She fought back tears. When she turned again to Raymond, she was smiling. Without the eye of the camera beaming down upon them, she straddled him, stuck a huge tit deep into his open mouth and plunged his erect little appendage into her vagina. Thereupon she bestowed upon him the best rotating fuck he was to experience for many years.

He drove his Continental into the Arboretum parking lot in Memorial Park. Raymond was puzzled. At high noon on a weekday the lot was practically deserted.

"There's no restaurant here." Raymond stated an obvious fact.

"I know, but at the last minute Sandra couldn't make it. So I thought we'd enjoy a nature-trail walk before lunch. The fresh air'll do us good."

"Sandra can't make it?" Raymond didn't want to walk on a nature trail with the hot August sun piercing through trees onto their backs. He didn't want to be alone with Lance Benson even if the man had become his idol. He wanted to be with Sandra, whore or no whore. More than once he had tried to call her, but each time the operater had stated emphatically, "I'm sorry, sir, that's an unlisted number." Finally, he'd asked Lance to contact her.

"I can do better than that," he'd offered. "How about the three of us having lunch on Thursday?"

Now here it was Thursday and, instead of the "charming little French restaurant in Memorial" Lance had mentioned, their destination had become this desolate place with no Sandra in sight. For *this* he'd had his hair styled, put on his best suit, and upset his mother by abruptly leaving the studio? He felt nauseated. Right now he should be supervising the restoration of a Lord Nelson sea chest or out at the Wesley mansion double-checking a questionable window measurement.

He found his voice, which like his mood had sunk deep into the toe of his black leather loafer. "Lance, Mother really needs me."

"She can wait." He was already out of his car and headed for the trail. Raymond Reese reluctantly followed.

Walking slowly, Benson pointed out various types of trees. "Look at that red oak. And that black tupelo."

His idol, Raymond decided, was a man of divers interests. He tried to get into the spirit of things, but his thoughts kept returning to his mother, bravely carrying on without him, and to Sandra Lowrey, deserting the one man who could truly protect and appreciate her.

"Why couldn't she make it?"

"Who?"

"For heaven's sake, Lance — Sandy!"

"Oh, she had a date with somebody who came in from out of town. She's a very unreliable girl, Raymond."

He died. Trees fell down around him and heaved up into boards for his coffin. Fickle, whorish Sandra. Suddenly, desperately, he wanted to get back to his mother.

"I've got to leave." He recoiled as a small striped snake moved across their path.

"You're afraid of snakes?" Lance laughed. "That one's harmless."

"It's not the snake."

Benson walked briskly now, as if headed for a specific place. The trail twisted. Branches, bent low from a summer storm, brushed against their shoulders. They crossed a narrow bridge. The trail cut deeper into the foliage. Raymond breathed heavily as he tried to keep up with his leader, who was covering ground in long, quick strides.

Abruptly he stopped. "This is a good place to talk," he said.

They had come to a clearing. A chapel among the trees. Benson placed a small white box on the weathered pulpit. Raymond thought of a Bible. Any minute he expected his leader to pronounce, "Our scripture for today is . . ."

His Adam's apple began its familiar lumping. His idol was acting weird. He would have welcomed the harmless little snake as his companion rather than this man who was staring at him now with an almost Machiavellian smile.

"Raymond, are you aware that Sandra is a whore?"

"I — I gathered as much." He didn't understand where this conversation was headed, but suddenly he detested Sandra Lowrey. Let her have an unlisted phone number. Let her go screw anybody she picked up at the airport, the bus depot, or along the side of the road. Sandra Lowrey had probably laughed at his clumsy efforts, laughed with Lance Benson while the two of them slithered around in that hideous bed. He wanted to tell Zoe Benson she was fine and good and had a cocksucker husband. He wanted to get back to his mother. Fast!

"You're astute to recognize that. But did you also know she works for me?"

"No." Fear prickled on his back.

"And in this box, Raymond, lies the product of her hard work. A superb videotape. Absolutely superb of a bumbling idiot humping a whore."

The coffin was nailed. Raymond Reese threw up. It was the French toast his mother had fixed for breakfast. He had eaten nine slices. Benson held out a handkerchief, which he refused. He would do anything, give anything, to destroy that tape.

"Tell me what you want!" He couldn't stop retching.

"One hundred thousand dollars."

"One hundred thousand dollars!"

"That's correct."

"Where would I get that kind of money?"

"That, Raymond, is your problem."

Raymond Reese bent lower to the ground. He'd never again so much as look at another piece of French toast. As for the money, somehow he'd come up with it. But one hundred thousand dollars! "Just take me home," he said.

"Would a cup of tea help?"

Raymond's eyes bulged. Then slowly his eyelids lowered until the edge of his vision blurred, until Lance Benson disappeared. Only a tall blond man who had no name remained. "A man," he thought, "who is insane."

As they retraced their steps, Raymond prayed that a snake would come out of the wilderness and strike his fallen idol. He would brazenly step over the body and rush headlong back to the calm, bland life with his mother. Such existence suddenly seemed a blessing.


Lance counted the money that Raymond had delivered to him in a small foil-coated box as if the bills were Godiva chocolates.

He looked up and smiled.

"Well, Raymond, weren't you fortunate to have had such a nice aunt?"

"Great-aunt."

"Whatever. The inheritance stood you in good stead, didn't it?"

"My mother would kill me."

"Probably so." He closed the lid then leaned back, silent, his fingers stroking the gold foil.

Standing before the impressive desk, Raymond Reese shifted on his feet and stammered, "I've — I've thought about it, and I'm going to resign from the board."

"Oh?" The swivel chair came forward. "How will you explain that to your mother?"

"I'll tell her —" He gulped.

"What? . . . You'll tell her what?" The sapphire eyes were glacial.

Raymond looked away.

"I guess I should stay on, shouldn't I?"

"That would be prudent. Besides, we need your imaginative thinking." The eyes remained frozen. The voice, however, had become light, airy. Without rhyme or reason, Raymond thought of summer sailing on Lake Conroe.

Benson slipped the box into a drawer. "Now, about the outstanding fifty thousand. The end of September, oh, around . . ." He studied his calendar. "Let's make it September twenty-eighth. That'll give you four weeks to come up with what you owe."

"Fine." Raymond felt as if he were thanking his blackmailer. Again, he shifted his weight.

Silence stretched taut, like a tightrope, between them.

"Raymond, are you waiting to be dismissed? If so, I can certainly oblige."

Raymond Reese scurried to the door.

"Oh, Raymond —"

He stopped, waiting for the dagger to pierce between his shoulder blades and burst out the front of his body.

"Next time don't bother with the fancy box."

# ✲ PART II

*Monday afternoon, September 12 —*
*Saturday morning, September 24*

ZOE BENSON unloaded her sack of groceries. She placed the items she had purchased in the refrigerator, then reached again into the pocket of her blazer. It had not gone away as she had hoped it would.

MRS. BENSON, TELL YOUR HUSBAND YOU WILL BE HARMED IF HE DOESN'T STOP, FOR "I AM A MAN MORE SINN'D AGAINST THAN SINNING."

"More sinn'd against than sinning" had a familiar ring, but she couldn't place its source. She ran her fingers through her hair — a nervous habit she had acquired that was childlike, appealing.

Here, at home, she could think. Obviously she had been followed. Unless the note was the work of a psychopath who had been there among the shelves, selecting her as the person he wanted to taunt, just as one might casually select one avocado or grapefruit over another. But he had known her name: Mrs. Benson.

So . . . she had been followed.

When and where had this person begun to trail her? What had she done today? The early hours had been spent in her studio. The afternoon had been spent with her father listening to Sibelius, talking, studying the angles of his face, wishing she could capture on canvas all that was there. She had tried once and failed. Perhaps she would try again . . . after she had finished the portrait of Sir Charles's child.

In the late afternoon she had left her father sitting in his small dusty study. She'd watched him turn again to a collector's volume of Greek rhetoric. The book was a gift he'd received from a former graduate student who had acquired an impressive teaching position and had not forgotten his mentor.

She had driven from her father's house in the university area to the theatre, where she'd returned some sketches that the costume designer had asked her to critique. This ritual, which had become irksome to her, was reenacted with each new play simply because Lance insisted, and the designer, a highly talented but docile lady, accepted the arrangement. As a result Lance was humored. Rarely was a costume redesigned. On impulse she'd stopped by her husband's office to announce that she was discontinuing the charade. Surprisingly he'd shrugged and said, "As you wish."

Then what? After leaving the theatre, where had she gone? Nowhere. She had driven the long stretch of freeway from downtown Houston toward home with the one quick stop at the store.

She stared now at her hands. Her thoughts, again, strayed. She noticed, as she sometimes did, that her hands were old hands. From painting since she was a child, she supposed, or, more logically, from an inherited trait. She frowned, feeling the lines crease into her forehead. She was aware that permanent facial lines were only faintly here and there. And those she did not mind. They were as friends. Especially the laugh lines etched fine and delicate about her eyes.

"Your mother's eyes," her father had told her often since that day, twenty-three years ago, when her mother had gone to the library and not come home. "She never regained consciousness," the doctor had said. "Some automobile accidents happen that way, and in this case it was for the best."

Strange, she thought, my thoughts keep veering. I should be thinking of this note, of what it means, but instead I think of my mother, my father. Well, no wonder, it was September, the first September in forty-two years that her father had not sauntered out excitedly, hesitantly — like a small boy opening a present, anticipating what was inside — to teach. And most of those many years had been spent at Crane University. But now retirement. It was September, and he was home. The first September. He had plans concerning what he was to do, but they had not, he told her, yet formulated.

About the note . . . she was going to assume that a person with purpose left it on her windshield. He'd said: "I am going to leave Mrs. Benson this note, because it is specifically for her. I will harm her if her husband doesn't stop." Stop what?

She poured a cup of coffee, then wandered through the house. It was a house old and beamed — a find fourteen years ago. Now, some said, it was worth a fortune, real-estate values having risen higher in Memorial than in the northwest or toward the Gulf. She went into the music room — so called because a piano was its focal point — and sat, drinking her coffee, smoking a cigarette.

Assuming she was the intended recipient — complete with name, no mistaken identity — that person, she then reasoned, must have followed her from the theatre. But she had not noticed one car, one person, trailing her bright red Toyota in and out of the traffic, though she was not difficult to follow. Once she'd even gotten a ticket for slow driving. It was just that she usually had so much to think about. The angle of a head; the space between the eyes; the flare of the nostrils; and, always, the play of light and shadow across a face. She lived, Lance complained, primarily in her own world. But why not? The chasm between them was great. That chasm might have been breached by children. "Please," she often used to beg, wanting at least one small round person, created from the two of them to see what they would come up with to love. "Forget it," he'd invariably say, "our lives are full enough without clutter."

"Clutter?"

"Clutter."

So there were no children. The chasm widened. Few good moments remained between them. She thought of sand shifting, filling the bottom of an hourglass, the top left empty. One day, when the unknown became less frightening than the known, she would have to leave. Perhaps months, not years, from now. If only Lance had kept the promise he'd made to her that night as they had lain close to the Pacific, their bodies entwined, the cool air as balm against their skin. If only flaws and seams and cracks, as in aging leather, had not shown through . . . In her husband. And in herself. For too long she had allowed Lance to submerge her very being. And though she still occasionally curved into the small of his arm, cooked his favorite foods, ignored his moods, she felt restless and remote. Angry. And sometimes sad . . . and something else. She felt dirty. Where did that feeling come from? She didn't know. She did know that for some time she had felt — without acknowledging its name or seeking its source — dirty. What was Lance doing and how would she be harmed if he didn't stop? Though she'd concluded her husband was a bastard, she'd assumed he had shown that side only to her. Maybe she had been naïve.

She mashed out her cigarette and decided to go for a swim. The small oval pool which they had built one summer with the help of four aspiring actors was a haven. She would dive deep, as deep as she could. For a time she would forget those questions needing answers. She would be able to do that with the water pressing against her, engulfing her. It was one solution she had found for getting away from it all.

"You think I like being a maid in this play?" She stood in the doorway of his office. "Hell, Lance, I was a sweetmeat *ven-dor* in the last one!"

Sandra Lowrey blew one long cool ribbon of smoke, aimed like the barrel of a gun, directly at him.

Lance Benson smiled.

"Really, Sandra, must you be such a poor sport?"

"Yeah, really."

He leaned back in his swivel chair and studied her.

Though she could lose some weight, there was a voluptuous quality to her that would be threatened by more than a five-pound loss. She would not hold up well in age, but at twenty-three she was a cherub. "You're a cherub," he said, hoping to divert her wrath.

"Aw, come off it, Lance. A cherub. My God." She sat down in the chair opposite his desk.

"Who's out there?" The tone of his voice darkened. With the new season upon him — and already pressing down hard — he had enough worries without Sandra Lowrey prancing in and out of his office.

"Don't worry. Everybody's gone. Even that crazy, loony, *absolutely* loony playwright."

"He's a hometown boy who made good. So don't criticize my choice."

"All right. All right." She smoked thoughtfully. Her eyes slightly squinted. "Look —"

"Yes?"

"Nothing . . . well, *yes,* something. You and I are getting into this pretty deep."

"I don't want to discuss that now."

"I do." She pouted. She could be such a nuisance, he thought. In fact, these last few weeks, most of the time. She whined a lot. But for now there was not too much he could do about it.

"What's on your mind?" He placed his pen on his desk, leaned forward and stared. The stare bored holes into her skull. "That look could kill," Zoe had told him once when they had been arguing about something trivial and long forgotten. He had replied, "You, Zoe, have a vivid imagination." But what she had said was true. His penetrating gaze was a potent weapon.

"I agreed to all this stuff for two reasons." The girl seated on the other side of his desk fidgeted. She was backing down before she even started.

"Oh?"

"Lance, smile. You scare me when you sit there staring." The gaze didn't waver. "OK, OK. Number one, I started doing this so we could get married . . . because you said you loved me. Right?"

"Right."

"But you also said it would help my career. Right?"

He nodded.

"Well, it hasn't."

"You've gained experience as an actress."

"Now who's going to do *that* on stage?"

"It frees you to express yourself more fully."

"In maids' parts?"

"Give it time, Sandra. Look, you were Maggie in *Cat on a Hot Tin Roof.* What do you think a repertory theatre is?" In a minute he was going to kick her out the door. Temperamental actresses were a pain in the ass. Especially this one. Though she was good at the job, he was beginning to wonder why he had selected her, drawn her into his project. The project itself — conceived to revive and challenge his senses and to amass his rightful fortune — was becoming quite an undertaking. And mainly because he was having to deal with this girl.

"Well, I . . ." She was becoming confused, as he had known she would. He could do that. Persuade, cajole, kick, smile, charm. Hadn't he turned some few blades of grass and dirt and broken glass on a used parking lot into this — a multilevel theatre?

"Go on." He smiled, deciding to give her a break. After all, he still needed her services.

"I started fucking old men so we could get married. Now that's the sum and substance of it."

"And to make money, lots of it," he reminded her.

"So we could get married."

"That's correct."

"Yeah, well . . . I haven't seen any money."

"Sandra, you have enough to live quite well." Goddamn her. Hadn't she been able to quit the drugstore crap?

"I need a new car."

"You need — what?"

"I saw this powder blue Jag —"

"Jag. You saw a Jag. Well, you just keep on looking at Jags. This conversation is terminated." He stood. Scare the pants off her was the way to do it. So help him, he had never struck a woman, but there was always a first time. She didn't know it, but she was pushing blackmail. The early stages . . . still, it was there.

"Lance, all I wanted to say was . . . I'm scared. I really am." She mashed out her cigarette. The full baby lips, smeared with pink, quivered. "I'm scared. I don't like doing this. And we haven't — been together, you know, in a long time."

"Six days." His mind could computerize, store away, any amount of information and churn it out again when needed.

"You remember? *Exactly.*"

"Of course." He reached in his wallet and extracted five one-hundred-dollar bills. He accepted only cash for everything — everything, that is, related to his project. And though most of the money went into his lockbox, he always kept enough available cash to meet certain expenses.

"This'll help, Sandra, but it won't buy a Jag. That's for later."

She took the money. He pulled a Kleenex from a container on his desk. Long ago he'd concluded that a wearisome task of any artistic director was dispensing tissues to highly strung actresses.

"We'll still get married?" She blew her nose loudly.

"When it's over."

"You're not getting any younger, you know."

At that he threw back his head and laughed. One remarkable thing about the girl was that occasionally she had accidental flights into wit.

"So I'm forty-six." He shrugged. "I'm Mephistopheles, didn't you know? I control the deals, and maybe I made a deal with myself that I'll be young forever. Now go home, Sandra. Relax, and tomorrow night —"

"Yes?" The hunger in her face would eat him alive if he let it. One big gulp and he would be gone.

"Tomorrow night it won't be one of the old ones — though they haven't all been old."

"It'll be you?"

"Precisely."

"Promise?"

"Promise."

That was the one way he could get rid of her. Demanding broad, but her anatomy was superb. Far better than Zoe's could ever be.

He turned out the light. It was time to visit the northwest bank.

Caroline Fletcher turned from watering African violets which she grew on long, narrow shelves of glass.

"You're home early." She expressed neither delight nor dismay. It was a fact. A little past five and her husband was home.

"I felt like taking off. Is that so unusual?"

It was, but she merely said, "Well, if you felt that way, Martin, you did exactly right." She kissed her husband's cheek. Thirty years of marriage had not altered but rather embedded in granite her ritual of kissing him with one light stroke of softness when he left in the morning and later when he returned.

"How do you feel?" he asked.

"Fine. I've had a good day."

Unconsciously he looked down to her blouse, gray silk to match her own thin, graying elegance. They both were thinking about the removal of what once had been small, firm roundness. Now the one-sided flatness. But she was alive.

"I did some committee work," she continued, "for the theatre."

"Oh . . . were you there today?"

She wondered briefly at the sudden edge in his voice.

"No, it was mostly telephoning — about the gala."

"Well, that's good." He seemed relieved.

"I'll get you a drink." She was already on the way to their bar.

Martin Fletcher III sank into his pale blue leather chair. He was tired. Tired of worrying about Caroline's health, tired of his ingratiating job. All he wanted now, he told himself, was Caroline to stay healthy — the cancer to be gone forever — and their expenses to be in line with what he was making and had saved. No, his thoughts wearily and fearfully backtracked. There was something else he wanted more. But that something else was inextricably tangled up in the other two — in Caroline's well-being and economics. Simply put, he wanted peace. A peace that was still unobtainable. There were steps to be taken first. Difficult, precarious steps . . . and today he had begun taking those steps.

He stared at Caroline's African violets and plucked at his moustache. Was it only a little more than two months ago — two months and not two years — that he had searched for some revived glory of his youth, which had never been glorious to begin with?

He got up quickly, as if fleeing his thoughts, and walked into the library. Perhaps the newspaper was there. Caroline had an annoying habit of moving it about the house. Ah, yes. He picked up the *Herald* from the table by the typewriter and returned to his chair in the sun room where his wife was waiting with his martini — that one cool evening drink — which he had taught her so carefully and with such devotion to make in those earlier years. The drink had gradually been perfected in much the same manner as had been the departure and arrival kiss.

"Perfect." He smiled, his moustache twitching. He was lucky to have Caroline. He knew it, had always known it. He had just panicked and forgotten.

They sat talking quietly, comfortable with each other. The sun slowly lowered. In the library, streaks of fading light hit upon the typewriter whose type size measured exactly twelve characters to the linear inch. A stack of bond paper lay nearby.

Lance Benson liked a big car. Controlling that much power with a slight touch on the steering wheel made him feel in charge of his destiny and that of everyone else on the road passing him by or pressing up behind him. A charcoal gray Lincoln Continental. A Cadillac was too flashy, but the Continental said and did precisely what he had in mind.

He passed a Mercedes, then slowed for a chemical truck. He

turned on the radio but quickly flicked it off. There was too much to think about. Thinking in a car made Zoe drive more slowly; for him thinking was simply a way of passing the time until he reached his destination. He'd be home by eight, barely. Going all the way out to the northwest, then back through traffic, was getting to be a pain, almost as much of a pain as Sandra Lowrey. Maybe he'd rent a lockbox in Memorial. What harm would it do? Still, the little northwest bank was hidden, and its hours — open till eight — suited his schedule. Only thirty minutes ago, he had placed in the steel vault twenty thousand dollars. But, damn, having to take Fletcher's money in installments! He had miscalculated on that one.

He smiled. The unpleasant thought of Fletcher led to thoughts of the others who had been agreeable. Not happy, but agreeable.

Money was coming in now. A person could go to prison for less than what he was doing. But he had outsmarted people all his life and he fully intended to come out ahead on this one. Solomon had paid in a lump sum. Reese needed two installments, which was understandable. But Fletcher — he'd have to put pressure on him for the outstanding fifty thousand. No way was he going to be a bill collector for some midget who kept wringing his hands and whining. "I've got kids in college, medical expenses for my wife . . ."

Despite its headaches, however, his project remained the greatest drama of his career. Not only was he the director, he was also the writer! Though all men probably have something to hide, he had not hired a detective to rummage through each victim's past. Rather, he himself, with their unwitting help, was creating the sordid evidence. And for his efforts he wasn't being doled out a meager salary decreed by a few pompous board members. Nor were his victims standing up in a meeting demanding his resignation. They knew better than to try that. "Why?" the loyal and perplexed majority would surely question. Any answer forthcoming could only be self-incriminating.

Though he was nearing the Bunker Hill exit, there was still time to think further about his project. About Hook. An image of Sir Charles Stanton, medals plumed across his chest, interfered. Perhaps he shouldn't touch the war hero, the proper gentleman, but damned if he could resist. If only he, like Charles Stanton, were "to the manor born," but he wasn't. He was Lance Benson, son of the nuts-and-bolts pusher, born in the sunken bedroom of a decaying house. He would become a Charles Stanton in his time. And that time would arrive just as soon as he wound up his work with the big one — the man named Hook properly hooked. First, Stanton; next, Hook. Then that would be it.

He would, of course, have to deal with Sandy. Pat her on the fanny and say, "So long, kid." . . . Hardly. Nothing short of a Clairol-commercial contract would shut her up. Well, he'd think of something. After all, wasn't thinking his specialty?

She neatly placed her wad of bubble gum back in its wrapper because maybe she'd chew it later. Sandra Lowrey liked to chew old gum. It was sort of like getting close all over again to somebody you hadn't seen in a while that you had liked, been crazy about, and they'd just disappeared. But with bubble gum it was different. If you put it back in its wrapper and put the wrapper some place you couldn't possibly forget, like on the kitchen counter or near your toothbrush in the bathroom, some place really obvious, then you could count on the bubble gum still being there. It didn't go away like people sometimes did.

Damn Lance. She turned on the hot water in the tub. He was treating her like an old shoe. Like a whore, was the truth of the matter. She watched the bubble bath form little mountains in her tub. Pretty soon she'd soak in all those foamy mountains. That should make her feel better.

She padded naked back through her apartment to the kitchen. Her eyes avoided the bed. It was a ridiculous contraption. To think in the beginning she'd thought it was the nuts. A pile of shit was what it was. Lance and his ideas. She poured a glass of wine. Lance was trying to get her to be more uptown, so here was this white-wine crap when all she really wanted was a cold beer. She'd have to walk back by that damn bed to reach the tub. Tonight she just might sleep on the sofa. The only time these days she liked being in that thing was when Lance was with her.

She sank deep in the water. Strands of hair, strayed from the ponytail she'd made, trailed down her neck. She didn't care. She always felt like some movie star when she filled her tub with bubble bath. Leaning back, she closed her eyes and sipped the wine. It didn't taste so bad tonight. Lance said you developed a taste for finer things. Like snails. Snails dipped in garlic butter. Escargot, he'd called them. But they were damn sure just little slimy snails. That was all there was to it. As far as she was concerned, a snail was a snail. You could call it any fancy name you wanted. She frowned. A whore was a whore. You could dress that up, too. Though she wasn't sure how. After all no man ever said he was having escargot tonight when he was having a piece of ass. *Her* ass! She sat straight up in the tub and got out quickly. Lance was just going to have to divorce that Zoe, soon; then marry her and get rid of that goddamn mirrored bed with all its contraptions. Remote control, my eye! All the stuff she had to think of, be in charge of. Let him try having that much on his mind at one time.

She pulled her old flannel nightgown over her head and went looking in the top of her closet for her one-eyed teddy bear. She hadn't done that in a long time. But, damn it all, she needed Rascal tonight. She hugged the worn little bear. "Fuzzy old thing," she murmured. Just let Lance walk in and order her into some flimsy black thing. No sir. Tonight it was the flannel, made out of East Texas flour sacks. That's all they'd worn at The Good Shepherd. They'd never even thought about it. Slipping one of those things over your head before you hopped into bed at night was just about the most natural, unthinking thing you ever did.

She sat on the floor, crosslegged, holding Rascal, flipping through *Cosmopolitan*. She peered closely at one of the pictures . . . here was this really classy-looking lady with frizzed-out hair. She just might get her hair done like that. She could do that now: afford new hairdos and silk blouses and jewels. Well, maybe not jewels, yet. On one score, however, she couldn't argue. All this was better than shifting from one tired foot to the other behind some drugstore counter. In a way, working there had been like standing behind all those unending piles of unwashed dishes at The Good Shepherd.

"She's a gutsy thing," everybody at The Good Shepherd had always said. Her brightest moments had come at Christmas when she'd acted in the pageant, starting out that first year as a camel and ending up by the time she was sixteen as Mary. She'd felt like some high, gold star shining down on the whole world. That's how she'd gotten the idea about acting; and she'd formed a plan. "I'll go to Houston," she'd promised herself, "get a job, save money, act in whatever happens to be there, and then — Hollywood." She'd be a real star. And she had carried out her plan —

at least the Houston part of it. Coming here with only three hundred dollars in her purse. "Natural talent," Lance had said. The only one at The Arch who hadn't had fifty-three thousand years of college and finishing school, and "professional acting experience." The only one.

She smiled and turned the pages of the magazine, not really looking at the pictures anymore. The only one. The gold shining star. From the East Texas orphanage to here. Not bad. Only thing . . . only thing. She'd miscalculated. She hadn't counted on Lance Benson. Hadn't counted on falling in love with somebody like that. And she sure hadn't counted on, all of a sudden, feeling so miserable. Not wanting so much to go to Hollywood. Not wanting so much to be a star. Just wanting Lance to marry her, take care of her, like a daddy would. Yeah, she reckoned, like a daddy ought to take care of his little girl. Lance was just going to have to take care of her. After all, that wasn't such a big, hard thing to do, was it? He loved her, didn't he? He'd said he did. He must. Making her do all those things in that bed with those other men was so he could take care of her in the end — soon. Wasn't that it? Well, wasn't it?

She closed the magazine. For a long time she sat on the floor, quietly.

Caroline had gone up to bed. He knew she would be propped against pillows, the night cream lightly rubbed into her skin. She would be reading. Lately she had turned to religious books: *God's Presence, Eternity Forecast, Preparing for the Hereafter.* Some few, thankfully, still had bits of earth clinging to their pages: *Life is for Living, Dynamics of Day-to-day Coping, Vibrant Now.* "For after all," she had told him, not complaining, not superior, simply stating, "when you've come close to — the other side — you begin thinking." Well, he was glad that, besides getting ready for "the other side," she was becoming interested in some of her previous pursuits. Her phoning today for the gala had been a good thing. He wished, however, he could lift the entire Arch Theatre and throw it deep into the bayou. Let the building become mired in mud and slime. In quicksand — all of it, every brick and stone, with its managing and artistic director inside, sitting behind his pretentious eight-foot mahogany desk. Whoever heard of one man being so presumptuous, so omnipotent, as to anoint himself sole managing and artistic director of a sprawling, prosperous, professional theatre? Who did he think he was? God Almighty himself? Being board members, Caroline and he should have had enough clout and foresight to prevent him from gaining and keeping such power.

But Benson's fist clenched about the theatre was not what was really troubling him. Rather, his problem was that same fist had been pushing down into his own throat. Pushing, pushing, until finally a hard knot had formed in his stomach. He sipped the milk and nibbled at the four crackers he allotted himself each night. This bedtime snack had become a ritual in his childhood and continued to be one even now. He had flavored the milk tonight with malt chocolate, for he needed to wash away the taste of bile. He could not decide whether the vile taste came from Lance Benson's manipulation of his life — prospering and destroying from that manipulation — or from his own reactions and actions. Was the thick sludge on his tongue simply the result of the revulsion he felt against what he, Martin Fletcher III, had done today? The step he had taken?

Zoe Benson was a nice lady. Wasn't she one of the few who had come for more than the single perfunctory visit when Caroline had been in the hospital? And she was smart. Didn't the exquisite portrait she had painted of Caroline hang over their fireplace? Didn't she, wasn't she . . . what? He gulped some milk and thoughtfully ate a cracker. He felt she was innocent. She, with her straight back and quick smile, certainly had no part in the dirty scheme of things. It was her husband alone who had played upon a weak moment, upon that carnal lust which springs from time to time in most men. In all men? What about priests? He hadn't been to confession in thirty years. Marrying Caroline had brought him over into the Episcopal Church; but sometimes — not often, but sometimes — and especially now with his wife upstairs so deep into *Eternity Now,* he wanted to go running back to one of those long, thin, black-frocked men of God. As a child he had thought of them as blackbirds hovering protectively, menacingly, over mankind. Ought he now to seek out one of them to confess his sin? But what sin? To which sin was the guilt attached? Surely, he rationalized, his sin of succumbing once to those baser instincts possessed by all men — except maybe priests — was understandable. His wife in the hospital; the breast gone. He had felt amputated of some vital part of his own body. He had felt frightened. And Caroline in her sedation had not needed him during that long night when Benson had led him to the girl.

He had gasped and wallowed in the warmth of her breasts, in their lushness, not realizing that all the while he was sinking into the moisture of her body he was also sinking into a whirlpool, a camera rolling as he writhed and turned and stared up at the mirrored reflection over their heads. The sin was not so much in that lost moment. He would not touch the girl again. He shuddered, repulsed, remembering how after it was over, as they had lain sprawled and naked, she had leaned over him to reach for an old piece of gum stuck to the nightstand. Popping it into her mouth, she had said, "Honey, you do that good. But you got to go home now."

Well, he was home now. But home had become a place where he paced and sweated and dug deep into his dwindling savings to come up with money for college educations and surgery over and beyond insurance coverage and house payments and boat payments and somehow, dear God, blackmail payments. Hadn't he dropped off his second installment at The Arch this very afternoon? And that is when the real sin might have been committed. He had seen her leaving the theatre.

Her back was that of a ballerina. He had always admired Zoe Benson's posture. He must ask her one day whether she had ever studied ballet. She reminded him of a gazelle.

The note, typed five days before, had been folded inside his wallet, waiting for just such an opportunity. He had not dared hope the chance would drop so easily into his path. Though he did not consider himself a creative person, he admired the originality of the wording. The threat, with its *King Lear* quote, should serve his purpose.

When she had driven away from the theatre, he had followed her, careful not to let his car edge up too close to hers. He did not intend to hurt her, unless that is, he had to. He only meant to frighten her husband. After all, Lance Benson must surely love such a lovely, intelligent woman. She must appeal to his finer nature, for hadn't the priests once said that all men, no matter how base, had somewhere — hidden, perhaps, but nevertheless there — a nobility which was like air, hazed and rarefied, ringed above mountains? Yes, Benson would want to protect his wife.

Still, he must not delude himself. Benson was not your ordinary man. He was a subhuman bastard who might care no more for his wife than he cared for a rose peddler waylaying cars on feeder roads. He might guard his marriage no more closely than he had guarded his friendship with a board member. He had tossed that friendship onto a garbage heap. Might not Benson's marriage land there too while the bastard laughed? Laughed uproariously, as he held the cassette over his head and refused to halt the blackmail, refused to return the fifty thousand dollars that had already been paid . . . The threat was a long shot. He knew that. But that threat and the others that were to follow were all the ammunition he had. They comprised his plan. His arsenal. And by aiming dead center at what he hoped was the correct target — Zoe Benson, the lovely porcelain wife — he would conceivably preserve life with Caroline as he knew it and wanted it always to be. Indeed, his own survival was at stake. His fight no less than jungle warfare. He had no choice but to proceed as if he could not fail. Surely no priest would condemn such an effort.

He finished off the last crumb of cracker and swallow of milk. He felt better. What he had done today was no sin at all. He needed no confessional.

Deciding to accelerate his plan, he reached for the phone. Step Two was to be implemented forty-eight hours ahead of schedule.

She answered as he had hoped she would. It could have been Lance, but it was Zoe. A sign that God was sanctifying and even guiding his plan. He let her say "Hello, hello . . . hello," then softly, but distinctly, he hung up. Knowing that she had heard the click, he visualized her listening to the line gone dead.

"Who was that?" Lance Benson asked through a mouthful of toothpaste.

"Nobody."

"Nobody?"

"I guess it was a wrong number."

"You *guess?*" He put away his toothbrush and came over to her.

"Yes, I guess. I mean, whoever it was hung up."

"Just like that?"

"Just like that . . . Why?"

"Natural curiosity."

"I see. Well, let's get to bed. It's after eleven, and I want to be in the studio by eight tomorrow."

After he had switched off the light, her husband did not reach for her. Rather, signaling that he wished to talk, he propped his arms behind his head. She had hoped he would turn over, as he so often did, and go to sleep. She didn't want to talk; she wanted to think. That call just now could have been from the same person who had slipped the note beneath her windshield wiper only hours before. And how could she talk about that when she had decided not to share the note with her husband? She would, instead, deal with the problem, should there actually be one, without Lance's help — or hindrance.

"How's it going?" he asked.

"What?"

"Your *work*." He seemed on edge lately, always on edge.

"It's difficult. You know, painting from a photograph of some-body's dead child. That still scares me. But not as much."

"Stanton will be over to see it at some point, won't he?"

"He said so."

"When?"

"I'm not sure." Why tell him that an appointment had already been made? "To see how it's coming, if you don't mind," Stanton had said. Such a gentleman. "If you don't mind." It was as if he understood that part of her which liked to keep a portrait hidden until it was completed; yet somehow it seemed right that the father see the face of his son in its evolution. She wanted that, so she had told him when he had called, "Wednesday, around four, will be fine."

"Let me know when he's coming to see it."

Too tired for an argument, she gently warned, "Lance, please, as we agreed, let's not mix your business with mine."

"Darling, all I want is to have a drink with you two. Is that so unreasonable?"

"I'll let you know." She moved farther away from him. Some-times when they got into bed she felt as though they were separated by the width of the Sahara. Tonight was one of those times.

"Try to make it soon."

"I will," she said and closed her eyes.

Lance Benson lay in the dark thinking. His thoughts were not about the wife beside him, nor were they about the theatre or the

troublesome Sandra or the whining Martin Fletcher. He was thinking about Charles Stanton, disgustingly upright, British, and elegant. He imagined Stanton in a velvet smoking jacket. And then
he smiled. It was a sardonic smile as he contemplated just what
Sir Charles Ashton Stanton's Achilles' heel might be.

Lowell Hook was not feeling well this morning. He coughed
and rang for hot tea, then forced his spirits upward. Even if thin,
blue-veined legs and a thoroughly undependable heart were what
he had now, he wasn't going to let either of those get him down.
He would apply mind over matter, so to speak. Besides, what the
hell! Wasn't he still able — still man enough — to dip down every
now and then into the earthier pleasures? That was proven fact.
Lance Benson had done him quite a favor some two months ago.
It'd caused his heart problem to flare up a bit, but he just might
take on another one of those evenings. He'd have to talk to Benson —
bright young fellow — about that. But not this week. He needed
to conserve his strength for a couple of board meetings. Being the
recognized leader of cultural endeavors was not to be taken lightly.
Having no heirs, he didn't want the city to get the idea it would
be better off having him dead rather than alive. He liked to keep
his hand in things. His God-given common sense consistently put
a lot of flighty dreamers on the right course. Still, you had to
dream, he knew that. Where would he be without all the dreaming
he'd done? Not here, that was for sure.

His eyes swept over the room in which he sat. The years had
not diminished his gratitude. Nor his amazement. On his walls
hung original art. On the table beside him sat a gold snuff-box
encrusted with jade. A Lopez sculpture stood in one corner. First
editions lined cherry bookcases. A Persian rug, dating into antiq-
uity, stretched beneath his feet.

To be surrounded by rare and beautiful objects not only gave
him pleasure and a sense of security but also kept him humble.
For those reasons, he had brought a few valuable possessions with
him three years before when, on his seventieth birthday, he'd donated his sixty-three-room mansion to the city. The grounds and
house were open now to the public; and he understood the tours
brought in a handsome revenue. Certainly he had no regrets about
giving up Bluebonnet Hill. During those last years, the place had
become a mausoleum in which he'd rattled around waiting for his

death. He had come here into the heart of the city, believing that
to be close to a city's pulse beat would make his own more alive.
It had been a good move.

Still, today he had rather be across town in the Buckingham
Club sipping brandy, playing a little gin rummy, and reminiscing
with old friends instead of here, encased in glass and marble.
Thirty-six floors up was, at times, too close to heaven to suit him.

Again he coughed. He tucked the cashmere lap robe closer about
his legs. Goddamnit, September, the hottest blazing month in
Houston, and he felt chilled. No doubt about it — you could ra-
tionalize all you wanted — old age was a pants' splitting pain in
the ass.

"Hello . . . Hello? . . . *Say* something."

The click and then deadness. It was the seventh call of the day.
Three o'clock in the afternoon. Each of the calls had come on the
hour. The first had occurred at nine o'clock, when she had been
at work. At three o'clock she was still in her studio.

With the first call, she had stopped work reluctantly, wondering
which of her friends was cutting into her concentration. But with
the other calls she had gone to the phone in the hallway as though
drawn hypnotically into the eye of a storm. After each call it had
become increasingly difficult to return to the work she must do in
order to be ready for Charles Stanton's visit tomorrow. When the
eighth call came, she would ask the caller to identify himself. She
would suggest to the person that perhaps mistaken identity was
involved. If that was not the case, she would demand a translation
of the cryptic note.

But there was no eighth call. She did not have the opportunity
that day to confront the enemy. She did, however, have time to
think, for she could no longer concentrate on the portrait of the
dead boy. She cleaned her brushes.

Lighting a cigarette, she stood at one of the tall windows, in
what once had been a cobwebbed attic, and looked down the three
stories into the half-acre yard. She stared as though expecting to
see her enemy prowling there, staring back at her through a
telescopic lens. No wind stirred among the trees. The water in the
oval pool was motionless. The enemy was not there.

She turned from the window. Her concentration centered on

her husband. Lance, the unfathomable Libra. Since their all-too-short vacation, he had been consumed with what she had thought was work: the mounting of a new play by a Texan who had made a name for himself on Broadway two seasons before. She had patiently listened as Lance voiced fears that the play was weak, that rewriting couldn't salvage it, that the audience would be lost in a maze of dark narcissism. Lance himself was narcissistic. Certainly she recognized that, but never before had she really considered that Lance the narcissist was capable of intrigue. She ran her fingers through her hair, shook her head. She felt she was shadowboxing. Someone out there, elusive and desperate, was threatening her because of something her husband was doing.

She left her studio and went out into the narrow hallway, which served as a divider between her spacious loft and Lance's small but special province.

Standing before his darkroom door, she hesitated, feeling as if she were about to read another's diary.

Recollections, memories, surfaced.

She thought of their trip abroad ten years before. They both had wanted to bring home with them the faces and the land. Across Europe she had painted, and Lance, frustrated, had watched. After that had come the still and motion-picture photography classes and eventually the darkroom. His interest, however, had waned. Boring easily, he mercurially shifted fom one pursuit to another. For months he would shun the darkroom altogether. But lately he had spent several long evenings there, cautioning her to leave him alone. Squinting, he would finally emerge from the darkness and present her with a handful of photographs as proof of the hard work he assured her had been in progress.

She thought of the note. And turned the knob . . . But the door refused to budge. Perhaps it was stuck. She jiggled the knob, then pushed against the paneling. The door was locked.

In ten years she had never known the door to that room to be locked. At times it had been left ajar, and more often closed, but never locked. She hardly could smash through the door without Lance's demanding an explanation.

The problem must be approached from a different angle. She walked quickly down the stairs and directly into the library, where her husband's desk was centered against two windows that looked out over willows and elms shading their front lawn. Again she hesitated. The serenity of the setting belied the task. That couldn't be helped. She opened a drawer.

In spite of an hour's search, the desk, filled with neat and orderly theatrical files, yielded nothing. There was not even a misplaced memorandum.

She threw up her hands and went for a swim.

Later, she called her father and asked if he knew the quote "I am a man more sinn'd against than sinning."

"It's Shakespeare, of course."

"Of course," she agreed, pleased that she had turned to him.

"From *King Lear*," he had said, then asked, "Why?" To which she had replied, comfortable in her lie, that she was helping this month with the theatre newsletter and the quote had come to mind for the Shakespearean puzzle, sometimes included as a filler. He had accepted her explanation and had told her he was sorting through memorabilia kept in a steamer trunk, and did she realize what a precocious little girl she had been, right from the beginning, pressing flowers between the pages of books, then tracing around their edges, and filling in the petals with bright splotches of watercolor? She had answered, "Well, why shouldn't I have been precocious? Look at my father." He had been pleased, and she had been sad.

At six o'clock she drove to The Galleria. She was determined to buy something youthful and colorful, because recently she had begun to feel old and faded. Lance had said he wouldn't be home until late. Though he was taking the playwright to dinner, he had not asked her to join them. Perhaps a silk dress and bright shoes would make her feel better. The simplicity of her thinking was absurd. She knew that. Superficialities would not lessen the uneasiness and distrust widening the gulf between her and her husband. Only now had she begun to realize that it had been three weeks since they had made love. Strange, she, of the highly passionate nature, had not missed that — making love with her husband. Her husband, keeper of a locked darkroom which always before had been open.

Victor Solomon poured a shot of scotch and took a deep swallow. He walked over to his desk, switched on the intercom, and informed his secretary that he was not to be disturbed for twenty minutes.

Stretched out on his leather sofa, he drank and thought. Ten o'clock in the morning. Too early to drink, he knew that, but he reasoned that one, maybe two gulps down his throat and into his stomach would lessen the agitation he had been feeling ever since the call had come from Bradshaw. Hell, even if Bradshaw was one of his closest friends, he was also his lawyer and being paid royally to keep the divorce, if it had to be, clean; to keep things *from* Roselyn; to leave his mind free to run an entire department store, for Christ's sakes!

In exactly one hour the first model would walk down the runway, and the Designer Salon's Fall fashion show would be off and running. Afterward he would be expected to be his usual charming self. Cheek-kissing some two hundred oohing and aahing ladies while they sipped his Dom Perignon, nibbled his caviar, and, he hoped, purchased many thousands of dollars' worth of cashmere, lamé, brocade, imported silk, and God knows whatever else struck their ridiculous fancies.

Damn Bradshaw. Better yet, damn Lance Benson. Blackmailing bastard. He wished he'd laughed in his face and told him to fuck off. But when a man has the goods on you . . . He got up and poured a second drink. And now here was Bradshaw informing him that Roselyn's lawyer was demanding — *demanding,* no less — an accounting for one hundred thousand dollars deposited and shortly thereafter withdrawn from his and Roselyn's joint checking account. In his haste to pay Benson, he'd forgotten that a day of reckoning would come. The monthly bank statement, showing deposits and withdrawals, would be mailed to their home. He imagined Roselyn opening the envelope and raising her delicate eyebrows as she noted that one hundred thousand dollars had been placed in an account seldom holding more than twenty thousand, and then withdrawn a few days later. That had been his stupidity. He should have done *anything* — stolen from the business; murdered Benson; sold his precious Beechcraft Baron, God forbid — anything rather than touch money that was in both his and his wife's names. But that had been the insurmountable problem: all his assets were jointly owned. He had borrowed the money against his and Roselyn's brokerage account. The margin account, with a small debit balance, held listed securities with a market value of over a million dollars. To cash the brokerage check issued by law in both his and Roselyn's names, he'd had to run it through their joint account at the bank. Panicked, he'd thought he had no alternative. He groaned, remembering how fortunate he'd felt that the court had not yet frozen their community assets. Dumb, dumb, dumb. He gulped his scotch. This was getting to be one big, fat, messy divorce.

His mind half toyed with the idea of leaving the store, driving over to Roselyn's house — hell, to *his* house that she'd kicked him out of — and forcing her back to the way she'd been before she got into women's liberation and all that crap and decided two could do it — "have fun," as she'd put it, "and be a success in some fulfilling job." Just what job, she wasn't sure, but she was goddamn convinced that a divorce would make everything fall into place. Well, what about the children? Was all this crap going to make everything fall into place for them? Rebecca called almost every day crying, "Come home, Daddy." And Chad was turning into a quiet old man at the age of eight. Christ! He needed another drink. He would have to think of something *good* to explain why one hundred thousand dollars had appeared and then vanished without one thin cancelled check to prove he'd bought additional securities or purchased a six-ton nugget of gold. Not only did Roselyn want her divorce, she also wanted his hide.

He looked out the window. Not a cloud in sight. What he really would like to be was an airline pilot. He'd like to chuck this crazy business of running the store, which his grandfather had so inconsiderately built up from a dry-goods corner operation into a multimillion dollar concern. And which his father had built up even higher. Now it was his lot to further the phenomenal rise. Well, if his son wanted to chuck the whole thing, that would be all right by him. He'd say, "Chad, you just go ahead and be a prize fighter, a golf pro, a clown in the circus. Be whatever you want, 'cause your old man at the age of forty-two almost walked out the door and became a real honest-to-goodness pilot." . . . Almost, but not quite.

Three drinks should hold him. He'd get back to Bradshaw later. That had been one hell of a night with Benson and what's-her-name, but damn if it had been worth all this. He brushed his teeth in the private bathroom next to his office. Might as well clear the scotch out of his mouth before he kissed the ladies. Looking into the mirror, he had no quarrel with the image reflected there: deep tan, jutting jawline. Dark, handsome bastard was how he thought of himself. Muscular, not an ounce of excess flesh. "The drinking'll get you one day," his doctor had warned.

"Well, not yet, my friend, not yet," Victor Solomon assured the devastating reflection.

He stepped into the reception area and smiled at his chic, blond secretary — the only kind to have in a place like this. Getting into the elevator, he impatiently pressed the Down button. He'd have to hurry to see how his razor-thin models were lining up for the show.

He had planned to make two more calls that day: the eighth at four o'clock and the last at five. But, unexpectedly, an afternoon meeting had been scheduled for Powell vice-presidents. Something from on high about the promotion of the new miracle roach killer, Lightning, that was guaranteed to act in one swift second. The product had reached the consumer market only twelve weeks before and was already taking the country by storm. Why the vice president of personnel should have to attend such a meeting was beyond him.

As he had anticipated, the agenda turned out to be nothing more than one long accolade for the public-relations division, whose promotional package was helping to make Lightning the most successful household aid in a decade. "Now to conquer the world!" the president had exclaimed. Well, he, Martin Fletcher, had his own deadly poison to put out into the world. It was a minuscule world, but it was his. He was going to rid that world of the menace that was preventing him from concentrating on killing roaches, shaving without nicking his chin, approaching par in his golf game, and making love to his wife. He was going to stamp out Lance Benson's blackmail scheme through Zoe Benson. And by now surely she was beginning to crack.

Zoe Benson was not beginning to crack. But she was beginning to feel caught in a vise whose pressure she suspected was intended for her husband rather than for herself. She was determined to get to the bottom of the frightening note and harassing calls. To find out the truth. Then she would act.

·　·　·

"Is tonight still on?" Sandy appeared suddenly in his doorway.

"Would you please lower your voice?"

She giggled and put her fingers, childlike, to her mouth. "Lance, I'm sorry." She was whispering now. "I mean, I just had to *know*."

"Tonight is still on," he assured her, then lowered his head to the papers on his desk. She was dismissed.

The happy child ran off to play maid on the stage.

"Raymond? . . . Raymond?" Winifred Adele Reese went calling through Reese Interiors for her son. "That boy! I can never find him when I need him." Her blue hair quivered. She twisted the diamonds on her plump fingers.

Finally!

She had discovered him in the workroom.

"Look, Mother, isn't this exquisite?" He held up a sample of silk brocade patterned with butterflies.

"Raymond, you are a love." Patting his cheek, she visualized tiny gold butterflies covering the Chippendale sofa they had recently purchased at a New Orleans auction. Reupholstered, the sofa would be stunning in the Wesley mansion. And Raymond had probably spent hours poring through textiles until he'd found, as he so often did, the perfect one.

She carried the swatch over to a window. "Perfect," she said, admiring the fabric as it caught the light.

So . . . the decision was made. Butterflies for the Chippendale.

She tossed the material onto a worktable. "Raymond, would you do something for me?"

He straightened, as if awaiting orders.

"Take my car and deliver the Ming vases to Irene Stanton."

"Yes, ma'am."

"Carefully. You understand?" She headed for the crated vases, chattering to her son as they walked. "I do believe Irene's fallen in love with all things Oriental ever since she and Charles went over there for him to receive another one of those honors. Imagine! This time in Taiwan, of all places. Well, Raymond" — she stopped, her destination reached — "I guess war heroes don't die. Like the song says, 'they just fade away.' " She rolled her eyes. "Though Sir Charles is certainly not giving the slightest indication of *that*, do you think?"

"No, ma'am." He picked up the crate.

"Oh — and Raymond?"

"Yes, ma'am?"

"*Thank you.* I realize the delivery men are perfectly capable of doing this, but Irene adores the personal touch."

"You can count on me, Mother."

"I know. Always." She blew him a kiss.

Raymond Reese drove his mother's Mercedes through traffic as if he were hand-carrying eggshells to the queen. The crated vases would not break there on the back seat, but he imagined that even a slight speed-up or a sudden braking of the car would smash each Ming into a million pieces. He would then stand among the bits of broken porcelain, while his mother retrieved two jagged edges from among the ruins and pierced one deep into his heart and the other into her own. Such would be her anguish.

But Raymond Reese, the worrier, had not one but two prominent worries on this particular September afternoon. The first was that he would somehow break the Ming vases. The second was that he had no means to amass quickly another fifty thousand dollars. He had come up with the first fifty from his inheritance — a modest sum left to him by a great-aunt of whom he was not allowed to speak because she was a Hamilton, though his mother had not objected to his taking the money. But fifty thousand more! If only his mother didn't clutch the purse strings so tightly in her pudgy little fists.

Feeling disloyal, he began worrying about calling his mother's beautiful hands pudgy. Well, they *had* been beautiful once. She had really been something — snaring all those husbands. But today, well, her hands *were* pudgy. At any rate, he was paid a flat salary the first of each month and bonuses whenever it struck her fancy. He, Raymond Billingsworth Reese, had a problem.

He would kill Lance Benson if he thought he could commit the murder without his mother's knowing. He would turn the car around, head for The Arch Theatre, and hit Benson over the head with one of the vases. If the bloody mission could be accomplished, then to hell with Lady Stanton's Ming. Such was the point of distraction to which Benson had driven him.

There must surely have been a better way than the one he had chosen to lose his virginity. But he hadn't done the choosing. Lance Benson had set him up.

Admittedly the experience had been mind-boggling. "You have a magnificent thing," the girl had told him; and he'd foolishly misinterpreted her smile. Incredulously he'd thought, "She cares. She really *cares* about me." He'd even liked her chewing bubble gum all through the act — right *through* the act. Keeping that wad of stuff in her mouth while she sucked on his magnificent thing. He'd liked feeling the wad there in her mouth every once in a while when it stuck up against him. And then the insertion! The real honest-to-goodness insertion. His virginal penis inserted into her not-so-virginal vagina! He was getting a hard-on just thinking about it.

At the very least the experience had made him determined to get more of it. Fucking. But he'd do it on his own. With some nice girl his mother selected. She would know best. In the meantime, he had to produce fifty thousand dollars or Benson would carry out his threat. What if his mother were told, were *shown*, the film! He ran through a stoplight. God, Benson was eating him alive.

The lights were out below, except for those in the corridors, which were kept burning through the night. All but the night watchman had left. It was safe. Lance Benson descended the winding concrete stairs into the belly of his theatre. His destination, specifically, was the wardrobe storage area. After some rummaging around, he knew he would find there exactly what he needed.

"Well, get you!" Sandra stood in her doorway surveying him.

"Are you just going to stand there?"

"I don't know. I'm not much on letting strangers in." She was being coy.

Damned if he was in the mood for this shit. He walked inside. "Not judging from your record."

"You bastard, that's unfair! Who put me up to this crap?"

The evening was off to a flying start.

He took off the wig. Wearily he sat down. "Sandra, my love, come here, and let's run through it again. We are doing this to realize a beautiful, happy goal, right?"

"Right." She smiled. The baby had been given the candy. "But I want to know why you're dressed up like Jack the Ripper?"

"Because it has occurred to me that from this point on it would be best if the same blond, handsome, devastating, married man were not seen visiting your boudoir night after night —"

"Night after night!" She was giggling now, snuggling up to him, as she got into the spirit of things.

"Well . . . as often as I can," he corrected. "At any rate, I have a black wig, a red wig, and one that's salt and pepper."

"Yeah, well, what about your tall, devastating, skinny frame?"

The girl, unfortunately, had a few smarts.

"I have thought of hunchbacks, canes, and such, but, ah, Sandra, there is only so much a man can do without ruining his beloved's reputation. I don't want people saying about you: 'That girl sure sees a bunch of weirdos.' "

She threw herself across his chest and cried, "I love you, Lance Benson. You are so *cute!*"

He grinned. Let her have her fun. He had decided to enjoy the evening, too. No need to mention that he had never once parked in front of her apartment. No need to point out that when he had selected this unit, located in one of the many sprawling, nondescript complexes thrown up about Houston to accommodate the thousands of young hopefuls pouring into the city, he had in effect buried her. In places like this few noticed or cared about their neighbors unless their own hedonistic purposes were to be served. And with his decreeing the pool off-limits, the clubhouse, the tennis courts, people off-limits, his accomplice might as well be Poe's Fortunato. Yes, having Sandra at Carrousel Square these last few months had worked well. Still, from the beginning he had protected himself further. Surgical gloves resided in the pocket of his car, awaiting that time when he might wish to enter her apartment without leaving his fingerprints. The wigs, taken from wardrobe storage, were simply added precautions.

"Now," he asked, "what's for dinner?" He began tickling her ribs, because suddenly he was in the mood to hear that high, childlike giggle and to watch those magnificent mammary glands quiver in delight.

She was not much of a cook, but she had tried, crying when the eggplant parmesan had rolled a bright, greasy streak down the front of her negligee. No, the big attraction here was not her cooking. At home Zoe would have prepared something cool and elegant. A shrimp salad would have been nice tonight. He reached for Sandra. "Leave the dishes," he said and began untying the ribbons of her negligee. As she stood in the middle of her tiny kitchen, he was aware that it was a ridiculous sight: the girl, holding a plate of leftover eggplant, while her clothes dropped to the floor.

"What are you thinking about?" she asked, leaning on her elbow, watching him stare up at the reflection of the man and the woman in the bed below.

"Nothing," he replied as he thought, "Three down, two to go." If only the footage on the old man had been usable! Then there would be no need for a retake. One false move and Hook would have his ass. Well, he'd just have to tread lightly, skillfully, and, above all, brilliantly.

"Come here, Sandra." He was aware that, at least for the time being, she was an indispensable link in the success of his project. "I believe," he said, pulling her close, "you definitely need more."

Two-thirty-five in the morning. Christ! He'd fallen asleep. He sat on the edge of the bed, his head between his hands. Too much wine, too much sex, and an eight o'clock meeting in the morning with the playwright about essential revisions. He groaned. Sandra, her body curled into a tight little ball, unrolled and blinked at him through the darkness.

He stood, anxious to dress and make a fast exit.

"You have to?"

Why did she invariably ask the same question? You could set your clock by it.

"Got to." His answer never varied. But he'd usually left by twelve. Now he'd have to pacify Zoe. What a bore that would be — listening to her bitch after he'd explained the obvious: he and the playwright had tied one on.

"Lance?"

He didn't answer.

"*Lance?*"

"*What?*" He had shouted. Controlling himself, he repeated, "What?"

"Can we get married soon?" It was a thin whimper in the dark.

"Probably."

He was almost to the front door when, padding barefoot and naked behind him, she said, "Lance, I've been thinking . . ."

Dear God, no, he thought.

"If we don't hurry up and finish this mess and get married — I mean, *soon* — then I'm —" She took a deep breath; he could hear her inhale. "I'm going to do one of three things. One: Tell Zoe about us. Two: Announce to the newspapers what's been going on — you know, in that stinking bed. Three: . . . Kill myself."

He supposed she had saved the last alternative as the ultimate threat. In actuality it seemed a lovely solution. He would wait, however, until his project was completed before he suggested that she select alternative three.

Tousling her hair, he said wearily, "Sandy, you're just 'full of sound and fury, signifying nothing' tonight, aren't you?" He was out the door before she could reply.

Walking to his car, he was conscious of the hollow sound his footsteps made on the pavement of the deserted street. He wondered if her threats had the potential of becoming realities. Sooner or later, he would have to deal wih Sandra Lowrey. It was not until he'd pulled into his driveway that he realized he had left the wig on the coffee table in her living room.

Wearing her old chenille bathrobe, she sat crosslegged on the floor in her bathroom. She was going to throw up. Any minute now. She didn't understand how one man could send her right up the wall in some kind of sexual frenzy — into some kind of mind-blowing, vaporized space where nothing — *nothing* — else mattered, and then when it was over that same man could make her feel so . . . so . . . she searched for the word. So like a whore? No. Dummy? No. Well, yes, to both of these, but neither was the word for which she was searching. She racked her brain. So what? How did he make her feel? And then she knew. Slave. So like a slave. She felt like Lance Benson's slave.

She stood up quickly and walked back through her apartment, as though looking for traces of the happiness she had felt with him. One evening in six — or maybe ten — was about all she was rating lately.

She turned on the lamp in the living room, because she hated darkness when she was alone. Suddenly she smiled and spoke aloud. "Well, what do you know?" She picked up the wig. Twirling it on a fingertip, she felt better. Lance would just have to make do with those other wigs he'd mentioned. She was hiding this one behind a box of old photographs, which she kept on her closet shelf. The wig would serve as her keepsake from a night when, to be sure, she hadn't gotten an engagement ring, but she had certainly spoken her mind right there at the end, and, above all, she had gotten royally fucked. Maybe up and about she was Lance Benson's slave, but flat on her back she was most definitely his princess.

Zoe Benson lay on her back, staring at patterns the tree branches made on the wall. Forty minutes earlier she'd awakened to find that the other side of the bed was as empty as it had been when she had fallen asleep at eleven.

Occasionally she glanced at the illuminated face of the clock or at the narrow streak of brightness across the bedroom floor. Though she liked to sleep in darkness, she'd left on the hall light. Lance had complained some years before that he didn't want to break his neck trying to find his way to his own bed, "for God's sakes."

She got up and turned out the light. Two-thirty was an all-time record. Maybe she, too, should be out in the night on her own, seeking excitement, indeed confirmation of life, rather than here turning to stone. She tried to go back to sleep, but thoughts kept intruding.

At least she wasn't afraid he'd been in an accident. During those early years, whenever he had been late she would frantically pace the floor or search through the Yellow Pages for someone to call: the police, the hospitals, the fire department — anybody to confirm that her husband was alive. Though she'd never actually called, she had worried until his car finally turned into the driveway. She would then run to the door and stand, waiting to fling herself into his arms. He'd stroke her hair and tell her how foolish she was and that she should know what a tyrant the theatre could be. But that had been back in the time when he had directed all the plays. She had watched his downward slide from directing eight plays in a season to one. Usually the first or the last. This season it was to be the last — so why had he taken the playwright to dinner? He wasn't even directing the play. And what restaurant stayed open until two-thirty in the morning? Bars were open. That was it. The playwright Biggs and her husband were sloshing down drinks while she lay here wide-eyed and angry.

. . . Or maybe he wasn't with Biggs. Maybe he wasn't in a bar. Maybe he was someplace else. Where? Doing what? With whom? No — to whom? She thought of the "man more sinn'd against than sinning."

Her imagination was running wild. What evidence did she have that would incriminate her husband? None. There was only one crazed note and several crank calls . . . and a locked darkroom. Not one of those, however, was concrete evidence against her husband. And he *was* her husband. Perhaps, for tonight, she should ease up on speculation and accept reality: Lance and the playwright were drinking themselves under a table.

At three-fifteen he slid into bed. Suddenly she wished he had not come home at all. Why bother? If only she could find the magic to reshape their marriage or the courage to leave it.

She heard him set the alarm. And then he stretched out, on his back, beside her.

Turned on her side, away from him, she again watched the shadows the tree branches made on the wall. She fancied she saw there a man and a woman. The man had a beak, like that of a bird, extending from the top of his head and the woman had only one large, hulking breast protruding from her body like the bow of a ship. "What grotesque figures," she thought, before she fell asleep.

"Let's have lunch today," Victor Solomon suggested to his lawyer.

"I can't today, Vic." Don Bradshaw spoke casually but firmly into the phone.

"I need to talk to you."

"I can imagine."

"Roselyn is giving me hell."

"Her lawyer's doing the same to me. Look, let's make it Friday."

"Friday? Christ, this is only Wednesday." Victor Solomon did not like being put off. Besides, he was beginning to sweat blood. Roselyn had called last night, using the suspicious one-hundred-thousand-dollar deposit and withdrawal from their joint checking account as an excuse for her rage. Ridiculous. These past eighteen years he had kept her well-supplied with jewels, minks, expensive foreign cars, and trips to exotic places.

"Sorry. It's the best I can do. I'm in court, old buddy," Bradshaw explained. "But Friday at the club, for sure. Twelve o'clock."

"I guess that'll have to do." Victor recognized that he had run up against a brick wall. Lately everybody else seemed to be calling the shots. First, Benson; then, Roselyn; and now his own lawyer, who was even designating the site for their strategy meeting. His gentile club, no less. Bastard! Just once it looked like Bradshaw should be able to control his obsession for the Buckingham's steak tartare. Victor gulped the early-morning scotch on his desk. Well, he would just have to ride out the wrath of his soon-to-be ex-wife. On Friday, Bradshaw, with his inventive mind, would concoct a plausible explanation for the missing money. As for himself, he was fresh out of ideas.

Lowell Hook sat in the Buckingham Club playing gin rummy with other sagging, but reigning, oil barons. The jokes were good, the brandy excellent, and he was winning. One never knew from one day to the next how one was going to feel. Yesterday he'd been wrapped in cashmere clear up to his chin. Today he was ready to take on a couple more rounds of gin rummy and maybe a brisk walk in the park before going home. The sap was rising. Next week, for sure, he was calling Benson. It was time to revisit that young lady who had raised his withering old penis to high heaven in that crazy mirrored bed of hers.

"Raymond?"

He jumped. She had startled him, coming up behind him and shouting his name like that.

"You're acting strange, Raymond."

"You're right, Mother. I've got — an idea for the Wesley mansion and I'm trying to pin it down." He was lying. Moving about the design studio — fingering objects, stroking fine woods, examining paintings — an idea *was* forming in his head. The idea, however, had nothing to do with redecorating the Wesley mansion. It had to do with how he just might possibly amass fifty thousand dollars.

Winifred Reese shrugged. If Raymond were "creating," she had better leave him alone. Still, walking aimlessly around the studio, like he'd been doing most of the morning, was strange. It definitely was not his usual method of coming up with an idea to transform a house. But who was she to question genius? She returned to her telephoning. How Caroline Fletcher had roped her into working on the gala right in the midst of the Wesley consignment she would never know. Besides, it was her son who should be doing this. He — not she — was a member of The Arch board. But she supposed organizing galas and such was, as the Colonel, her dearest husband, would have said, "woman's work."

She picked up the phone to inquire if Hannah Niday Florist would be interested in donating thirty dozen roses, twenty potted ferns, and sixteen gardenia garlands. "You're a saleswoman; you can do it," Caroline had coaxed. A saleswoman, hell. She'd have to be Jesus Christ himself to convince one florist to contribute all that. Six florists, maybe. Yes, probably six. She sighed and went to work. "All in the name of art and civic pride," she reasoned, forgetting about Raymond, who at that moment was unlocking the studio's vault. Quietly he stepped inside and slipped a small eighteenth-century music box out of its case and into his pocket.

Sitting at his IBM Selectric, Martin Fletcher carefully typed an address in capital letters. He then centered and pasted the label on the front of a package. There was no return address.

At four o'clock he said goodbye to his secretary, left his office, and drove to the downtown post office.

The postal clerk assured him that the package would arrive at its destination "no later than Friday, but probably Thursday afternoon."

"That will be fine," said Fletcher, his moustache twitching, his palms perspiring.

Step Three had now been activated. It was a step he had hoped would not have to be set in motion. But Step One — leaving Zoe Benson the note on her car windshield — and Step Two — calling her, then wordlessly hanging up those many times — had not brought the desired result. Lance Benson had not come to him and said, "I'll lay off if you'll lay off." So the harassment was to continue in a deadlier way. Step by step, terror must be layered over the Benson household. Benson must be made to realize that he, Martin Fletcher III, meant business.

He stopped off at a corner drugstore for a limeade. Monday he had arrived home early from work. Here it was only Wednesday. No need to arouse Caroline's suspicions that all was not as it should be. He longed for an after-work martini, but there must be no hint of liquor on his breath when she greeted him with the ritualistic evening kiss.

Stirring the ice in his glass, he frowned. There were three plausible explanations for Benson's silence. One: Zoe Benson had not told her husband about the note and the calls. But if that were true, wouldn't she be an unusual woman? Such incitement would normally propel a member of the female sex into a state of utter panic. Surely she had told him! Explanation Two: Benson, the subhuman, truly did not care what happened to his wife. He simply ignored her fright. Or . . . He moved on to Explanation Three. Here he took a long sip and squinted. Others were being blackmailed. If that were the case, Benson would not know whom to contact. Which of his victims was victimizing him? He shook his head. It was too farfetched. Why would a man of Benson's position risk everything by spreading blackmail over the city of Houston? No, there was only one blackmail scheme afoot. And that scheme was the result of Benson's lighting suddenly and unexpectedly upon a sitting duck — a man vulnerable in his grief and anxiety. He had led the sitting duck to an actress-whore who must surely be servicing Benson himself. But what of the film? That was one hell of an expensive setup to blackmail only one man. To snare Martin Fletcher III. Maybe the camera had other uses. Perhaps it was Benson's own personal toy.

He finished the limeade. It was entirely too perplexing. His guess was that Zoe Benson, for whatever reason, hadn't talked. At any rate, Step Three was about to lower several more tons of tension down upon that fine lady's shoulders.

He looked at his watch. He could go home now to Caroline. It had been a long day during which he had recommended hiring two marketing experts to work exclusively on Lightning, attended three meetings, rushed out at noon to make his purchase — which he embellished and packaged behind his locked office door — and then, finally, he'd gone to the post office to mail what he considered to be an ingenious creation.

It was time, he reasoned, for an evening of relaxation.

Driving home, he hoped Caroline had had a good day. She was getting back to being her old self. But then she was spunky, that woman. Briefly he wondered had it been she rather than Zoe Benson who had received a threatening note and anonymous calls, would she have come to him. Certainly. For didn't they share everything? Everything, that is, until now. Well, he was about to put an end to a sordid chapter in his life — in their lives. Caroline need never know.

He was home. He straightened his tie and walked in with a smile to assure her that it had been a hectic but normal day.

"Here's a nice interview with Biggs," Charles Stanton commented as he passed a page of the paper across the breakfast table to his wife.

"Biggs?" She lifted her head from the sports section.

"Nelson Biggs, Irene. The Texas playwright with the new play." He was resigned, but disappointed, that she was only mildly interested in the arts.

"Oh." She glanced at the interview. "I'll read it later," she said, returning to tennis and golf.

"Well, I must be off." He gulped the last of his coffee.

"Oh, darling" — she put aside the paper — "I did tell Caroline Fletcher I would work on the gala. I said I'd do favors."

"I'm glad." Kissing the top of her head, he again noticed that the cropped auburn hair was becoming increasingly streaked with gray.

"I thought you'd be. There's a meeting at her house this Friday."

She walked with him to the door.

"Isn't it rather late to be thinking about favors and such for something only a month away?"

"Absolutely, but you know Caroline. Even though she had that operation, she didn't want to give up the chairmanship. Anyway, she's going full steam ahead. I thought for favors — fans for the ladies and Lord knows what for the gentlemen." She shrugged. "It's a flapper theme — something about the roaring twenties — to tie in with the play. Think, Charles . . . something for men."

"I will." He smiled. "It will be given top priority." She kissed him perfunctorily as he picked up the briefcase he left each evening in the foyer of their River Oaks home.

Though his schedule at Royal Petroleum would be full today, he planned to leave early and drive out to see the beginning stages of David's portrait. For years he had resisted having a painting of their son. David's image could only serve as a reminder for that which he needed no reminding. Didn't he see the boy's eyes no matter where he looked? He had finally decided, however, that, if having the portrait meant so much to his wife, he would commission the work. Perhaps the gift would give her solace. Perhaps it would slow her down. She ran from tennis to golf to talking more to their neighbor, Bonita, than to him. And, finally, in the late hours of evening she ran to brooding.

"Tennis when you get home?" she called after him.

"Probably." His probablies were almost as good as promises. She smiled and waved as he backed the maroon Daimler out of the driveway.

Consoling himself with the knowledge that having a tennis court in his own backyard made it easier to placate his wife, he turned on the FM radio and headed for downtown Houston.

Oblivious to the admiring stares passers-by gave his magnificent car, he listened to Mahler's Fourth and contemplated negotiations concerning the black gold of the North Sea.

"He's gone," she whispered into the phone, then asked herself, "Why am I whispering?" It was the maid's day off. Both she and Bonita knew that. And weren't Wednesdays always their special time? Fortunately Bonita never had to worry about husbands and such. For twelve years she'd been a widow, her husband having died neatly and quietly in bed one night.

"I can't today."

"I don't understand."

"I just can't." There was a pause before she said softly, "Forgive me, Irene, but I can't."

Irene Stanton sat beside the phone long after the brief conversation had ended. Bonita would explain to her soon, she knew, what was coming. "I am tired of living alone," she had hinted. "I am beginning to see someone — no, he isn't after my money. . . . Yes, I think I can. It's worth a try. You do it with Charles. You love Charles. You love your life with him. You just don't like — that. Well, I'm going to try to like that again. I'm lonely. Do you understand? I'm lonely."

"It's here," Irene Stanton thought. "Bonita is leaving." She closed her eyes. As long as her son had been alive, she had been able to submerge that part of herself which was different. Her single-minded goal had been to be a loving mother and proper wife. Indeed, to be the proper Lady Stanton, wife of the war hero and the best man who ever lived. With each year, however, it had become increasingly difficult to play the role she had selected for herself. And when David — her only child, because she could have no others — had drowned, she had desperately needed to accept and nourish her difference. She had turned to Bonita, much as she had turned to the girl in boarding school those long years ago, after her father had died and she had felt so alone. Then, she had sought out the tall, thin, fragile girl — "the girl with the long blond hair," she'd called her — and loved her with a fierce passion that had gripped her until the handsome Sandhurst cadet, recipient of the Queen's Medal, had appeared. Here, she'd thought, was her opportunity to be as other girls. She would submerge her difference.

Charles and she had played swift, firm tennis together. They had attended the theatre and concerts and gone punting on the tributaries of the Thames. But the rumbles of war had sounded over their heads. Suddenly there were to be no more tennis games, plays, and concerts. No more boating. Charles was going. And then he was gone. In one extended battle he became a hero. There were other battles. He became a leader among boys his own age and men old enough to be his father. She had turned again to the girl, smoothed her long blond hair, held her, and loved her. Then one day Charles, the glory blazing as a halo about his head, had returned. The war was nearly over. Her mother, his parents, and almost everyone else, including Charles, had urged, "Marry. It's time." Confused, she had answered "Yes." The tall, frail girl had gone into the bathroom and hanged herself. No one had understood why this lovely, winsome creature had done such a thing. No one except Irene Rowland. For years now she had lived with that knowledge shelved in some far corner of her brain.

There were no high peaks of sexual excitement with Charles as there had been with the girl. He and she made love politely in "the British way," as she called it. Gradually all sensations which started and swelled in the lower part of her body became anesthetized. Deadened. Until, that is, the time of her son's death.

Bonita, lonely and seeking solace after the death of her husband four months earlier, had been there across the street. She had come as a friend. And each, in her separate grief, had clung to the other.

In the beginning they had shared morning coffee, and then trips to the museum because Bonita enjoyed them and tennis because she enjoyed that, and afternoon tea and finally ... it had happened. For twelve years now their relationship had continued. Though all along she had known deviation was not truly Bonita's nature. Bonita was not haunted by that special difference which was so much a part of her own being.

Her eyes remained closed. Bonita Graves was going on beyond her. They would be friends — awkward friends, at best. Bonita would marry the fine gentleman, recently divorced, who was not after her money but was genuinely taken with her. And Irene? "What of Lady Stanton?" she asked herself. Almost fifty-six years old and alone. She had Charles, dear unsuspecting Charles. Yes, she had him. But in that more important way ... she was alone.

She opened her eyes and went upstairs. Quickly she dressed for the morning coffee at the British embassy. Though she had previously declined, she would arrive and explain that unexpectedly she had found — much to her delight — that she could attend. She would be welcomed. Lady Stanton was invariably greeted with open arms in whatever social arena she cared to venture.

Zoe felt the stream of hot water run down her back and, turning, into her face. She grimaced and adjusted the temperature. "Now, as cold as I can stand it." Finally, she stepped out of the shower and vigorously rubbed her skin with an oversized towel. It was as if she were trying to scrub away the dirty feeling which, reason told her, stemmed not from anything she had done but rather from whatever it was her husband was doing — had perhaps done last night until three in the morning.

When he had left for work earlier than usual, she had pretended to be asleep. She didn't want to open her eyes and see in her bedroom a man whom she was beginning to consider a total stranger. It was unsettling to know the shape and size of the moles on his back, his food preferences, his expressions of pleasure and pain, his favorite books, his political bent, the length and width of his body — and to awaken one morning realizing that she knew not at all the breadth of his mind.

The ring jarred her thoughts. Eleven o'clock. Her unknown adversary was reestablishing contact. She would pick up the phone and demand that he either identify himself or go to hell. Today she was in no mood to deal with shadows.

"Zoe?"

It was Caroline Fletcher inviting her to a gala committee meeting.

"I'm working on a portrait." She gave her standard excuse, for she was asked to attend in an ex officio capacity far more theatre meetings and teas than she possibly could or would. Because she liked Caroline, she added, "The painting's a birthday present, and I don't want the birthday to come and go without the gift."

"I can appreciate that." Caroline laughed her high, lilting laugh. It reminded Zoe of wind chimes. "I believe the committee's on the right track, but I'd like your thinking. After the meeting on Friday, could I mail you a memo?"

"Of course. And maybe lunch next week?"

"I'd love it."

She unwrapped the towel from around her body and began dressing. Caroline was special. Perhaps she should have accepted. It was just that this morning she wished she had never heard of The Arch. She wished she had never auditioned for Hedvig when she had been twenty and the theatre had relied on amateurs. She wished she'd never met Lance Benson, with his head full of dreams she'd thought she understood and loved enough to make her own. She wished she had listened to her father who, through all the years since her wedding day, had remained silent and watchful. Suddenly she wished she could ask him what, in all that silent watching, he had seen that she had not seen.

She studied her reflection in the mirror. Scrubbed and glowing, her face belied the deadness inside her. When Charles Stanton arrived, he would never suspect that the woman greeting him longed to pour out her misery to a friend. Despite his formal manner, he looked as if he were capable of listening quietly — of really hearing what someone was saying and not saying — then offering sound advice and, above all, keeping another's secret. He seemed that kind of person. She recalled the hour they had already spent together, photographs of his son stretched out between them. "This one is my favorite," she'd said, looking down at the boy gazing up at a star on top of the Stantons' Christmas tree. "Yes . . . it's mine, as well." He'd smiled. And she'd noticed how white and straight his teeth were, but she had also observed his eyes. Pools of reflection, in that moment, revealing pain. Yes, Charles Stanton would make a trusted confidant. But she scarcely knew him. And though there were those to whom she might turn, she didn't want to do so. What if her somewhat intriguing story accidentally slipped from one friend to another and then on to another? A brushfire spreading! Frequently she turned to her father. But she would not burden him at a time when he was trying to find his way out of the wilderness of retirement. So there was no one . . . There was her work. She could lose herself in that. Suddenly she was seized with an overwhelming urge to paint. She hurried up the stairs. Most of her morning had been spent searching for evidence which she knew lay behind the locked door of Lance's darkroom. Until she found a way to enter that sacred vault, she was wasting her time.

The drawing was already on canvas. She would plunge into the color. It was going to be, after all, a fine portrait.

Stanton arrived five hours later to see a woman with a smudge of paint on her nose and a small, pleased grin turning up the corners of her mouth. As she led him inside, she took off her work smock.

"I must be a mess. I just got carried away." She looked sheepish.

This is an adorable woman, he thought, realizing he had never noticed before. He quickly dismissed the observation. Long ago he had settled into his good but dull marriage, asking himself only once or twice why he had married Irene Rowland. He had concluded that the romance and excitement of going away to war, combined with pressure from relatives, had swept him into some high, adventurous moment that had swiftly turned into a lengthy chronicle of life after festivities. Still, he loved his wife. She would never suspect some unnamed need lay dormant inside him, for almost from the beginning that need had been consciously submerged. Sir Charles Stanton smiled at Zoe Benson and said simply, "On the contrary, you look enchanting."

"You've got to see." She took his hand and led him up the stairs. Only on the second stairway did she let go and rush ahead of him into her studio.

She's like an excited child, he thought. Once in the studio, she became shy again. "I'm into the color — you realize there's a lot more to be done. But . . ." She paused. "What do you think? I never knew your son, but I think" — she looked at the enlarged

photograph pinned on a board near her easel — "I think maybe —
well, what do you think?"

He stared at the boy's eyes staring back at him. He turned away.
Damn Irene for wanting this. Damn himself for giving it to her.
The painting would hurt him every day of his life. He must say
something. Compliment her, he supposed. She was a craftsman
and an artist. He must not be insensitive to her feelings. "Yes,"
he said. And then he repeated, "Yes."

Her face broke into a relieved smile. "Then let's have tea.
Unless . . ." She hesitated again. "Do you want to suggest anything?" He knew she was afraid he would tamper with her work.
It was hers. He would not. Indeed there was no need to change
even the tilt of the head, the curve of the mouth. He smiled. "Tea
would be fine."

She poured the orange pekoe from a small china teapot. There
were lady fingers. He was amused. Americans, anxious to please
him, were forever serving him tea. He would have enjoyed relaxing
over a gin and tonic. He sipped his tea, then suddenly surprising
himself, he asked, "Do you mind?" and loosened his tie. She laughed,
"Actually, I'm relieved. I've always thought of you as being —
well, formal." He wondered if he dare ask for the gin and tonic.
Deciding why not, he said, "The tea is delicious, but what I'd really
like is —"

"A drink?"

"Precisely."

She let him fix the drink himself. Watching him, she said, "I
never realized that a person who's seen — been in — war — could
have the hands of an artist."

"Are you surprised?" He raised his eyebrows.

"Oh no, I didn't mean you *couldn't* have beautiful hands. It's
just —" Flustered, she stopped.

"My father was a surgeon and perhaps I inherited the hands
from him. I've never created anything like a painting. But I fancy
myself as somewhat sensitive. A man doesn't always kill because
he likes to, you know." He stirred his drink and looked at her
over the glass. "A man does what he has to do. And, hopefully,
it coincides with his idea of honor." He took a sip of his drink.
"God, I sound stuffy. Forgive me."

"No, no, you sound — like my father."

"Oh?"

"That's a compliment."

"Then I'd like to meet him."

"That would be nice." She smiled into his eyes.

Seated again in the living room, they spoke of The Arch, the opening play, of travel abroad, music, of paintings they both admired. Unexpectedly the conversation became difficult. He felt uneasy. He should leave before he began asking this woman to tell him about herself. Her work told him more than her words. And yet it did not tell him enough. He stood abruptly. "I must go. Thank you. I realize my seeing the unfinished portrait was not your first choice."

"No. But I'm glad you came." She held out her hand. Small and blue-veined, the hand he held briefly was stained with the flesh tones from his son's portrait.

"May I meet your father soon?"

"If you'd like."

"I'd like that very much."

Driving home, he wished he had requested that the finished portrait, sight unseen, be delivered to his office. It would have been better that way. The stirrings inside him were disturbing. He turned on the radio and headed for the freeway. Remembering suddenly the tennis match awaiting him, he veered down a side road leading through Memorial Park. He had decided to take the long way home.

Closing her front door, and for a moment leaning against it, Zoe Benson felt as if a strong gust of wind had blown into her house and into herself. She no longer felt dirty.

Later, diving deep into the pool, she realized there had been no anonymous calls that day. Perhaps evil was only a mirage. An undefined sense of peace enveloped her.

The early-morning conference with the playwright Biggs was over. Lance stretched his arms. The late night had gotten to him. Bleary-eyed, he drank bitter coffee and felt no better. It would be another thirty minutes before the theatre came alive — before his phone started ringing and the hectic impresario business struck in all its fury. He sweetened his coffee. Nelson Biggs was an idiot who probably had only one good play in him and that play had burst into brilliance on Broadway two seasons before. This morn-

ing he had suggested that Biggs revise the second act of his new
play, pointing out that the director — a mild-mannered man on
leave from one of the more successful eastern theatres — had commented that the two major characters were acting like ships passing
in the night. For emphasis, he'd quoted the director: "Sooner or
later the ships have to signal or the play's sunk." At least Biggs
had agreed to return to his aunt's house in the Heights and try for
a rewrite.

It occurred to him that Zoe and he were beginning to act like
the major characters in Biggs's play. Two ships passing, never
signaling. Maybe he should have guarded his marriage investment
more wisely, for he still needed that cover. Until recently Zoe, in
her love for him, had reminded him of Tolstoy's Anna Karenina.
And while he could not reciprocate with such fervor, he had, until
recently, tried to be a good husband. He'd have to admit, however,
that from the very beginning he had occasionally treated her like
shit. It was like when he'd been a kid he hadn't been afraid to
kick his dog, because he'd known the old hound would come
bounding back across the yard to lick his hand. Sometimes he'd
give Bailey a good kick just to watch it all happen. Well, Zoe had
taken the shit smiling. Christ, smiling! Like Bailey. These days,
however, she hadn't been smiling. And she was taking very little
shit.

He almost wished for the early years of their marriage. Then
they had been called "the golden couple." Unfortunately, the gold
didn't glitter so brightly now. It was his own doing. Of that, Zoe,
as well as he, was aware. Hadn't she been pretty outspoken about
his shortcomings? That night in California when her charms had
weakened him — passion, again, sidetracked him — he'd made a
promise he couldn't keep. And though she hadn't kicked him out
of the house yet, one minute she was obnoxiously opinionated and
the next inscrutably withdrawn. Like her old man wrapped in his
cocoon of literature, she could instantaneously curl up inside that
other world of hers. But the cocoon was woven now of more than
her work. Threads of discontent were part of the protective covering.

Well, he had far greater troubles than whatever tempest might
be brewing at home. His project and unavoidably his theatre must
take precedence over a recalcitrant wife. So long as she did little
more than complain or withdraw — the latter she had magnani-

mously done this morning — he wasn't going to worry. He would give the marriage more of his attention, but only enough to stave off a crisis. After all, at the opportune time he intended to leave Zoe Benson high and dry.

With that decision made, he glanced at his watch.

Sandra would be in for the afternoon rehearsal. He'd have to remember to tell her to keep the wig out of sight until he had a chance to stop by her apartment. The prospect of a visit from him should make her happy. But damned if he was up to another one of those nights. Besides, keeping her pacified was beginning to gall him. Soon — very soon — he would plop her down on top of old Hook. He picked up the phone and dialed.

Without identifying himself, he spoke softly. "Raymond, I'm denying your request. Fifteen days from today should give you plenty of time." He hung up before Reese could reply. Tilting back in his swivel chair, he smiled as he imagined a sweating, pimple-faced Raymond Reese scrounging around for what would be mere chicken feed to a man like Lowell Hook.

Lawrence Harrington woke early, as was his custom; and, after his morning cup of tea with the thin slice of apple-buttered toast, he went for his customary walk. The daily outing had been inserted into his schedule during the last few months . . . since his retirement.

He walked briskly down Sunset. Though the street was quiet, life was beginning to stir. A boy on a bicycle threw newspapers onto lawns. Cars occasionally passed, bearing, he imagined, overzealous workers anxious to reach their offices before the phones started ringing and the real world flung itself into motion. It was Wednesday. "Hump day." He smiled to himself. Students had always been more attentive, their backs slightly straighter, as they sat at their desks. On Wednesday. He had supposed weekend plans like bright-colored tops were beginning to spin in their heads. He liked Wednesdays, too.

He loved this neighborhood, where he had lived for more than thirty years. The houses stood under arches of trees as though they had not been built but had sprung up whole to grow mellow in the late afternoon rays of the sun. He walked the full length of the street, then retraced his steps.

There was correspondence awaiting him. He made it a practice to keep in touch with ten or so of those who had been his more promising students. They were teaching now in places as far-flung as Oxford, England, and as nearby as San Antonio. After attending to his correspondence, he would read and listen to music. Perhaps he would walk over to the museum and view the Pissarro exhibit which would be gone soon. To New Orleans next, he understood. Zoe had mentioned that she would like to see the exhibit. He should probably wait a few days until the two of them could lunch in the tearoom and study the paintings together.

He stretched his back and rubbed his eyes after completing his letter to the fine young fellow — not so young now, he imagined — who was teaching at the University of New Mexico. The letters he wrote were primarily philosophical treatises. This one had dealt with the implication of the Heracles' *ex machina* concluding Sophocles' *Philocetes*.

He sealed the envelope then stared out the window at the small, neat patch of yard where he often worked with his hands. He liked to watch things grow, push up through the earth into flower. Sophocles, he reminded himself, had written *Philocetes* when he had been well into his eighties. Amazing. He, Lawrence Harrington, must rid himself of the heavy feeling that at seventy he was finished. Didn't he have the same penetrating mind he had possessed when he had written his seven books? They were reference books placed on the finest university shelves not only in this country but also abroad. When would his next book be written? Would there be a next book? Surely the impetus would come soon. For years he had been intrigued with Euripides' women. Why not compare and contrast the dominant ones — Medea, Phaedra, Hecuba, Andromache? Certainly all of Crane University's resources were available to him and would be until his death. And, during his research, he could travel. He would like that.

He turned from the window. Eight o'clock. This time last year he had been walking into the classroom to teach a graduate seminar on Homer. He and the students had dug beyond the obvious into the nuances. For forty-two years he had helped to unearth ideas and bring them to fruition in young inquiring minds. And always, with each class he had taught, he had learned. Well, he would get a grip on things soon.

Perhaps he should have married again. A woman in the house would have been good for both Zoe and him. But there had not been anyone in all these years whom he had loved enough to say, "Here, put your clothes in her closet, sit at the dressing table where she sat, share my bed and my thoughts day in and day out." It had not happened that way. There had been women, but no special woman. He and Zoe had survived. His daughter had somehow gotten through those difficult teenage years when she had needed a mother to tell her things which he could not. He recalled only a month after his wife's death Zoe had started her first period. What could he tell her? He had said, "How lovely. You have become a woman." But there had been no way he could add, "I know how it feels."

He must quit thinking so much. Pushing his mind back through the long, narrow shadows of the past was not good. He must look ahead.

He would go next door and share a pot of tea with his neighbor. She was a plump, endearing lady who could abruptly jerk him back into the present with her talk of grandchildren and recipes and church bazaars. Soon, he told himself, soon, he would reach for a star and "if his reach should exceed his grasp," at least he would have tried. He thought suddenly again of Sophocles. The Greek, he reminded himself, had been an old man when he wrote *Philocetes* and, incredibly, had still gone on to write the far greater *Oedipus Coloneus.*

He would not, after all, visit Mrs. Beardsly next door. Instead he would list the ideas he held in his head that might possibly evolve into a book. Only then would he seek companionship.

Seated at their dining room table, Zoe and Lance Benson ate poached salmon. Candlelight from the candelabras flickered into the dark corners of the room.

From time to time Lance attempted casual conversation. Zoe answered his questions, recounted the trivia of her day, but he noticed that there was a tenseness in her voice and an impenetrable shell had again formed around her.

Over melon and chocolate wafers, she finally made the comment he'd been expecting and for which he was prepared.

"You were so late last night. It was three o'clock."

"Drank too much with Biggs." He squeezed a sliver of lime over his melon.

"I thought as much. Still — I didn't appreciate it then. Or now."

"I'm sorry, Zoe." He thought of Biggs's characters — ships passing in the night — and redoubled his efforts. "It won't happen again." Then he added, with the charm which once could bend her in whatever direction he chose, "You look lovely . . . except you're too far away."

She didn't bend. Instead she spoke formally.

"Then we'll have coffee in the music room."

His eyelid quivered. He sipped from a glass of water. Coffee in the music room. At times he felt like a stranger in his own house. He could remember suppers around a metal table, its white enamel chipped, in a steaming kitchen, his father often in his undershirt and his mother, overweight and overbearing, sloshing down heavy bowls of stew before them. His wife was a snob. He was repelled and attracted. The repulsion sprang from the roots of his heritage, the attraction from his conviction that he belonged in the milieu of the Zoe Harringtons of this world. He had merely been misplaced at birth.

She stood and snuffed out the candles.

He pushed back his chair and followed her out of the room.

Zoe Benson handed her husband his black coffee, then stirred a lump of sugar into her own Lenox cup. Her thoughts turned, as they had repeatedly over the past hours, to her afternoon visitor. Suddenly she wished that instead of Lance, Charles Stanton were there. Together they would listen to *Daphnis et Chloé,* or perhaps a Brahms symphony. And afterward the quiet would not be strained as it was now between her and her husband. Her husband, she felt, was a liar. A liar who had remained out in the dark or somewhere in lights apparently brighter than in this house until three o'clock in the morning. He was also a stranger with a locked darkroom, a stranger who was somehow responsible for the note left on her car windshield and for the deathly silent phone calls with their disconnecting clicks. Yes, she would much prefer Charles Stanton beside her. She lowered her head and dwelled on her private thoughts.

"It's time Stanton came to see your work, isn't it?"

He had read her mind. She hated the evening. It didn't matter that her husband had told her she looked lovely. His words meant no more than the air through which they had traveled across the expansive table. She might as well sound the evening's death knell.

"Actually he dropped by this afternoon."

Lance lighted a cigarette, closed his lighter, and stared. The eyes cold, blue marble.

That was to be expected.

She stirred her coffee, which needed no stirring.

"I specifically remember telling you I wanted to be here when he came." His voice was low, controlled.

She looked down at the ring on her finger, then met his stare. "I decided we needed the full time to discuss my work . . . not yours."

She waited for the explosion.

It did not come.

"I see." A thin stream of smoke blew across the room. She watched the smoke hang in the air. The tone of his voice lightened. He smiled. "Well, it's no great catastrophe. Actually I've been wanting to give a small buffet supper — one of our Sunday affairs. We owe quite a few people socially, so let's make it a little larger group than usual. We'll invite the Stantons —"

"Lance, you're still trying to mix your business with mine."

"Let's not be paranoid, Zoe. Charles Stanton, may I again remind you, is a board member. And I can assure you I will not mention your painting. Now we'll go ahead with it this Sunday."

"This Sunday?" She straightened.

"*This* Sunday, Zoe."

"I can't." Her mind was racing ahead now. She needed to work on the portrait, to take her father — lonely in his retirement — to the museum.

"Can't or won't?"

"Lance, it's too late to invite people."

"Look, it's no big deal. Call tomorrow morning. Start with the Stantons. If they can come, I want it Sunday. *This* Sunday, Zoe. I'll make the list."

"*You'll* make the list?"

"*I'll* make the list."

Mentally she balanced above uncertainties. But she knew she wasn't paranoid. She stared at this complex man who was her husband.

"Then, Lance," she spoke evenly, "you just go ahead and make your list."

"Meaning, I take it, you may not like it but you're agreeable?"

The smile remained cool and unwavering.

"Meaning, I'll do it to keep peace in the house. But this is the last party I'm giving for a very long time . . . and I think you should understand that."

She left the room.

Uncharacteristically he called after her.

She kept walking.

Lance Benson did not go after his wife. Instead he sat staring at the door through which she had made her dramatic exit. Unexpectedly he had thought again of Bailey. He shook his head, then reached for a notepad. His left eyelid twitched. He couldn't get rid of an image. His old dog, still, tire tracks imprinted across a broken skull.

Climbing the stairs, Zoe fought back tears. The evening could definitely be labeled a disaster. And as for on beyond this evening . . . Her husband, she knew, would never change.

"These are the people I want."

Reluctantly she placed the book, whose pages she had been mindlessly turning, on the nightstand and examined the list.

She counted the names.

"Thirty people for a small buffet supper?" She raised her eyes to meet his.

"That's right." He picked up her book. "Henri's *The Art Spirit*. Don't you ever get tired of reading this stuff?"

"Art is my avocation as well as my vocation." She took the book from him and returned to the list. The names included — and the names omitted — puzzled her.

"Why not the Fletchers?" she asked. "Caroline would enjoy getting out after all she's been through."

"We'll have them another time."

"Or Victor Solomon. He needs friends now."

"Another time, Zoe." His voice was insistent.

"Sandra Lowrey." She laid down the list. "Why, Lance?"

"Why not?"

"That's not good enough. I mean, we hardly know the girl. And she's not going to be comfortable around people like the Stantons and these others — some of whom are just —"

"People we owe socially."

"That's true, but why this actress?"

"Stanton admired her performance."

"In what? Certainly not in *Cyrano*. She had all of three lines."

"Since the snob in you is rampant tonight, I'll invite Sandra myself. But I'd appreciate it if you'd take care of the rest."

He began unbuttoning his shirt."

"I would like to invite my father."

"Fine. Have him for tea sometime."

"Lance, he's lonely!"

"Zoe, invite the people on the goddamn list! I admit it's a social occasion, but it's for business purposes. Your old man would bore everybody with all that Greek crap."

"He never bores."

"Let's just say he'd mystify."

"You're probably right. Sandra Lowrey wouldn't understand the first thing about Aeschylus." She returned to her book. The words blurred. Briefly she wondered if she was jealous. That idea she dismissed. Something else — having nothing to do with her marriage — was disturbing her. If only she could examine what was in Lance's head. If only . . . what was the use? She switched off her bedside lamp.

The sense of well-being she had experienced after Charles Stanton's visit had disappeared. In its place was an uneasiness that tightened her chest. She fought irrationality. An oppressive force seemed strong in the air that she breathed. Silently, she began repeating the almost forgotten words of Psalm 121.

During the months after her mother's death, she had repeatedly turned to that psalm. Now, after all these years, she sought refuge there. Somehow in those ageless words she found comfort. And slept.

Martin Fletcher awakened with a hard-on. Hope coursed through his veins. For weeks now he had looked down and seen limpness. But he was becoming stronger. The fear was lessening. Revenge and redemption would make his life right again.

He reached for Caroline, asleep on her side, her hands folded as in prayer against her cheek. He pulled the white satin gown above her waist. She smiled; her eyes remained closed. For the first time since she had come home from the hospital, Martin Fletcher, maintaining a respectable erection, was able to make love to his wife.

· · ·

By two o'clock Zoe Benson had invited to a Sunday buffet supper twenty-nine of the people whose names were on the list Lance had presented to her the night before. The questionable thirtieth guest, Sandra Lowrey, was to be invited by Lance. Of the people she had called, twenty-four had accepted in spite of the invitation having been extended only three days before the event. She supposed that was a compliment. Irene Stanton had graciously replied, "How lovely! We'll look forward to it."

She ran her fingers through her hair. That was done. For a while longer, however, she sat smoking a cigarette, her legs propped on a coffee table. Her thoughts stayed on the party and on her husband.

When she had married at twenty, it had not entered her mind to omit from the ceremony the promise to obey her husband. The word, seeming to bear no import, had slipped from her lips as naturally as the wedding ring had slipped onto her finger. In agreeing to Lance's party — for it was his — had she relapsed into that unquestioning, submissive role? Maybe, but only temporarily. Finally she had become too tired — too tired of it all yesterday evening — to fight until she had won.

She stood. Regardless of her feelings, the party was set. She would open the door of their home at approximately seven o'clock Sunday evening. Ironically, her one consolation was that Charles Stanton would be among the guests.

Walking to the mailbox, she began thinking about the portrait. The boy's eyes, which Charles had said were identical to Irene's, needed to be filled with light.

The mail was late. Empty-handed, she turned back toward the old stone house which she had claimed as her own from the moment she had walked up its curved driveway some fourteen years before. Explaining that repairs were needed, the realtor had brought her here late one winter afternoon. The neglect, the cold, and the darkness had not blighted her perfect house.

Glancing up at the third-floor windows, she frowned. Her perfect house was no longer perfect. For an instant, imagination soared to that one locked area. Seven vultures loomed black on rafters; one of them — which one? — poised to strike. She shook her head. This whole thing was getting to her. Without Lance suspecting, she would have to find a way to enter the forbidden room and rid her house of whatever flaw was there.

His index finger moved slowly down the yellow page. Raymond was convinced that only a name worthy of the item in his pocket would halt his finger's downward slide. Certainly Corral Center, Lone Star Pawnshop, and Jimmie's Quick Cash did not merit the slightest consideration. He paused at Harold's, Inc., but moved on after noting that Harold's ad promised money right on the spot for everything from ten-gallon cowboy hats to plastic flowers. His finger abruptly stopped. The Medici Shop. Christ Almighty! With a name like that the place could be hocking holy water fonts adorned with the Virgin Mary, Roman amphoras, croziers of carved ivory. Raymond Reese was on his way!

Three gold-painted balls hung over the doorway of the narrow little shop on Congress Street. Inside, Raymond blinked through musty clutter toward a weasel-thin man with stooped shoulders, a graying mane, and a jet-black moustache that looked as if it had been penciled above his upper lip. He was tagging a Shirley Temple doll straight out of the 1930s.

Raymond wondered where the doll was to go, for every conceivable space seemed filled. Articles were hung, propped, and strewn above and around him. Wicker baby carriages, horsehair love seats, Oriental screens, wind-up Victrolas, and stereoscopes were juxtaposed with papier-mâché statuary, galvinized washtubs, presto cookers, tasseled batons, and overstuffed pink satin rosettes. A 1942 Magnolia's Best calendar, with its picture of the Dionne quintuplets riding Shetland ponies, hung lopsided on the wall behind the counter at the back of the store.

The Medici Shop was not as Raymond had visualized. But it would have to do. He cleared his throat. The proprietor looked up.

"I — uh, have something to pawn."

The silent man waited.

With three steps Raymond reached the back of the store. Carefully he lifted out of his monogrammed handkerchief the miniature child's drum and placed in on the counter. Its sides were laced with thin strips of twenty-four karat gold. Tiny drumsticks encrusted with ruby and diamond chips lay crossed on top of the drumhead, which he opened to reveal a velvet-lined jewelry compartment. Strains of Haydn's *Toy* Symphony began tinkling merrily.

"It dates back to the eighteenth century — as you can probably tell." He had decided it was best to flatter the wordless proprietor. "Flute pipes instead of metal teeth explain the slightly different sound from that of today's music boxes." He spoke quickly and nervously. "And, of course, the rubies and diamonds alone are worth a small fortune."

The man asked one question. "Is it hot?"

"What?"

"You know, hot — stolen?"

Raymond reddened. "Of course not."

Oram Balzer had been a pawnbroker for three decades, minus the five years he had resided in the Huntsville State Prison. He recognized a hot item when he saw one, especially when the thief was personally presenting the merchandise. Even a well-dressed thief. So what? He had seen them all.

Balzer held the tiny drum in the palm of his hand. He thought how much his mother would have loved to own such a beautiful little toy. It *was* a toy. A remarkable, valuable toy. She would have rocked in her straight-backed chair at the institution — insane asylum, they'd called it back then — and held the drum close to her ear, listening to its music and repeating over and over, "Mine, mine, mine. Thank you, Orie. Thank you, thank you, mine." He placed the item back on the counter.

"Five hundred dollars."

"I beg your pardon?"

"Five hundred dollars."

"For something worth thousands?"

"That's it." Balzer shrugged.

"Well, that's *not* it!" Indignantly Raymond whisked the little drum into his handkerchief and back into his pocket.

"Wait." Balzer studied the agitated young man who was about to march his alligator loafers straight out the Medici door.

These past seven years Balzer had contacted the Dallas people on only four occasions. He was a respectable man now. A good family man. But that was part of the trouble. A responsible father must provide for his brood. And lately his youngest daughter with the mysterious 162 IQ had been loudly protesting, "I don't *want* to be a nurse. I want to be a doctor — a cardiologist! Can't you understand?" Then there was his oldest daughter, sweet Claudia, who never requested, much less demanded, anything. Didn't she and her veterinarian fiancé deserve a really special wedding?

"You want to hock or sell?"

Raymond gulped. "Well, I don't know."

"You have anything else? To sell?"

"I — I might."

"How much stuff?"

Raymond plunged into a fifty-thousand-foot ocean. Waves engulfed him. He came up floating. "A truckload."

"You're kidding?"

"I'm dead serious." He straightened to his full six feet.

"What's the merchandise?"

The recitation began: "A black-and-gold lacquer Louis Sixteenth desk, a neoclassic pier table, a veneered mahogany commode à vantaux mounted in gilt bronze, a hand-carved Tudor armchair, imperial Satsuma vases, a pink-marble Florentine mantel, a Kashan rug, a love seat dating back to —"

"Hold it! I get the idea."

"It's legal . . . but we'd have to move everything at night."

"Legal, but a night job. Sure."

"During the day it's a thriving business establishment. Which I own — well, I own half of it."

"And the other half?"

Raymond hesitated. "That's the reason for doing it at night."

Balzer's eyes narrowed. He was thinking. Obviously the kid was in trouble. Desperation fairly dripped from his pores.

Shifting gears, Balzar got back to specifics. "What kind of money are we talking about?"

"I'll need to receive —" Raymond cleared his throat. "Fifty thousand dollars."

Oram Balzer relaxed and smiled, revealing a diastema between his two front teeth. "What's your name, kid?"

"Raymond. Raymond Reese."

"And the name of your business?"

"Reese Interiors."

"I've heard of it. Pretty high-class. Well, call me tomorrow evening, Raymond. At six. In the meantime, leave your box here. I'll give you two thousand dollars."

"But it's worth —"

"Two thousand dollars."

"All right, as a pawn. *Not* a sell."

"I understand." Balzer wrote out the ticket. Tonight he would contact Benny Fein. "Long time no hear," he imagined Fein saying in his low gravelly voice. Balzer pictured Fein shifting in his chair, leaning closer to the phone as he listened to the descriptions of the Tudor and Louis-whatever business unearthed as a result of this amateur kid walking into the Medici.

"Remember, six tomorrow, kid."

"Right. Six o'clock. Thank you, thank you very much, Mr. —"

"Balzer. I look forward to doing business with you."

As he was leaving, Raymond couldn't resist asking, "Mr. Balzer, how did you name this shop?"

"I didn't. Bought it from an Italian fellow who was hung up on fancy names and things. Those gold balls out in front, for instance? A coat of arms, he said, for this Medici family." Balzer smiled his gapped-toothed smile. "He'd have liked your music box, Raymond. Probably given you a lot more for it. But then, that's life, isn't it?"

"I guess," Raymond agreed faintly. He would throw up if he didn't get away from the Kewpie dolls and the ostrich boas, the Japanese fans and the cracked washbasins and the — Christ, he was leaving his mother's prized music box here amid the fake tiger lilies. He must be insane. But then he was playing an insane game, wasn't he? With an opponent who was equally crazed.


"You've got to be kidding!" She reknotted the shirt to reveal more midriff.

"Sandra, must you show bare skin when you come to work?"

"Well, look who's getting to be Mr. Prude. Christ!" She rolled her eyes and popped her gum.

"And that goddamn bubble gum —" Lance Benson took a deep breath. He mustn't let this girl — this mere but essential instrument — get on his nerves to the point that he crushed her skull between his bare hands. His only excuse would be that the girl was beginning to weigh like an albatross around his neck.

He pushed a penciled sketch and seven one-hundred-dollar bills across his desk. "Go to Neiman's —"

"I like Solomon's."

"*Neiman's,* Sandra. Buy a dress with classic lines. Like in the sketch. Stick to black, it's your best color. Get black evening sandals and have your hair done. Keep it long, but maybe with some kind of rolls in front. I want you to look like you stepped off the cover of *Vogue*."

"Wow!" She counted the bills. "This next one's pretty important, huh?"

"Very. And he'll only go for class. Pure class — which is what I expect you to exude Sunday night."

"Right under Zoe's nose?" She giggled.

"Don't bring her into this!" He was surprised at the sharpness in his voice.

Sandra straightened from her slumped position. "Well, fuck you! And let me tell you something else you can do. Start preparing that bitch for what's coming up."

He spoke evenly in spite of the bitter taste in his mouth. "It's too early for that, Sandra."

"Too *early?* The way I figure it is, I've got to hit the sack with this very important person and then one more time with sweet old Mr. Hook. And that's it! After that, it's you and me. You and me, Lance. Because that's the way it was supposed to be from the time I was a little girl wishing on a star right outside my window. And I'll tell you something else — I pray to God every night He'll forgive me for what I have put myself and those people through. The only thing that keeps me going is I know — I mean, I *know* — it's for a good cause, the *best* — you and me forever!"

"That was quite a speech."

She was blinking. Sniffling. "Hell, you got a Kleenex?"

"I keep them . . . for such dramatic moments." He was back in control. But he felt the control was temporary.

"Sandy?"

"Yeah?" She blew her nose loudly.

"Come here."

"Where?"

"Around here." His voice was smooth, coaxing.

He pulled her onto his lap. "We want the same thing." He kissed her neck.

"Promise?"

God, what a bore! Still, he liked burying his face in her hair. He was reminded of the fresh, clean scent of ocean air. Perhaps, later, he would live beside some great body of water.

"I promise." He had delivered her favorite lie. She burrowed against him. He thought of a mole.

"Look, you'd better go." He eased her off his lap. "The rehearsal's about to start."

He'd said the wrong thing.

Her lips curled into a pout. A persimmon. "They sure aren't going to be looking any time soon for the maid."

"Oh, I don't know. I hear she's dynamite."

"Well, if she's such dynamite, why isn't she —"

"Patience, Sandra . . . please. Now go!"

"Yes *sir!*" She saluted him, her heels clicking to attention. Then she grinned and puckered her lips. "One more kiss?"

He complied.

The girl would never, ever stop, would she? It could go on forever.

"Buy the dress, Sandra, and tomorrow evening I'll look you over."

"Anything else?"

"Of course," he lied. His plans did not include touching her. "And get out the wig I left over there the other night."

"Gotcha." She turned at the door. Again, there was that mischievous little-girl grin on her face. "What if I don't give it back? I mean, it's kind of cute and I like to wear it myself."

"Just have the wig out, Sandra."

"And if I don't?"

"Look, what's going on?" He dug his fingernails into his palms. Right now he wanted this girl out of his office, out of his life. The sooner the better.

"I *told* you."

"And I *promised* you." The voice was steel. The blade of a hunter's knife.

"OK, OK. I got it." She raised her hands over her head and shook them as though she were ringing a tambourine. "I got it. Lord, help us all. I got it!"

She was gone. Out the door.

For a time he sat at his desk. Still. Silent. Gradually he relaxed. His fingernails stopped digging into the palms of his hands. He lit a cigarette and leaned back in his chair. Slowly his mind began weaving a strange, dark mosaic of color and motion. A pattern of action, undefined as yet, began evolving out of the swirling mass.

He searched for a progression of steps that one by one would lead to cutting the cord from around his neck. The albatross would then fall into the sea.

. . . Death was not so bad. After all, he reasoned, such was the fate of every living organism. It was not true that death and taxes were both inevitables. Once born, a person had only one inevitable. Why not devise a plan whereby Sandra Lowrey would undergo what she, along with everyone else, must surely know is life's great unavoidable experience? The plan, however, would have to be foolproof so that no one could ever link his name to her death.

It was a thought. Frightening, distasteful — yet somehow fascinating. Maybe he should secure a handgun, which he would avoid registering . . . But a bullet was mundane. The challenge would be in figuring out a more intricate means for someone to succumb to the ultimate.

He'd better stop this! Hell, he was dressing up murder with fancy words. He tried to let go of the idea. But the idea held fast, twisting, curving, embryonically growing.

. . . He would get a gun. Daily he would search the classifieds until he found an advertisement for a small automatic, which he would keep locked in his car awaiting that time when he would have no further need of Miss Lowrey's services. The gun would merely serve as insurance should all else fail . . . But surely he could persuade Sandra to step out of his life. Could he? Would she? Hardly. Regardless of what he might offer her. Damnit! With every breath she drew, the girl pushed him to extremes.

Sandra dead. That was hard to imagine. His stomach turned; his eyelid flickered. "Sandra Lowrey dead." He sounded the words in his head. He tasted the syllables on his lips. As horrible and farfetched as it seemed, the girl's death was probably the best solution.

Mashing out his cigarette, he spoke briskly into the intercom. "Suzanne, bring me the newspaper, please."

Stretching to relieve the cramped muscles in her shoulders, Zoe looked at her watch. Two hours had passed. She had discovered that when working in her studio time often became relative. She stood back and studied the evolving portrait of Stanton's son. More than the eyes, the hair was giving her trouble. It needed highlights.

Perhaps streaks of summer sun. She washed her hands and hung her smock on its hook. She had done enough for the day.

The mail had arrived.

Crammed into the box were two department-store statements, an invitation to a Texas Children's Hospital benefit, a brochure advertising the new roach killer Lightning, an announcement of a gallery opening, the current issues of *Psychology Today* and *Texas Monthly,* and a package addressed to Mrs. Lance Benson. She noted there was no return address. Christmas was three months away. Her birthday wasn't until April. She fantasized. With its Houston postmark, the package might contain a gift from her husband. In the early days of their marriage, Lance had occasionally mailed her presents. Or — even more imaginative — hidden them about the house. A gold chain in the cookie jar, a china dolphin in the linen closet, ivory combs in the medicine cabinet. On their first wedding anniversary a telegram had arrived with a single line from John Donne's "The Good Morrow": "I wonder by my troth, what thou, and I Did, till we lov'd?"

Would receiving an unexpected gift from her husband mean as much to her now as it had more than a decade ago? Of course not, but it might offer reassurance that he was indeed the same man she had married. No matter what the package held — diamonds, sea shells, or Cracker Jacks — she wished it were from Lance. That would be farfetched but nice.

She hurried into the house.

And screamed.

She flung the box across the kitchen. The coiled snake lunged from tissue and bounced against the refrigerator. Its black body streaked with blood-red fingernail polish.

With her hands to her mouth, she whispered to no one, "Dear God in heaven."

Finally, she reached down to lift the repulsive object. Six feet of synthetic rubber unfurled. The creature's tail hit the floor to circle again on the tile.

Between fingertips, away from her, she carried it outside.

Deep in the garbage, among potato peelings, broken glass, and old newspapers, she buried the evil thing, its stiff red tongue jutting narrowly from a slitted mouth. Every fiber of her being cried out, "To hell with evidence! Let it rot! Let it disintegrate! Let it be carried off *today*. This minute!"

Running down the long drive to search the street, she wondered if it was even garbage pickup day. She didn't know. She couldn't remember. No. The truck came on Friday. And today was . . . today was Thursday. She sneezed. Then she sneezed again and again.

She hurried back into her house and up its stairs for her pills. Swallowing the Ornade, she noted vaguely, as if from a distance, that three capsules remained in the bottle.

Only after she had poured coffee and lighted a cigarette did she look for a card in the box. Her hands were shaking as she unfolded the single sheet of bond paper. The type was elite.

"And the Lord God said unto the serpent . . . 'I will put enmity between thee and the woman.' " Mrs. Benson, I repeat, tell your husband you will be harmed if he doesn't stop, for "I am a man more sinn'd against than sinning."

She studied the label. Strange. A different typewriter had been used to type the address. How quickly she had latched on to false assurances simply because there had been no anonymous calls during the past thirty-six hours. All that time her assailant had been somewhere in Houston, eating, sleeping, no doubt poring over the Bible and Shakespeare, waiting to spew his poison directly into her house. The proof lay coiled in the garbage.

In order to think clearly, she would have to calm down. She stared out the window at a willow and breathed deeply. The hay-fever attack, brought on by ragweed and trauma, had passed. She could think now.

Why was she the target? If the notes were to be believed, her husband was harming someone who reasoned that Lance would be scared off if she were threatened. This person had counted on her turning to her husband. Because she had not done so, the warnings had continued. Even now, however, she would not confront Lance. Nor would she seek help from the police, for that would surely mean news leaking to reporters. She would figure this out for herself.

She poured more coffee, then sat thinking, scrawling question marks on a scratch pad. Suppose Lance wasn't guilty? Her antagonist might well be an unbalanced actor, enraged that he had been denied the role of King Lear in last season's production.

Even as she considered the possibility of her husband's innocence, the question persisted. What was Lance doing and to whom? She thought of the times he had returned home in the early morning hours. She thought of his refusal lately to discuss anything other than the superficial. Most of all, she thought of the evenings he had closeted himself in his darkroom. She stared intently at the willow. Its tangled branches swayed in the wind. The sky had darkened. Rain would come soon. Suddenly she knew how she could open the locked door.

Lance would have to be at home. And asleep. She imagined him supine, arms folded ceremoniously across his chest, his mouth slightly open. What if he awakened? She pushed that thought from her mind.

The vision of another viper flashed before her. This one was not made of cheap rubber and smeared with nail polish. This one possessed a ruby eye and a coiled tail studded with emeralds. Purchased in Carmel last month, the jeweled asp lay resplendent on Lance's desk.

Early Friday morning, a garbage truck wheeled into the Bensons' driveway and took the snake away. The evening before Lance had asked, "How was your day?" His wife had replied, "Just a typical day," and resumed reading her book.

"Jesus!" Don Bradshaw ordered another Jack Daniel's rather than the espresso with which he had intended to round off his favorite meal — the Buckingham's steak tartare. His client and good friend had just told him an incredible story.

". . . So you've got to come up with an explanation that'll make Roselyn apologize for even *asking* about the money." Victor Solomon wished they were sitting in the Texas Tinhorn right now. He'd loosen his tie and take off his jacket. He wiped his forehead. It was as hot as the hinges of hell in Bradshaw's club. Earlier the waiter had mentioned something about a temporary malfunction in the air-conditioning system. Solomon had assumed that the aloof superiority of the Buckingham's members alone would have cooled the place down to its usual perfect chill. "It's nice to know," he'd teased his WASP companion, "that you people need a little help like the rest of us to keep from working up a sweat."

The two men were easy with each other. Along with enjoying a trusted attorney-client relationship, they shared an interest in poker, duck hunting, and deep-sea fishing. On numerous occasions they and their wives had skied in Aspen and scuba-dived off the northern coast of Jamaica. There had even been talk of an African safari. The women had stated emphatically that they would love it provided they could keep a respectable distance from the hunt itself. Strange, Solomon often mused, that his and Bradshaw's business affiliation, as well as their friendship, had begun with something as simple as their firstborns becoming best friends in nursery school.

"You should have come to me before you paid off the bastard." Bradshaw stared into his drink. He was thinking.

Solomon breathed more easily. His lawyer would rescue him.

"What I shouldn't have done was screw that girl." He was simply filling in the silence.

Bradshaw's head jerked up. He fixed a penetrating gaze on his friend. "I've been telling you to slow down on that score for years. Look at the mess it got you into with Roselyn."

"Don't preach. Besides, that wasn't all that did it. She's become a women's libber."

"I doubt that."

"You don't think so?" A flicker of hope stirred in his constricted chest.

"Not according to what she tells Connie. And, by the way, they're both damned mad I'm representing you. I probably should have stayed out of it."

"What did she tell Connie?"

"That you're a bastard. Which tells me, if you'd do some re-forming — like cut out the broads and the liquor — you might get your wife back."

"The broads I'm getting a little sick of. The liquor" — he touched the ice in his glass — "I can stop any time." They both knew he was lying. Solomon took a swallow of scotch and felt as if his one trusted friend was warming his insides. Conceivably even Bradshaw would let him down.

"Well, I'll just say this as your friend, not as your lawyer. If you want her back, which from all appearances I'd say was the case, then I'd recommend you get down on your knees, ole buddy, and tell her exactly how you feel."

"Not a chance." He signaled the waiter for another drink.

"OK. Back to legal counsel. Why in God's name did you use that joint brokerage account?"

"Obviously to get quick cash." Solomon was becoming irritated.

"You and Roselyn don't have a money fund with your broker?"

"Oh, I got one when they first came out, but I never bother to use it."

"Well, for your information, that happens to be a setup through which you could have gotten the money without Roselyn's knowledge. You could have written the check directly on the account and had your statements mailed to the store." Don Bradshaw leaned back in his chair and studied his client's reaction.

"Son of a bitch." Revelation shot off sparks in his head.

"Enough said. Now, for an alibi. I've come up with something. It's tricky, and we'll need to cover ourselves in case anything unexpected appears in court. But at least it's a reasonable explanation."

"Go on." Solomon stirred his drink.

"We all know the one thing you'd rather do than drink is fly. Right?"

"I can give up the drinking." Again irritation, mixed now with defiance, tinged his voice.

"Answer my question."

Solomon hesitated, then conceded. He smiled slightly. "Fly and screw. My wife, that is."

"Back to counsel as a friend. Go to her and tell her exactly how you feel."

"She kicked me out of the house. Remember?"

Don Bradshaw, a devoted family man equally as handsome and twice as shrewd as Solomon, sighed. "Back to legal counsel. We agree you like to fly. In fact, you've got an obsession for anything to do with flying. Especially antique planes. Remember the time in Boca Raton when we drove over a hundred miles just so you could see some antiquated crate rumored to have been flown by a World War Two ace? Remember that?"

"It was an interesting plane."

"To you. And you can bet your sweet ass Roselyn remembers that little trip, complete with flat tire, because it made us miss a party she and Connie were all fired up about."

"So?"

"So, I've done some thinking . . . You needed cash to buy a World War Two plane from an out-of-state collection. You've put in the order for the plane, which won't be delivered for several months. But your cashier's check — covering cost of plane and expenses for getting it here — was required before delivery. That will be our explanation for the missing one hundred thousand. What you'll need to do is locate just such a plane in case you actually have to buy it. I'll reluctantly, *reluctantly* you understand, lend you the money since your assets are frozen, then you can pay me back as soon as the divorce is final. With luck you won't have to buy the damn thing. I'm counting on Roselyn's lawyer accepting our story without digging around for evidence."

"Such as?"

"A duplicate of the cashier's check. But even to consider such a possibility would be borrowing trouble. Roselyn's going to accept the plane fabrication simply because it sounds like something crazy you'd do."

"Thanks."

"You're welcome." Bradshaw continued: "You could even tell her you're planning to resell it, though — if you're going that far — you'd for sure better have a plane in mind and a potential buyer lined up . . . What do you think?"

"I think," Solomon stared directly into Bradshaw's eyes, "my personal lawyer is a damn sight smarter than that bunch we've got representing the store."

Bradshaw smiled. He had hoped Solomon would eventually see things that way. Quickly he returned to the immediate business. "I'm confident that I can explain all this to Scruffy Dawson's satisfaction. He's a reasonable man. Roselyn made a damned good choice of lawyers. But I want to be sure there aren't any loopholes. Discreetly begin inquiry about World War Two planes for sale in other states. *Discreetly.*"

"No problem." Solomon was becoming intrigued with the idea of owning a vintage fighter craft. "I'd love a P-51 Mustang; but, for the money, it'd probably have to be something like a North American SNJ-5 or a T-6 Texan."

"Sounds good. Now another thing."

"Christ! There's more?"

"This plane crap can be made believable, but it's a lot of non-sense. Roselyn's a sensible woman who loves you."

"That is *not* legal counsel."

"Shit! How many lawyers would offer to lend a client one hundred thousand dollars? I figure my generosity gives me privileges."

"True."

"So I suggest you tell Roselyn you got mixed up in some crazy blackmail scheme, which happened as a result of one of your drunken episodes. During the separation, right?"

"Right."

"In short, tell her the truth. I also recommend that you two have a sober —you did get that word — sober — "

"I heard you."

"Then consider having a sober, *honest* talk with your wife. You probably haven't had one in — how many years?"

Solomon shook his head. "I don't know. I honestly don't know."

"Good, we're getting somewhere. She might surprise you. After all, she and Connie already have brochures from Tree Tops. And you've got to admit that would be one hell of a trip."

"You and I could still go."

"You think Connie'd let me get all the way to Africa without her? Besides, Vic, face it, it'd be a lot more fun with them along. Right?"

Solomon hesitated. "Right," he said and looked down into his drink.

"What I'm suggesting, Victor, is that I'll support you in covering for the missing money, but I want you to consider telling Roselyn the truth — or half the truth if that's all you can handle — but get back with her. It's what you want. Pride is a word, that's all. Just a word. And, misplaced, a damn poor one at that."

Subconsciously Don Bradshaw was reflecting the influence of his dead parents. He was the son of a father who had been a Methodist minister and a mother who had majored in Eastern philosophies back when most of her Bennington classmates were gliding through elementary-education courses. It wasn't that either of his parents had been opposed to divorce. They had simply been opposed to the dissolving of any relationship whose reason for being was love, no matter how complex that love might be. For all the shortcomings of Victor and Roselyn Solomon's marriage, Bradshaw sensed the union was based on that intertwining which his mother had once compared to the roots of a live oak spreading shade over half the little Rhode Island town in which they'd lived.

"I'll think about what you've said." Solomon gulped the last of his drink. "In the meantime, go ahead and contact Dawson."

The two men rose from the table. The Buckingham's air-conditioning began working properly. Solomon observed that it was as if his lawyer had arranged for a hot seat in which his client was to squirm and roast for two and a half hours. Bradshaw's suggestions, however, were intriguing. Should he actually consider getting down on his knees to Roselyn? All along he had envisioned her bending contritely before him. The reversed image was sobering. But whether or not Bradshaw's reconciliation scheme would succeed, one thing was certain. His lawyer hadn't failed him. During the long and trying luncheon, an alibi for the missing money had been established.

As they stood beneath the green canopy stretched over the entrance of the sixty-eight-year-old granite building, Bradshaw remarked, "Funny thing. Lance Benson could have fooled me. He's a real sickie, isn't he?"

"For sure."

They were both silent. Bradshaw wanted to say more, but he'd said as much as he dared. He patted his friend on the back and headed back to his office.

Alone, Victor Solomon swore. He was remembering the dinner date he had scheduled for tomorrow evening. The woman, recently divorced, was remarkably beautiful. She was also highly attracted to him. Suddenly he wanted nothing more than to slice up through the clouds in his silver plane.

Stopping at a pay phone, he called his secretary to tell her he would be out of the office for the remainder of the day.

The meeting had been a success. Caroline Fletcher lightly touched the chignon at the nape of her neck before moving about her town house emptying ashtrays, carrying coffee cups into the kitchen, gathering pads and pencils which she'd made available to committee members.

Her home was pleasantly quiet. The enthusiastic chatter of the ladies had pleased her. The ideas had been good, and the reports of action taken or about to be taken were encouraging. But she was tired. Though her red-blood count had built up again to a satisfactory level, she still needed, as she told Martin, "to prop my feet up every once in a while and have a little rest."

Yesterday evening she had had such a rest, with Martin gently rubbing her shoulders until the muscles had relaxed and she, with closed eyes, had imagined the two of them on a long, halcyon journey. She'd imagined they were in New Delhi. She'd worn a pale lavender sari and her breasts had been small and high and rounded. Abruptly she had opened her eyes, thanked Martin, and hurried to fix his martini. With or without two breasts, she'd reasoned, she was still the same efficient and somewhat endearing woman she had been before the operation. Hadn't Martin and she finally made love only that morning? She'd heard that often after a mastectomy it is the woman, rather than the man, who avoids physical contact. Conversely she had welcomed her husband's body pressing down upon hers. The bond between them had been renewed. And when Martin had returned home from work, he'd seemed happy — relieved of some heavy burden which for weeks now had etched lines, as though with a stylus, onto his face. Apparently he had taken the operation far more seriously than even she. She wished he would join her in reading about life's significances and insignificances, its strange yet magnificent easing over into infinity. Suddenly she'd felt guilty that she had even imagined herself gliding in lavender, the lost breast restored to her. There was no room in her life for wistful thinking. Organizing The Arch's Fall gala, with its guest list consisting solely of those people who encouraged and contributed to the arts, was an important responsibility. Clearly there would not be the Olympian theatre rising amid Houston's skyline without the support of those who recognized an artist's work as an essential rather than a frill. She'd felt revived and her smile had been bright as she'd handed her husband his martini, perfectly mixed and chilled.

Straightening her town house now, Caroline Fletcher mentally reviewed the morning meeting. Irene Stanton's recommendation for favors — fans for the ladies and desk pads in the shape of Gatsby's yellow roadster for the men — was perfect. Winifred Reese had miraculously secured commitments from six florists. Roselyn Solomon, continuing to serve in spite of her recent separation from an Arch board member, had announced that the invitations were addressed and sealed for next week's mailing.

Suddenly remembering that she had promised Zoe Benson a

summary report, she hurried into the library. "Dear Zoe," she typed, "I think the Gala is going to be one of our best. Here's a brief rundown of what came out of today's meeting . . ."

She touched the keys lightly and rapidly. The elite letters rushed onto the crushed bond stationery. Whipping the page out of the typewriter, she read what she had written then hastily signed: "Affectionately, Caroline."

By four o'clock Friday afternoon Martin Fletcher was beside himself. The scene he had walked through a thousand times in his mind had not shifted over into reality. No later than this very morning a shaken, ashen-faced Lance Benson was to have contacted him. "Leave my wife alone," he was to have pled as he returned the fifty thousand dollars already delivered into his grubbing hands. Each time Martin replayed the scene he'd felt a thrill similar to that experienced whenever a particularly cool, dry martini slid down his throat.

But something had gone wrong. Why else was there this silence? He stared at the phone on his desk. His anguish was probably due to a fucked-up postal system. A snail-paced mail delivery. That was it. He'd have to be patient. The lifelike snake would arrive in the Bensons' mailbox tomorrow. Saturday. That would be even better. Benson would conceivably be at home when his wife screamed.

Still, he must be prepared — if necessary — to activate Step Four of his plan. He left his office and walked slowly to the elevator. The weight which had lifted from him for a brief while yesterday had descended again. He frowned. The lines remained rigid in his face.

The elevator sped downward to the basement. Hesitantly, Martin stepped out into a long gray corridor leading to the "dungeon," as employees jokingly referred to the research department, whose locked doors opened only to scientists and their assistants, government inspectors, security personnel, and the company's upper echelon.

Fletcher, whose vice presidency placed him among the privileged few, signed the registry and entered the "dungeon." He walked between the prison rows of vermin. Blinking his eyes against the bright glare of overhead lights, he ignored the spiders and ants, the flying roaches, the rodents. He walked on until he came to the section for which he was looking.

Snakes slid, crawled, and slept entangled in their own length, awakening briefly to flick onto their tongues experimental poisons mixed with deceptive food which at mealtimes was shoved into their cages. Some few lay dead or dying; others, recently brought into captivity, coiled sleek and fat.

"Can I help you, Mr. Fletcher?"

Martin froze. As though disembodied, the voice had crept up behind him. He turned. It was one of the scientists.

He moistened his lips. "Yes, I need to know who's doing the company's reptile trapping. We're — updating our personnel files."

"Oh, it's the same man we've used for years."

Dimly Fletcher recalled the scientist's name. Dr. Vincent Gerard was making things difficult. "Yes, but I'd like to see his information card to check it against our records." He gambled that a scientist whose head was immersed in his own poisonous sprays would be unaware that personnel kept no records of outside contractual workers.

His gamble paid off. Dr. Gerard did wonder, however, why the vice president of personnel stood before him seeking information that could have been obtained in a single telephone exchange between secretaries.

Smiling politely, the scientist turned his visitor over to a tall, thin-lipped woman who, after twenty years as departmental receptionist, had begun to resemble her reptile assemblage. Efficiently she xeroxed the information card.

Averting his eyes from the caged vermin, Martin thanked her and left. The information he needed was tight in his hand.

As the elevator rose, he studied the xeroxed page. Name: Frazer Thompson. Address: 613 Old Mill Road, West Columbia, Texas 77038. Ph: (409) 345-8901.

Five messages awaited him on his desk. The last one was pure gold. Benson had called. So, the package had been delivered. The imagined scene could now become reality.

"Fletcher here returning your call." The authority rang bell-like in his voice.

"Fletcher, one word."

That word, Martin knew, would be surrender. His threats had paid off. He thought of the time he had stood in Benson's office and handed over the first payment. Dangling the videotape cassette, the bastard had sneered, "You look pale, Martin, as if a snake just spit at you." At that moment Martin's scheme had begun its slow, embryonic curving around Benson's throat.

"The word, Fletcher, is boredom. I'm bored with you. Bored with your little installment plan. I want the rest of it — all of it — fifty thousand dollars by Monday, September twenty-sixth."

Fletcher held a dead connection against his ear. He had not been given the opportunity to utter a single syllable beyond his opening identifying statement.

His beloved scene lay smashed at his feet. Stunned, he searched in his desk for a 5-mg Valium and quickly pushed it into his mouth. Obviously, his package still resided in the US post office waiting to be delivered in tomorrow's mail. If only he could hold on for a few more hours, the scene would then become whole, crystalized. Actualized. The way it was supposed to be. The way it was going to be. He had too much at stake. He was in too deep. He put his head on his desk and waited for the Valium to take effect.

But what if something went wrong? He lifted his head. The muscles in his neck twitched. What if the toy snake made no impact? What if? What if? If necessary, if necessary, if necessary — the words throbbed against his temples — if necessary he would contact Frazer Thompson and proceed with Step Four. The muscles relaxed. He lowered his head again to his desk and waited.

He stared at the pay phone. The call had been made. Balzer's slimy words had come from the other end of the line. "A black truck will pull into the back alley. There'll be the driver and one other man."

"You'll be there, won't you?" Raymond had asked, the question pushing its way over his thumping Adam's apple.

"No, kid, I'm just the go-between, remember? But you got yourself a good deal."

"I'll need the fifty thousand immediately."

"That's the only way we do business. You deliver the merchandise, we deliver the cash. Ten o'clock, Friday night, September the twenty-third."

Exactly one week and four hours from this very moment.

Raymond felt as if he had made an appointment with the mortician to scoop out his entrails and stuff the remaining vacuous body into a box. There would be no soul left to float up into the ethereal beyond. He had just sold his soul. And for what? To whom?

As he got into his 280 ZX, Raymond Reese was mortally afraid. Though not a particularly religious man, he was trembling. Religion to him was reciting the Episcopal litany by rote on Sunday mornings, his mother mouthing the words beside him. That was religion. God was remote in His heaven. But suddenly the presence of the Omnipotent filled his little car. The question pounded: Why? Why? WHY, RAYMOND? Oxygen was being extinguished. Hoarsely he answered aloud, "To keep my mother from knowing. To keep Mother and me unchanged!"

He drove aimlessly through the crowded streets. His mind searched for weaknesses in his plan and found only moral deficiency. Logically the plan should work. Friday had been selected because the design studio was closed on weekends. Not until Monday morning would it be discovered that the items were missing. And never would his mother suspect that her own son had smashed the backdoor lock and yanked out the alarm system's wiring. She would accept that a burglary had been committed in this city where the crime rate was gaining national prominence. Sinking weakly into a chair, she would instruct him to call the insurance company and, he supposed, the police! The thought made him grip the steering wheel. His knuckles whitened. But hadn't Balzer assured him that the truck would speed straight through the night into Mexico? The heirlooms would be sold there beyond the reach of US law enforcement. Only the insurance company would suffer. Each item had been photographed and scheduled on a policy. The monetary loss to his mother would be recouped; Lance Benson would be paid off. As for himself, Raymond vowed that he would pursue only those post-debutantes who nightly swallowed their birth control pills and fucked for their own harmless pleasure rather than for some conniving blackmailer.

He felt better. Even a little hungry. Still, he drove on. At nine o'clock he turned toward home. There was no place else to go.

His mother would be worried. He imagined her pacing the expanse of polished floor, twisting the rings on her pudgy fingers, moving often to the casement windows to peer out into an empty driveway. "Where *is* that boy?" She'd be sobbing.

He would tell her he had stopped off at Scruffy Dawson's for a drink. She would be relieved and then pleased that such "in" persons as Scruffy and his adorable Missy had sought his companionship. Enfolding him in her plump arms, she would not scold but simply ask that he call next time.

Together they would go into the dining room to lamb chops with mint jelly, parsley potatoes and spinach salad, and icebox lemon pie, which their faithful cook, Mattie, had been instructed to prepare for their evening meal.

"Golgotha," she thought, laughing hysterically as she pressed her legs together and spread her arms out from her body. Flat on her back and staring at the ceiling, Irene Stanton imagined herself crucified. The cream satin comforter on which she lay became for her the coarse boards of a cross. She wondered how long she could remain motionless in the blood-red position of crucifixion. "If Charles could see me now," she thought. "If the British ambassador, the queen could see me; if the proper, high-spirited ladies of The Arch gala committee could see me; if my little eighty-six-year-old mother, her smile fading into cracks of tissue-thin skin, could see me; if the whole world could see me; if Bonita — Bonita who has caused this crucifixion — could see me; if God — surely He can see — God who made me different. Look, You can see! I am hurting, bleeding internally, because my lover wordlessly, kindly, sadistically, has left. She has chosen man over woman, she has chosen the natural way, she has no longer chosen to choose me."

Irene Stanton did not move. She closed her eyes and held her breath. In a few minutes she would gather the threads of her life into a tight little ball and get up. She would pry nails from the palms of her hands, she would walk calmly into the bathroom, brush her teeth, wash her face, and comb her graying hair. She would slip from her robe into slacks and a blouse. Vibrantly she would greet her husband coming home late from a meeting and tell him they must go for a long, brisk walk because her day had not been the best, and did he realize that in exactly one week she would be fifty-six years old, which was somehow quite different from being fifty-five and certainly no cause for celebration. She would silently demand that in exchange for her confidence he tell her something complimentary and consoling. She imagined the sharp intake of breath if she added to her confession, "I want to go to a gay bar tonight. That would cheer me considerably." She envisioned bewilderment and horror sliding down the smooth narrow face at the thought that his wife found exhilaration in watching perverts play. "No, Charles, no," she would clarify. "Though your wife, and mired in age as if in quicksand, I would be going to seek, to partake. Rather than a voyeur, I would be the aggressor, the hunter stalking the young, firm prey — I would be — I would be despicable." She moved on the bed. First her arms. Then her legs, cramped from their taut, still position. Slowly, she curled into an embryonic ball and wished she were dead.

"Got it!" she cried, clutching the cassette to her breast, as though it were a lifeline thrown across water. She neatly rearranged swirls of purple moiré over the VCR equipment, then hopped down off the chair she had dragged over to her bed.

"Now what am I going to do with it?" she asked Rascal, who sat propped in a corner, silent, his one eye cocked at an angle.

"You're no help," she scolded. "But that's OK," she added, as if the little stuffed bear were a person whose feelings she had hurt.

It was OK because a film of her and Lance was just something she had to have, for her very own, to use whenever, however, she pleased. And the moment she got the hang of plugging that thing into her television set, she'd be able to play the film any time she wanted. If she felt lonely, she'd pop up some popcorn, open a cold beer, then sit, like she was at the movies, watching herself and Lance making love. She'd see the black dress she'd tried on for him tossed to the foot of the bed, hear him exclaim, "God, you're beautiful!" She'd watch herself arching over him, him throwing her on her back, sliding her under him, like "Me, Tarzan. You, Jane." All that would be on film! And if Lance, who could act like a bastard, ever entertained the slightest notion of staying with Zoe and ditching her — after all she'd been through — then she would have the cassette, wouldn't she? She'd be able to say, "Well, Lance, you taught me maybe one thing too many." She smiled, her green eyes sparkled. He'd never even recognized the trick he'd taught her. There he'd been unzipping his pants while she'd stretched, her hands going up and behind the headboard, and the tape had begun slowly unwinding as that machine she'd finally figured out how to use recorded Sandra Lowrey and the great Lance Benson in bed. Whatever would he think of that? But she'd never really have to use their love-making against him, would she? To even think he might stay with Zoe was a sinful, outrageous thought. That marriage, which was no marriage, had not been made in heaven. There weren't even any children. Poor man! Those she fully intended to give him. Yes, God wanted them together — producing children who would never, ever, be put in an orphanage. As for the film, on their first wedding anniversary she would bring it out and say, "Surprise! This is you and me, honey. And we two are fantastic!"

For now, however, she'd better keep her surprise hidden.

"This is our little secret," she cautioned Rascal as she tucked the cassette beneath lingerie. She thought of the wig, which she had most assuredly "forgotten" to give Lance tonight. First the wig and now the film! Her souvenirs were mounting.

Uncharacteristically Lance unloaded groceries while Zoe moved to other tasks. From the final sack he took out a small jar filled with fine white powder and read aloud the label: "Lightning." He fingered the skull and crossbones.

"Caroline's been raving about it, so I thought why not?"

She watched him study the ingredients as if he were reading a remarkable new play.

He looked up. "Fletcher's insect killer sounds like it could wipe out the entire roach population of Texas."

"That's the claim." She tied an apron around her waist.

"Let's test it."

"Now?"

"Now."

He was already spreading a thin white stream across the counter. Assiduously he searched for a roach, then dropped it into the powder. As though stuck by lightning, the roach died instantly.

"Interesting," he said and left the room.

She put the dead insect into the trash compactor, wiped up the powder, then placed the jar beneath the sink. She was not going to let such erratic behavior spoil her good mood. The Sunday buffet would be a success. Suddenly she decided to invite her father. So what if Lance had insisted he not be included? She went to the phone and, though her father declined the invitation, she was delighted to hear that he would be having dinner tomorrow evening with friends — two professors, like himself experiencing their first unfamiliar month of retirement.

"Kelli has firm nipples and a flat stomach," Victor Solomon silently observed as he looked at the long tanned body spread out before him.

"Kelli — spelled with an *i*," she had murmured earlier over dinner at Tony's.

"Nice." He'd lifted his glass. His eyes had extended the invitation. She had accepted. And he had signaled for the check.

He circled a taut nipple with scotch, then placed an ice cube from his mouth against her breast. She screamed a small, delighted scream. Sexy, he decided, dropping the melting cube back into his glass.

He sighed. "Nobody," he thought, "will believe this. Tomorrow probably not even myself."

He got out of the lady's bed with its down pillows, its scent of Chanel, its frilly lace, which softly rubbed against his skin. He pulled on his clothes while Kelli Mayfield, a recently divorced, highly desirable, mother of two children (safely tucked away for the weekend at their father's ranch outside Austin), watched propped on her elbow, the sheet pulled up to her neck like a bib.

"Did I do something, say something?" she finally asked as he slung his tie around the unbuttoned collar of his shirt. Her large violet eyes were wide and unblinking as if, by staring at him long and hard, she might understand what she had done to short-circuit the physical attraction that had sparked between them.

"You didn't do anything, Kelli. It's me." He stood beside the bed and looked down at the lady, who was trying hard now to keep her lips in a straight, sure line. "You're lovely. Let's just say — I changed my mind."

She lifted her chin slightly, then with distinct breeding, sipped from her glass of wine, and said, "If you unchange it, Victor, don't come back here."

"I won't," he promised and left.

Kicking pebbles on the way to his car, he kicked himself. It had taken getting all the way into another woman's bed for him to realize how single-mindedly he wanted to make love to his wife — with his wife. He wanted Roselyn to hold him. To trace the hair on his chest with the tips of her fingers. To assure him everything was going to be all right. He wanted to hold her. To feel her familiar skin, smooth from the bath oil she used each night. He wanted to promise her everything was going to be the same, but somehow different.

Monday he would send Kelli Mayfield two dozen long-stemmed yellow roses with a note of apology. Her only failing had been that, stretched out there on her king-size bed, she had been unable to become Roselyn Cohen Solomon. And that, unfortunately, had made all the difference.

His left eyelid twitched as he read in Sunday's *Herald* an obscure two-line advertisement. His daily search through the classifieds had ended. Perhaps he would have his handgun by dusk today. Though Zoe was busy in the kitchen, he still crept stealthily up the stairs to make his call from the third floor.

"I'm inquiring about your ad in today's paper."

"Yeah?"

"The gun's in good repair?"

"Sure is. My wife just doesn't want it around, what with the kids getting into everything."

Lance laughed easily. "Well, my wife wants it because she's afraid to be alone at night."

"Sounds like we may have a deal."

"Precisely. I'd like to drive over today and pick it up, if you'll tell me where you live, Mr. —"

"Mason. Harvey Mason. Out in Avon, but today's no good. We're heading for Galveston."

A wave of irritation swept over Lance Benson, but he quickly reasoned that he had no immediate use for the gun. "No problem," he said. "How about tomorrow?"

"Well . . . ," Harvey Mason hesitated. "I'll be home around six."

"Fine. Just give me the address — I'll be there."

When he hung up the phone, the eyelid was still. He went into his darkroom and locked the door behind him. For twenty minutes, he reviewed the notes that filled most of the pages in his legal pad.

Though he had accomplished a great deal since July, much remained to be done. Perhaps even an extinction. The gun was simply a precautionary measure. A more subtle and creative method was to be used in bringing about, if needed, Sandra Lowrey's demise.

Stretching, he stared into space. The image of Sandra, dressed in her new black dress from Neiman's, the hair rolled back from her face, rose before him. Such a lovely broad. He had ended up taking her to bed Friday evening. Unfortunately, in succumbing to her charms, he'd forgotten to ask about the wig. But it should have been out on a table, waiting for him. Damn bitch! Damn stupid and complaining bitch. Well, he would show her. If he had to, he would show her in spades. He had made that decision.

His thoughts turned to the upcoming party. And to Sir Charles Stanton. Sandra had her instructions to ease her way through the guests to his side. "Keep talk to a minimum," he'd cautioned. "The communication is to be with your eyes, your body. Slow, easy, and subtle, Sandra. Always subtle."

"Gotcha," she'd said and popped her gum.

"And get that stuff out of your mouth *now*. And keep it out!" he'd ordered.

Her eyes had filled with tears and her lower lip had protruded, but she'd gotten rid of the gum, muttering, "Mean old man, mean, mean old man."

"Look, Sandra," he'd explained, "I just don't want the East Jesus Orphanage to show through."

With that she'd thrown a pillow hard into his stomach and screamed, "The name is Good Shepherd — The Good Shepherd Baptist Orphanage, you understand, and it taught me a whole lot more than how to chew gum, thank you!"

He'd had little choice but to fuck her again. It had been either that or slap her full across the face. He hated noisy broads. Zoe, at least, kept her voice in a lower register. But lately there was that detachment and — what else? Anger? He would have to get Zoe Benson back in line. He rubbed his forehead. Christ! There was so much to think about, so much to keep under control. It was enough to make him walk out the door and board the next plane for Zurich. But he couldn't. Fletcher and Reese still owed him money. And then there was Hook. Christ Almighty! Hook was left dangling. Next week he would have to rectify that. But, for now, attention must be paid to Stanton.

He turned out the light and locked the door. He would steal up behind Zoe, who was probably stirring her creole, and playfully kiss her neck. Startled, she would be either annoyed or pleased. Women were a strange lot. A man never knew what to expect. But surely Zoe's behavior of late was due to his neglect. He would do better, be better. Tonight he would make love to his wife. He didn't want her asking questions, the answers to which might turn her into a moralist, mouthing the outrageous profundities of her old man. She was, after all, her father's daughter and ultimately that made her a pain in the ass.

Victor Solomon rang the doorbell four times, then used the key he had secretly kept. The massive front door of the large, old Georgian house, in which he had lived for fifteen years, opened. He stepped into the wide foyer, with its cool white marble, its brass-potted ferns, and tapestry hangings. Only the faint, persistent sound of dripping water jarred the silence. He made a mental note to have the powder room's faucet repaired as soon as he moved back into his house — the house where Roselyn and their children had remained, while he had carved out misery for himself in a dismal high-rise whose occupants consisted primarily of oil barons' widows and affluent ex- or about-to-be ex-husbands.

"Anybody home?" he called out into the silence.

Often on Sunday afternoons Roselyn took the children to the movies. Rarely had he gone along. "Sunday is a family day," she had insisted, but he had ignored her insisting. Perhaps at this very moment they were munching popcorn in a darkened theatre, while somebody else's happiness loomed bright and promising before them. Certainly the children had not had much happiness of their own lately. As for Roselyn . . . he couldn't say. If you believed the society columns, she was up to her ass in happiness.

He poured a drink, then walked through the rooms of his house. No one disturbed his solitary viewing. He entered the master bedroom and stretched out on the chaise longue. He sipped his scotch. Should he leave Roselyn a note? "I'm sorry. Please call me." He scribbled the message, then shoved the paper into his pocket. Hurriedly he left the room.

After rinsing his empty glass, he placed it neatly on a shelf in the bar. Roselyn need never know she had had a visitor. He got into his car and drove back to his apartment. There was still time to catch the beginning of Cable's Sunday-afternoon movie.

·  ·  ·

Sir Charles Stanton shrugged into a navy blazer and studied his wife as she turned critically before the full-length mirror in her dressing room. Clearly she was unhappy with her reflection.

"You're immensely attractive," he assured her.

"Attractive is a weak word, Charles." She brushed past him to drop, with emphatic boredom, a few cosmetics into her handbag.

"We don't have to go, you know."

"It's too late to cancel."

"The Bensons would understand."

"Understand what?"

"That you don't feel well."

"I didn't say that."

"Irene, you don't have to *say* anything." He moved to encircle her in his arms. Wearily he thought, "She still wears the tragedy of our son's death like a badge." He thought of the portrait Zoe Benson was painting. For the hundredth time he wondered if he had made a mistake. Though Irene had insisted she needed a remarkable resemblance of David to make her feel better, he feared the reverse would happen. In less than a week he was to present the completed portrait to his wife on her birthday. Could that impending date be depressing her? She hadn't said. But aging was reputedly more upsetting to women than to men. He would plan a surprise celebration to help her feel young again. Perhaps then she would throw back her head and laugh that hearty laugh of hers. Lately she hadn't laughed at all. And her smile had been no more than a thin veneer, covering what he suspected was some deep inner turmoil.

He felt as if he held a statue. He tightened his hold. Gradually she responded. Her fingers touched the wrinkles at the corners of his eyes.

"You look so serious."

"I'm worried about you, Irene. I want to help but I don't quite know what the trouble is."

"It's nothing. I simply — you know —"

"No, I don't know."

"I miss David."

He relaxed. So that was it. The unrelenting but, at least, the familiar.

Irene Stanton bit her lower lip. It was true. She would never, ever, stop missing her son; but she had chosen to hide behind that acknowledged hurt rather than admit to her husband that which could never be openly acknowledged.

"We must go," she said, quickly kissing his cheek. She would try to be her old self. "Old self," she thought wryly. "That's what I am — old, old, old."

"If you're sure . . ."

"Of course I'm sure. Even doubly sure," she added, laughing the hearty, beautiful laugh he had missed. "We don't want to be late for the Bensons."

"Yes," he said, thinking somewhat guiltily of Zoe. "They're nice people."

Lance Benson surveyed the table. And approved. China, crystal, and sterling, arranged buffet-style, gleamed on white linen. Tapered candles rose on either side of an antique tureen filled with daffodils and irises.

In the kitchen Zoe gave final instructions to the twins — neighboring high-school girls who helped on such occasions.

The doorbell chimed. The Bensons moved quickly into the foyer to greet their guests.

Thirty minutes into the cocktail hour, Lance Benson's eyelid was twitching. He prided himself on his ability to size up a situation quickly and accurately.

Sandra Lowrey's smashing good looks were being admired by every man in the room — except one. And that man was smitten with another woman. Sir Charles Stanton was smitten with Zoe Harrington Benson. Lance longed to crush the glass in his hand and grind the broken bits into Zoe's face. How dare she! How dare he! Oh, it was all very subtle. Nothing overt. But the eye contact, the laughter, the repeated coming together after mingling for a time with other guests, were all unmistakable. While Sandra, goddamn her, was prancing unheeded, like a well-instructed little puppy, practically beneath Stanton's feet. It was a wonder she didn't trip him.

His eyes narrowed as he observed Stanton's wife: an aging dull-haired lady, short and wide-hipped but somewhat regal in her mauve silk. Had he been Irene Stanton, he would have pushed Sir Charles out the door and taken him home. Instead she seemed oblivious to what was going on. Holding a drink in one hand, while the other lightly caressed the single strand of pearls that dropped below her full breasts, she spoke softly to Sandra.

Stanton and Zoe — Irene and Sandra. Standing together, the four formed a tight circle. But it was as if the circle was halved.

"Excuse me," he apologized, not having heard the question.

"Is this second play of Biggs's a departure from the socialistic bent of his first?"

"Decidedly."

"Good!"

"Yes, you must see it." Without another word, he moved away from Kelli Mayfield and her escort, the chairman of Spur Oil.

He joined a group standing next to the dichotomized circle. Charmaine Norwood, an architect whose passion was global travel, was holding court. As she expounded on the grandeur of German opera houses, he nodded occasionally and studied what was transpiring practically at his elbow.

There was something interesting in the way Irene Stanton was approaching Sandra, something in the way . . . something in the way . . . what was it? He had a full view of her face. The expression was animated. She laughed often and quickly.

"If you could see England, my dear, you would love it."

"I *imagine* so," Sandra gushed and brushed against Sir Charles.

A slight frown crossed the older woman's face, but she continued talking. "Getting out into the countryside is such a joy."

"Oh yes, ma'am."

He cringed. Don't call her "ma'am," you klutz.

"At The Good Shepherd —"

He would strangle her!

"That's the church my family and I — uh — attended — we used to have picnics."

Good, she had covered her slip.

"How lovely." Irene Stanton leaned closer. Her fingers stroked the pearls.

Something clicked. Irene Stanton was approaching Sandra Lowrey as a man would. That was it! Her manner was that of an older man seducing a young girl. But he must be wrong. He *had* to be wrong. Not Lady Stanton, not the wife of the knighted hero and savior of us all. Not the cream of the elite, not . . . Was he wrong?

He glanced at Stanton and Zoe, then back at Irene and Sandra.

If one weren't looking for deviant behavior, one would never suspect. But he was looking, scrutinizing the woman's every move. And there it was. Shit! Suddenly he felt like a kid again, buck-naked and eager, rushing out into Lake Ontario to splash water high into the air. Goddamn it! He was right! He sensed it. He knew it. After all, wasn't he a past master at sizing up situations and people? He was exactly right! And this way — this new means to entrap the arrogant Sir Charles — was even better.

"You got rocks in your head or something?" she whispered indignantly as she tossed her blond hair and turned to walk away. He grabbed her arm, then quickly looked to see if any of the guests clustered in groups around the pool had noticed.

"The rocks are going to be over our future, sweetheart, if you don't watch out." He spoke low and smiled. Anyone observing them would think they were discussing an upcoming production. Well, they were. Of sorts. "Now listen, we're about to go in for dinner. People will scatter over the house to eat. Sit with her, lean over and touch her as you talk, and don't — I repeat, *don't* — leave this party without an invitation for lunch tomorrow. You understand?"

"Lance, that's a very nice lady. And nice ladies are not *queer*."

"Just do as I say, Sandra."

"Lance, I can't. I'm not —"

"Not what?"

She faltered. "You know — *strange*. I'm not strange, and I don't want any old woman, *any* woman, doing that to me . . . Lance, please, I just can't."

"Not even if I tell Zoe I want a divorce?"

Her eyes widened. Then narrowed. "When?"

"Just as soon as you do this."

"Why can't I do it, like you said, with her husband?"

"Because her husband happens to be interested in my wife."

"Oh!" She glanced through the French doors into the living room as though expecting to find Zoe Benson, enraptured, in Stanton's arms. All she could see was a multicolored haze of indistinguishable bodies. Damn, she thought, if only I had on my glasses. As soon as she became Mrs. Lance Benson, she was going to buy herself a pair of violet-tinted contacts. She would go swishing up and down theatre aisles looking like Elizabeth Taylor.

She turned again to her future husband. He was a bastard, she knew that now. For sure. Listening to him spewing out that filth he expected her to wallow in caused something inside her to die. She wondered if her heart would ever again stand on tiptoe, roll over, and lie palpitating on the ground before him. No, he shouldn't have asked that of her. But he had. And she would do what he wanted, because they were, fuck it all, in this together for life. That had been preordained. And she guessed — she *knew* — she loved him.

"OK," she sighed. "Next thing I know you'll want me to do it with an elephant."

Lance Benson threw back his head and roared. Several people turned and smiled at their charming host and the beautiful young actress. A few of the more bitchy women wondered why Zoe had allowed this devastating creature to set foot in her house. Unanimously the men who had witnessed, but not overheard, the exchange envied the artistic director. Obviously his life was one big bowl of cherries.

From a third-floor window, Zoe looked down at the guests clustered around the pool. She saw without seeing, for her mind was elsewhere. She was waiting for some strong, final word of approval or disapproval from Charles Stanton, who stood not far from her, staring wordlessly at the nearly completed portrait of his son. Because he had insisted on seeing the painting, she had brought him to her studio.

Suddenly her eyes focused on a man and a woman below. She watched in disbelief as her husband roughly jerked Sandra Lowrey to him. There was hostility yet intimacy between Lance and this woman, who surprisingly had come here tonight in a designer dress which, according to idle cocktail chatter, Kelli Mayfield had almost purchased for herself.

She stared intently at the two figures. They stood close together now. Were they arguing? She couldn't be sure. Certainly they were not director and actress rehearsing a scene. Nor were they merely host and guest conversing. What were they? What was their relationship? What did they mean to each other? She sought instant identification. A label to paste across each of their foreheads. A tag to slap on baggage. A banner to fly from the rooftop. Anything to identify them as something other than that which she suddenly knew them to be. They were what they had probably been for some time — lovers.

"It's incredible."

Startled, she turned.

"Zoe, what's wrong?"

"Nothing, I was just — checking on my guests."

Charles Stanton glanced out the window. "They seem to be having a good time."

"I hope so." She tried to clear her mind. "I haven't got the hair right, but — you do like the portrait?"

"Immensely."

"Thank goodness. Well . . . I've got to get to the kitchen." Her laugh was small and unnatural. "The twins are better than the best caterers, but occasionally I need to supervise."

"You're sure there's nothing wrong?"

"I'm sure." Suddenly she longed to take this man's hand. To hold on tight.

The telephone ring broke the moment. She hurried into the hallway.

There was silence on the other end of the line.

She waited for the click before she hung up.

"Wrong numbers are aggravating, aren't — Zoe, what is it?"

"You're right, they *are* aggravating. Charles, I really must get you back to the party."

"Blast the party! What's wrong?"

"Nothing."

He lifted her chin. "Tell me."

She shook her head.

For the rest of the evening, Zoe Benson avoided three people: her husband, Sandra Lowrey, and Charles Stanton.

Martin Fletcher stared at the phone. What had he hoped to gain by calling her? Had he expected her to say, "Just a minute, my husband wants to speak to you"? Had he expected her to accuse him? — "It was you who sent that filthy snake!" What *had* he expected? Indeed, when he heard her voice, he had almost asked, "Did you receive my latest warning?" The words had not come. Like a coward, he had hung up. He knew no more now than he had known five minutes ago.

Knotting his hands into fists, he glanced distraught about his bedroom. From a corner a black-hooded priest rose twelve feet into the air. The towering figure demanded retribution. But for what? From whom? From Benson? It was Benson, not he, who should be penitent. He, Martin Fletcher III, was simply the instrument necessary to bring a disloyal servant to his knees.

He unclenched his fists. "Face it," he ordered himself, "the package was either lost in the mail or Zoe Benson has iron guts and a closed mouth." The time had come to proceed. He dialed the West Columbia number.

Frazer Thompson deliberated, then allowed it would take him a couple of days to catch "a fine one."

"I'll drive out and pick it up on Wednesday." Martin spoke in a voice pitched higher than usual.

"No, better give me till — oh, 'long about Friday morning."

Fletcher looked at his bedside calendar: Friday, September twenty-third. "I'll be there," he confirmed in his disguised reedy voice.

He put down the phone. The black-hooded figure disappeared. Step Four had been activated. He would try to relax. Calling downstairs to Caroline, he suggested they go for a walk in the woods that stretched beyond their town house.

"I'd love it," she said, turning the oven temperature to low. Her roast could wait indefinitely. Perhaps after walking they would make love. He had not touched her since that Thursday morning.

As they stepped out into the approaching night, Martin commented, "You and I need to walk more to get in shape for the years ahead."

Caroline glanced at her husband. Lately he spoke often of the future. "What," she wondered, "does he find wrong with the present?"

"Got it!" Sandra whispered as she sailed past her host. "Twelve o'clock. Tomorrow."

"Glad you could come." Benson responded formally, but he winked and she grinned. He was remembering. Thrown impossibly far, the bone had been returned to him tight in Bailey's mouth, the old dog's sides heaving as his breath came in short, rushing pants. Only a worthy leader demanded and received such devotion. He wished he could pat Sandra rewardingly on the ass, but he supposed the wink would have to suffice. On the other side of the foyer, Zoe, looking pale but lovely, was saying good night to the

Stantons. With some amusement, he wondered if Sir Charles, Lady Stanton, and Sandra Lowrey would be walking together to their cars.

"That was a marvelous party!" Irene Stanton exclaimed as her husband wheeled their maroon Daimler out the Bensons' driveway.

Charles smiled in the dark. Lights from a passing car flashed on their faces. He glanced at her. "It's good to see you happy again. We should socialize more often with people you enjoy."

"I think maybe you're right. Our circle of friends has been limited. And the demands on our time —" She made a wry face. "It *is* tiring, Charles."

"I know."

For the remainder of the drive each was immersed in private thoughts.

Within Charles Stanton a battle raged. The battle swirled in disturbing yet exhilarating patterns. "My God," he thought, "it's been years since I've been this attracted to a woman! When last was it? Perhaps in school. I can't remember. When did this begin — this fascination with Zoe? I think maybe the day she opened her door and there was a smudge of paint on her face. An aliveness about her from working hard at something she loves. This is insanity. It must stop at once. Why did I ask to meet her father? I'll cancel. Tomorrow, early, I'll cancel. Besides, what was I thinking of? Taking off on a Monday, despite the meetings and the pile of work on my desk, to spend time with an aging scholar. Ridiculous! To spend the afternoon with a woman surely twenty years younger than I whose husband heads an organization on whose board I sit. Bloody ridiculous! I'll cancel . . . but perhaps I shouldn't. I saw the look on her face in her studio, and then after the phone call — the way she avoided me for the rest of the evening. She's afraid of something. I'd help a total stranger if he was in trouble, so why should I turn my back on someone I like — hell, someone I find myself thinking about obsessively — wanting to make love to her, to know everything about her? Well, I'd damn sure better get this thing back in control! Irene's a fine, good woman whose moods keep me constantly walking a tightrope, but I'm committed to her. I'm concerned about her. I somehow feel responsible for her stability. I am — I am — attracted like hell to Zoe Benson! I won't cancel tomorrow. We'll be friends. That's all. Good, close friends."

Within Irene Stanton, there raged no battle. Clear, unadulterated resolve lifted her spirits. Her thoughts fairly soared: "When
I walked into that room and saw her, just her back, the same as
I'd seen her that night at the gala, the long blond hair — I knew.
I knew that was the girl, the girl who reminds me so painfully of
Priscilla. Priscilla who went into the bathroom at boarding school
and hanged herself because I chose Charles. And now, with Bonita
making her choice, I have another chance. It's as if Priscilla is here
again. This time I'll make it up to her. I know Sandra's not smart,
not fragile, like Priscilla. She's not refined. But she's young and
eager. She'll trust me. Charles will never suspect. It's another chance.
I'm going to take it! I'm going to be the greatest lover that girl
has ever known. She will never, ever desert me for a man. Charles
will never know. The way she looked at me, touched me as we
talked — nothing was said but we both knew. Tomorrow she'll
come for lunch. And still nothing will be said. The maid will be
there and I have that damn tea at three, but there'll be other days.
Perhaps I can go to her apartment. We could meet there. Oh, she
made me feel young again, beautiful myself! Thank God, Charles
didn't hover over me at the party. That he let me find my own
way. Oh, Charles, if you only knew the way I've found. The way
I *had* to find. Forgive me, but this will make our marriage better.
I promise."

They were home. Impulsively Irene Stanton leaned over and
gave her husband a hug. "I was proud of you tonight," she said.
"As I always am. People look up to you, Charles . . . and I love
you."

"What's this all about?" He smiled quizzically at his wife. He
felt guilty.

"I don't know. I simply wanted to tell you that."

Unlocking the door which led from the garage into their house,
he reaffirmed his decision. Zoe Benson would remain his friend,
no more, no less. Lately Irene seemed to need his support and
reassurance even more than she had at the time of their son's death.
He was not going to fail her.

He flipped on the kitchen lights. They stood in sudden brightness. Irene blinked and laughed. "Let's take wine up to bed and
read for a while. I'm in such a good mood I couldn't possibly go
to sleep just yet."

Pouring the Chablis, he determined to dispense temporarily with embassy dinners and charity balls and to concentrate on relaxed social evenings. Next Friday he would definitely give a surprise dinner party to celebrate his wife's birthday. He'd invite the Bensons and a few others she'd enjoy.

She paid the twins and told them good night. Alone she walked through the downstairs rooms. Except for fresh flowers on the dining-room table, no evidence remained of the party. She glanced at the grandfather clock. One-twenty. Lord, she was tired. She supposed her unfaithful husband had been asleep for hours.

For a few minutes, she sat on a lower-stair step and pondered the revelations of the evening.

. . . Whatever her convictions about Lance and that girl, it was best to remain silent. Though logically it made no sense, she intuitively felt that the affair was somehow connected with the threats and the telephone calls, which could not be coming from anyone who had attended the party. That last call had slashed into the cocktail hour while her husband and Sandra Lowrey had stood arguing, laughing, out by the pool.

Keeping quiet would be hard. How she would love to shake her sleeping husband and demand an explanation, announce a divorce! To show her hand now, however, would be foolish. Lance would only lie. Deny. Smoothly and adroitly. As for leaving him, that would inevitably come . . . but not until she had unraveled the mystery.

She rubbed the back of her neck, ran her fingers through her hair.

Were she not exhausted, she would quietly lift the chain of keys that lay each night on Lance's bureau and go up to the darkroom. That had been her plan. She took a deep breath. Regardless of her exhaustion, tonight was the night.

She slipped off her shoes and climbed the stairs.

He met her on the landing.

"Lance, you frightened me!"

"Your own husband frightened you?"

"I thought you were asleep."

"Obviously I'm not. Let's go for a swim."

"At this hour?"

"Why not? We've done it later than this."

"I'm too tired."

"Come on." He took her hand. "A swim'll make you sleep better."

"Lance," she protested as he led her down the stairs, "I'm going to pass out as soon as my head hits the pillow."

"After we swim."

They had reached the foyer.

"Let go of me, please." She spoke straightforwardly, politely, as if asking someone to pass the butter.

"Why?" He focused an icy stare on her.

"Because. I've already told you."

"Why?"

"All right . . . because I don't feel like swimming with you." She turned to leave, but he pulled her back, roughly, to him.

The scene she had witnessed from her studio window only hours before flashed before her. Resolve disintegrated, and she lashed out, "Slinging women around seems to be your style lately!" She bit her tongue.

"Explain that!" He tightened the grip on her arm.

The damage had been done. The plunge taken.

"If you'll let go of me." She met the cobalt stare.

"Very well."

She was free; his hands had gone deep into the pockets of his robe.

". . . I saw you and that actress out by the pool."

"Oh." He shrugged. "Is that all?"

"Is that *all*?"

"You're jealous?"

"Absolutely not! What concerns me is —"

" 'The lady doth protest too much, methinks.' I'm flattered, but surely you don't think Sandra Lowrey would interest me?"

"Lance, please." She put her hand up as if to halt the lies which would be coming now, fast and predictably.

"Zoe, listen! The girl had too much to drink and was raising hell about the roles she's been getting lately. Things got out of control for a minute, that's all. Surely you noticed before it was over I had her eating out of my hand."

He reached for her.

She sidestepped.

"That's the truth. I swear it. Now, let's go for a swim and afterward maybe I'll be more convincing."

"Spare me," she said and walked up the stairs.

His words, soft and distinct, followed her.

"You're wrong, Zoe."

In bed she lay rigid. Questions pelted, as hail raining down, into her tired brain.

What if she were wrong? What if Lance were telling the truth? How could he be? Why hadn't she held to her initial resolve? Why was she so confused?


Lance Benson dropped his robe and dived into the lighted water. Surfacing, he noticed that a few dead bugs and fallen leaves floated beside him. He had planned and wanted to seduce his wife. Slowly and artfully. Instead he had been forced to assuage a recalcitrant bitch who alluded to information she was not supposed to have. It was a good thing he was a fast thinker.

. . . But what did she know? He suspected not very much. Besides, why be overly concerned? A wife didn't run to the police about her husband. Unless that husband had pushed a knife against her throat. Certainly he had no intention of harming Zoe. His only desire was ultimately to leave her alone. Once he was out of the country, he didn't care if she went to the police, Charles Stanton, or anyone else she chose. He shook water from his face. Maybe it wouldn't be Stanton. After the cocktail hour, she had said little more than two or three words to him. He had observed them. Stanton's eyes had shifted repeatedly to Zoe, but invariably she had been talking to other guests. She'd probably reasoned that she had devoted enough time to the pompous dignitary. Yet . . . He swam underwater. He could have sworn she was attracted to Stanton as, he had no doubt, Stanton was to her. And he was seldom wrong.

He surfaced thinking of Sandra Lowrey. Now there was someone you could depend on. Too bad she was a whining nuisance demanding marriage. He pictured Sandra leading Irene Stanton into bed. "Goddamn, shit!" he said aloud. Charles Stanton would put himself in hock for the next fifty years to keep that incident from becoming public knowledge.

Vigorously he swam twenty laps. It was unfortunate that Zoe had elected to take herself upstairs. Tomorrow evening he would wine, dine, and, he hoped, charm her back into submission.

He congratulated himself. The swim had not been solitary after all. His thoughts had been companion enough. For a time he sat on the edge of the pool. He lit a cigarette, inhaled deeply, and stared at the fading stars. Had he not had to go to work tomorrow he could have sat there until dawn, feeling comfortably pleased with himself.

Her designer dress lay in a heap on the floor. The makeup remained smeared on her face while she slept. Sandra Lowrey had come home from the party feeling, as she'd complained aloud, "like two cents."

The next morning she awoke before dawn and walked dazed through her apartment. Huddled over the kitchen counter, she rubbed her swollen eyelids and waited for water to boil. She tried to make sense of the dream that had pushed her into wakefulness.

The letters of her last name had been scattered in broken pieces on the splintered floor of an old tenement house. Wearing a thin white slip, she had bent shivering in dark cold, trying to gather the emerald chips of her name, which kept slipping through her fingers. She had cried, "It's my name. My beautiful, beautiful name!" Suddenly coming toward her had been a woman with thick white arms and lines through her hair that sloped like scars into her face. Terrified, she had run from the shadowy room of her nightmare into the glare of her own apartment — and Monday. She had run into Monday. The day she was to have lunch with Irene Stanton.

Sipping instant coffee, she unlocked her door and reached for the morning paper. She read no more than the headlines. Trouble in the Far East. Shrugging, she dropped the paper on the coffee table. There was trouble enough inside her tiny apartment. Inside Sandra Lowrey. "My name, all broken like that," she sorrowfully moaned. Talking to herself was a habit she had acquired as a child when she'd discovered the meaning behind there being no brothers or sisters, only nameless others joined to her in a chain without any blood links.

"My name," she repeated. Remembering, she frowned. Brother Stevens had explained to her that he had personally selected both her middle and her surname. She had come to them, he'd said, with one word — "SANDRA" — stitched neatly on the small pink blanket. He'd added Christine in honor of his own little girl, who'd died one night in her crib without a mark on her. Christine was passable, she guessed, but it still gave her the creeps knowing she was named after somebody who'd died like that. Nine days into life and she'd died. He'd chosen Lowrey from the big brown leather book of names he kept in his office because of "its poetic quality," he'd told her, "its lyric beauty, its aristocratic ring." Lowrey. Immediately she had loved the name. At times she even convinced herself that she didn't want to know her real name. What if it was something common like Brown, or foreign like Kraus, or, God forbid, ugly like Turnipseed? As for her given name, Sandra was all right — a good name. Brother Stevens had stressed that her parents were probably God-fearing people, for didn't Sandra mean "Helper of Mankind?" She had dug her toe in the sand and questioned even then whether all parents who named a daughter Sandra knew its lofty meaning. "Helper of Mankind." Well, she was that now, wasn't she? And for sure mankind was about to include, not just figuratively but literally, woman. If she didn't add sugar to this shitty instant coffee, she was going to vomit on the morning headlines. Damn Lance for putting her on a diet. So what if she had gained a pound or two? Hadn't she been last night's sensation? She stirred gobs of sugar into her cup, then swallowed deeply.

Five hours remained before she was due at Irene Stanton's house. But first she had to stop by the theatre for "instructions." Dear God — she put her face in her hands — when would it end? Whatever was she to do? Damn! She'd broken a fingernail. Probably she'd become disfigured like that while frantically searching through her nightmare for bits of her name. That particular fingernail, long and gleaming red, had been her pride and joy. She blinked to keep from crying. Slowly the room blurred.

She cried until her shoulders shook and she gasped for breath. Her fingernail was broken. Who wouldn't cry? She sobbed loudly, hoping someone would hear. The only problem, she told herself, was there was no one within earshot and if there was what difference would it make? Who would care? Who cares about anybody? "But *I* care. I care about Lance," she sobbed. "I care about Brother Stevens, who named me; about some of the nice ones, not the snobs, at The Arch; about a whole bunch of people — that's who I care about!" She left her coffee and went into the bathroom. With thoughtful tenderness, she wrapped a Band-Aid around her broken fingernail.

·    ·    ·

Lowell Hook awakened just as Sandra Lowrey was reaching for the morning paper on her small front patio. He rubbed his eyes and rang for Mrs. Mabry to bring hot tea to his bed. It was early, damn early, for any intelligent person to be awake, but the older he got the less sleep he required. This past year his pattern of awakening to morning darkness had petrified into routine. "If it's before daybreak, keep your hair net on," he'd apologized to his housekeeper. "But just get the hot tea in here fast." Agreeable enough, she usually included two blueberry muffins on his tray. Once she'd even brought in a rose at 5:30 A.M. Eyeing the dewy thing, he'd exclaimed, "Mrs. Mabry, you have indeed outdone yourself, but if I accept a flower at this ungodly hour, I'm a bigger fool than you are to bring it in here." Primly she'd replied, "I expect you're right, sir." With blue hair net over plastic rollers intact, she'd removed the bud vase and returned to bed.

Waiting for his tea, he relived the fogged dream which had come to him during the early morning hours. The sky whirled with yellow dust. Birds with soft wings filled the pockets of an old sweater, hanging loosely about his shoulders. A frightened young woman, her hair in long blond braids, came running toward him. In her terror, she ran on beyond him. The birds streamed from his pockets to fly ahead of her. No longer afraid, she turned, smiling, and beckoned. Suddenly young again, he ran toward her, then beyond to stand on a hill, the sky now still and translucent. The birds rushed to form a thin blue rainbow about his shoulders. The old sweater disappeared. He motioned to the girl to come ahead. Slowly, as though moving through clouds, she came running, smiling, her arms outstretched. The dream ended. He didn't understand. He was left with a sense of loss. An uneasiness stirred in the pit of his stomach.

The girl reminded him of the young actress he had determined to see this week. "To see, hell." He chuckled to himself. "To fuck!" The chuckle slid into a cough. It was to be a busy week: three meetings, a concert, and a small but important dinner party at his home next Saturday in honor of the mayor, who was seeking reelection. He thought again of the illusive, ethereal girl of his dream. He thought of Sandra Lowrey. Only earthiness clung to that one. Still, she and the girl seemed merged. In spite of his crowded schedule, he promised himself that in the next day or so he would contact Benson.

Fluffing his feather pillows, he sat up, eager now for Mrs. Mabry to bring in his tray. He missed the lumberjack pancakes of his youth, but certainly hot tea and muffins would begin his day in a most digestible fashion.

"Good Lord!" Balzer and his cohorts were getting the better end of the deal. Scrutinizing the list he'd compiled, Raymond realized that without stripping the studio he could easily assemble a truckload of antiques worth well over two hundred thousand dollars. In exchange, he would be receiving a mere fifty thousand! Thoughtfully munching a chocolate bar, he drew heavy lines through items seven and eight. The Chippendale candle stand and Queen Anne card table would definitely stay. After all, this wasn't a flea-market giveaway. Now, should he cross off the Hepplewhite chair? His mother's voice rang out for him through the studio. Hastily cramming the sheet of paper into his pocket, he reminded himself that he still had several days in which to decide what went and what stayed.

He gulped the remaining chocolate and answered, "I'll be right there!" Reaching again into his pocket, he pulled out a second list. Neatly typed on Reese Interiors' pale gray stationery were ten names. Beside each was definitive information: year of debut, phone number, and address. Proudly he would present the list to his mother. As he explained its meaning, a puzzled but delighted smile would surely cross her face. And then he would wait. It was she who was to judge and pronounce the winner: the young lady destined for a Thursday-evening dinner date with Raymond Billingsworth Reese!

Though he couldn't remember the source of the quote, "The time for action is now," he thoroughly agreed. In this one troubled week he intended to pay off Lance Benson and launch what he hoped would be a meteoric dating career.

She supposed it was the most splendid house she'd ever seen. Certainly the ceilings were the highest, the paintings the finest, the china the prettiest. Oh, she hoped one day she and Lance would live like this. The thought gave her courage to glance questioningly across the table set up especially for them in the sun room "because it's my hideaway, my favorite place in the entire house," her hostess had confided girlishly.

Irene Stanton touched her hand. "What is it, dear?"

Sandra spooned the soufflé from its fragile little chocolate pot. She shook her head and lied: "I'm just so happy. I was wondering —"

"Yes?"

She was glad Brother Stevens couldn't see her. Right now he was probably saying grace over the long rows of children who were waiting to scoop mashed potatoes and English peas and slabs of spam onto their plates. He would be ashamed of her for taking advantage of this poor, queer old lady who was starved for nourishment beyond that which the chicken salad filled with seedless grapes and freshly shelled walnuts, the fruit cup, and the tea rolls with rich spun butter, could provide. Lady Stanton was starved, while she, Sandra Lowrey, tucking an extra pound under her belt, was stuffed.

"What were you wondering, dear?"

Sometimes when she got to thinking hard she forgot another person was around, even the very person she was thinking about. "Just that . . . could we — see each other again?"

The older woman dabbed yellow linen at the corners of her mouth. "I don't know why not. Perhaps tomorrow even. I'd like to see your apartment. Would that please you?"

"Oh yes!" Her heart sank. So it would happen just as Lance had predicted. Did he always get his way?

Irene Stanton pushed back her chair. "Come, I'll show you the rest of the house. Then I must run. There's a tea I've promised to attend."

Together they walked through the tapestried rooms.

"Beautiful. Just beautiful." She was dazed.

"I'm glad you like it. We have a tennis court in the garden. Do you play?"

"Well, I like it, but I don't know how."

"Oh." A dullness came into the lady's voice. Quickly the lilt returned. "Never mind. I'll teach you."

"Yes, ma'am." She bit her tongue. Lance's instructions at the theatre this morning had included: "Do not, under any circumstances, say 'yes ma'am' or 'no ma'am.' "

Irene Stanton turned with a cool smile. "Call me Irene. And no 'yes ma'ams' or 'no ma'ams,' please."

Another point scored for Lance. She would just have to trust him. Tomorrow she would close her eyes and somehow get through the ordeal. After that there would be Lowell Hook and then she was home free. She and Lance could soar to the moon and build there a house exactly like the Stantons' palace. All shiny and glistening. She was reminded of a prism.

"Tomorrow at two?"

They stood looking down upon the hedged garden, the swimming pool, and tennis court.

"That'll be fine — Irene."

"Good. I'll walk you to your car."

Sandra consoled herself. In five minutes she would be out of here, hitting the freeway and heading straight for Carrousel Square. She needed to sit in a corner, chew a big wad of bubble gum, and hold on tight to her teddy bear. Kind one-eyed Rascal would comfort her.

Standing at her car, she resisted the impulse to wipe her hand hard across the cheek the lady had kissed. This was a grade-B British movie if ever she'd seen one. Seen one? Hell, she was *in* one.

She again lied: "I've had a lovely time." Brother Stevens would at least have approved of her manners.

"So did I, dear." She wished the woman would stop calling her "dear." "Until tomorrow."

Lawrence Harrington waved goodbye to his daughter and the distinguished guest she had brought to his home. Bending over a flower bed in his small front yard, he pulled stray weeds and worried that he might have dominated the conversation. Much of their talk had revolved around Western man's debt to his Greek forebears. "Particularly in literature," he had suggested. "Consider Shakespeare, O'Neill, Joyce, Faulkner. Indeed there is a continuum from Homer to Philip Roth's *Portnoy's Complaint* and on beyond."

"Certainly," Sir Charles had agreed, "though obviously our indebtedness is also reflected in architecture, government, education, mores —"

"Sculpture," Zoe had interjected.

He had smiled then pointed to the tray of cheese and fruit. "Observe, traditional fare offered guests for centuries in homes of even the simplest Greek peasants. It seems we are linked irrevocably to a past culture whose impact defies our comprehension."

Eventually he had shifted their conversation to other topics. "Tell me, Sir Charles," he'd asked, "what is your assessment of the current OPEC situation?"

Dropping the pulled weeds into a container hidden behind a wax-leaf ligustrum, he paused to squint at the afternoon sun. It was time to go inside. For the next hour or so he would take notes for the book he knew now he must write. The book was not to be, after all, a study of Euripides' fascinating women.

For four nights and five days an idea had reverberated in his head, demanding that he at least try to write about a subject which others before him had tackled — some succeeding, most failing. Undoubtedly overambitious and somewhat pretentious in scope, the book would require vast research, travel, compilation, correlation, and long hours at his typewriter. Still, the idea refused to let go: he felt compelled to explore good and evil. Both, he believed, existed. Rejecting The Fates of his beloved Greeks, he favored free will. Man he saw as basically good but his choices as sometimes questionable. Therein, he reasoned, a person brought either order or havoc — good or evil — into his life and the lives he touched. He had often admonished his students as they examined history to keep in mind that "professed well-meaning intentions are rarely acceptable excuses for catastrophic results."

He would tell only Zoe of his plan to trace the threads of good and evil interwoven throughout literature — starting with the Greeks. It was to be an overwhelming project. Perhaps he would never write his book on Euripides' ladies, for he suspected he had just secured lifetime employment under the guise of authoring one book which might well stretch into ten.

His thoughts veered sharply. Frowning, he sank into a porch rocker. His mind became a *tabula rasa* upon which a sketch was drawn.

| Good | | | Evil |
|------|---|---|------|
| Sir Charles Stanton | Zoe | | Lance Benson |

What did it mean? Zoe's name seemed caught — suspended. He rocked and nodded to Mrs. Beardsly backing her car out of the driveway that lined up evenly against his property. Literature, he mused, only reflects man's state. What was the state in which his daughter found herself?

He was being overdramatic. To be sure, Charles Stanton radiated a certain charismatic light; but Lance, though no favorite of his, did not emit darkness. Or did he? He tried to remember when he had last seen his son-in-law. It had been approximately two months ago. Still, after all these years, the left eyelid had nervously quivered and the words had slid as though greased from Benson's mouth.

He shook his head. The slate disappeared. He would have a bit more cheese, then begin work on his book. Certainly, whatever his motivations, his son-in-law's choices — marrying Zoe, building a theatre — were commendable. Lance Benson was contributing to the community; and Zoe was still with him, wasn't she? Perhaps his daughter's decision to marry this man had been right. As for himself, he had simply been reluctant to relinquish his only child to someone who had appeared out of nowhere. That was it. He was an old man holding on to an old grudge.

"I'm impressed with your father," Charles Stanton remarked as Zoe drove him back to his office.

She smiled, though she continued to look straight ahead.

"Do we really remind you of each other?"

"Definitely." She turned and smiled into his eyes.

"I was particularly intrigued with his concept of hubris. I think we all stub our toe on that tragic flaw at one time or another, don't you?"

"I'm not sure. I just know a person is bound to fail if he sets himself up as some kind of demigod." She thought of her husband and changed the subject. "Did you like my father's humor?"

"That was a pleasant surprise. I'd never before heard Odysseus described as a 'lousy navigator.' "

They both laughed.

He shifted to face her. "Now . . . it seems to me since we've established that your father is outstanding; that I'll have the portrait picked up on Thursday; that you'll come to my dinner party for Irene this Friday; that you and I are friends —"

"Such a recitation!" She was pleased but uneasy.

"It seems to me that now is the time for you to tell me what's bothering you."

"Charles." There was protest in her voice.

"Zoe." He matched her protest with insistence.

"I can't."

"Why not?"

"Because . . ." She shook her head. If she made herself vulnerable to Charles Stanton, she would end up being more miserable than she already was. She would want to call him daily; unload her problems onto his shoulders; seek his reassurances; and, finally, ultimately, run straight into his arms.

"Zoe, I'm your friend, remember?"

"I remember." She bit her lip.

"Then promise me something."

"What?"

"Suspicious, aren't you?"

She laughed. "All right, I promise. What?"

"If you need me, you'll call."

That would be easy enough to promise, for she did not intend to allow herself to have that need. "I promise," she said.

The struggle began. Lance Benson was driving his Lincoln Continental through Houston's five o'clock traffic. Caught in the teeming mass of cars pouring out of the city, he spat out the word, "Avon!" Harvey Mason lived one hell of a way from civilization. Resigned, he settled back for the hour it would take to reach what he already knew would be a squashed box of a house, with a scraggly yard and an attached garage. A barbecue grill, tricycles, beanbags, and jumping ropes would be blocking the driveway. Thank God for Zoe's inheritance. He had never had to settle, even temporarily, for life in an armpit suburb.

Glancing in the mirror at the red wig and moustache, he fancied he looked paradoxically seedy and distinguished. He loosened his tie. Walking with a slight stoop and speaking in a gravelly voice, he would become Fenton Jennings. He was rather enjoying selecting his pseudonyms. He stroked the moustache with his fingertip. "Well, get you!" he said aloud. He was aware that he was repeating what Sandra had said the first time he had appeared in a wig. She'd asked if he were Jack the Ripper. Then he had been irritated. Now he was intrigued. He imagined her beside him.

"Wait and see, you whining bitch. Just wait and see. Even complaining this morning that your precious cunt wasn't to be passed around to women. As if that were your decision." . . . He didn't want to kill her. Surely the gun would never be used. But why wouldn't she stay in line? Behave? Well, if she forced him to extremes, he would at least give her a peaceful death. He thought of the swift, sure stillness of the roach dropped into powder. Sandra Lowrey would die like a roach.

He was there. After parking his car three blocks away, he walked until he found Harvey Mason's carbon copy of all the other little clapboard houses lining the treeless street. Each seemed struggling for its own identity. Some were painted in bright colors; others were weighed down with window boxes and grillwork.

He stopped before a house with shutters, tiny crescents carved into their centers. Stepping over a tricycle, he reached the front porch and rang the bell.

A child peered from behind the screen door.

"Is your father home?"

Wordlessly the little girl ran for her parent.

A woman, perhaps in her late twenties, whose prettiness seemed dulled by exhaustion, came to the door. "Run play, Jenny," she instructed the child before letting him inside. "Harvey had to work overtime, but he said you'd be coming about the gun."

"Yes. We talked on the phone." He concealed his elation. It would be easier to deal with Mason's wife. She looked as if one strong gust of wind would topple her.

The gun lay on the coffee table. She handed it to him. He knew enough about firearms to recognize the Smith and Wesson .45 caliber automatic. He cocked its hammer. Startled, she jumped then laughed apologetically. "I'll be so glad to get rid of that thing."

"I don't blame you." He smiled sympathetically. "With small children around."

"That's it exactly!"

"As I explained to your husband, I don't care for guns myself, but I'm frequently out of town and my wife wants protection. How much are you asking?"

She hesitated. "One hundred and fifty . . . but it's like brand-new."

"Sounds fine."

She broke into a smile. He noticed a chipped tooth.

"Well, I'll just get the paper Harvey says you have to fill out. He's already signed it."

In a moment she would return with the Firearms Registration Form which he had been afraid she would have and which he had no intention of touching. Neither Harvey Mason nor he was going to register the sale of the gun.

She returned with the yellow form.

"It's not required, Mrs. Mason."

"That's what Harvey says. But he wants to mail it in anyway. Just to show he doesn't own it anymore." She looked down at the form, then up at him. "So if you'll answer a few questions."

"Like 'Have you ever been convicted of a felony?' Which I haven't. 'Have you ever been treated for a mental disorder?' Which I haven't." He focused the sapphire stare full upon her chipped tooth. She blushed. "Forms are a pain, aren't they, Mrs. Mason?"

"They sure are. Harvey goes up the wall getting all that income-tax stuff together every year."

"It seems we're of the same mind." He smiled. Again she blushed. "Why don't we forget the paperwork?"

Her eyes widened appreciably. "Oh, I don't know! Harvey's not here, and I just don't know."

He sighed as though hurt that she might have misunderstood. "Mrs. Mason, would I be here if I wanted the gun for something other than additional security for my wife — though it'll probably stay in a drawer. But you understand how some women are afraid?"

"Oh yes, that's why we got the gun in the first place, what with Harvey sometimes working the night shift."

For a moment they both were silent. His closed wallet between them.

"Look, I'll tell you what let's do."

"What?" She pushed a wisp of hair, strayed from her ponytail, out of her eyes. He was reminded briefly of Sandra.

"Simple. Give me the form, and I'll have my secretary take care of the nuisance."

Still she hesitated.

"It's all right, Mrs. Mason. I'm a lawyer."

"A lawyer?" She breathed deeply. "Then it should be all right."

"Of course."

She relinquished the form.

He opened his wallet.

"Actually, I'm a trial lawyer." He was placing bills, crisp as if freshly printed, into her palm. "So you can see why my wife imagines — though it's only her imagination — prowlers."

"Goodness, I would think so. I know I would."

"Well, it looks like we're all set." He closed his wallet, the yellow sheet folded inside replacing the bills. "You have your one hundred and fifty dollars and I have the gun for my wife. Thank you."

"Thank *you*." She had already stuffed the money into her jeans pocket.

The child named Jenny stood in the driveway silently watching as he walked across the shallow lawn. She found her voice: "Where's your car?" He never acknowledged her question. The child, he observed as he strode steadily and quickly away, was considerably smarter than her mother, who had not even bothered to ask his name.

She saw butterflies bursting from cocoons, tulips pushing through earth, sparrows peering out of shells. Ridiculous! She longed to stand barefoot in mountain streams, to climb rainbows, to run a marathon and win. Absurd! She pulled her car into the garage, then walked back down the graveled driveway for the mail. What she had was an impossible schoolgirl crush on Charles Stanton. So what if they both liked chocolate ice cream and he commanded vast oil fields and destinies of men? So what if he was a gentleman and an intelligent, sensitive human being attuned to her needs? So what? It should, and would, come to nothing. But at least, thank God, her fantasies took her mind off fear, off unanswered questions to which she must soon find answers.

She opened the mailbox. One letter was inside. Typically, efficient Caroline had promptly mailed the summary of Friday's committee meeting. Walking slowly toward the house, she opened the envelope and began reading. Abruptly she stopped. She held the paper up to the sun. She stared at the type. Dropping the envelope, she ran into the house to spread the anonymous notes alongside Caroline Fletcher's report.

She reached for the phone. Though she wasn't sure what she would say, she knew that she must speak immediately to this woman who was supposed to be her friend; this woman who beneath her professed fondness — "Zoe, dear, how are you?"; "Zoe, darling, how good to see you!" — must surely harbor a calculated desire to have Zoe Benson's brain scooped out of its skull and served on a platter. Whatever have I done to her, she wondered. What has Lance done? Where does Sandra Lowrey fit into all this? Or does she? Whatever — ever — have I done? What — ever —

The phone kept ringing. No one answered.

She made coffee then sat at her kitchen table. There had not been the slightest reason to suspect that a woman — most likely a jilted lover — had written the notes. By hiding behind the quotation "I am a man more sinn'd against than sinning," Caroline had thrown off such suspicion. Now it seemed so clear. She frowned. Again she wondered about Sandra Lowrey. Maybe Lance had dropped Caroline for Sandra. But it was the wife, not the new mistress, who was getting the threats. That made no sense. Yes . . . it made sense. Maybe. But why had Caroline typed the gala report and the notes on the same kind of paper, using the same typewriter? Did she *want* to reveal herself? If so, why in this subtle way? And why now? Because she'd gotten no results? This was all ridiculous. Fifty-year-old Caroline Fletcher was hardly Lance's type. Nor did she seem a woman who would even remotely consider having an affair. But couldn't appearances be deceiving? She ran her fingers through her hair. Nothing, absolutely nothing, made sense.

Refolding the letters and clipping them together, she decided it was just as well that Caroline hadn't answered. The confrontation should come later, when her thoughts were ordered and her words carefully measured.

Tomorrow she would call and suggest that they meet for lunch to discuss the gala. Over salad she would ask, "Why not have the theatre filled with daisies?" Over coffee she would ask, "Why, Caroline, are you threatening me?"

It was still light outside when they left their house. Wearing sunglasses, they peered at one another. Neither could see the other's eyes.

Their destination was Fleur-de-lys, a restaurant they had frequented in the early days of their marriage. Over the years, however, they had not returned to the quiet little café where violinists strolled and an iris was placed on each table.

Calling earlier, Lance had suggested what he had not suggested for some time: "Let's go out for dinner tonight."

"Tonight?"

"Tonight, so don't cook."

"I already have."

"Save it."

Now, at the Voss stoplight, he turned to her. "After Biggs's play opens, we'll go away for a weekend. Maybe New Orleans. Would you like that?"

She answered simply. "I don't believe so."

"Just think about it, OK?"

She stared out the window, across Memorial Drive, at the Racquet Club. How long since she had played tennis there? Or anywhere? She had never been good at the game, but she had tried and soon she would again because trying represented a whole other life that needed to be reclaimed.

"I can do that," she said.

"Good." He reached for her hand.

She studied his hand over hers. Tonight's display of affection could only be because her husband wished to dispel her suspicions about his having an affair with Sandra Lowrey.

She withdrew her hand and turned again to the window. They were passing Steak 'N Eggs. How often, in other years, Lance and she had hopped into their car at some ungodly hour to speed up Memorial Drive to that little building, stretched lighted and windowed on a slab of concrete, like a dining car stalled in the night. Only there could they satisfy sudden cravings for what they both deemed "the world's greatest waffles." She smiled. Back then she rarely questioned her husband's motives. Had he told her that clouds were made of oyster shells and trees of twisted coat hangers, she would have thought "How strange," but accepted his pronouncements. It had been as if she expected him at any moment to walk on water. Well, she had been a fool. But surely there existed a firm middle ground on which she could stand and accept at face value most of what he said and did. Instead, she found herself questioning every word he uttered, every move he made. When he left for the theatre, she suspected he was going elsewhere. Perhaps at one time he had gone to a now discarded Caroline Fletcher. When he appeared distracted, she imagined dark thoughts coiled in his head. When he insisted on going out for dinner, she wondered why. Why ever on a Monday night would he dismiss beef stew, already simmering, to take her to a place to which they could never really return? She knew why, didn't she? The motive was transparent.

They were there. Removing her sunglasses, she tried to open the glove compartment. Doors slammed in her head, keys jammed against metal.

"Lance, this is locked."

"Oh, is it?" There was an edge to his voice.

"Why?"

"I've got a new script in there."

"It's that important?"

"Just leave your sunglasses on the seat, Zoe." He got out of the car.

As they entered the restaurant, he linked her arm through his and commented, "You're beautiful. Surely you know that."

"Pretty, maybe. Interesting, possibly."

"Beautiful."

They were led to their table, which overlooked a courtyard, a fountain in its center. Seated, she watched the water spill from the cupped hands of a stone child.

Over the rim of her wine glass, she observed her husband's attentiveness. The evening seemed interminable. Finally, he ordered trout meunière for her and veal medallions for himself. She listened and thought wearily that now there were two locks to be opened. And the keys to both hung on a chain in Lance's pocket.

She looked down at her hands. Her fingers were laced together. Locked. She unlocked them and reached in her purse for a cigarette.

He struck a match. She leaned to the flame.

Their eyes met, and he smiled. Such cool, blue eyes, she thought. And felt sad.

"What're you thinking?"

". . . That this was a nice idea." She had given a strange mixture of lie and truth.

Later he would want to make love to her. She would be agreeable, perhaps even passionate. It had been days since they had touched. But for her the merging of their bodies would be a sham. They could no more return to making love than they could return to this place from their past.

.   .   .

Propped on pillows and sipping Perrier, she was reading *Ms.* when the ring jarred into the luxurious calm of her evening. Lately she had been on a merry-go-round of cocktail parties, sports events, and intimate little dinners with men who were, she had concluded, as chauvinistic as her soon-to-be ex-husband.

She answered the third ring.

"Roselyn?"

Her back straightened against the pillow.

"What is it, Victor?"

There was a pause, as if he were searching for the reason he had called. "Could I speak to the children?"

"No, you may not speak to the children. Do you realize it is ten-thirty at night, and they've been asleep for an hour?"

"No, I guess I didn't . . ."

"Victor, are you drunk?"

"Do I sound drunk?"

"Frankly no, but to call at this hour and ask to speak to the children . . ."

"That was an excuse."

"Oh?"

"I was just wondering how you're doing."

Roselyn Solomon reached for a cigarette. "All right. And you?"

"Fine."

She was disappointed.

"Roselyn . . . we ought to have dinner and discuss all this."

"Our lawyers are doing the discussing for us."

"You think that's right?"

"I suppose. Don explained to Scruffy about the hundred thousand — and I must say, Victor, that's a lot of money for an old plane. But it sounds like something you'd do."

"I could unbuy it."

She laughed. "That doesn't sound like you."

"I'm changing."

"Oh?"

"Does that interest you?"

"Victor, to interest me you'd practically have to have a lobotomy. And since you've called, I expect half the money when you sell that antique plane. I'm getting my life in order without you and your drinking and your — Listen, I expect to do very well.

It looks like I'm going to be on the staff of a women's magazine that's got good backing and will be published right here in Houston."

"What're you going to do, model jumpsuits for it!"

"You see, that's what I mean. You're a bastard, Victor, a real bastard. For your information, I'm going to write. If you remember, I do have a journalism degree. You do remember? No, you probably forgot that along with all the other important things, but I'm telling you — I'm warning you —"

"Roselyn, let me tell you something!"

"There is nothing you can tell me, absolutely nothing."

She slammed down the phone. The glass of Perrier toppled over. On her knees and close to tears, she dabbed at the spilled mineral water. Changed or unchanged, Victor Solomon was not going to interfere with her life. She was going through with this divorce. She was going — The phone rang again. She refused to answer. On the twenty-second ring, she picked up the receiver and said, "Yes, Victor?"

"Roselyn, now you listen to me. I've stayed sober all evening for this talk. You can do your women's lib thing. You're a fine writer. You're right, I'd forgotten. I forget a lot of things. You can do anything you want except flit around town with those studs you've latched on to."

"Now wait just a minute."

"No, you wait! You can be independent, but married to me! You hear?"

She was silent.

"Are you there?"

"I'm here."

"Well?"

"And what would you do differently?"

"Everything. I promise."

Again there was silence before Roselyn Solomon answered softly, "I wouldn't want everything changed."

"Roselyn —"

"No, don't say anything else. Let me think. And please don't call again. At least not tonight."

For a time she remained still, her eyes closed. She was remembering nineteen years ago: the ball at which she had been crowned a UT beauty and he had come up to her and said, "I'm Victor

Solomon and you're just about the prettiest girl I've ever seen."
She was remembering long walks — their arms about each other —
across the campus; the loss of her virginity in the back seat of his
Mercedes (he was the only boy she'd ever dated who owned his
own Mercedes); the beer busts at which he had drunk too much
(but then she had been only mildly irritated), the parties at which
he had flirted outrageously with other girls (but then she had been
only faintly amused). Never once had she felt threatened by either
the drinking or the other women. Not then.

She fluffed her pillows, straightened the comforter. Her thoughts
stayed on the worn path of her past. The inevitable marriage had
come. She had quickly forgotten that once she had dreamed of
scooping international spy stories, announcing Paris couture to the
world, writing of the Olympian torch burning over Garmisch-
Partenkirchen. Her ambition for a Pulitzer Prize had been replaced
by her expectation of a perfect marriage.

From the start, however, the marriage had been flawed. Liquor
and other women had never given perfection a chance. No longer
had she been mildly irritated, faintly amused. She had been outraged, humiliated. But she had kept those emotions bottled up
inside, the corners of her mouth turned up until one day the lips
refused to tilt into the frozen smile. The dam burst; the mountain
erupted. She had left Victor Solomon, whom she loved — whom
she missed even now with the same fierce passion she had brought
to their marriage. The passion had simply become fraught with
exhaustion.

She would have to think. Victor would have to change. Should
they reconcile, the children would be happy. Rebecca would stop
biting her nails; Chad's grades would improve. She would still
pursue her modest writing career, which eventually might become
more than modest. No longer would she be alone, nightly double-
checking doors and windows. She would resume making love with
her husband. In the past months she had taken three lovers. With
none had she achieved the completeness that had been hers during
the years of her marriage.

She turned out the light and lay in the dark wondering if he
was drinking now. That he had remained sober until ten-thirty at
night was indeed an indication of change in Victor Solomon.

.   .   .   .

Promptly at nine o'clock Tuesday morning Zoe Benson began debating whether or not it was too early to call Caroline Fletcher. She decided it was not; still, she hesitated. During the night she had awakened with incriminations against Caroline churning in her head. This morning, however, she was confused. Surely other homes, or offices, had elite typewriters and Eaton's bond stationery. She unloaded the dishwasher, turned on the washing machine, swept the kitchen floor, and dialed the Fletchers' number.

Caroline answered the phone.

"Good morning. It's Zoe."

"Zoe! You must have received my memo."

"I did, and it's typically thorough."

"Thank you, but we missed your ideas."

The woman sounded sincere. Innocent. Perhaps she was. Surely Lance had not taken proper Caroline Fletcher to bed? Recalling last night and his ardent efforts to arouse her, she briefly considered that his sole preference might be his own wife. No, she mustn't be a fool. She reminded herself of her husband's encounter out by the pool with the actress who had been wearing a designer dress that he had, no doubt, selected and purchased. Logically, an affair between Lance and Sandy was probable; between Lance and Caroline, improbable. If Caroline Fletcher were threatening her because of something Lance was doing and must stop doing, that something did not have to do with sex. It had to do with — what?

"Zoe?"

"I'm sorry."

"You do like the favors?"

"They're perfect."

"Good."

She had always admired the musical lilt in Caroline's voice. This morning, however, the sound grated against her nerves. She forced herself to continue. "We mentioned last week that we'd have lunch soon."

"And I said I'd love it. Let me look at my calendar."

"I thought today." Never mind that she must work in her studio. Never mind anything. She needed to look directly and immediately into the woman's eyes. That would tell her more than anything Caroline Fletcher might deny or admit.

"I can't today." The lady sounded genuinely disappointed. "I have a doctor's appointment. Routine, but nevertheless there. Let's see . . . Friday is free."

"Not before?" She realized she was pushing.

"Is Friday bad for you?"

"No, no, Friday's fine. Why don't we meet at the Confederate House — around twelve?"

"I've written it down. Now tell me how you've been — what you're painting — how's Lance? It's been ages since we've *really* talked." Caroline laughed. "But maybe we ought to wait until Friday."

"We probably should."

"That makes more sense."

The magical, but now obnoxious, lilt vibrated against her ear. "Fine," she said. "I'll see you then."

It was done. Finished. Until Friday. She went upstairs and showered. Two bright spots shone in the remainder of her day. One: her father called to thank her for bringing Sir Charles, whom he considered "remarkable," to visit him and to tell her — the excitement strong in his voice — that he had begun research for a book which he would describe to her later. Two: after five long and uninterrupted hours, she completed her portrait of David Stanton. It was, she knew, the best work she had ever done.

Irene Stanton soaked for thirty minutes in perfumed water; applied color to her age-spotted face as though she were a Flemish painter struggling in vain to create a masterpiece; combed and recombed her shampooed hair; slipped into black lace underwear, reserved always before for Bonita; tugged slenderizing slacks over her broken-veined hips; buttoned peach silk across her pendulous breasts; gave final instructions to her maid, who noted that "the old girl never looked better"; and drove breathlessly from her River Oaks home to Carrousel Square.

Sandra Lowrey dashed home from a morning rehearsal that had run overtime and quickly showered. Chewing bubble gum, she splashed on her favorite cologne (so what if Lance said it was tacky?); stepped into black bikini underpants, reserved always before for men; braided her long blond hair into a single plait; stroked a dab of Fire Ice lipstick across her mouth; and pulled jeans up over her hips and a pale blue T-shirt down over her braless breasts. She was ready. Out of breath, she collapsed on the living-room sofa. Tight in her hand was the necklace with its tiny chip diamond that Lance had given her. As if it were a rosary, she stroked the gold chain and repeated aloud, "It'll be a piece of cake, it'll be a piece of cake." Finally, she took the gum out of her mouth and clasped the necklace around her neck. For the remaining three minutes, she stared at the clock. Irene Stanton, she knew, would arrive precisely when the toy cuckoo flew out of its tiny house.

She opened the door to her afternoon guest. Within thirty minutes they discovered simultaneously that both were wearing black lace underpants.

"How did I get here?" Sandra agonized, as the older woman took command of her body in the mirrored bed. Lance's instructions became superfluous, for Irene Stanton hungrily, expertly, had taken over! Once in her ardor the lady called out a name. Vaguely, through an electrical haze, Sandy wondered who Priscilla might be. And to her absolute horror, she was allowing herself to be brought to a climax.

When finally it came her turn to do to Irene Stanton half of what had been done to her, she distastefully took the woman's bulbous, sagging breast into her mouth. At first she nibbled gingerly. Then suddenly she began tugging and sucking. She whimpered as an infant seeking milk from a mother's breast. Harder she sucked. Deeper. But there was no milk. There was no mother. There was only this frenzied lady, her back arched, her head thrown back, pushing her down, down, down, until her mouth reached that damp, dark place like her own and she thought she would vomit. She tried to return to the breast, but the lady's hand was firm on her head. Closing her eyes, she pretended that Lance's penis was full in her mouth. Lady Stanton moaned and thrashed, yet her grip remained like stone. "Brother Stevens," she silently cried, "Lance, anybody, God, dear sweet God, make the lady come!"

Drenched in perspiration, Irene Stanton finally rose from the bed. She lifted her crumpled clothes off the floor and went into the bathroom.

Sandra sank into a corner of the living-room sofa. Every bone in her body ached. Her teeth chattered. She was sure she had a fever. Perhaps she would die. She touched her broken lips. They were swollen, as though a blow had been struck across her mouth.

When Lady Stanton emerged from the bathroom, she appeared composed. "Like she's been to a garden party," Sandra thought dully.

"We must visit again."

She nodded and tried to smile. Pulling her robe about her, she padded barefooted to the door.

When the silver-gray Jaguar was out of sight, she went to the phone only to discover that Lance was in a meeting.

"Oh."

"Would you like to leave a message?"

"No . . . Yes! Yes, tell him to call Sandra."

Let him throw a tantrum about her leaving her name and unlisted number. She was sick of the shroud thrown over their relationship. She was sick of being afraid. And when somebody was sick like she was, especially if there wasn't any mother or father around, it was important to be able to turn to the person who was supposed to love you as much as you loved him.

She filled the tub with water. Surrounded by steam, she sat scrubbing her skin until it burned red. But the shame of her climax with another woman clung to her soul.

Pulling on her flour-sack nightgown, she returned to the sofa. With Rascal in her arms, she fell asleep waiting for Lance to return her call.

Irene Stanton drove eighty miles an hour on dirt roads. She had been wrong. Never would she return to the young girl, whom she suspected was not, after all, of the nature that she herself was. But why had the girl pretended to be the same? All the signals had been there. Perhaps she expected money. Reeking of dime-store cologne, Sandra had rapidly been transformed into a mockery of Priscilla. Only the hair remained the same. The sole reason then for continuing with the imposter had been her own unadulterated lust. She had bought satiation with betrayal. Betrayal of Priscilla; betrayal of her twelve-year relationship with Bonita; betrayal of her husband; betrayal of herself. What if her dead son, floating in some bodiless awareness, had observed what had gone on in that monstrous bed? Her foot pressed down. The speedometer needle shot to ninety-five.

A siren brought her to her senses. Pulling her car over, she decided she wouldn't argue.

"Lady, are you all right?" A policeman peered in through her lowered window.

"I'm fine."

"Then what's your hurry?"

She shook her head.

He inspected her driver's license. She suspected he was noting her River Oaks address.

"Suppose I follow you home?" He leaned closer. She could smell garlic on his breath.

"No! ... Just give me the ticket, please."

"You got it, ma'am!" He flipped open a pad and began writing. Handing her the innocuous-looking slip of paper, he observed, "It's like you're about to thank me."

She dropped the ticket into her purse and smiled. "You're right, officer. Thank you." It was small punishment for what she had done.

She started her car and drove slowly. After a few miles, the policeman sped past in a swirl of graveled dust. When she estimated that he was approximately ten miles away, she again eased her car over to the shoulder. There, by the side of the dirt road, she removed her slacks and peeled off her underpants. She tossed the dampened silk into an open ditch.

"I don't think you should," he said to her back. She was watering African violets.

"Martin" — she placed the small, hand-painted watering can on a table and came to perch on the arm of his chair — "I'm fine. I live a normal life now. Remember?" She smoothed his thinning hair. "I admit I need rest, but I know my limits." She returned to her violets.

"You forget we've got the Stanton dinner party that evening. And I think going out for lunch on the same day is too much."

"Surely you're not worried that I'll get fat."

He looked at her thinness. She was teasing him when he was in no mood to be teased. Not now. Not when he was being forced to use his wits after a trying day at the office. Caroline and Zoe Benson must not spend time together. What trouble, he speculated, could their luncheon bring down upon his head? Probably only a pile of granular nothing rather than the shit he anticipated. Still, the risk was there.

"We could always stay home Friday evening." He hoped she would take his suggestion as a threat.

"Not go to Charles's party for Irene! Now that's ridiculous. And so is the other."

"Caroline, please."

She left her violets and sat in the wingback chair across from him. "I'm fine, Martin. Are you?"

"What do you mean?" He stirred the olive in his martini.

"I don't know. You just seem — not quite yourself lately."

"Office tensions."

"You've always had those."

"Look, Caroline —" he stood — "I'm going to get out of this suit." He paused at the doorway. "I just don't want you to overdo, that's all."

Changing into his baggy Bermuda shorts, which offered relief from the binding three-piece suit, Martin Fletcher knew that he dare not press further. He would have to take his chances. He looked in the mirror and saw worry. He tried smiling. "Think pleasant thoughts," his wife sometimes admonished when catching him in a scowl.

He stared at his mirrored image. The lips tight together, he asked himself what possible good might result from the two women's being together. Not a single positive answer came to him.

Only as he walked down the stairs to rejoin his wife did the flash explode in his head: Zoe Benson, who had kept her mouth shut all this time, would not confide in Caroline. They were casual friends. The two women would exchange gala ideas and a few harmless intimacies. So let them have their little lunch. Encourage it. Zoe Benson would then be out of her house for approximately two hours on Friday. Perfect!

With a broad grin on his face, he hurried on down the stairs and into the sun room.

Taking needlepoint from his wife's hands, he hugged her and apologized. "I'm sorry, Caroline. It'll probably do you good to get out of the house."

She kissed his cheek, then straightened a cuff on his bright plaid Bermudas. "I promise it'll be a decidedly brief lunch."

"Oh, I think you should take all the time you want. Just plan on having a nap before we go out that evening."

"Good idea." She stood. "Now, would you like to eat inside or out?"

"Surprise me," he said. "You always arrange things perfectly."

It was to be a western barbecue. Dressed in her Sasson jeans and a white satin shirt, Roselyn Solomon sat with her children while they ate early dinner. The baby-sitter stood at the sink slicing bananas for ice-cream sundaes the children were to have after they finished their green beans and drank their milk.

The doorbell rang.

"I'll get it," Roselyn said, wondering who it might be. Cramer Jordan wasn't due for thirty minutes. Passing a mirror, she admired her new frizzed hairdo.

She opened the door.

"What have you done to your hair?"

"Updated it. What do you want?"

"To come home."

He was inside.

"I have an engagement."

"Cancel it."

"It's a little late for that, don't you think?"

Rebecca came running out of the kitchen. "Daddy, Debbie'll make you an ice-cream sundae."

"Sounds fantastic!" Victor Solomon swooped his daughter up in his arms and buried his nose in the fold of her neck. She giggled. Roselyn frowned.

"If you won't cancel, I'll baby-sit," he offered.

"Debbie's hired for the evening."

"No problem. I'll pay her double and drive her home."

"Goody!"

"Rebecca, I thought you liked Debbie."

"Not if Daddy can stay."

"Victor, see what you've done!"

"Look, Roselyn, it's harmless. We'll have sundaes, watch television —"

"Chad has homework."

"Fine. We'll do homework, then watch television, and when you get back I'll be here."

"Victor, it's going to be a late evening."

"Only if you want it to be."

"Please, Mommy."

She sighed. "All right. Just get in the kitchen, Victor, and don't come out, please, until I've gone."

Rebecca squirmed out of her father's arms.

"Roselyn, you're sure you won't cancel?"

"Positive."

"Then I'll be a spectacular baby-sitter!"

She glared at her husband. He smiled into her glare. Standing between them now, Rebecca looked from the glare to the smile. "Daddy's prettier than you are, Mommy."

Her glare softened into a smile. "This is ridiculous," she said.

"I would say so, yes. Wouldn't you say so, Rebecca?"

"Yes." She giggled.

Victor Solomon laughed one long laugh which rolled into others. In spite of herself, Roselyn joined in his laughter. Rebecca began laughing, too. She wasn't sure what it was they were laughing about; she only knew it felt good to be doubled up, her mother and father suddenly happy again. She almost called her brother to come out of the kitchen, so that the four of them could stand there laughing together.

Victor Solomon touched his sleeping wife's hair. The new frizzed styling was rather chic. He could live with it.

When she'd returned home at eleven-thirty, he had been just sober enough to talk sensibly and she had been just drunk enough to listen. He had contemplated meeting her at the door and booting Cramer Jordan straight down the Georgian steps and out into a magnolia tree. He'd relished the idea of the bastard dangling precariously from a broken limb with a blossom stuck up his ass. That would teach him not to mess around with a good friend's wife.

Restraining himself, he'd waited for Roselyn in their bedroom. When she'd entered the room, he'd risen from the chaise longue and toasted her with Perrier, which he had poured into his glass rinsed clear of scotch.

How long had they talked, he wondered. Not long enough to

smooth out all the rough-edged hurts. But long enough for him
to lead her across the room into bed. Tomorrow he would move
in permanently. He had promised to remain faithful and sober.
To be faithful presented no problem. To be sober? He would stay
as sober, he rationalized, as his thirst would permit. At any rate,
the marriage was going to work. And he had not had to make a
single confession about Benson's blackmailing him to the tune of
one hundred thousand dollars.

"Well, it's about time you got here!" She hadn't bothered to
change out of her faded nightgown.
"You look like a sack of flour."
"That's about what I feel like." She lifted the can of Lone Star
and drank deeply.
"I see you're reverting to old habits."
She wiped her mouth with the back of her hand.
"And I see you're still playing Halloween." She pulled at the
fake red moustache. He knocked her hand away.
"Lance, I'm sorry. It was just a bad, bad scene, that's all."
"I'll be the judge. Where's the cassette?"
"Right there, your majesty." She curtsied low and pointed to
the top of the television.
"And the black wig?"
"Don't know where it is."
"Repeat that, please."
"I threw it away," she lied. "Right into the dumpster." Her
hand zoomed out from her body.
He was reminded of a scarecrow flailing against wind. She top-
pled slightly. "I hate a drunk. And let me tell you something else."
He fought to keep his voice even. "That you threw away the wig
is stupid, and I don't like stupidity but it's forgivable. That you
left your name and number at my office is malicious and is not
forgivable. I don't like that. I don't like malicious people."
"Well, look who's talking! What do you think you're doing to
all those poor slobs?"
"What we're doing, Sandra, what *you and I* are doing, is not
malicious. We are simply offering pleasure in exchange for money
they'll never miss. Money you and I were not born to. They were.
And such money needs to be shared — divided up among the more
deserving."

"Sweet old Mr. Hook started out from nothing. He told me he did."

"You were not supposed to talk to 'sweet old Mr. Hook.' Your job is to keep your mouth shut and screw. Your job —"

"No!" She stamped her foot. Often as a child she had wanted to do that very thing, but she had feared Brother Stevens and Miss Traylor would think her sinful. Now, by damn, she was going to stamp her foot, hard. "No! My job is to become your wife. Did you tell her that?"

He was silent.

"Did you tell her? Did you tell her you wanted a divorce?"

"I haven't seen the footage. If you have performed in an exemplary manner, then of course I'll proceed with our agreement." He turned to leave.

"No, Lance, wait! Listen!" She stumbled over to him and held on tightly to his lapels. "Listen, let's go away now."

"There's still Hook."

"No, I mean *now*. I mean, because, listen, it took everything I had to do what I did this afternoon, and then you didn't call me back and you didn't come until now. And I sat here with this knot, this *knot*, Lance, swelling in my stomach like it was gonna push up into my lungs and burst. I mean kill me it was so bad. I was so afraid, and I needed you. I need you now and I don't like all this and I just want us to leave this place, please, please!" She tightened her grip.

He wanted to get away, to hit her as he left; he wanted to see blood spatter over white walls. He wanted, he wanted. He did the opposite of what he wanted to do. He held her.

"A little while, Sandra," he coaxed, "hold on for just a little while longer."

He started to lead her into the bedroom, but she pulled back. "No, just hold me. Hold me, please." She wished she had a rocking chair so that she could curl up in his lap and have him rock her, sing her, to sleep.

He stroked her hair. "A little while longer, Sandra. I promise."

"You promise, promise, promise? Because if you make a promise you're supposed to keep it."

"I know." He kissed the top of her head. "Now I have to go."

"No! No, goddamn it. No." She pulled away and put her hand

to her lips, still swollen from her afternoon with Irene Stanton. "Please, don't leave."

He spoke in a low voice. "You want me to see the footage, don't you?"

She shook her head.

"The sooner I see it, the sooner we can be done with this."

She stared at him solemnly then slowly she nodded and went into the kitchen. He followed to take the unopened can from her hand.

"What?" She appeared dazed. "What're you doing?"

"No more." He opened the refrigerator, removed the four remaining cans, and calmly began pouring their contents into the sink.

"Stop that!"

"You've had enough."

She struggled for her beer. "Says who? Oh, you're high and mighty, aren't you? Well, have you ever before seen me drunk?" He continued his silent pouring. "Have you?"

"I'm seeing it now."

"That's right, *now*. A little tipsy." She laughed weakly. "Whoopee!" She spun her finger in the air. "Big deal. Lance, please stop!"

He left her the final can. Temporarily she was pacified.

"Thank you." She wiped her finger across her nose. "This is my first and my last drunk. But, I tell you, I've been in one hell of a mess today waiting and waiting and waiting for you. I mean, it's after eleven o'clock and you're just now getting here!"

"I had a meeting."

"I've been scared!" She hiccuped. "And you tell me you're leaving now — to go to her —"

"To go home, Sandra, to view footage."

"Well, that's where she is, isn't she, and you're leaving me here with one lousy can of Lone Star? Well, fuck you!"

He had had enough. "That's right." He headed for the door.

Quickly she blocked his path. "You're not going to leave me, you hear!"

"Try me!" He pushed, harder than he had intended. She fell over a table, a lamp overturned.

He bent down to her. "Are you OK?"

Whimpering, she rubbed her shoulder. "You struck me."

"That was hardly a strike."

"You struck me, you struck me, you struck me." She spoke in a high singsong voice. "You struck me, yes you did, you struck me, little eyes and hands and feet unseen say and saw you struck me."

"And you," he said rising, straightening the overturned lamp, "are an obnoxious drunk. Get some sleep and I'll talk to you tomorrow. We'll move fast on Hook, and then that's it."

"You struck me, you struck me, you struck me," she continued with her song.

"All right, you're goddamn right. I struck you!" He leaned down again close into her face. "And if you don't get hold of yourself I'll do more than that!"

"Such as?" Her large green eyes looked questioningly into the ice-blue stare.

He restrained himself. "I will," he said evenly, "turn you across my knee and spank you."

She smiled.

Amazing. He had stumbled upon the key to restore order.

"Do it now," she said. "Do it now, please."

"No, but you be a good little girl, you hear? A good, good little girl."

Meekly, she nodded. "I want Rascal."

"What?"

She pointed to the sofa.

He brought the old one-eyed teddy bear to her. Then he knelt beside her. As he stroked her hair, she smiled again and lifted her face for a kiss on the cheek.

He let himself out the door. Looking back, he stared for a moment at the girl, holding her teddy bear, huddled in a corner.

Fear and bewilderment infrequently beset Lance Benson. But those two emotions were upon him now. What if Sandra Lowrey, huddled in her corner, were actually Fritz Delmar, the tenth-grade discard, come back to haunt him? What if Sandra Lowrey was crazy! Or on her way to being crazy. Where would she run to hold on to sanity — into the bright glare of the police station, or amid the harsh clatter of newspaper rooms? Only two nights ago he had thought of her as someone who, in spite of her threats, consistently came through for him. How much longer could he depend on her to do that? To perform remarkably and silently? To perform at all?

He pulled his car into his garage and sat in darkness. Slumped. Thinking. Tomorrow he would call Hook. Time was running out. The girl, not he, was beginning to call the shots.

He hit the steering wheel. Damned if that was so! He was not going to let the reins of power slip through his fingers into the hands of an idiot girl. Into the hands of a sidekick. He calmed down, sank lower, and closed his eyes.

It had been one bitch of a night. He hadn't lied to Sandra about having a meeting. For four hours he had sat hunched over Biggs's badly rewritten script. Never before had a play in his theatre balanced so precariously on the precipice of its opening. He blinked. Straightened. Christ, he was falling asleep! There was no way he could coherently critique the footage of Irene and Sandra. Instinctively he knew it was good. He would hold off the viewing until tomorrow. But there was something he must do tonight.

He entered the silent house and crept up the stairs, past his sleeping wife, on into the master bath. Quietly he opened the medicine cabinet.

Three allergy capsules remained in the bottle. He needed at least two in case one failed to accomplish his purpose. It couldn't be helped. He left Zoe a single capsule.

Avoiding familiar creaking steps, he stole back down the stairs. Carefully he pried open the capsules and shook their contents into the kitchen sink. He replaced the medication with Lightning, which had so dependably exterminated the roach. Whether or not the insecticide would work as reliably and swiftly on a human being, he didn't know. His not knowing was, indeed, one of the reasons a loaded gun lay hidden in his car.

He dropped the capsules into an envelope, which he sealed and placed in his wallet. After Hook and Sandra were successfully videotaped, he might have to go to her. "To help you sleep, darling," he would say as she swallowed the poison with water he would bring to her bed. Then he would stretch out beside her. He would wait and see.

He turned out the kitchen light. Though exhausted, he didn't want to sleep just yet, to lose awareness, consciousness. What if he dreamed of the twins, that grotesque skull expanded to join with his?

For a time, he sat in the music room. He stared into space. Through his project he had outdistanced boredom, but he had not counted on this unsettling feeling. This — what was it? "Be a little man," his mother used to order. For as long as he could remember he had hated that expression. "Be a little man." What did it mean? Be a gentleman? Be a fucking ass-hole? Why was he remembering those loathsome words? "Be a little man. Be a little man." Shit! As soon as he collected his money and got out of here, he was going to be a giant. As much of a giant as Lowell Hook had been in his youth and was even now. He was going to be that powerful. He was going to be a titan, no less, towering over midgets. Toppling deformities. But why was he always "going to be"? Going to be.

"Who's there?" Zoe, apprehension in her voice, was calling from the top of the stairs.

"Go back to bed. I'm coming up."

For a brief moment — and then the feeling was gone — he wanted his wife to hold him. She was sane and sensible and beautiful. She was his wife. Sandra Lowrey was a scrap of cloth he had used to wipe up slime. A cleaning rag soon to be thrown away. He shook his head. He must get hold of himself. There must be no dent, no chink, in his armor. Each of his victims possessed an Achilles' heel, but not he.

Standing, he thought again of Sandra clutching her teddy bear. He would be among the first to arrive at the funeral. Sorrowfully he would insist that the tattered little bear be placed beside its mistress. He walked through the scene in his mind. Damn, it would make a good movie! Caught up in the drama of what would appear to be her suicide, he felt better. He would be able to sleep now.

He climbed through the dark to bed.

She had agreed to the loan of her dearest material possession for two reasons: Barbara and Forrest Wesley were currently her most important clients, and their request, springing from Forrest's serving on the exhibits committee of the Museum of Natural History, was rooted not in personal gain but in an honest desire to mount an extraordinary display of heirlooms belonging to the city's citizens.

The eighteenth-century music box had been given to her by the Colonel when he had been dying of cancer. The gift, he'd said, was his tangible promise that, since their time together had been cut short, they would spend their next incarnation enjoying a long and happy life as simple and loving artisans. No one, not even Raymond, suspected the box's significance.

Each year, on the anniversary of the Colonel's death, the treasure was brought out of the vault. She would lift the tiny drumhead and listen to Haydn's *Toy* Symphony, her eyes misting over. She would then slip the jeweled box back into its velvet case and replace it among those items too valuable to display in the studio. On other infrequent occasions she would share its remarkable beauty with a friend. Such had been the case soon after she secured the Wesley contract. She and Barbara Wesley had become better acquainted over lunch; afterward, warm with wine and excited over their deepening friendship, she had allowed her client to see — and even hold — the magic box. The result of her impulsive act was that the box was to leave its nesting place to be ogled by thousands. But perhaps the Colonel, himself a showman, would have approved. After all, the exhibit, which was certainly praiseworthy, would be over in two months and the treasure — the tangible promise — returned.

Winifred Reese's hand was on the vault, when chaos broke loose. Henri, her little French wizard assistant, came whirling toward her. The draperies hung no more than ten minutes ago in the new presidential suite of First National Bank were swinging an unheard of three and one-half inches off the floor! Reese's Interiors could afford an occasional mistake but never one as alarming as this. Amends would have to be made immediately by no less a personage than herself. Grabbing her purse, she headed for the door, only stopping at Raymond's desk long enough to instruct him to take the music box "carefully, precious, very, very carefully" to the museum. In her haste to soothe the president's secretary, who she understood wielded more power than the executive himself, she failed to notice the panicky expression which descended and froze, mask-like, over her son's face.

.    .    .

The Tyrannosaur skeleton towered above him. Twisting his neck for a better view, Raymond wished he could will the dinosaur into life. Astride the giant lizard, he would thunder through the streets of Houston until he reached The Arch Theatre, where he would command the reptile to flatten the place like a matchbox. Benson would escape from the marble ruins only to be run down. The Tyrannosaur's bony head would ram the bastard's groin, and that would be that.

Raymond walked out of the Museum of Natural History. The music box was delivered, but the experience had cost him fully ten years of his life. He wondered if his hair had turned gray.

He had returned the two thousand dollars to a surprised Oram Balzer. "So soon?" Balzer had asked, raising his bushy eyebrows.

"So soon," Raymond had echoed, extracting additional bills from his wallet. He'd forgotten he'd have to pay a fee just to retrieve what was rightfully his. Rightfully his mother's. Christ, he'd thought, what if the little drum were now in the hands of a collector? Or worse! Burned in an arsonist's flames. Drowned amid burst water pipes.

Balzer had vanished behind a narrow door. Raymond had held his breath.

Balzer returned.

Raymond breathed.

Placing the music box on the counter between them, Balzer had lowered his voice. "You haven't changed your mind about Friday night?"

"No!" Raymond's Adam's apple had jerked above his button-down collar. "Have you?"

"Who me? Never. A deal is a deal."

Pausing now to study his reflection in the lily pond near the museum parking lot, Raymond Reese saw that his hair had survived the morning's trauma. A dull mouse-brown mop still flopped atop his head. His emotions, however, were mixed. Perhaps a rich thatch of steel gray would have made him appear mysterious, even desirable, to Melissa Stebbins, the post-debutante whom his mother had selected and who had accepted his invitation for a quiet little dinner for two tomorrow evening at the Rainbow Lodge. He hoped she liked desserts. Judging from her ample figure, he suspected that together they might gorge their way through an entire walnut pie which, with a wave of his hand, he would casually yet masterfully order.

Sir Charles Stanton stood at his window looking down thirty-three floors to mounds of new construction rising like pyramids in downtown Houston. . . . Perhaps if he took Irene away. It wouldn't be a business trip but an excursion to explore mountains and rivers — and each other. Would she like that? Last night, when he had reached for her, she had involuntarily shuddered. He had not touched her again. This morning, however, he felt renewed in his determination to help her. They could go to France, or Switzerland, or . . . Egypt. Yes, Egypt. She cherished a photograph, yellowed with age, of her maternal grandparents astride camels, the Sphinx in the background. He would suggest Egypt. Together they would pose on camels . . . He wasn't sure. Maybe Egypt was a bad idea. Her jubilance after the Bensons' party had lasted a mere two days, and then last night she had sunk again into her dark, isolated depression. She had not rallied at his suggestion that after dinner they play tennis. Instead she had sat there at the table, toying with her food, until finally she had pushed back her chair and said, "Forgive me, Charles," then gone upstairs to bed. He prayed that the surprise party on Friday would help, that his gift would work the miracle she had insisted would happen only if she had a portrait of their son.

Inadvertently he thought of the artist. The woman. How different Zoe was from Irene. How beautifully alive! And strong. Though something was obviously troubling her, Zoe Benson was like a determined little general guiding her own destiny. And yet, there was a vulnerability about her. He needed to see her.

He turned to his desk and shuffled papers. Debating. What harm would there be in at least hearing her voice? What harm in calling to verify the time a delivery van would arrive at her home tomorrow for the portrait? What harm? The debate, which had been no debate at all, was concluded.

"Charles!" She recognized his voice. "It's finished. Absolutely finished! And I can't wait for you to see it. In fact I want to deliver it myself. Is that all right?"

He hesitated. "You don't mind?"

"I have to be downtown tomorrow."

"Then you name the time."

"No, you. You're the one with the busy schedule."

He laughed. He felt better already. "Let's see. How's three o'clock? Here in my office."

"Fine."

"I'll have a porter meet you in the parking garage to carry it up. And, so that you won't be disappointed, I'll be very British and serve tea."

Lance Benson was disgusted with himself. He had been at the theatre for five hours and had not yet found the wherewithal to pick up the phone and call Lowell Hook. He was intimidated. But he couldn't back out now, not when he was so near the finish line. Not when — the childhood memories were crowding in again. Close to him now was a fifteen-year-old boy trying out for football, making the team, then the day before the big game telling the coach, "My parents don't want me to." The truth was that the boy had asked himself, "Who wants to have mashed-in guts, knocked-out teeth, and a bloody nose?" The answer had been, "Not me." Not for all the touchdowns in the world. After the lie, the boy had slunk off to a John Garfield movie. Later in the afternoon he and old Bailey had gone for a walk beside the still gray lake.

He decided to see what was happening in rehearsal. Xeroxed pages of the final rewrite had been handed out that morning. He'd snap a few pictures of the cast then develop the film tonight in his darkroom. That way he would have something to show Zoe when he emerged from viewing the footage of Irene and Sandra. Sandra!

Sitting in the last row of the darkened theatre, he watched her flitting around the stage with her feather duster. She made a damn good maid. And to think she'd wanted to play the heroine, a character of somewhat tragic dimensions. Well, he was glad she was holding together. Amazing. He'd been afraid she'd be in a straitjacket by now.

The break came. He scowled at her swaying up the aisle toward him. There was no escaping. She would find him underneath granite, on top of clouds, suspended over water. She would ferret him out to suck from his strength.

"I guess I tied one on last night, didn't I?" She groaned, holding the side of her head.

"I suggest you not do that again."

"Lord, help us all, I won't." She rolled her eyes and slurped down a coke.

"You're blowing your diet, aren't you?"

"Look, kid" — she popped the blasted gum — "this is glue to hold my insides together. I'm feeling better, but I'm still rocky. I don't like all this, but I'm a survivor. I am a survivor, and don't you forget that."

"How could I? You keep reminding me."

"You're damn right. You know, I was thinking about something you said last night. See, I wasn't so blotto I blacked out everything. You said you were born poor. Well, I didn't know that about you. I mean you never said. I got the idea you and she were born with these little silver — what do you call them? — demitasse spoons in your mouths. But, Lance, because you and I come from sort of — not exactly but sort of — the same place, that makes us, don't you see, all the more belonging together."

He wanted to kick her back up on the stage. How could he have revealed himself, even inadvertently, to someone who could not begin to comprehend the strains of royalty, in terms of rights and intelligence and talent, that coursed through his veins? She was incapable of understanding. She might be a survivor, but look how she had survived: a worm slithering in dirt.

"We'd better not talk any longer. People will be wondering."

"Lord," she rolled her eyes, "the unapproachable Mr. Benson. Why don't you put on your little red wig, sweetie, then nobody'll know it's the great Lance Benson who I'm talking to?"

"To whom, Sandra, whom."

"Who, whom, it!" She squinched her lips into a silent, puckered kiss. "I have certainly gotten hold of myself enough to finish off one more, so long as it's a man —" She switched abruptly. "How was the video? Was it — how was it?"

"I haven't seen it."

"You haven't what?"

"I'll look at it tonight. Now move, Sandra!"

"But you said you were going to —"

"Move!"

"OK. OK. But I got to tell you this one thing."

He sighed.

"I woke up this morning hung over, but thinking, 'Sure you can do one more.' One more for us, baby, one more and then —"

He stood. "Since you seem to have diarrhea of the mouth and refuse to move your ass, I will move mine, which is not nearly as distinctive." He brushed past her and walked down to front row center, where Nelson Biggs sat wringing his hands, blinking his eyes.

"Lance!" The playwright leaped up and extended a weak handshake. "The rewrite's great, don't you think?"

"It'll do, Biggs. I think we may even have ourselves a play."


Though he needed no reminder, the notation was printed in small, neat letters at the bottom of the page for Wednesday, September twenty-first: "CALL L.B.!" The exclamation point translated into "Don't procrastinate."

It was too bad that the girl had an unlisted number. Somehow it would have been easier to speak directly to her. Still, Lance Benson was a good man. Hadn't the screwing after all these years been Benson's idea? And in the two months since the young man had not asked a single favor in return.

He was tempted to hold off, but seeing the girl again had become an obsession. Since early Monday morning when the dream had awakened him, she had crowded into his thoughts during board meetings, dinners, and half-dozing naps. She was there. Everywhere. Besides, once a commitment to do something was down in his calendar, he made damn sure he followed through. Though this had been one ball-busting week — and he was only halfway through it — he was determined to screw the girl on Friday. The next day he would remain in his bed and recover. When the mayor and his wife arrived for dinner Saturday evening, he would greet them a happier man, having experienced that swelling in his loins and done something about it. What had the girl said the last time? He hadn't forgotten. "You are such a lover," she had said. He picked up the phone.

"I'm sorry. Mr. Benson's in rehearsal."

Damn, he was not accustomed to turbines remaining still, oil derricks churning air, when he pressed a button.

"Have him call me the minute he walks in his office, you understand, sweetheart?"

"Yes sir, Mr. Hook, the very first thing."

Scanning *The Wall Street Journal,* he waited for the phone to ring as if he were waiting for a gusher to spew rich dark oil over his withered flesh.

Had he been a religious man, he would have interpreted the message on his desk as a sign from God that the project had His blessing. The message had come just when his own determination was faltering! Though he didn't know what Hook wanted from him, he damn sure knew what he wanted from Hook.

Dialing Hook's number, he felt the adrenaline flowing, the pulse quickening. He was about to reel in the big one.

"Lance, how are things down at your place of business?"

"Couldn't be better, sir."

"That's what I like to hear . . . Look, I don't beat around the bush. You know that."

"Oh, I know that." He laughed, but he was perspiring.

"I've been thinking about that girl."

Christ Almighty, the fish had jumped into the boat!

"Well, as a matter of fact, sir, she's been thinking about you."

"What'd she say?"

He heard a pitiful eagerness in the old man's voice. So the giant was mortal. Somehow that was a disappointment.

"Just that — well, frankly, I think she'd like to see you again."

"You do, huh?"

"I do."

There was a pause.

"Think you could set it up?"

"Probably so. How about —"

The old man interrupted. "Friday night, eight o'clock."

Shit! There was no way he could get out of attending Charles Stanton's party on Friday. He'd have to think fast. Not only was Hook ready to move, he knew exactly when he wanted to move. It was best not to tamper with the old man's whim. He would attend the party but leave Sandra a number where he could be reached in case, God forbid, anything went wrong.

"I expect it'll be fine with her, sir, that is, if you don't need me to drive you over. I have an engagement."

Hook chuckled from deep in his throat. "Benson, the way I figure it, three would be one hell of a crowd anyway, don't you think?"

Together they laughed.

"Then you've got yourself a date."

"You can speak for her like that?"

Quickly he covered himself. "I'll check, of course — as a matter of fact, she's in the theatre now."

"Benson, you're a good man."

"I damn sure try to be," he said jokingly.

"Don't we all. Well, call me so I'll know what to count on."

"Give me twenty minutes."

"That's the kind of action I like. In thirty minutes I'm leaving for the club, so hop to it."

"Yes sir." He wanted to vomit. What was he? A caddy on a rich man's golf course? Well, shortly he would be the one wielding the stick. And, if he ordered Lowell Hook to bend down and pick up dirt, the old buzzard had just better "hop to it."

Exactly twenty minutes later Lowell Hook printed on his calendar page for Friday, September twenty-third: "8:00 P.M. — S.L." Beside Sandra's initials he scrawled in his usual florid script the word "Confirmed." For emphasis, he drew two lines beneath the word then added an exclamation point.

He wrote her address on an outdated calendar page, which he irreverently tore out of the leather book and carried for the next two and a half days in his pocket. His hand went often to the slip of paper. That simple gesture made him feel thirty years old again.

A Texas sunset greeted Victor Solomon as he walked out of the apartment building that had been his hollow home for the past three months. He threw the final load of suits into the back seat of his car. Glancing up, he observed that the sky seemed filled with cotton candy. Sunday he would take his family to the zoo. They would spread a quilt on the ground. Roselyn and he would sip lemonade and talk, while pink confection smeared sweet and sticky over their children's faces.

Wow! He had a hard-on from just observing. For a moment he was tempted to sell the videotape to a porno company. Sandra was really getting in there. Maybe she was a little queer herself. So why was the bitch upset? She'd obviously enjoyed herself. And, hell, she knew he was open-minded. Look at her going for that nipple. Some nipple! If the circumstances were different, he might seduce Lady Stanton himself. He ran the tape three times and almost masturbated. Christ Almighty! Either performance could win an Oscar. Irene Stanton would hock the family heirlooms to keep such dynamite out of circulation — meaning hand-delivery of the cassette to her husband.

After the ten o'clock evening news, Martin Fletcher hastily typed nineteen succinct words while Caroline was upstairs showering. He rolled the paper out of the typewriter and smiled.

Zoe Benson feigned sleep. And waited. Her husband lay on his back, hands folded across his chest. He began breathing deeply, evenly. One o'clock. He was asleep. She crept barefooted from the bed and lifted the chain of keys from his bureau. Then she began her slow, steady descent.

Cautiously she opened the door that led from the kitchen into the garage. She fumbled for the key to open the glove compartment of his car. The third key on the chain slid effortlessly into the lock.

Lance had lied. There was no script filling the tiny space. Only road maps and cigarette packets. Slipping her hand beneath the maps, she touched something soft. She lifted the maps and saw there a ghastly mass of red hair. Beside it was a matching moustache and another, less offensive, wig. Straight from The Arch's prop department, she decided. But why were they here?

There was something else, hidden behind the wigs. At first she wasn't sure. It looked like black rubber tubing. She pressed the object with the tip of her finger. It was cold and hard to her touch. Suddenly she knew. She lifted out the gun. Why had she never once suspected that locked in her husband's car was this hideous thing? She had considered coke, which he occasionally used. She had thought of letters from Sandra Lowrey or from some other woman. But never a gun.

Whatever was in his darkroom? What did he do in that place where tonight he had again spent long hours, emerging finally with photographs he had taken during a rehearsal: Sandra Lowrey waving a feather duster; the director, pointing authoritatively, a cigarette dangling from his lips; an actress she didn't recognize weeping copious tears. Looking at the developed photographs, she had seen nothing that warranted his spending that much time in seclusion. Perhaps he had been dissecting and cremating remains. Her imagination was running wild. Hadn't she once smelled smoke coming from that very room?

She replaced the gun and the disguises — for she knew now that was what the wigs and moustache were — beneath the road maps and cigarette packets. Then she relocked the compartment and quietly reentered her house.

She straightened and climbed the stairs.

As she passed the door to their bedroom, she asked herself how she could ever again sleep with a man she no longer knew. A man who frightened her. Who owned a hidden gun.

She groped her way up the final flight of stairs. The first key on the chain fit the lock. She turned the knob and stepped inside the forbidden room.

As fluorescent light flickered over her husband's desk, she blinked, then slowly looked around. No cadavers in gunnysacks swayed from the ceiling. No cremation urns loomed tall and sinister. Nothing was changed — except — yes, something. Why was there a television set in here — and a videocassette recorder? She had not been aware that Lance owned such expensive equipment. Had she known she would have recorded Channel Eight's "Artists at Work" series. Strange, she thought, how the mind bumps into trivia when it confronts complexities too bewildering to grasp. A desk drawer was locked. Again she fumbled with keys. And dropped them. She heard noises. Footsteps. There was no place to hide. No time to lock the door. She hurried into her studio and stood at a window, waiting, her heart pounding, as she looked down on shadowy outlines.

Overhead light shattered the darkness.

"What do you think you're doing?"

"I couldn't sleep."

"So you crawl up the stairs, through pitch-black dark, to stand at that window?"

"I needed — I *need* to think."

"You need to see a psychiatrist."

"Because I can't sleep?"

"Because you're lying!" He was towering over her now, the breath of his recent sleep strong in her nostrils.

"Why would I lie?" She fought for control.

"My keys, please." He held out his hand.

Her eyes never left his face as she dropped the keys on the floor.

"Pick them up, Zoe."

She didn't move.

"Pick them up."

The sapphire eyes remained on her, challenging her stare, as he stooped and scooped up the keys. Wordlessly he walked out of the studio. And into the darkroom.

She followed.

A pool of light shone down on his desk.

"I see you left in a hurry." He turned to her. "Well — now you know."

She waited.

"You know, my impatient little fool, what your Christmas present is." He smiled, but the left eyelid was twitching. "It was too good a bargain to pass up, so I went ahead and bought it, then hid it up here, and began locking the door. Oh, I admit I've selfishly come up from time to time to watch a few old movies I'd taped. But you couldn't allow me that one simple privacy, could you, without becoming suspicious? What did you suspect?"

She was confused. Her Christmas present. Hidden. That made sense. She thought of the gun. Was that a present, too?

"The worst," she said.

He studied her face, then smiled. "Zoe, let's display a little more trust, shall we?"

"If you'll stop acting so mysterious."

"Mysterious?"

"*Mysterious.*"

He pulled her to him. "When I was only trying to hide your present?" He kissed the top of her head. "Come on, loosen up."

She remained rigid.

He led her outside, into the hall, his hand firm on her elbow.

"I suppose," he sighed, "I should go ahead and bring the set downstairs, but I'd prefer to keep it here until Christmas."

"Why?"

"It *is* your present, Zoe."

"I see." Again they matched stares. "And I imagine Christmas morning you'll put a bow on it." She thought of the wig. "A red bow."

"Something like that. But I'll also give you something else. Now, do you suppose we could pretend this never happened?"

". . . I don't think so."

"I suggest you try."

She had pushed him to the limit, the edge of the cliff.

He bent to relock the door.

She gave another shove.

"Why do that? I mean, I know what's inside."

He didn't budge. The key turned in the lock.

He switched on the hall light. "There's no need to break our necks getting back to bed. Surely you agree with that?"

He kept asking questions; he kept smiling, but the voice and the eyes were cold. She hugged her arms to her. Her heart and her brain wouldn't fall out of her body if only she kept her arms close together and walked quickly and steadily through the glare of light. Her husband had lied to cover his fear of what she might know; she had accepted the lie to cover her fear of the man.

The master bedroom loomed as a cavern. For a moment she considered bolting. But then the mystery might not be solved, the wrong against someone out there wronging her exposed. Ideally, rectified.

She retreated to her side of the king-size bed. Before Lance stretched out in the regal straight-spined position, she heard the distinct click of metal against wood. Her husband had placed the key chain on the nightstand beside him.

It was past noon before Victor Solomon looked up from his desk and realized he had spent three hours engrossed in work. Beginning again with Roselyn had infused vitality into his professional life. He reflected upon last night's move back home. It had been good. More than good.

He closed the thick file labeled "INDIAN FESTIVAL." In the upcoming year the store would again devote the month of February to honoring a foreign country. England, Spain, and Belgium had already been recognized. Now, India. The festival would be spectacular. He visualized his store transformed into the streets of Bombay. Bazaars would house hammered brass and enameled silver; Kashmir shawls; spices, teas, and coffees; thin glass bracelets, gold filigree earrings, agate necklaces; leather-tooled books of Rabindranath Tagore's poetry and Brahmanic philosophy; wood carvings and stringed instruments; Agra rugs; indigo cotton selwars; jewel-studded turbans and hand-woven tapestries. A commissioned painting of the Taj Mahal would rise to the ceiling in the tearoom where exotic curry and a special sugar-cane dessert would be served. Dark-haired dancers would perform on the mezzanine. Throughout the store models would shimmer in gold-threaded saris. And, finally, India's consul would speak at a black-tie dinner.

This morning he had discovered that a myriad of details had been overlooked. His notes covered thirty-five legal-size pages. The entire afternoon would be spent dictating memos. These past few months he had been away, mentally nose-diving. But all that was changed.

He began projecting. Already his committee had recommended that Ireland be honored a year from now. Ireland? He stretched. Why Ireland? Why any foreign country? Why not the United States? Why not depict a particular era? Say, the forties. That time of bobby socks, angora sweaters, taffeta evening gowns — and war. The backdrop for a fashion show — he saw models in goggles — might be a World War Two plane. He would tell Roselyn that had been his sole and secret reason for his seemingly extravagant purchase. Incredible! Happiness made his mind click like a computer. He was off and running a whole year ahead of schedule. But didn't he need some reward for this extraordinary brain-work? He went to the liquor cabinet. Twelve-forty-five. Had he been at lunch he would already have downed two scotches. He poured a drink.

Stretched out on his leather sofa, he sipped and basked in his creative sunburst. He closed his eyes. Gradually his thought processes slowed, warmth flowed in his veins. Thank God, he thought through a haze, that a married man still maintains blocks of time in which he is alone to do what he pleases. What he pleased to do was drink. One scotch, maybe two, and then he would call in his secretary for dictation. Also, he needed to search the *Trade-Plane* ads. All along, from the moment Bradshaw had given him the idea, he had known that one day he must own a vintage craft.

His glass was empty. Momentarily he left the sofa. He reminded himself of the agreed-upon ritual begun last evening. Wine with dinner, no more. When he had poured his third drink, he raised his glass to his reflection in the mirrored bar.

"My last," he said aloud, "until tomorrow."

Irene Stanton hung up the phone. The taste of straw was in her mouth. She didn't know what she felt. Pleased, puzzled, repelled? She was reminded of the confusion she'd felt her last year in school when it had seemed past time to decide what one wanted to do with one's life. "Professional tennis player," she'd finally announced proudly, only to become confused again when her mother had responded, "Absurd! Proper ladies play tennis for amusement, never for money."

Well, there had been no need for either her mother's alarm or her own confusion. The war had come and, near its end, the compliant daughter had married Charles.

Seated now in her white wicker rocker, she was surrounded by lemon-yellow brightness. Yet the sun room was no longer her favorite. Sandra Lowrey should have been served lunch on scarred linoleum rather than here on fine linen. She went into the garden and felt better.

Why had Lance Benson selected her to chair — how had he put it? — "the most important committee this theatre will ever have formed"?

"Then why not my husband?" she had asked.

"Because this committee needs a woman's guidance. And if you'll have lunch with me tomorrow, I'll be more specific than I care to be over the phone."

She had thought, "Tomorrow. My birthday." There were no plans other than those she had requested. A quiet dinner at the club, just Charles and herself, and afterward dancing. She suspected her husband would give her an exquisite piece of jewelry. He was prone to such extravagance. Why not surprise him with a gift in return? She had little love for the theatre, and even less now. But should she accept this rather mysterious chairmanship, Charles would be pleased. Always before the insignificant committee work she'd done had been merely to assuage his disappointment that she did not share his artistic interests.

Strange that suddenly Lance Benson was calling her, an obvious token worker, urging, "We want you to head the most important committee this theatre has ever formed." More important than the building committee that Lowell Hook had steered eight years before? The ongoing play-selection committee? "What committee could this be? And why me?" she wondered. In spite of wanting to please her husband, she would refuse if the duties entailed contact with the actors and actresses. Sandra Lowrey must never again touch even the sleeve of her blouse, the edge of her life.

On her fifty-sixth birthday she would reach yet again for beginnings. She would somehow dredge up strength to start anew. To become a decent person and the wife her husband deserved. Conceivably this chairmanship would help.

"Tomorrow is free for lunch," she had said and noted, as if from outside her own body, that the man's choice of restaurant was superb.

She would hear him out. She would separate her shame from work for the theatre upon whose board her husband sat.

Carrying marigolds into the house, she walked with determination. Perhaps flowers would overshadow the humiliation she felt each time she entered her once-favorite room.

"You mean, while I'm buck naked playing with Methuselah's ding-dong, you're going to be at the *country* club?" Her mouth twisted into a crimson sneer. "I can see it now — you sloshing down champagne, eating a big old fat lobster; and *her,* fresh out of the beauty parlor and wearing some gorgeous little thing she just happened to pick up at Solomon's, hanging all over you." She plopped down in a chair across from him and scowled.

He counted to ten. Sandra Lowrey had inflated ideas. He should never have permitted her to enter his social circle for even one evening. And wearing a designer dress, no less! She was the hired hand, but already she saw herself as his wife.

"Have you an alternative?"

"Yeah. Tell her you want a divorce, like you promised, and take me. We can do Hook the next night."

"Hook is calling the shots, remember? As for the other," he had no trouble lying, "I've already told her."

"You did?" She straightened, then bounded for his lap, smothering his face with sloppy kisses. "What'd she say? Tell me! Every single word, every pause, every scream. Everything!" She bounced like a fat child on his knee.

"How much weight have you gained?"

"Three pounds. Don't change the subject. What'd she say?"

"Get your tonnage off me, and I'll tell you."

Playfully she stuck out her tongue then returned to her chair. "Now. What'd she say?" Like a schoolgirl, she sat erect, hands folded in her lap.

"I believe she said, 'Go to hell.' Not verbatim, but that was the gist of it. Still, I think if we bide our time —"

"Bide our time!"

"A month, Sandra. Surely you can tolerate a month. Some divorces take years. This one won't." Recalling that she viewed promises as sacred, he added, "I promise."

"OK." There was reluctance in her voice. He blew streams of smoke through her silence. "Look, Lance, about tomorrow night . . ."

"Yes?"

"I just don't like the idea of you being off somewhere like that, I mean, always before I've *known* you were easy to reach if — well, what if the camera busts right through that damn mirror or something?"

"That's absurd."

"I know, but we're in this together."

He stood. "Sandra, you have the number. I'm available if you need me. In fact, if it'll make you feel better, you may call just to touch base as soon as Hook leaves your apartment. Now" — he began guiding her to the door — "do you feel better?"

"Yeah. Yeah, I guess so. I mean, yeah, I feel lots better." She smiled.

For a moment he winced. The child with the teddy bear. The trusting little girl with the woman's body that had gotten her into such trouble. He must be tough. His goal demanded that. Still, he was not a monster. He kissed her. "Good," he said. "Very good, because you should. Everything's going to be all right, Sandra. I promise."

She nodded, then held up the slip of paper he had given her and read aloud, "529-8090."

"Precisely . . . that's where I'll be."

"Gotcha. And I'll be" — she put her hand up to her mouth and grinned —"performing superbly. Like you said I'd done with that old woman. You said I was a great actress 'cause you knew I didn't like it. Well, I hated it. But I'm an actress, and you'll see again. I'll show you just how big a star I can be. And when you see tomorrow night's footage — wow!" She rolled her eyes heavenward. "You'll be so proud of me!" She faltered. "And then that'll be it, won't it? I mean, really *it*."

"It," he repeated. "Finis."

"Then can we — I know this sounds crazy, but can we build a bonfire and burn that bed?"

"You want to do that?"

She nodded again. This time solemnly.

"Then we'll have the biggest bonfire in town."

She threw her arms around his neck. "I love you, Lance Benson. And you know what we'll do?" Her eyes danced.

"No, tell me."

"Right over that roaring flame, we'll toast these little bitty marshmallows. A whole sack of them."

"And you'll gain three more pounds." He laughed and removed her arms from about his neck. Doubts were again worming their way around the lining of his brain. His stomach felt queasy. The girl was getting to him. He had to get her out of here. Now. For some unknown but surely imbecilic reason, tears were stinging his eyes. A whole goddamn sack of marshmallows, a bonfire of twenty-one hundred dollars worth of bed. The kid had obviously hated the whole show. Zoe would never have done half of what Sandra had done for him. "Out," he said. And she was gone.

Zoe placed the portrait in the trunk of her Toyota then set out for Charles Stanton's office. Her afternoon would be full. After tea with Charles, she would visit her father. But first she must stop by the bank to deposit the check she would receive for the painting. It would seem strange to accept money from the man whom she'd dreamed about last night when finally she had fallen asleep.

Iron doors had stretched endlessly across a moor. There had been no walls or ceilings, only doors with Charles Stanton trapped behind them. Weighted with a heavy chain of keys, she had unlocked door after door. But she kept dropping the keys as she looked over her shoulder to see if the Cyclops was nearing. Though miles away, she could hear his footsteps sinking craters into earth, could see his bloodshot eye bulging from his forehead. Wearing mud-caked work boots and a long muslin skirt, she had been a turn-of-the-century peasant struggling with the keys, with the heavy doors which opened then slammed shut. She must reach Stanton, a man of undefined time and place, who was suffocating behind those doors though the fresh, clean air of the moors surrounded him. As a key twisted in the final lock, she had awakened, not knowing if she had saved either of them — Stanton from his wall-less prison; herself from the Cyclops.

She drove slowly. Trucks roared past on the freeway. One driver yelled, "Park it, lady!" Her foot pressed down on the accelerator. Her thoughts trailed in dust. Last night she had failed. Why today was she undaunted? Why more determined than ever to search the darkroom, when she was also more afraid?

While dressing this morning, she had imagined tattooed on her arm a number, signifying one of thousands. A label: Abused Wife. But where were the bruises, the blackened eyes? No matter, she felt battered. The abuse was real.

She exited off the freeway onto the downtown ramp and counted small blessings. There had been no insidious phone calls since Sunday evening. No bomb had exploded in her mailbox. Perhaps Caroline Fletcher was waiting to slip arsenic into her salad at lunch tomorrow. Perhaps she, Zoe Benson, was losing her mind. A sane abused wife kicked her husband out the door or packed her own bags and left. A sane threatened person turned to the police. Why then was she intent on staying with Lance until she had discreetly and completely unraveled the mystery? Certainly she no longer cared to live out her days with Lance Benson. To think she had wanted to have his child! And yet, he had reassured her that he had kept the door locked to hide her Christmas present. What was real? What was unreal? Maybe the threats were coming not from Caroline but from Lance himself, intent on driving her insane. No, today one simply divorced an undesirable spouse unless huge sums of money were involved. Besides, was she so undesirable? She thought of the overtures he had made to her only three nights before.

She needed to talk to someone. Though she had not wanted to trouble him, she would turn to her father.

Pulling her car into the garage, she saw an attendant waiting to carry the portrait. "Considerate, but unnecessary," she thought.

"A healthy woman without a bruise on her body could easily carry twice the weight of an oversized portrait."

Charles Stanton stared at the painting. ". . . You knew my son."
"I wish I had."
"So do I."
He turned the portrait to the wall. "Now, let's have that proper British tea I promised you."
She drank from a bone china cup, ate scones with raspberry jam, and felt safe. Their small, inconsequential talk often lapsed into silences. Between them, she sensed, existed something elusive and special.
Finally, wanting to stay, she said, "I've got to run."
"And that," he said, "is regrettable."
Leaving, she felt grateful that her fears had subsided simply from being near this man with whom there had been nothing more physical than hands touching as he thanked her for the painting.

After she had gone, Charles Stanton turned the portrait from the wall. The boy's eyes were Irene's. He moved to the window. Looking down into traffic, he contemplated reality. The reality was that he no longer wanted to live with his wife, who would no doubt stand for hours before their son's portrait and, contrary to her protestations that she would do otherwise, grieve incessantly. He no longer wanted beside him in ceremonial lines a woman with a smile masking depression. He no longer wanted to scramble about tennis courts breaking his back to match expertise. He no longer wanted to hold a frigid body only to merge into a vacuous oneness.

Well, it didn't really matter, did it, what he wanted or did not want? He picked up the phone and informed Irene that he would be home early for tennis. Soon he would take her to Egypt. He would wrap her in antique jewels. Exotic fabrics. He would buy her a new car. A spectacular set of golf clubs. He would drag her kicking and screaming from moroseness. He was thankful that an oasis existed in the desert. Seeing Zoe Benson fostered in him not weakness but strength to give to Irene what he could not give to another man's wife.

.   .   .

Ignoring the savings account she shared with her husband at Memorial Drive Bank, Zoe deposited the five-thousand-dollar check from Charles Stanton into a separate account, which she opened in her maiden name. The address she listed was the home of her childhood.

"Narcissus," he said thoughtfully in answer to his daughter's question, "Why didn't you want me to marry him?" Lawrence Harrington spread his hands as though studying the lines in his palms. "From the beginning he reminded me of Narcissus." He folded his hands. His slender fingers rose to form a steeple.

"In love with his own reflection."

"Yes."

He carried dishes from the table to the sink. She helped him. He had suggested that she call her husband to tell him she would be staying for supper, but she had said, "No. I'll stay and he may, or may not, wonder. It doesn't matter." He hadn't pressed.

"Let's go out on the porch."

They laughed for they had spoken in unison.

They sat in twin rockers. He listened to crickets. He would miss their sounds when winter came.

In darkness they rocked. She talked. Gradually his rocking stopped. He stiffened. And then he felt helpless. Once as a child Zoe had cut her leg on barbed wire. The pain had been real but easy to alleviate. He had washed out the wound and applied peroxide then salve. After the dreaded tetanus shot, he had read to her until she fell asleep.

"What will you do now?" he asked.

"I don't know."

"You must go to the police."

"I can't."

"You must."

"I have no real evidence. Notes, and a silly toy snake that I threw away. But from whom?"

"Your husband has a gun hidden in his car."

"That's not necessarily unlawful."

"Zoe, at the least I want you to pack your things and move back here. Tell him you need to think about the marriage. That you need time. Surely you can do that."

He waited through her silence. She was thinking, perhaps, that his suggestion was a possibility.

"I've considered that. I even put the check for the Stanton portrait in a savings account under my maiden name and I listed the address as here. Maybe I should . . . this weekend. By then I could have all this — intrigue — figured out."

"*Now*, Zoe. I think now. I'll go with you to get a few things, then tomorrow we'll move over most of what you'll need."

"My studio." She laughed. He heard unfamiliar bitterness. "I can't bring my studio, can I?"

"No." He laughed as well, because he sensed she needed that. "But in time you'll return to your home. It was bought, if you remember, with your inheritance."

Abruptly she stood. She leaned against a post that was entwined with dried wisteria. She pulled at fading blooms.

"I can't move out just yet," she said. ". . . The time's not right."

"You'd better consider the threats."

"I don't think they're coming from Lance."

"Zoe, for heaven's sake, they're there because of something he's doing!"

"I realize that. Still, it seems to me —" She didn't finish the sentence. Instead, she bent and kissed his cheek. "It'll be all right. Now, I've got to get home."

He walked with her to her car. Helpless. Damn helpless was what he felt.

"Look, I have an idea." She was already in her car. "When you go abroad to research your book, I'll go with you. I'll be your assistant."

"Then we'll leave tomorrow."

". . . You really want me out of there, don't you?"

"Yes, because you don't have a typical marriage gone wrong. You have something far more serious. Something neither you nor I understand. The pieces aren't fitting together. It's —" He thought often in dark mythological images. "You're caught in a labyrinth."

"That's strong imagery. Save it for your book. I'm just glad you shared it with me . . . And thank you for listening." She patted his arm; he felt patronized. For an instant he was angry with this woman, this child conceived of his flesh and blood. The anger dissolved. She had come to him, he knew, to talk, to have her father listen; but the solution, the momentum building to action must come from within herself.

He kissed her good night, then watched as she backed her Toyota out of his driveway. He wondered if Lance Benson was waiting for her at home or if even now he was speeding toward the actress Zoe had mentioned or toward some other equally questionable person.

Her mind raced as she drove slowly home. Thoughts were spiraling, darting, springing from questions to images and back again. She was reminded of the piano lessons she had taken as a child. How she had loved the pieces with the little dots above or below the notes indicating an abruptly changing rhythm. Why then did she so dislike the fact that her thoughts were coming now in staccato rather than in a smooth, thin ribbon of legato? Only staccato. Would Lance be at home when she pulled into the driveway? Why had she not thought to ask Charles Stanton which of Sandra Lowrey's performances he'd admired? Lance had used Charles's praise as his excuse for inviting Sandra to their party. But it had been Charles's wife, not Charles, who had spent almost the entire evening with the actress. She rubbed her forehead. She must remember to ask him. Surely he had not been impressed with her in *Cyrano*. But did it matter? What mattered? Narcissus: Lance staring at his own reflection, preening before his Olympian beauty, the iceberg points frozen in his pupils. How often the pupils of those eyes contracted. They would be huge luminous orbs, then suddenly pinpricks of blackness encircled in irises of clear sapphire. Never had she seen such eyes. Narcissus. She hoped he fell into the pool of his self-adoration. The image would then become as distorted as was surely his mind.

Staccato. Her bed in her father's house. The quilt, embroidered by her paternal grandmother, had remained all these years neatly squared over the mattress. Its white background matching the white iron of the bed. There were patches of little girls, sunbonnets hiding their faces as they stood with their water sprinklers over delicately stitched flowers. What would it be like to sleep again beneath that quilt? She should have stayed the night.

Staccato. Her father's pupils had been large when he spoke of his book. But had they become minute as he listened, there in the dark, while she told him more than she had intended?

She tried to think of something pleasant. Of her visit with Charles. Of Charles. No, that wouldn't do. She thought of Eddie. Why him? Why would she think now of Edwin Landrum? Maybe because she longed to snuggle beneath the patterned quilt of her childhood. Eddie had been a part of that time — both before and after she had become aware that pain and horror could seem more real than people. In spite of that experienced reality — her mother dead, half her face ripped off in the automobile accident — in spite of the pit in her stomach filling up with anguish and fear, emptying, filling up again, she had survived, somehow continuing to feel loved and protected. Eddie Landrum had contributed to that stability. They had shared wooden puzzles in kindergarten, hopscotch in grade school, hayrides in junior high, dances in high school, and an engagement in college.

Had she married Edwin Landrum she would be living now in the long, narrow, award-winning house he had designed. It was made of glass. She would be sending him off each morning to the architectural firm begun by his great-grandfather and entrusted through lineage and talent to him. To be passed on one day to Eddie's son. Or, perhaps, to one of his daughters. Had she become Eddie Landrum's wife, she would be car-pooling children. Long ago she would have filled her womb and given her breasts over to sagging so that she might thrust milk into the bird-like, trusting mouths of her babies. Where were her babies? She was a barren vessel into which birth-control pills were endlessly poured. Edwin was happy, she supposed, with Evelyn Thornton. E&E had been printed in silver across their wedding reception napkins. E&E: a contented pair. She supposed. She knew. She was glad. Last December she had spoken to the two of them during the intermission of a play. He had smiled warmly, yet impersonally, the years having erased the hurt and anger over her rejection. While he had gone for coffee, she'd stood talking with his wife. Evelyn: tall, slender, chestnut hair swinging in a page boy off her shoulders, a chic and efficient Junior League vice president. Evelyn Thornton and Zoe Harrington: cheerleaders, once, jumping and twisting and screaming. Together they had spelled out "VICTORY," neither suspecting that Eddie — "Zoe's shadow," as her college roommate once described him — would one day be Evelyn's, rather than Zoe's, husband. E&E: Evelyn had sought and pursued, asking anxiously, "Zoe, do you mind?" Fingering the small diamond given to her only the week before by Lance Benson, she had quickly replied, "Of course not. Why should I?" And truly she had not minded. Solid, reliable Edwin Landrum had set off only infinitesimal sparks in her life, whereas Lance Benson had ignited some high meteoric flame that coursed through her entire being.

Had she married her childhood sweetheart would she still have had to abandon the causes for which she'd fought throughout her school years? Probably so. Eddie had stood on the sidelines, patiently waiting for her to "settle down." Marriage to him would have been placid. Her excitement generated by children and work. Maybe that would have been enough. Certainly barring tragedy — which one could never be sure would or would not happen — she would have lived out her days as Mrs. Edwin Landrum. And it would have been a good life; not sensational, but good. Well, she was glad she had turned her back on that good, unsensational life. But why, why, dear God, had she chosen what and whom she had? Why him? Why life with him? Why had she not packed the steamer trunk at the foot of her bed and gone to study art in Paris? Her father had offered that. Why, why, why? She thought of the first time that clear, strong, sapphire stare had turned upon her; and she knew the answer.

The walnut pie remained untouched on Raymond's plate as he studied Melissa Stebbins's round face. Though not a pretty woman, she had an infectious laugh and a repertoire of witty stories which put him at ease. He had only to listen and respond, while marveling that her eyes and short curly hair were an identical shade of chocolate brown.

"Picture this," she said, finishing off her pie. "Here I am about to win the blue ribbon, I'm sure of it, and the damn nag sits down right in front of the judges' stand and rolls over. It was all I could do to hop off. Twelve-years-old and disgraced. I refused to go back to that camp." Shaking her head emphatically, she laughed at herself. "Now tell me one of your most embarrassing moments."

They were playing childhood memory games. He thought of always being chosen last for team sports in gym, of Scruffy Dawson throwing an arm around his shoulders, defending him: "This is my best friend." Raymond squirmed. "Oh, I can't think right now. Tell me another one of yours."

And she was off again. Moving on to Sweet Briar college days then beyond to the present.

"We're gearing up for our annual auction," she said, referring to her programming job at Houston's educational television station. "One man wants to donate a giraffe. Can you imagine who — even if it does benefit the station — is going to bid on *that?*"

"Maybe me," he said shyly over his lumped Adam's apple.

"You?"

"To help a lady in distress."

"My hero!"

Together they laughed. No doubt about it, this woman gave him courage in his attempt to appear as cool and debonair as Scruffy himself, or as the other one — the bastard.

Pushing aside his thought of the repulsive yet hypnotic Benson, he waited for Melissa's upcoming story. He wondered if she spun out her entertaining sagas in bed. That would be the one place he would want her to keep quiet and concentrate on him.

Some time later he called for the check. They were the last to leave the Rainbow Lodge. His mother had been right. Long ago he should have pursued some nice, refined woman who might be no raving beauty, but who was at least approachable and decent.

He gulped. "Would you — this Sunday — like to have brunch? And maybe afterwards . . . tour Bluebonnet Hill."

She smiled deeply enough for him to discover a dimple to the left of her mouth.

"I'd love it," she said. "You know, I used to go there before Mr. Hook donated the place to the city. My grandmother and he date — I guess you'd call it dating." She giggled. "They attend musicales and things like that. But mostly, I think, she does the asking."

Guiding her outside, he cupped her elbow and walked tall. A breeze stirred the skirt about her tanned, sturdy legs. He looked down and wondered. Miracle of miracles: Melissa Stebbins, who had strong, fine legs and a quick mind, had accepted a second date with him! If only tomorrow night he did not have to crouch in his mother's studio waiting to open the door to thieves. If only two months before he had pursued this sensible girl rather than fallen into the chasm where Sandra Lowrey had cost him a virtual fortune, as well as untold anguish.

Holy Jesus! Even waiting for the valet to bring the car, Melissa was launching into yet another story. Tightening his grasp on her elbow, he tried to concentrate on her tale of a woman deciding to have braces at the age of thirty-six. It was useless. There was no diverting his thoughts from the gloom and destruction which could descend upon his shoulders within the next forty-eight hours. A woman's teeth behind little wire fences. Big deal. By Saturday morning his entire body could be behind bars. He, Raymond Billingsworth Reese, could be in jail! There would be no Sunday brunch, no visit to Bluebonnet Hill.

Tipping the valet, he gave a monosyllabic "Yes" in answer to Melissa's question, "Did you wear braces in high school?"

"The inevitable fate of us all," she moaned.

Suddenly he saw before him the image of Sandra Lowrey. She was smiling, her teeth white and even. How, he wondered, had those teeth developed so perfectly without the orthodontic help taken for granted by this woman standing now beside him and by, he supposed, himself?

"Look at that," she said softly and blew a bubble so big it covered her nose, then exploded into a pink mass on her face. She pulled at the sticky goo and leaned closer to her television set. Her fingertips touched the screen, stroked Kris Kristofferson's back. She felt lonely. Her hands closed tightly around the cassette she'd made of her and Lance. If only she could hook the VCR up to her TV! What had she been thinking of? She didn't even have an instruction manual, much less the strength to haul that contraption down from the top of her bed. Still, she was glad she'd made the tape. Maybe she wouldn't wait until their first wedding anniversary to present her surprise to Lance. He'd know how to set the thing up and together, right away, they could watch themselves. Sure he already had a tape which, like a meanie, he wouldn't let her see. But that one had been made before they'd gotten to know each other — really know each other — before they'd started touching the backs of each other's souls. Her tape, she just knew, would show him all that. Maybe then he would appreciate her more.

The screen rained snow. 2:00 A.M. The world was signing off.

Her apartment got suddenly quiet. Except for the cuckoo clock ticking away in the living room. It was eerie.

She drew her legs up under her flannel nightgown and thoughtfully chewed her gum. If only her phone would ring and it would be Lance saying, "Honey, I know it's late, but I just decided . . . who needs any more money! Tomorrow night's off."

Tomorrow night, hell; it was already Friday. "Tonight . . . tonight's off," he'd have to say, if he called her this minute.

She twisted around to stare at her little pink princess phone. It didn't ring. And it wouldn't.

Slowly she blew another bubble. If she thought God had somebody else in mind for her — somebody decent and *outstanding* waiting around the bend (maybe nobody as fine as Kris Kristofferson, but somebody who was OK), somebody she couldn't see quite yet — then she wouldn't be here when old Mr. Hook showed up. He could just stand outside ringing her doorbell, letting it ring and ring, until finally he'd give up — "Nobody home" — and walk away.

But the Lord didn't have anybody else in mind. Not for her, He didn't. Lance was the one she'd prayed for and gotten. His soul touching hers.

Barely.

The bubble popped.

She would be here, where and when she was supposed to be.

Purposefully, she walked across the room. Placing the cassette back among her lingerie, she blinked and scolded herself: "Be happy, Sandra. It's almost over."

Lowell Hook lay in his silk pin-striped pajamas, his arms behind his head, as he looked across his darkened room to glass doors. The drapery was drawn back so that he could observe the soft glow of light which arched upward from the city below. His city. How right he had been to move into its center. He breathed deeply. The pain in his chest subsided. He thought of ringing Mrs. Mabry for tea but decided hot tea halfway through the night would only sharpen his wakefulness. Besides, the old girl wasn't getting any younger. She needed her sleep.

Sipping iced water poured from the thermal pitcher kept beside his bed, he considered canceling his engagement with Sandra Lowrey for tomorrow evening. This week he had pushed himself too hard and too fast. And the truth of the matter was that during the past twelve hours he had become more excited about his decision to donate funds for a new burn research center at the medical complex than he was about screwing the girl. On balance, however, he should probably keep the appointment. Perhaps he would spring from her bed as from a Fountain of Youth. But wasn't that a myth? The folklore of a brave, new country. Still, he had always enjoyed the story. In spite of its ending. A painting of Ponce de León hung in the library at Bluebonnet Hill. He wished he had brought it with him.

Tomorrow he would give his chauffeur the night off. How long had it been since Jason had had a Friday evening to do as he pleased? Informing Mrs. Mabry that he would be dining with friends, and that by no means was she to wait up for him, he would then drive himself to Sandra Lowrey's apartment, where he would suggest that she plug into her tape deck country and western music rather than the Tchaikovsky she'd played before. The classical befitted only the ethereal lady he would have cherished and married had she materialized. But she had never appeared, never come. The Sandra Lowreys of the world had had to suffice.

He placed the glass on his nightstand, crossed the room, and closed the drapery. Perhaps he could sleep now. At least he had reached a decision. He would proceed with his plans for tomorrow evening.

"Happy birthday."

"Bonita?"

"I'm sitting here, having coffee, wearing this absolutely beautiful hapi coat you brought me from China, and all of a sudden I thought, 'This is silly. Just because we've stopped — the other — is no reason for us to stop being friends.' Besides, I know it's your birthday, and I've just ordered flowers. I told the florist to write on the card 'Happiness always,' which I truly mean. Irene, I wish you and Charles the kind of happiness I seem to be finding now myself." Bonita Graves expelled a sigh. "There. In one huge rush, I've said everything."

Irene Stanton paused. She rearranged the salt and pepper shakers on the table in the breakfast alcove where she was seated. "Thank you. I'll look forward to the flowers. And yes, I agree, it's ridiculous to have things awkward between us. After all, we are neighbors. The other day Charles asked if we'd had a quarrel." She gave a short laugh. "I told him you were busy with your new man. But I am happy for you."

"And we can be friends?"

"I don't know why not." She placed the shakers on opposite sides of the table. "Now I really must run. Thank you for calling."

"Irene?"

"Yes?"

"It's not all right, is it?"

She hesitated. "Not yet, Bonita. Give me time. I really can't say any more, please." She hung up the phone. For a while she sat motionless, though she knew she should leave for her hairdresser appointment if she was to be on time for the luncheon which held such promise.

What a godsend that Lance had offered her a chairmanship so important he was unwilling to discuss it until they could meet! For she had decided. To become the wife Charles wanted, she must work — and work hard — for the arts. Surely Sandra Lowrey would not be involved. The girl was a peon.

She should hurry.

Still, she sat. She felt she was not alone. Images crowded against her: Bonita, aging — as was she — in the pink silk hapi coat, a dragon's fire flaming across her back; the young girl, Priscilla, no, Sandra Lowrey, whose hair fell like rays of sunlight below her shoulders; Priscilla, dead, the cord of her purple robe looped over the bathroom door. Priscilla, Bonita, Sandra. Standing, she accidentally knocked over a shaker. Salt streamed to the floor while she rushed from the room to set in motion the activities of Friday, September twenty-third — a day signifying for her fifty-six years spent upon this rotating, spinning planet. If only, she cursed, the damn sphere would slow down long enough for her to regain her balance.

Lance Benson toweled his face after a meticulously close shave. He reached in his closet for a navy pin-striped suit. When he greeted Irene Stanton at lunch today, he wanted to appear his authoritative best. He pushed aside, however, his white shirts. Pale blue would emphasize his blue stare, which he intended to bore with laser precision straight through her skull. He would, of course, smile during the meal. No need to arouse the suspicions of other diners. His tactics with Lady Stanton would be the same as those he had used on Martin Fletcher. Over coffee he would place the cassette on the table between them.

Behind him, Zoe sneezed. She reached into the medicine cabinet for her allergy pills. How convenient that he should be standing here, calmly buttoning his shirt, when she discovered the bottle contained a single pill. He wondered what her reaction would be if he were to inform her that the missing two resided in his wallet, the capsules filled not with Ornade but with Lightning. He selected a navy silk tie.

"Funny."

"What?"

"I could have sworn I had more pills."

"I've never known an artist who wasn't absentminded." He knotted his tie and waited.

"You're not taking them, are you?"

"You're the one with allergies, Zoe."

"I know, but this is so strange."

He stepped into his trousers. "Do you make it a practice of counting your pills?"

"No, but usually I don't get down to one."

"Maybe the maid popped a few."

"Hardly. She thinks even aspirins corrode your insides." She swallowed her pill. "It just seems strange, that's all."

"Absentminded." The tone of his voice was affectionately chiding. She responded by turning on the faucet. He slipped into his coat and tried again. "What's on your agenda today?"

Splashing water against her face, she said, "Not much. But, Lance, please get home early so we won't be late for the party."

"I've told you, Zoe, Charles Stanton is too important a board member for me to consider, even remotely, being late."

"Good point." Water splashed on the sleeve of his suit. He stepped out of the stream of attack.

"I'm leaving now."

She made no comment. He hoped she drowned in the torrent of water aimed, he suspected, more at him than at her face.

·   ·   ·

The two-lane highway rose and coiled and curved like a black snake with a yellow stripe down its back, Martin Fletcher observed, as he drove farther away from Houston, out of Harris and Fort Bend Counties and on through the gray-shingled little Texas towns, their dirt rodeo rings, Baptist steeples, cotton gins, roadside cafés, and one-pump filling stations checkering the landscape. The Brazos River charted his course as he crossed its muddy foam sometimes on smooth concrete, more often on rutted macadam bridges constructed decades before for mule-drawn wagons. On he drove past the statue erected amid live oaks in memory of a mystic believed to have been buried upside down. Sixty miles he traveled, and then he was there. He sought from a postman on foot the whereabouts of a winding dirt road which led out of West Columbia to a yellow house, high on stilts, set against swampland.

Ten minutes later he parked his car in a graveled driveway. Frazer Thompson, a ruddy, weather-stained man in his fifties, wearing faded overalls and a bright plaid shirt, greeted him with a slap on the back. He held out a box from which Martin recoiled. Thompson threw back his head and roared.

"I see more city folks do that. Look, think of this little box like Alcatraz. No snake's gonna get out of here unless you slide this bolt. Like so."

Instinctively Martin jumped.

"Hey, relax, I'm not gonna open it up. But what you've got in there, Mister, is a fine five-footer that normally would have taken quite a spell to catch, 'cept the damn critter was like waiting for me. Coiled up on a rock right outside his den. Yes sir, I just reached down with my snake stick, dropped the noose nice and easy over that sleeping dude's head, and all of a sudden I had myself one big old mean rattlesnake that didn't like it *at all*. But he's settled down in there, leastways for a while."

The wood-slatted, thick-screened box sat squat on the ground now between them. Frazer Thompson waited for his money.

Martin counted the bills into the outstretched palm, then stood back while Thompson lowered the box into the trunk of the car.

"I don't sell many single ones. Mostly I trap 'em for the biological lab at that Houston insecticide company. Powell. You know the one I'm talking about?"

"I've heard of it." A high reedy voice came from Martin's throat.

"But for them I get in my pickup and deliver. They use the venom, I 'spect in serums. Never questioned them too much about what they do with the beauties. They want all kinds. Couple of times a year I even go down close to the border for some of the ones you don't see around here. Now the zoo gets theirs from all over the world, so they don't need me. Well . . . if this one here is gonna be a pet, watch it."

"No . . . no, it's not."

Martin knew he was expected to fill the silence with an explanation of why he had driven more than fifty miles to have a five-foot rattlesnake placed in the trunk of his car. His strategy, however, had never included fabricating an explanation for his purchase. Money was all he had brought. That, he concluded, should be enough.

"Thank you. Well . . . I'll be on my way."

"It was a pleasure. Can't say that about all of them. But this one, yes sir, like I told you, the way I caught it and all. You be sure and tell your friends if they ever need a rattler, or a water moccasin — we're big on those around here — that I'm their man."

"For sure," promised Martin as he started his car to head back toward what he deemed to be civilization.

Irene Stanton was late. Beneath Flemish paintings on the wine damask walls of Aylmar's, Lance Benson sipped a Gibson and waited. He studied the faces of other diners. A few were familiar. Not that it mattered. He was often seen with one or more theatre patrons in Houston's fashionable restaurants. Anyone recognizing him would assume that this was just another business luncheon. Besides, Stanton's wife would hardly qualify as a femme fatale with whom one would be having a rendezvous. So confident was he of his reasoning that he had chosen a table rather than a booth. The scene could be played before an audience. Irene Stanton was far too composed a lady to let her prim upper lip drop even a sixteenth of an inch.

Today, in all areas he felt brazenly self-assured. He tracked three lines with his fork on white linen. His project was divided into three sections. First, the entrapment. Second, the blackmail. Third, the escape into a life where demands placed on him were to be placed there solely by himself. He would become, so to speak, captain of his own ship. It was this third segment with which he concerned himself while he waited for the lady who, he imagined, in her righteous superiority, probably thought no more of inflicting a fifteen-minute wait on him than she did of demanding that her maid stay late to polish silver. Well, he would show her. He would show them all, because his day was coming. And that day concerned him now.

He had thought that after collecting his money he would hastily flee, leaving behind his professional and marital life in ruins. With the rest of the world at his disposal, he would have no need to return to a country whose success lay more in imitating other cultures than in forging ahead. And, when it did forge ahead, look at the results: "Frontier Crude," he called it.

But now he had begun to rethink his strategy. After all, the project had progressed amazingly well. Only Sandra and the confronted victims knew that his interests lay beyond theatre, hearth, and home. To everyone else — excluding Zoe, the suspecting wife — he appeared to be an exemplary public figure. Perhaps he should, as his father used to say, "cool his heels" and remain in Houston until the season's end. He could announce in March that he would not be returning the following year. With two years remaining on his contract, he would fabricate an excuse. Probably something about poor health. The blackmailed board members would openly express regrets but staunchly support his resignation. In June he would take his hard-earned money and leave. That would be the better way. Why scurry off into the night like a common thief, when he could exit if not in glory as a revered king, at least in a small burst of recognition as a fine public servant?

Today he would inform Irene Stanton that she had exactly ten days to deliver five hundred thousand dollars. Tonight Sandra would successfully videotape her liaison with Hook. On Monday he would ring the old titan's doorbell and, with cassette in hand, demand one million dollars within the next twelve days. Fletcher's final payment was due Monday morning, and Reese's would be forthcoming on Wednesday. Things were being tied up neatly. And with a twenty-four-karat gold chain!

He frowned. There was still the problem of Sandra Lowrey. A few days ago he had almost been eager to kill her. Killings, however, could be messy. Roaches he had no trouble exterminating; but, as the time approached, he again had doubts about permanently stamping out a human being. Even if she was a troublesome broad, she had been loyal. Noisy and quarrelsome, but loyal. Perhaps he could silence her with fifty thousand dollars. That would leave him more than enough. Why be greedy? He would instruct her to resign immediately from The Arch and move to New York where he would establish theatrical contacts for her. He would assure her that at season's end he, as a divorced man, would join her. Instead, he would never see her again. With luck she would become immersed in toothpaste commercials. As for himself, he would touch down in New York just long enough to board a plane for Zurich. The gamble was that she would keep her mouth closed rather than risk destroying herself in an attempt to bring him down.

Well, he could decide later what Sandra's fate was to be. Should she persist in causing trouble, she would become her own executioner. He would merely be the instrument. If there was a God, he, Lance Benson, would be judged guiltless. But there was no God. Only the godlike. The verbal, two-legged mammals with power and money.

He moved his fork over lines lightly pressed into linen. The lines became firm. His decision was made. For the time being he would forget the shots, the passport, the plane ticket. He would bide his time. Until June.

Sipping his Gibson, he watched the maitre d' lead Irene Stanton to the table. The bitch had arrived. He was about to send her into a heat from which there would be no relief. In full public view, a moaning, arch-backed writhing would be inappropriate. And, heaven forbid, "inappropriate" was not even a word in Lady Stanton's proper British vocabulary.


He rose and kissed the lady's cheek, her face still flushed from the heat of the hair dryer, and listened to her fluttering excuse about a sudden urge to banish the gray, which had taken longer than she'd expected, and she knew it was foolish to do that anyway, but it was her birthday.

"Ah, your birthday! This calls for a celebration." He promptly ordered an impressive wine, which she sipped while calming down into her regal ladyship image.

Nibbling at an artichoke, she contributed to the small talk he sensed was frustrating her. Too proper to ask outright about the chairmanship, she was waiting — the rabbit's nose attuned to the carrot. He enjoyed an unspoken tension mounting to the climax around which his little drama was being staged.

She buttered a croissant. "Isn't it lovely that Roselyn and Victor have worked out their difficulties?"

He straightened slightly. "I didn't know that they had."

"Recently. It's infinitely better for both of them. And, of course, for the children."

"Of course." So, his timing had been perfect. The possibility of a divorce-court scandal had spurred Solomon to hand over one hundred thousand dollars with no more comment than "Get out of here, you bastard." Now if there was some way he could squeeze an extra fifty thousand out of the happily reunited husband, he would. Being a man of his word, however, he had not kept a duplicate tape. The goods had been delivered and that had been that.

He poured more wine into Lady Stanton's glass and admired her breasts pushed sedately against pale yellow Shantung. With modest pride, she informed him that it was she who had selected favors for the upcoming gala. He was aware that she was saying, as though serving in tennis, "Hit the ball, please, with some discussion of the promised chairmanship."

Instead, he spoke of Caroline Fletcher's mettle. "Chairing the gala in spite of her recent misfortune."

His eyes shifted again to Irene Stanton's chest. This time she became aware. Touching the pearls at her throat, she glanced around the room. Nervously she nodded at someone she recognized.

When coffee had been served, he slammed the ball unexpectedly into her court.

"By the way, Sandra Lowrey was sorry she couldn't join us today."

"I beg your pardon?"

"Well, I know you're fond of her."

"Fond is a bit strong. She's a pleasant girl."

"Yes, she told me you thought so."

The facade was being stripped. Disregarding formalities, she struggled to gain control of the conversation. "Perhaps we should discuss the chairmanship you mentioned." Both hands were in her lap. He imagined her clutching her Gucci purse ready, if need be, for instant flight.

"Oh, that. The concept for that particular committee fell apart."
He spread his palms, shrugged, and smiled. "Sometimes a brilliant
idea goes that way." The sapphire stare bored dead center into
her eyes. She didn't flinch.

"Then why are we having lunch? I mean — this is delightful,
Lance, but *really*." She forced a laugh. For that and the returned
stare, he admired her. The indomitable, insufferable British! He
reached in his pocket.

"There's another pressing matter." He placed the cassette,
wrapped in white tissue, on the table. "You might say, Irene, that
this is a birthday present, except for one thing. It has, my dear, a
very expensive price tag."

She reached for the cassette. Quickly he pushed it beyond her
grasp.

Leaning forward, he spoke softly. "You know, Lady Stanton,
in my opinion you're definitely one hell of a butch."

Across town another luncheon was taking place. Surrounded
by the Confederate House's portraits of yellow-sashed generals,
Zoe Benson and Caroline Fletcher exchanged pleasantries, minor
confidences, and gala suggestions. Over vichyssoise and salad the
ideas sparked. Several times Zoe had to remind herself that she
was here to extract a confession. Once admitting her guilt, Caroline
would then explain why she had written the threatening notes,
made the anonymous phone calls, sent the odious toy snake.

Over coffee Zoe began questioning her own sanity. There had
been genuine affection in Caroline's greeting. And, once seated,
they had entered into virtually nonstop conversation.

"I have a confession, Zoe."

She tensed. Here, unexpectedly — and voluntarily — it came.

"Don't look so startled. This is nothing momentous. It's just
that since the operation I have become, well, *aware* of a Power."

She was both relieved and disappointed. Caroline was referring
to her newly acquired interest in religion.

"It's a force I'm trying to tap into. To be *used* for." She laughed
self-consciously. "Do I sound like a fanatic?"

"No, no. I think — it's wonderful."

"I've been reading about religion. Various religions. We can't
ignore that there are over six hundred million Hindus in India.
We have to recognize similarities in all religions. Confucianism's

system of ethics, Buddhism's Eightfold Path, Christianity's Beatitudes." Again she became self-conscious. "I sound like a lecturer."

"No, don't apologize. It's what you believe in . . . and you want to share that."

"Yes . . . I do." Caroline Fletcher continued with her confession, so different from the one dreaded but sought. "You won't believe it, but I've even started going to church regularly. A lot of the ritual I don't relate to; but, still, my being there is a statement. Of sorts."

"I can believe it, and I admire you." She did not add that she had been brought up to find her own religion in trees and mountain streams, in faces and ideas, and honorable work. She looked down at her hands. Sometimes she felt they were permanently stained with the flesh tones of her portraits.

"I knew you'd understand. Because I've always thought of us as being somewhat alike."

She nodded. It was true. Years before Caroline had come to her door with a walnut cake and a thermos of coffee and announced, "I want to get to know you, not as the wife of the director of our theatre but as yourself." Their friendship had begun that day.

"Well . . ." Caroline glanced at her watch. "I promised Martin I'd take a nap before the party tonight. But . . ." Her eyes twinkled. "I'm going to jog a bit first. I've gotten back into that."

"Caroline?" If the question were going to be asked, the time was now.

"Yes?" The gray eyes opened wide. "Is something wrong?"

Zoe studied the eyes. And looked away. "No, I was just going to say I'm glad the four of us will be at the party tonight."

"Absolutely!" Caroline laughed her magical laugh. "And isn't Irene going to be thrilled that Charles has done this?"

Together they walked to the parking lot, Caroline summarizing the gala details they had discussed over lunch, Zoe answering once and for all the question she had asked not Caroline Fletcher but herself. The woman was innocent. Were Caroline, who was above average intelligence, her enemy, she would never have used the same typewriter to type both the notes and the committee report. More important, treachery was not in her nature. The woman was her friend as surely as she was hers.

When Lance had asked this morning, "What's on your agenda today?," her reply had been an evasive: "Not much." She could readily have said, "Lunch with Caroline." The answer would not have aroused the slightest suspicion. She was convinced there was no connection, other than that of director and board member, between her husband and this woman, who stood now no more than two feet away from her.

The question was answered. Caroline Fletcher was not the person she was seeking. She would have to look elsewhere. If only she weren't so tired. And wherever, dear God, was she supposed to look?

Willows, magnolias, and live oaks shielded the Bensons' property. Passersby rounding a curve of Memorial Drive could see no more than the slope of a gabled roof and the end of a drive leading through dense foliage. Parked deep in the driveway now was a black Buick Regal. At the back of the house, French doors were ajar. Upstairs a squat, moustachioed man stood inside the master shower stall, adhering a sheet of bond paper to the wall. After stepping out of the stall, he placed inside, where he had stood, a wood-slatted, black-screened box about the size of a filing drawer. He turned the box over on its side. Carefully, as though the slightest noise would explode the house into a mushroom cloud, he slid the container's bolt. The top fell open to become a gangplank, slanting down to the tiled floor. Without the slightest hesitation, the man slammed the shower door.

For a moment he leaned against the bathroom wall and breathed deeply. He wiped his clammy hands down his pant legs. Glancing about the room, he spied a dressing stool. "That'll do," he said aloud.

Balanced on the tiny stool, he peered over the top of the shower door. The box remained as he had left it. For ten minutes he stared. Suddenly his attention became riveted by motion inside the stall. The tip of the tail appeared first. The five-foot rattler was emerging from one confinement into another, where it would remain trapped until someone opened the door.

Quickly the man walked down the stairs and out the French doors, which twenty minutes before he had jimmied with an American Express card. He got into his car and backed out the driveway.

Martin Fletcher drove well over the speed limit away from the Bensons' house. He glanced furtively out the window. His mind raced around irrational tracks. No one must recognize him, for surely he would be suspect. He was supposed to be in his office, wasn't he? Noting the time, he estimated that Caroline and Zoe should be finishing their luncheon. Why hadn't his threats gotten through to the bastard? Why was he being forced to commit this monstrous act? He had broken into a house and left there a poisonous snake coiled in a shower stall into which the man or his wife would undoubtedly step within the next twenty-four hours. He hoped the rattler wouldn't strike. A terrified but unharmed Benson would calm a hysterical wife, steer the reptile back into its box, and read the note taped to the shower wall. This time he had written as openly as he dared. Nothing biblical or Shakespearean was contained in the terse words. Benson would rush to meet his terms. Surely at last he was in control.

But was he? Gripping the steering wheel, he wheezed out a curse. Man's very existence seemed to hinge on unanswerable questions. A Catholic church loomed ahead. He was tempted to veer into its parking lot. He would slam open the heavy doors and demand of a priest that all his whys — the whys of the universe — be answered. The car willed itself past the church. His hands relaxed on the wheel. The Valium in his desk drawer would at least dissolve this knot in the pit of his stomach. The questions senselessly circling in his head would vanish.

The Buick Regal sped on into town. Routine shuffling of paperwork suddenly seemed a blessing.

. . . One of these days I'm going to pop in for a surprise visit! I sure do like living in Houston, but I miss everybody at The Good Shepherd. Course I don't miss washing all those dishes. But I'll bet by now some rich Baptist has donated one of those brand-new industrial dishwashers you were always talking about.

When I get a real big part I'll send you tickets to come on down to Houston and see me. Maybe you can even bring along a couple of kids.

Well, rehearsal's about to start up in a few minutes, so I'll close for now.

Don't take any wooden nickels, you hear?

> Love,
> Sandra (Lowrey)

P.S. I know you're both real busy, but if you ever get a chance please drop me a line. I'm sorry I haven't kept in touch except for Christmas cards, but I'm not much of a letter writer. I sure am going to do better on that score.

"On that score and a few others," she thought, addressing the envelope to The Reverend Harmon Stevens and Miss Lela Traylor. She stretched. Actually there were ten more minutes before rehearsal resumed. The upcoming scene opened with her spilling coffee on an Oriental rug. She was supposed to slap her hands up to her face like she'd just spread leprosy over half a continent. Silly play. Stupid part. At least for a split second she would have the stage all to herself.

She guessed she should've stayed in character rather than sit backstage writing a letter. But suddenly an overwhelming urge to contact The Good Shepherd had propelled her straight to Lance's secretary. "Can I borrow something to write on?" she'd asked. A preoccupied Suzanne Porter had torn sheets from a notepad and, without looking up, handed them to her.

Realistically she could begin planning a trip back home now. In a couple of months Lance would have his divorce. He had promised her. They would be rich, she supposed, as a result of the sinful acts she had committed in that awful bed. But after tonight she could turn her back on the shame she had caused and suffered. The degradation — a word Brother Stevens had used a lot in connection with sin. Maybe she and Lance could leave this place altogether. On their way to California, or wherever they'd be heading, she'd make him stop by The Good Shepherd. That was her fondest dream. Her noblest plan. And people with such a plan needed to write home, didn't they, to say that they would be coming soon? Well, she'd written. They could be expecting her.

The Good Shepherd was not the best kind of home. But it was home. In a way, it had been like a strange country through which she'd roamed looking for her mother and father, in haylofts and behind old upright radios and sheets flapping on clotheslines, but never finding either of them. Still, the people there had been kind, the bed soft, the black-eyed peas digestible, the clothes serviceable. "Let's face it," she whispered aloud, "I miss the place."

The Good Shepherd had been the place where she'd earned her white leather Bible. Stamped in gold on its cover was her name — her beautiful name, given to her by Brother Stevens, about whom she had fantasized, then prayed to God the Father, the Son, and Holy Ghost to forgive her. She'd quickly sought a substitute upon whom to fix her adoration. The substitute, however, had turned out to be no more substantial than sawdust slipping through her fingers. Billy Pickens was a boy with a dimple in his chin and muscles which rippled beneath bronzed skin whenever he jack-knifed into the lake, where summers they'd swum among mud and grass and little silver fish. She'd gone one afternoon with Billy deep into the woods. Picking blackberries for Sunday-night cobbler had ended up with her on the ground and him on top of her, and a sharp sudden pain piercing straight through her insides. Afterward had come the guilt, and then the fear that they had started up there inside her sixteen-year-old body a living, growing organism. Strange, she'd almost wanted that. A baby, small and dependent, to be her very own. But the fear was greater than the desire. For days she'd mumbled the Lord's Prayer and questioned what would happen to the acting career upon which she'd already decided. She'd run to the bathroom repeatedly to pull down her pants and see if her period had started. Never before had she longed to have a period. She swore she would bathe her face in her own blood, so welcome would be the warm, sticky dripping between her legs. "Just come, just come, just come, damn you!" Finally, she'd awakened one morning and it had been there, the bright red stains on her sheets. She'd gotten down on her knees and prayed, "Thank you, thank you, God. I'll be good forever." And she had been good, not once thinking about Brother Stevens in that way — not even with her new awareness of what a man's thing actually looked like; she'd just pretended he didn't have one. Never again did she give Billy Pickens the time of day. She read her Bible from cover to cover. She assumed more chores than were required. She sang nursery rhymes to the younger children, poured grape juice for the Lord's Supper, polished shoes for Visitors' Day. Yes, she had been a good girl. All that time. Until Houston. Until Lance Benson.

Oh, there had been others before Lance. But they had been just good, honest men she'd turned to when she'd felt so lonely she'd thought she would die. All of them were big, muscular, and handsome, but a little too dumb and unambitious. The first one she'd met in the drugstore when he'd come in off his delivery route to buy bubble gum. They'd had that in common, and they'd had contests to see who could blow the biggest bubble. After a few months he'd left her to go back to his high-school sweetheart. She hadn't minded. A shoe salesman had come along. He'd sold her a pair of red sandals. They'd just walked out of Foley's together, him taking his coffee break. He'd taught her that sex didn't hurt and wasn't sinful. Being in bed with him had felt warm and good. And fun. Taking her little yellow birth-control pills, she'd never had to worry about that other — that other she wanted but was afraid of and didn't want to have happen except with somebody special, somebody to whom she was married. Then the mother, and the father, and the baby could all live together, sharing the same last name. The shoe salesman had moved to Omaha, where his brother lived. She hadn't cared. By then the pizza-parlor manager had appeared. She'd met him one night when she kept leaving her pizza to put quarters in a jukebox that played hits of the fifties. She'd always liked that kind of music. The new one had a water bed, a dachshund named Droops, a habit of tickling her until she wet her pants, and an attentive ear for listening to her troubles. Life with him had been fine. Fine, that is, until one day a spotlight had caught the gold in Lance Benson's hair. Encircled by light, he had stood tall and lean like Brother Stevens. Successful, brilliant, and gorgeous, he'd seemed everything she'd ever wanted. That night she told the pizza-parlor manager "adiós," nice and friendly, while the two of them sat on the edge of his water bed. Then she'd gone straight home to kneel and pray that Lance Benson would notice her. For four months nothing happened. But suddenly, when she'd seemed to be making no headway, God answered her prayers.

The way she figured it was that all the pain she was undergoing now, all the humiliation, was some kind of testing. If she could emerge from fire and brimstone unscathed, she would have proven herself. She would have become of strong mettle, deserving of her reward: happiness ever after with her prince — who admittedly was a bastard, but that was only because he'd come from a bad place in his own childhood and was stuck now with Zoe, who must be some kind of bitch — she had to be. Those were the reasons he was like he was — mean, horrible, and despicable. But that was now. When she became Mrs. Lance Benson, he would be transformed, surely, into what she'd thought he was in the beginning, when he'd stood before her in a circle of light.

"*Miss* Lowrey, would you care to join us?"

She guessed she hadn't heard when he'd called the first time. Well, the director, who was no Kazan, didn't have to be a horse's ass.

She wadded her gum neatly into its tinfoil. Shit! There wasn't time to get into character. But who cared? Not when the part was that of a nameless walk-on maid whose one glorious moment came from spilling coffee on a fake Oriental rug.

Well, soon it would all be over — maids' parts, strange bodies on top of her, loneliness. She could stand a little more. After all, tonight was the last time she would ever again sleep with anyone other than her future husband.

She sailed on stage. Too late. She'd forgotten to bring the goddamn coffeepot.

Drapery blacked out the bedroom. A damp cloth lay across Irene Stanton's forehead. Motionless in the wide bed, she had resumed her position of despair. Terror rendered her immobile. Five hundred thousand dollars. Wherever was that amount of money to be gotten without turning to her husband, the one person above all others who must never know? Shame paled her cheeks. Lance Benson and that slut had strapped her into a vise which would press against her skull until bone shattered and she became totally mad. That would be acceptable, if memory could be obliterated. He had given her ten days to deliver the money. It might as well be ten seconds. If she didn't comply, the man would no doubt carry out his threat.

"*Her Ladyship and the Actress* is a charming title, don't you think?" he'd asked, outlining his plan to sell the cassette to a porno company. "You can, of course, sue." The cold stare had stripped her naked. "Regardless, your reputation and your husband's career will be destroyed."

First would come Charles's hatred, then his desertion. How could it be otherwise? She wouldn't blame him. Hating herself, she longed to abandon her own body, so despicable did she find the flesh and blood, the appetites that had led her foolishly into the vise, pressing harder now against her temples. She should be bathing, dressing. Any minute Charles would be home. He would expect to find her radiant, ready to celebrate. She'd hoped their evening — the two of them alone over dinner, then dancing, and later in bed — would offer proof to both Charles and herself that she was becoming the wife he deserved . . . That hope had vanished.

She struggled to move. It was useless. She would plead a splitting headache. They would have soup at home. The thought of New England clam chowder, his favorite, propelled her out of bed. She leaned over the toilet bowl and vomited.

Slipping out of her robe, Zoe headed for the bathroom. When her hand was on the shower door, she changed her mind. A long hot bubble bath would revive her for the party tonight.

While water steamed into the tub, she stretched her tired muscles. She was not sure which ached more — her body or her mind. Tension had built over lunch as she sat waiting for Caroline to reveal a guilt that was not there. Afterward she had hurried to the library for an "Art in Your Environment" meeting, then to the drugstore to refill her allergy prescription, and finally to the museum bookstore to purchase a gift for Irene. The beautifully illustrated *Renaissance Games* lay wrapped in bronze tissue on the bed. She'd wanted to show the book to Lance; but when it was past six and he hadn't appeared, she'd gone ahead and wrapped it. A card waited on his bureau for his name to be scrawled, hastily no doubt, alongside hers.

With the gift and her evening bag in her lap, she sat in a straight-backed chair in the living room, smoking a cigarette, watching the minute hand of the Atmos clock, and waiting.

The back door opened.

She met him in the kitchen.

"There's no time to shower."

"I'm dressed."

"It's black tie."

He eyed the long beige lace. "So I see." He brushed past her.

She called up the stairs to a retreating back. "We're supposed to get there before Irene."

Abruptly he turned and came back down the stairs to stand three steps above her. She thought of the Cyclops in her dream.

"You know, Zoe," he spoke softly, "you are beginning to remind me of my mother, a most decided nag."

She bit her lip. This man who had waylaid her life was not going to ruin her evening.

"Just hurry," she said and returned to the living room.

Ten minutes later he reappeared, the golden hair neatly brushed, the black tie properly straight. "Let's go." He tossed the signed card into her lap.

She rose quickly and walked ahead of him into the garage.

"Amazing," she thought, "he had it perfectly timed." They would arrive approximately five minutes before Charles Stanton escorted his wife into a room filled with friends singing their birthday greetings.

Finally! She whirled out the door, a whiff of gardenia perfume left swirling in the air about him. Raymond breathed a relieved sigh.

Rarely did he lie to his mother. In this instance, however, lying had been his only recourse.

"That's even better!" she'd exclaimed, a ringed hand patting his cheek, when he'd apologized for being unable to escort her to the party because he was taking Melissa Stebbins to dinner.

"This time out near Clear Lake." He'd compounded the lie. "So don't wait up."

"I wouldn't dream of it," she'd said, her violet eyes twinkling.

Five seconds after she'd left for the Stantons' party, Raymond looked at his watch. In approximately two hours he would be aiding and abetting thieves in order to pay off another thief. The bizarre scheme indicated he was either brilliant or stupid. He wasn't sure which. Of one thing he was certain. He was desperate.

For all he knew, he could be murdered tonight. After loading their truck, Balzer's cohorts might spray him with bullets. His body probably wouldn't be discovered until morning. At least his mother, confident that he was out with Melissa, would get her rest.

Bending before an open refrigerator, he peered inside at coconut meringue pie, then closed the door. Somehow it seemed inappropriate to eat. He would play solitaire until the time came to meet his destiny head-on.

At precisely 8:00 P.M., Sandra Lowrey, wearing a tie-dyed hostess gown, hooped earrings, and bronze sandals — because she wanted to look like a casually elegant lady rather than a whore in a black negligee — opened the door to Lowell Hook, who stood

inside her front patio holding a chilled bottle of Dom Perignon
and a cattleya orchid he had lifted from an arrangement floating
in crystal on his dining-room table.

"Miss Lowrey," he said, as though they had been introduced
no more than five minutes before.

"Mr. Hook," she replied and stepped to one side of the door.

Entering, he presented her with the flower, which she pinned in
her hair.

They would be forty-five minutes late for their own party. It
couldn't be helped. The miracle was that he had gotten his wife
out of bed, dressed, down the stairs, and into the car. He was
exhausted.

"Wait here, dear, I've forgotten cigarettes." He closed the door
of the Daimler. She smiled, as if through a drug-induced haze. "Is
she taking something?" he wondered, knowing even as he wondered that there was no such medication in their house.

Charles Stanton walked purposefully through the downstairs to
a storage closet. Hidden behind boxes and trunks was the portrait.
Carefully he carried the painting of his son into the living room.
He removed its brown wrapping, then propped the portrait against
a wall. Quickly he averted his eyes.

When they returned from the party, he would bring Irene here
to this gift which caused him such pain. She had no right to insist
on her need being met while ignoring his own equally desperate
need. From now on he would avoid entering this room. For all he
cared, she could convert it into a shrine.

He felt in his pocket for the less private gift which he would
present to her among friends. The emerald necklace would enhance
her coloring, even more so now that her hair was once again a
vibrant auburn. What the dickens had possessed her to do suddenly
what months ago he had encouraged her to do? Unquestionably
she was acting strange. In one day she had both colored her hair,
which was a positive step forward, and retreated back into her
own private gloom. Seeing her with the sheet pulled over her head,
he'd almost blurted out, "Damnit, Irene, there are twenty people
waiting to shower kindness and love over you, so stop wallowing
in whatever it is you're wallowing in!" Instead, he had drawn her
bath and lifted her from the bed. When he'd slipped on his dinner
jacket, she'd asked, "For just the two of us?" Feeling hypocritical,

he'd replied, "And who is more important?" That had somehow helped. She'd even hurried a bit. But still the glazed expression shrouded her face.

Walking back through the foyer, he noticed again the exquisite flowers Bonita had sent for Irene's birthday. And yet his wife's closest friend had declined his invitation to the party. Women. They were more than he could fathom. One woman — one woman alone — seemed different. He shook his head and hurried. Tonight was pivotal. He was surrounding Irene with people she enjoyed. He was giving her the gift she had repeatedly requested over the past twelve years. If this evening failed to return to him at least a semblance of the woman he had married, perhaps a psychiatrist could succeed where he had failed.

"We're off," he said, sliding into the driver's seat.

"Wonderful." Her voice reminded him of dry, crackling leaves.

She stared straight ahead at the garage wall. Old tires, ropes, and watering cans hung there. Nothing remarkable. Still, she stared. He backed the car out the drive. The garage door came slowly down.

Inside its white-tiled prison, the reptile dozed. Occasionally the pointed head would rise from the thick brown coil, then lower again to rest on a diamond marking.

T. D. Bass swaggered down the sidewalk in front of a row of apartment buildings. He hiked his holster and shifted his five-channel scanner from one hand to the other. Friday night. HPD was gearing up. All week-end long radio calls would be coming in over his scanner, making his balls fairly ache he wanted so bad to be chasing down the live ones. Instead, for the past month he had been stuck as a security guard in a complex where he had nothing more exciting to do than tone down beer busts, run off winos, and warn guys to quit growing marijuana on their patios. If just once something really big broke in this place, he'd be first on the scene. Maybe then he'd be reconsidered for the police academy.

The calls raced on statically. The world of handcuffing crime was passing him by. Rounding a curve, he whistled softly. "Jesus!" Switching off his scanner, he walked over to the Fleetwood Brougham parked in front of a corner unit. For sure nobody around here owned this mother. He glanced at the apartment number. Eighty-eight. Figured. The good-looking broad who kept her ass tight and her nose in the air had a sugar daddy who was visiting tonight. Probably she'd recently latched on to him, for this car hadn't shown up before. He'd have remembered, waxed to perfection like it was, and custom-painted a deep English racing-green.

He walked on. Seeing that car was probably going to be his one big thrill in a long and boring evening. Resigned, he flicked on the scanner and straightened his shoulders. "Walk tall" had always been his motto. "And with a swagger." That never hurt anything.

Guests mingled in the Alcott Room as they waited for Charles Stanton to appear with his wife. Though the drinks were plentiful and the hors d'oeuvres superb, most occasionally glanced at the time and questioned why the guest of honor had not arrived.

"André does wonders. It's a coup for the club, whisking him away, like we did, from Paris," Amanda Stebbins remarked, daintily wiping pâté from a corner of her wrinkled mouth. Slightly deaf in her left ear but never admitting it, she leaned closer to Winifred Reese.

"Two evenings straight they're having dinner together," Winifred was saying. "As much as Raymond wanted to be here, he obviously wanted to see Melissa more."

"I'm delighted, but, Winifred, are you sure? Melissa stopped by my house not thirty minutes before the party on her way to the airport."

"The airport?"

"She said something about having dinner with a friend from college days. Seems he'd flown in to interview at Texas Eastern."

Winifred Reese carefully placed her daiquiri on a Chippendale table and lighted a Silver Thin. "Oh well, you know young people," she said. "Raymond probably got his dates mixed up." Exactly what, she wondered, was her son doing tonight if he was not out with Amanda Stebbins's granddaughter? Without demanding an accounting for his activities — after all, he was thirty-one years old — she would demand an accounting for the lie.

"What's that?" Amanda hated to ask, but Winifred's statement had fallen on that damn left ear. "Oh, yes," she agreed, having heard this time. "Young people are hopelessly scatterbrained."

Glancing about the room, she sighed, disappointed that her dear friend and contemporary had been unable to accompany her. She had brought along his regrets and a gift — two sterling goblets from his personal collection. His instructions were that at midnight Irene and Charles should drink from the goblets to help ensure a prosperous and happy year. "How like Lowell," the old lady thought.

Nearby, Roselyn Solomon, stunning in white silk, commented, "Tuesday we leave for Cozumel."

"In the Baron?" Lance asked, mildly interested. His eyes repeatedly shifted to the door through which Irene Stanton might or might not enter. "Perhaps she's taken to her bed," he thought, not sure whether to be dismayed or amused.

"Oh, it's always in the Baron. Sometimes I get nervous, even though Victor's an excellent pilot. The children adore going up with him. We're taking them along, you know."

"How old are your children?" He stifled a yawn. References to children invariably bored him.

"Five and eight," Victor Solomon answered, joining them. "Roselyn, Harriet Clements is asking about shops in Cozumel, so why don't you fill her in?"

"That I can certainly do."

"Unfortunately, you speak the truth."

"Women are an expensive necessity, aren't they, Victor?"

"Oh, Lance, you're as bad as my husband! Male chauvinists, both of you. But Victor's doing better." She touched his cheek and noted approvingly the Perrier with a twist of lime he was distastefully but willingly nursing. "Now if you'll excuse me, I'll go chat with one of my kind."

When she was beyond hearing, her husband spoke softly yet distinctly: "Benson, I don't like bastards talking to my wife."

"Surely, Victor, you don't think I'd spoil your reunion?" Lance took a sip of his scotch. "As I told you, I'm a man of my word."

"Stay that way." Victor Solomon walked away. He had decided to trade in his Perrier for scotch. Roselyn wouldn't deny him one drink. After all, this was a celebration, even if the guest of honor was nowhere to be seen.

Caroline Fletcher stopped him midway to the bar. Silently he cursed, but listened to the astute lady's reaction to the store's upcoming festival.

"Vic, I've just heard from Roselyn you're doing India this year. I think that's wonderful. But I have a request. Please stock your book department with lots of Eastern philosophy."

"We'll do that, especially for you, Caroline." God, he thought, it's easy to be charming.

"I'm honored." She bowed her head, accepting his mild flirtation. "Seriously, the library at the Jung Center has an excellent selection, but I've just about exhausted it."

He smiled. "Persuade ole Martin to buy you a few saris to go along with the books."

"I'll do that," she promised, remembering her fantasy of only the week before. Swathed in lavender, she had journeyed with her husband through the mystical East. Unconsciously her hand went to the breast which was not there. She turned to other guests. Victor continued down his path to the bar.

Martin Fletcher searched Zoe Benson's face. The shower door had not been opened. Why else would she be standing here, her ballerina back straight and unbroken, her smile radiant, as she told him that he and Caroline must come to dinner soon? His eyes shifted to her husband conversing with Herman Mallory, the heart surgeon who had recently operated on an Arabian sheik or some such honored personage. Short of leaving the party, he did not intend to acknowledge Benson's presence. When next they spoke it would be after that shower door had been opened and Benson came running to meet his demands.

"I'm lying," thought Zoe. "I won't be asking Martin and Caroline to dinner soon. Not when I'm about to move back to my father's house." She changed the subject. "Caroline tells me you're going to build a retreat up near Austin. Such beautiful country. The hills and all."

"Oh, that's not for some time. But we'll definitely build."

As Martin Fletcher rambled on, Zoe became aware that he was perspiring heavily. "Is he sick?" she wondered. She looked closer, forgetting to listen. His eyes kept shifting as he gulped his martini. Recalling that it was she who had come over to him, she thought, "It's as if he doesn't want to talk to me." His face blurred. She saw before her the memo from Caroline and the notes from her unknown assailant. She saw the identical bond stationery, the identical elite type. She saw something else — a package label. Its type was pica. Perhaps the label had been typed on an office typewriter. She studied Martin Fletcher. Perspiring, nervously shifting from one foot to the other, he was not as she had ever before seen him. She glanced across the room at her husband. If she could place them side by side, line them up like toy soldiers in combat, then perhaps she would know what now she only suspected.

"Martin" — she interrupted his florid description of historical sites surrounding Austin — "you've got to hear Lance's personal testimony about your new insecticide. He did an experiment with Lightning that was absolutely astounding."

In one gulp he finished off his martini. "It's potent, all right. Look, Caroline is signaling. I suspect she wants to be rescued from Amanda. Shouting at that deaf ear gets to be a strain." He was gone.

So Martin Fletcher no more wanted to speak to her husband than he had wanted to talk with her. She sipped white wine and tried to imagine short, balding Martin Fletcher, fussy as an old maid, as her enemy. Somehow it didn't compute. Unless — unless Lance had driven this mild, gentle man to desperation.

People began singing. She turned quickly and saw Irene Stanton's hand go to the pearls at her throat. A frightened look crossed her face. "She's not pleased," Zoe thought and hurried to give her a hug.

Irene's body was rigid. "How are you, Zoe?" she asked coldly, then moved on to Marion Martinique, wife of the museum curator.

"What's wrong? What have I done?" Zoe wondered, running her fingers through her hair. For a moment she worried that Irene sensed and resented her closeness to Charles. Her eyes met Charles Stanton's stare.

"I misjudged," he said. "Obviously my wife doesn't like surprises."

"Charles, she's overwhelmed, that's all."

"You're probably right." He studied his wife as she responded, stiff-backed and proper, to congratulatory remarks. He wished he had left her staring at the garage wall. He moved closer to the woman in soft, beige lace, who seemed softness itself.

"You are so lovely."

"This sounds strange: but so are you."

"Well, Charles" — Lance stepped between them — "for a while there we wondered if the honored guest had skipped the country."

"No, Lance, just detained."

Voices rose to a higher pitch. A golf champion spoke to a horticulturist about a tournament in Palm Springs; a patent attorney marveled at the phenomena of Astroturf and Xerox in the company of the wife of the British consul and a gynecologist noted for jogging ten miles daily; Winifred Reese discussed eighteenth-century writing tables with Victor Solomon, who was downing his third drink, while Roselyn Solomon, pretending not to notice, exclaimed to Caroline Fletcher that after the Cozumel trip she would be writing professionally.

Dinner was announced. Guests moved toward circular tables spread with pale green organdy and decorated with larkspur and roses. After finding her place card, Irene Stanton excused herself. For a time she hovered in a stall of the ladies' room. When she emerged, her head was lifted. Clutching a lace handkerchief, she reentered the room and walked to her appointed place. The dinner partner to her left rose to seat her. "Surprised?" he whispered, leaning close to her ear.

Placing her napkin in her lap, she replied, "Under the circumstances, Mr. Benson, devastatingly so." Sitting quite still, she watched her friends and enemy rise to toast her on the evening of her fifty-sixth birthday.

He crouched in the dark waiting, the back-door lock smashed with the hammer he had held in his gloved hand. The alarm box's intricate wiring dangled to the floor as if someone had silenced a warning with one swift, disemboweling thrust.

From across the street a neon sign flashed fluorescent blue into the studio. Outside cars passed on wet pavement. Rain had come suddenly and as suddenly stopped.

The slightest noise made Raymond's spine straighten. His ears strained toward catastrophe. His bones ached from being immobile. Should he move, the entire Houston police force would descend upon him. Twice he thought he heard a truck pull into the back alley. Twice he was disappointed but, at the same time, relieved.

At twelve minutes past ten, two men with stockings distorting their faces — "like *Clockwork Orange*," Raymond thought — appeared in silhouette against the single window in back of the store. Raymond jerked upward. His arm had gone to sleep. Violently he shook it and lurched for the door.

"Reese?" A guttural voice came from behind the stocking of the taller man. His short, barrel-chested partner remained silent.

"You're from Balzer?" Raymond squeaked. His throat was raw from the incessant lumping of his Adam's apple.

"Correct. Now let's move it out."

"I — I expect the fifty thousand first."

"After the truck is loaded. Understand?"

Wordlessly he nodded.

The tall man unfolded a sheet of paper. "OK, I'll call; you point; and we'll do the rest."

Raymond recognized the itemized list that Balzer had requested.

"Tudor armchair."

Raymond pointed. The burly man swung into action.

"Florentine mantel."

"Louis Fourteenth marquetry bureau."

With each item called, most surprisingly correctly pronounced, Raymond pointed and the burly man, or both he and his leader, heaved.

Through the rain, which had begun again, heirlooms, strapped to a dolly, rolled out of the store and up into the truck.

Within thirty minutes the job was completed. Bills were counted into Raymond's palm. The short man slammed the truck door and padlocked it. The tall one waited in the driver's seat. When both were inside the cab, the truck slowly backed out the alleyway and disappeared. Rain began coming down in bucket-loads.

The roar of *La Mer* crashed impressionistically upon the old man's eardrums. He rode the high fierce waves, his balance precarious as the surf smashed against his body. The young woman was riding him as he was riding the waves. He struggled to gain control, to mount her. But she was the stronger; she retained her dominant position until she became the sea itself. Her mighty cunt snapping, sucking, tightening over his throbbing penis. He would drown. His arms flailed, his temples pounded, his heart beat wildly against the unrelenting rage of the sea, against the tenacious sucking up of his body. From far off a storm was swirling in; he would be swept into its vortex. His fingers dug into the mound of flesh, the firm, dry land. Moisture, seepage, torrents of water flung him further into the depths. The storm rose from within himself; his heart would burst with the pressure, the crescendo, the cymbals crashing, the engulfment coming. "God, oh God!" he cried. As the waves thundered over him, he called upon Zeus.

The salad fork bearing hearts of palm to his mouth never reached its destination. The maitre d' bent down to him. "There's a call for you, Mr. Benson. If you'd like, you may take it in the manager's office."

"Thank you." Excusing himself, he left the room and strode purposefully down a long corridor leading to the empty office.

Though he had encouraged Sandra to call after Hook had left her apartment, he felt uneasy. What if something had gone wrong? He had stopped by earlier to insert the cassette and to give her the reassurance she seemed to need constantly. "Break a leg," he'd said, finally leaving her and the video equipment in operable condition — "raring to go," as she'd put it, after he'd pumped an inordinate amount of confidence into her shallow brain.

Surely his apprehension was unfounded. He would hear only elation now that the ordeal was over, the bubble gum popping, no doubt, into his ear, as she proclaimed that she'd just given the greatest performance of her career.

"Finished?" He spoke lightly into the phone.

"Lance, get over here fast! Right away. I mean — *hurry!* You've got to —"

"Hold it!" Alarm sirens screeched in his head. "What's wrong?"

"He's dead."

"What in the hell are you talking about?"

"He's not breathing. He's dead! I can't stand it. I gotta get out of here. You told me everything would be OK, and he's dead!"

"For God's sakes, calm down! Now . . . what happened?"

"We were in bed, everything was fine. The video was going, we were at it, and he had a heart attack. Oh God, it was awful! I'm leaving. I can't stay here!"

"You're sure he's dead?"

"Yes! He's right here beside me, for Christ's sakes! Oh God, I almost called an ambulance. But I thought no, you'd know what to do. I don't know — maybe I should get help. Maybe he's alive. There's a security guard here. Maybe I can call —"

"Stop! You did the right thing."

"I don't know, I just don't know. I don't —"

"*Sandra, you did the right thing!* Now, sit tight. Don't call anybody. Don't do anything. I'll be right there."

"Promise? You've got to promise!"

"You're goddamn right I promise!"

"He put down the phone and muttered, "Christ!" For a moment he stared into space; then abruptly he turned and spun into action.

"Zoe," he said quietly to his wife, whom he'd beckoned to from the doorway of the Alcott Room, "Biggs is bombed out of his skull and threatening suicide. I've got to get to him."

"I didn't know he had a drinking problem — just a writing one."

"Your humor is misplaced."

"I'm sorry. Can I help?"

"Yes. Without being specific, express my apologies for leaving early and have someone drive you home."

"Of course."

"Good. I'm leaving now."

"Lance?"

"Yes?" Impatience was strong in his voice.

"Your fabrications are extraordinary."

He left without comment.

Waiting for the valet to bring his car, he attempted to light a cigarette. His hands were shaking. He threw the cigarette and charred match into the shrubbery. Lowell Hook dead. Impossible. Not the seemingly omnipotent man whom he'd once called Zeus. Where in the hell was the valet? Hadn't his order been to "rush it"? He stepped back closer against the building. The rain was coming down in sheets.

He would have to think fast. If he could think at all. He only hoped the broad, who had apparently fucked Lowell Hook to his death, was doing exactly what he'd told her to do, which was to sit tight and do nothing. He should have instructed her to hold her breath, then maybe by the time he got there she'd have keeled over alongside the old man.

Rain beat against his car as Lance Benson sped across town. Thoughts pummeled his brain. There were no heirs apparent — no blood relative for him to blackmail into preserving Lowell Hook's respected name. The old man's estate would be dissipated by the museum, symphony, theatre, and medical center. How the hell did one blackmail inanimate organizations? The million dollars he'd planned to collect might just as well be put underground with the deceased.

Rage tightened his muscles as he neared Sandra's apartment. How dare she? How dare she forget to turn on the video that first evening when Hook, panting like a schoolboy, had come to her? How dare she stupidly ignore the symptoms of a heart attack? How dare she fall apart now when composure was imperative? From its inception, Sandra Lowrey had been the weak link in his otherwise infallible plan.

His car skidded through a stoplight. He cursed. His foot eased on the accelerator as he fought to control his rage. Suppose, miraculously, Hook was still alive? With his own breath, he would pump additional life into the old man's body and keep it there. Suddenly he formulated a simplistic but immediate objective. He would accept reality as it existed in Sandra's apartment and proceed on the basis of that reality.

The complex appeared dimly through the rain. He steered his Continental into a parking space beside the old man's Fleetwood. Why not be obvious? After all, he had been summoned by Lowell Hook's mistress — who happened to be an Arch employee — to rush Mr. Hook, if need be, to the hospital.

Quickly he unlocked the glove compartment of his car and slipped the loaded gun into his pocket. Working the surgical gloves down over his fingers, he reasoned that he was as prepared as anyone could be for whatever situation awaited him.

He was coming. She had to hold on to the knowledge that Lance would be here soon. Lance who had caused all of this. Lance whom she wished she'd never met. No, she mustn't think like that. She had to trust him, to believe he would make everything right. Though the connection was dead between them, she still gripped the phone. Finally, she turned to face the old man. Had he stirred; was he in a different position? "Please, please, dear God," she prayed, "let him live!" He had brought her an orchid, poured champagne for her, talked to her as if they had been on a date, until she'd felt comfortable, until she had willingly, though guiltily, taken his hand and led him to the bed — that hideous contraption she would soon send up in flames. How she wished she had played the country and western music he had requested rather than that awful classical junk Lance had already set up. The cymbals had crashed into their eardrums until Lowell Hook's heart had burst. She hadn't done that, had she? Not she. The music had killed him. Lance had killed him. "Please, dear God, not me," she wailed and pushed her head against the sunken chest. There was no sound. No movement. She wanted to shake him, to cry out, "Live, damn you!" Instead, she covered his naked body with the sheet, neatly tucking its edges about his shoulders. He was so frail. Jabbing her fist into her mouth, she fled into the living room to crouch in a corner, her teeth chattering, her body shaking. If Lance didn't bring the old man back to life, she would tear at the bastard, calling him "Murderer!," clawing at his face until there was blood. She would run into the street screaming that a terrible wrong had been committed. Afterward, she would crawl on her hands and knees to the altar at The Good Shepherd and beg for forgiveness, Brother Stevens's palm cool on her head — that is, if he would touch her, touch the sin oozing out of her pores, staining her skin, dripping blackness onto the chapel's deep crimson carpet. If only her teeth would stop chattering, if only she could stop shaking. It was so cold. If only Lance would get here. If only, if only . . . tonight had never happened.

She ran for her teddy bear, her eyes shifting to the bed then quickly away. He hadn't moved. "He's just asleep, that's all," she said aloud. "Asleep." Standing on tiptoe, she grabbed Rascal from the top of the closet.

Fearfully, clutching the tattered bear, she hurried to crouch again, waiting, in her corner.

The key turned in the lock. She rushed to the door.

"Where is he?"

"In there! Oh, Lance, you've got to —"

"Has he moved?"

"Nothing. He's dead. I know he's dead!"

Clutching Rascal, she watched as he bent over the old man. Prying open the shriveled lips, he sent deep rushes of air out of his own lungs into the gaping mouth.

"What're you doing?"

Ignoring her, he pushed gulp after gulp of air into the old man's mouth. Five times he stopped then stooped again to his task. Finally, he began pounding his fists on the narrow chest.

"You'll hurt him! Stop it. You'll —"

"Shut up!"

At last, his arms hanging loosely at his sides, his breath coming in short quick gasps, he stood looking down at the dead man.

"It's no use."

"What do you mean?"

"I mean what I said. You fucked him to death."

"What do you mean, I fucked him to death? I did what you told me to do. He's not dead! You were supposed to fix it!"

"You don't 'fix' death, Sandra!"

"You were supposed to!"

"*You* were not supposed to let him die. But your stupidity. Your —"

"Stop it. I'm not stupid. Or maybe I am stupid. But I'm not a murderer. You are. You're a goddamn fucking murderer, and he was so kind. He brought me champagne, he brought me an orchid — you never brought me anything like that, not even a dandelion. Just this stupid necklace — *that's* what's stupid!" She tore the chain from her neck and threw it at his face. The hard little diamond struck his nose. He didn't flinch.

She stared into his eyes, her hand to her mouth. Then, still holding Rascal, she moved to fling lingerie from a drawer.

"What do you think you're doing?"

"This — you see this?"

He was over to her fast, reaching for the cassette she was waving above her head.

"It's you and me, you bastard! See, I'm not so dumb?"

He gripped her wrist. Rascal flew across the room. She wanted to go to him, but she stayed where she was and bit hard, deep, into Lance's hand.

"Bitch!" He released her. But quickly he was reaching out again.

"Oh, no, you don't!" She darted into the living room. "This one's mine. It's you and me." She was screaming louder now. "And I'm the one who's going to show the world a thing or two. Tell everybody what you did. Tell — no, Lance, don't, please, please, don't —"

The cassette fell to the floor. He bent to claim it.

She leaned against a wall. Whimpering, rubbing her arm.

"Now, Sandra, I want you calm." His left eyelid was twitching
like crazy.

Like crazy. Crazy, crazy, crazy. The words beat against her skull.
She stared at the red marks on her arm.

"Oh, God, I'm so scared," she whispered. And then her head
lifted, her eyes widened as she looked, horrified, at this man whom
she'd once wanted to marry. "You didn't fix it. You made it
worse . . . I gotta get out of here!" She headed for the door.

But the fist closed again around her wrist.

"You're *hurting* me!" she cried as he dragged her through the
living room on into the kitchen. "You've got gloves on! Why are
you wearing goddamn fucking gloves?"

"There's a dead man in there!"

"Let me go! I gotta get out of here!"

"Shut up, Sandra!"

"No, no, no!" Her head swung back and forth, back and forth.
"Killer, killer, killer!"

"Listen to me!"

"No!"

With his free hand, he held a glass under the faucet.

"What're you doing?"

"What does it look like? Trying to calm you down. *Help* you.
Listen, I was wrong."

"You're admitting it? The murderer admits it!" She began laughing hysterically. "The great Lance Benson made a mistake. Big,
big mistake."

"All right! I admit it! . . . And you're not stupid."

She stopped laughing.

"You're smart."

". . . Why? You tell me why! Because I've got that tape?"

"No, Sandra, *I've* got the tape. But I admire your spunk for
making it. Your intelligence. Now . . ." He released her and opened
his wallet. "I want you to take this."

She stared at the tiny blue and white capsule.

"It's a tranquilizer. I take them occasionally myself."

For a moment she hesitated, then she began shaking her head
again. She turned and ran back into the bedroom. She had decided.
He could keep the tape. She would get Rascal and leave.

Quickly he was behind her. "I said, *take this*, Sandra." He pried open her fingers and placed the capsule in her palm. "We're in this together. I know what's best." He spoke softly, coaxingly. "You're smart. Very smart. But you've been through a lot. You can sleep. You won't have to think."

Again she hesitated.

"And while you're sleeping, I'll do the thinking."

Her head snapped back.

"No!" She flung the capsule across the room. The glass spun out of his hand. "No! I'm sick of your thinking. You're not going to dump his body in some lake. That's what you'll do, I know it. But I won't let you — I'll tell first! He deserves a fine Christian burial. *And he's going to get one!*"

"Listen to me!"

"No! Not ever again!"

The force of his slap sent her sprawling across the dead man. Breathing hard into her face, he bent over her, his expression strange, like she'd never seen before.

"You want to go to prison?"

"No! But that dear kind man is dead!"

"And for that you could get twenty years to life. Plus you're a blackmailer! You want to become an old woman rotting in jail?"

"What about you!"

"Think about yourself!"

"I gotta get out of here!" She struggled to free herself, but she was locked in iron. Arching her back, she summoned all the strength in her body and sat up to begin clawing, screaming, "You killed him, you killed him, you killed —"

With one thrust of his hand, the pillow smashed down over her face, pushing her back against Hook. A front tooth loosened; blood trickled into her throat; the pillow dug deeper. She gasped for air, but the pillow kept grinding; the cartilage in her nose snapped. Her arms waved; he let them wave. She couldn't speak; she couldn't breathe. Twice she tried to tell him she was sorry, he knew best, she would be a good girl, she would obey him, if only he would give her, please, please, give her air.

He had committed what he considered to be the unpardonable sin: he had lost control. Momentarily he had become one of "them." The unreasonable people. Balanced on a thin line, he had toppled over into that enemy camp where, in a fit of passion, he had killed Sandra Lowrey. Perhaps he would have killed her anyway. After all, he had offered her the capsule and there was a loaded gun in his pocket. But killing Sandra should have been the result of his coolly deciding that her death was logical and desirable. Looking down at the broken nose, the lifeless body, he knew that he should have soothed her, led her into delivering a beguiling public statement. "He was a wonderful man. I've loved him for years, and I'm grief-stricken. I feel like a widow," she would have confessed. They could have pulled it off. For surely he could have seduced her again into doing whatever he wanted. But no! Like a stupid fool, he'd lost all reason when she'd produced that tape then started raving about Christian burials, about telling people. And she'd kept calling him a murderer, which he most certainly was not. At least he hadn't been until five minutes ago.

Sandra dead. Christ Almighty, he had killed her! If only he could relive the past hour. She would still be alive. Under his direction, she would have performed. Sandra would have jumped through the burning hoop. Well, there wasn't time for remorse. There was only time, and not much of it, to save his own hide. At least he wouldn't have to listen to her hysterical babbling ever again. Never! The finality frightened him. Nor was there time to think about that. He lifted her from Hook's body. Two of them. That made the whole thing possible. He stripped off her robe and tossed it to the floor. She lay naked now beside the old man.

He felt his reasoning powers returning as he smeared blood from her mangled face onto Hook. Lowell Hook had killed his mistress. Her blood should be on his hands. He'd hit her, then smothered her with a pillow, but the strain had overtaxed his heart. He had died instantly beside the woman he'd murdered. Logical. Plausible.

On his knees, he ran his gloved fingertips over the plush carpeting. The necklace was easy to find, but where was the capsule she'd hurled across the room? After ten minutes he stood, deciding to resume the search later.

Standing on a chair, he lifted the camera and video recorder from the board which hung, camouflaged by the mirror, over the canopied bed. Next he unhooked the remote control from the back of the headboard.

Loading the video equipment into the trunk of his car, he was thankful for the blinding rain, thankful that it was a Friday night when most of the complex's occupants were away, probably draped over bars. He closed the trunk and dashed back through the downpour into the apartment.

With a clean cloth he'd found in a kitchen drawer, he spent twenty minutes meticulously wiping surfaces. Counters, glasses, lamps, doorknobs, tables, faucets — anything on which an incriminating fingerprint might have been left from his afternoon visit. He was aware that Sandra's prints were also being removed from her own apartment. It couldn't be helped.

Again he bent to the floor. Where had the fucking pill landed? Beneath the chest, inside the open closet? He gave up the search. No one, he reasoned, would be going over the place with a fine-tooth-comb. Blatant evidence pointed to a lover having killed his mistress. Homicide had an open-and-shut case. There would be no cause for him to become involved, other than as Sandra Lowrey's former employer. Should he be questioned, his answer would be definite: "I make it a practice never to pry into the private lives of employees."

He glanced at his watch. Eleven-fifteen. He'd better get home. His excuse for leaving the Stanton party would be that he had become ill. Granted, he'd told Zoe he was going to Biggs, but he had cautioned her to avoid being specific. No one — and certainly no one as dense as Biggs — must become involved in his alibi. As for the call he had received during dinner, he was completely mystified. When he'd picked up the phone, there had been only the dial tone. He had gone directly from the phone into the men's room, where he had thrown up. "Probably something I'd eaten earlier in the day," he'd say if it came to that; then he'd elaborate, "I'd mentioned to my wife, as we were driving to the party, that I didn't feel well. She can verify that, of course." And she damn sure better.

He'd have to rush now to reach home before Zoe. He needed to lock the video equipment and gun in his darkroom until he could properly dispose of them.

From the bedroom doorway, he looked back at the two figures. Lowell Hook and Sandra Lowrey. Christ, he'd never intended his brilliant plan, which suddenly did not seem brilliant at all, to come to this.

He flipped off the living-room light and left.

The rain had stopped. Headlights from a passing car flashed into his face. He froze in the glare. Far down the row of apartment buildings, a man, probably a security guard making his rounds, was slowly coming toward him.

He slid behind the wheel of his car. Suddenly reversing his decision, he returned the gun to the glove compartment. After the events of the past hour, he didn't dare lock the automatic in his darkroom. It was possible, though God forbid not probable, that he would have future need of the weapon. He backed out and drove away. With luck, he would be in bed when Zoe arrived home.

"It's like a wedding cake," Irene Stanton thought as she blew out the candles, then stepped aside for the waiter to slice through the scrolled icing. Soon she would be freed from the net drawing her tightly to these people whom she scarcely knew, who knew her not at all, though they were joined together by that illusive word "friend."

She unwrapped her gifts. The book from Zoe and Lance Benson she vowed to toss into the trash can. The one blessing of the evening was that Lance had left the party. Perhaps the phone call that had sent him away had been from some other desperate victim. She willed the blackmailer to his death. Her problem would then vanish. But would it? The cassette would remain, waiting to be discovered, among his possessions.

Her smile hardened as the emerald necklace was clasped about her neck. She had hoped for a portrait of their son. But Charles's gift, while disappointingly predictable, was exquisite. Their eyes looked beyond each other as she and her husband toasted another year with champagne from the goblets given by Lowell Hook.

At twelve-ten the guests began to leave. Victor and Roselyn Solomon were among the first. She was not surprised. Victor's words had become increasingly slurred, while Roselyn's lips had narrowed as though a slit had been slashed into her lovely face.

Soon she could chip the frozen smile from her own mouth. Thanking the departing guests, she loosened her hold on the lace handkerchief, wadded now into a damp little ball. Amanda Stebbins fluttered an ivory fan and exclaimed, "An incredible evening!" The Alcott Room emptied. The party was over. She turned to thank her husband; instead what she said was, "Let's leave."

She wanted only to hurry home and again pull the sheet over her head.

They were taking her home. These two people — one she trusted, the other she viewed as a probable enemy. From the back seat she stared at the shadowy figures. How freely Caroline chattered, how silently Martin sped toward Memorial.

"Well, that was a birthday Irene'll never forget. But she seemed so quiet. Did you notice that, Zoe?"

"Maybe she was just overwhelmed."

"I know I would be. Martin, prepare me, please, if you ever do something like that."

"I'm afraid throwing a party's not my style."

"I like your style." She leaned over and patted her husband's cheek. "The people there were fascinating. I never realized Dr. Mallory, in spite of all the surgery he does, is into archeology. Did you, Zoe?"

Thankful that Caroline's comments required little more than yes or no responses, Zoe Benson tried to unravel the events of the evening.

There had been not the slightest hint of jesting when Victor Solomon, losing his balance even as he leaned against a wall, had said with a sneer, "Your husband, Zoe, is no gentleman."

"What do you mean by that?" she'd asked.

Struggling through an alcoholic haze, he had adroitly backed down, twisting accusation into flattery. "What I mean is, he's so successful at running that theatre of his, he makes the rest of us legitimate businessmen look sick. You know, sick?" He'd belched and walked away. Turning back, he'd said, "Hey. Forget what I said, OK?"

"OK." She'd smiled. But she had observed a strained, almost frightened, look on his face. "Don't tell Lance," was what he had meant. Perhaps Victor was her enemy. No, her enemy was the man driving her home. Martin Fletcher, perspiring, anxiously avoiding both her and Lance, nervously blinking when Caroline had said, "We're dropping Zoe off." But why, she wondered, had there been no calls or notes, no second synthetic snake — nothing — since Sunday evening. Maybe Lance had stopped the blackmailing. "Blackmailing." Her spine straightened against the leather upholstery. Strange: she had stumbled upon that word. Was Lance blackmailing innocuous Martin Fletcher? And possibly powerful Victor Solomon? About what, for God's sakes? She ran her fingers through her hair. Nothing made sense.

"Didn't you adore Lowell's gift and his request for the toast? That man is incredible! How many buildings, do you suppose, are named after him?" Caroline was waxing eloquent on the philanthropic nature of Lowell Hook.

Martin continued to drive in silence.

"I know that The Arch couldn't have survived without his backing," Zoe contributed; then she closed off her thoughts and wrapped them like a cloak about her.

Who had called her husband away from the party? Only pride had stopped her from asking the maitre d' if the call for her husband had come from a man or a woman. Perhaps it had been Sandra Lowrey, not Nelson Biggs, who had threatened suicide. Through the phone the girl had screamed neglect, and he had rushed to calm her.

"I'm sorry, but Lance had to leave," she had said, without explanation, to Charles Stanton, who had simply raised his eyebrows and commented, "That's too bad."

Seated on Charles's left, she'd had the perfect opportunity to ask which of Sandra Lowrey's performances he most admired.

"Should I have admired any of them?" he'd asked.

Flustered, she had quickly mentioned another actress whose talent was undisputed.

"Now there's a woman Houston is fortunate to have." He'd warmed to the subject. "Her Desdemona a few seasons back was remarkable."

"Destination reached," Caroline trilled as Martin turned into the drive. The gabled house loomed in darkness. She had left the porch light on, but now it was off. That meant one thing: Lance was home.

"The taxi service was superb!" She got out of the car. "Martin, aren't you going to walk Zoe to the door?"

"Well, of course, if she'll slow down."

"No, it's all right, really."

But she waited.

As they silently made their way beneath the arched willows, she debated whether or not to confront this man walking closely behind her. Should she ask the question she had once planned to ask his wife, she would speak with authority as if his guilt were fact.

"It's slippery," he cautioned. Their footsteps made hollow sounds on the flagstones, still damp from the rain.

At the door, she faced him, her decision made.

"Martin . . . why are you threatening me?"

His small almond eyes darted back through the willows, then returned to her face.

"Zoe, I didn't mean — I only meant — I guess, then, the snake got to you, didn't it?"

"All of it, all of it, Martin, got to me. *Why?*"

"Just make Lance call, like I said."

"Like you said?"

"I can't talk to you, Zoe. Just to him. I'll just talk to him. I didn't mean to hurt you. I only meant — Look, I'm sorry it worked out this way." His fingers plucked at his tie, his eyes shifted from his shoes to her chin. "I've got to get back to Caroline."

"Martin, what you've got to do is talk! Because, if you don't, I may go to the police."

"No! No!" He glanced over his shoulder. His car was hidden by trees. Still, he lowered his voice as if he feared Caroline were at his elbow. "Lives, *lives* you understand — Caroline's — will be destroyed. Now I've got to go. Please just make Lance do what I said."

And he was gone, a hunched-over man, suddenly old, scurrying over flagstones to his wife.

Entering the dark house, she felt apprehensive but also relieved. Her enemy now had a face and a name. And he seemed far less threatening than Lance, far more frightened than she. Her question had obviously sent him reeling. Why else would he have thought he'd instructed her to have Lance call? Each word of those notes was imprinted on her brain. There had been no such demand. No matter, the "man more sinn'd against than sinning" had given her the evidence she needed. Tomorrow she and Lance would talk. And it would be she who called the shots. Conceivably her questions would be answered, the blackmail — regardless of its provocation — stopped. The end of the tunnel was in sight. She felt as if she were running — perhaps in slow-motion, but nevertheless running — toward an opening, out into light.

She went into the kitchen to stand at the sink drinking orange juice. She was stalling. She recognized that. If only Lance were someplace else and it were Charles Stanton who was upstairs waiting for her. In her room. In her bed. She would curve against his back and he would turn, draw her close, so close that their bodies would blend, move, as their minds already did, in rhythms harking back to beginnings. Somehow it no longer seemed wrong to have such thoughts . . . But it was wrong. Charles had a wife.

Once during dinner their knees had touched beneath the table. Instantaneously they had both pulled away. Their eyes had met. Wordlessly, she had shaken her head. He had turned to the museum patron on his right and she to the lawyer on her left. When next they spoke, the conversation had been about the rain pounding against the windows. The unspoken between them, however, had coursed as strong and as deep as water flowing from its source.

Groping once more through darkness, she felt as if she were sinking into an abyss rather than climbing the stairs in her own home. Her muscles strained against fear. She must get hold of herself. A sleeping Lance was harmless. Still, she was afraid. And tense. The day had stretched through miles and miles of revelation. She felt as if she had walked those miles across her own back. Perhaps a shower — the water as hot as she could stand — would relax her.


Quietly opening the door to Raymond's room, Winifred Reese saw that her son was in bed, the door to his bathroom open a crack so that a sliver of brightness cut through the blackness. As a child, Raymond had insisted that light kept Frankenstein away. The habit of not sleeping in the dark had persisted. "What frightens him now?" she wondered. Surely the image of the hulking monster had long since vanished.

Relieved that Raymond was at home, asleep in his own bed, she reflected on where he might have been that evening. What had he done? She had no idea. Clearly he had not escorted her to Irene's party; and, according to Amanda Stebbins, he could not possibly have had a date with Melissa. She wouldn't awaken him, but tomorrow she would expect an explanation for the lie she had gladly accepted as though she had just been handed a prewar Doulton. She closed the door and continued down the hallway. In spite of her concern, she refused to set the alarm for daybreak questioning of her son. Blessed Saturday had arrived. She intended to sleep until noon.

As his mother stood in his doorway, Raymond Reese felt like Judas Iscariot. Blood money lay in an envelope beneath his pillow.

He dared not breathe. He squeezed his eyes tightly shut. Tomorrow — when he would have to face her and lie once again about the dinner date — would come soon enough. He planned to mention that both Melissa and he had selected lobster thermidor as the entree and strawberries Romanoff for dessert. Now he wanted only to be left alone, to travel in his mind for the thousandth time the route along which he imagined Balzer's men were speeding into Mexico. Where were they now? How close were they to the border? Would they pass over into safety with ease or with difficulty? He visualized for the hundredth time the studio stripped of its heirlooms. Still, he consoled himself with the knowledge that he had left behind three-fourths of the stock. Stock! He felt as if he were speaking of cattle. His mother referred to each and every antique as one of her precious babies.

When finally she left, Raymond jumped out of bed and threw open his bathroom door. Light pierced to the darkest corners. Such protection was essential if he was to survive. Had he believed in sleeping pills, he would have popped several into his dried-out mouth. He was convinced, however, that medication was detrimental to the digestive system, and he fully intended to keep his stomach in cast-iron condition. How else could he continue his association with culinary delicacies? Nothing, he vowed, was going to take away from him the one uncomplicated pleasure in his life.

"Now." He untied the linen handkerchief.

The blindfold fell from her eyes.

She blinked, then stared. And, finally, she knelt before the portrait propped against a wall. Her fingers traced the delicate nose, the shape of the dark eyes so like her own. She caressed the streaks of sunlight in the brown hair. And then she cried. Because she had been wrong. The portrait did not change anything. She could stand for hours before this resemblance and life would never spring from the canvas. David would never return to erase her guilt. She had left him in the lake. He was dead. Charles had done a terrible thing. No matter how she had pled for the portrait, he should have kept this haunting reminder from her. He had never understood or met her needs; and he never would. Her fingernails tore at the canvas.

"What're you doing?" He jerked her to her feet. Sobbing, she beat against his chest. But it was someone else, not she, it was some other crazed fifty-six-year-old woman tearing at her husband's face. She saw blood there. He stood immobile. It enraged her that he had seen and felt more in battle: her clawing and beating made no dent. She made no dent. Her clenched fist, raised in midair, dropped to her side.

"I'm sorry," she said and stretched to her full short height. "You were right. I was wrong. The portrait doesn't bring him back." She dabbed at the blood on her husband's cheek. "This isn't like me, you know that, Charles."

"I know." He drew her into his arms.

She heard a deep weariness — or was it resignation? — in his voice.

"Whatever have I done?" she thought. "I will always fail him. Always. And myself. I will always fail myself."

"Irene, you need to get to bed."

She nodded.

As he led her up the stairs, she asked, childlike, "You'll get rid of the painting?"

In the early morning hours, Irene Stanton left her sleeping husband and crept downstairs into a guest room. There she sat at a black lacquered desk, beside a four-poster bed in which Churchill had once slept, and wrote unsteadily on lilac stationery. She inserted the scented sheet into an envelope, which she then addressed in a barely legible scrawl to Charles Stanton.

Hurriedly she left the room to walk through the downstairs into the garage.

She lifted the coiled rope from its hook on the wall and knotted a noose in its thickness. Carrying the rope, she reentered the house and walked purposefully back to the guest room, on into the bathroom.

She opened the linen-closet door and tossed the rope over its top. She closed the door, then tugged on the rope. The rope held fast. She propped the envelope addressed to her husband against a crystal bowl filled with soaps. Then she placed a stool beneath the dangling noose.

For a time she knelt beside the tub and tried to pray. No words came. She held out her hands. "I'm trembling, I'm so afraid," she thought. "I can't do this." She weighed her alternatives. They remained more unbearable than the solution toward which she now groped. She was able to pray. It was a prayer seeking courage and forgiveness. But mostly courage.

She stood. For a moment she hesitated. Then she stepped on the stool. The knotted rope slipped over her head and down around her throat. She kicked the stool from beneath her feet.


Zoe undressed in the pitch-black bedroom, where her husband slept. She draped her dress over a chair. She dared not search for a coat hanger, for fear the slightest noise would awaken him. Naked, she walked into the adjoining bathroom, then closed the door before switching on the light. Her need for hot water pouring over her body, relaxing her, was urgent. Besides, the odds favored that Lance would sleep through the sound of running water. The doors and walls of the old house were thick, the construction dating back to 1912.

Later she was to recall what happened next in colors and shapes — the squares of white tile; the brown spotted body; the pointed head; the narrow flicking tongue; the rectangular white page, its sparse message typed black in upper case, taped to the wall. And sounds. She would remember a shrill hiss — cold water thrown on a hot iron — and a rattle — hard little beads rolling against the plastic insides of an infant's toy.

Zoe Benson opened the shower door and the snake lunged; she slammed the door, screaming, as the reptile lurched forward. A hairline crack skittered down the frosted glass ruptured by the force of the slam and the reptile's weight thrown against the door.

He was there immediately.

"What's going on?"

She pointed. "Don't open it!" And then, grabbing a towel to wrap about herself, she ran, a cool, hard voice in her head, ordering, "Get the keys, go to the car, bring back the gun." Clutching the key chain, she tore down the stairs, out the door, into the garage, then back through the house as she gripped the revolver.

The snake had to be killed before it killed them, before it gulped the entire house down into its long repulsive body.

Balanced on the dressing-table stool, Lance was peering over the top of the stall when she returned with the gun.

"Here. Kill it!"

He took the gun from her, and slowly pointed it, not at the snake, but at her.

"Let's talk." He motioned with the gun that she was to go into the bedroom and sit on the bed.

As he stood over her, the nozzle angled down into her face, the cool, hard voice inside her head took over again.

"What do you think you're doing?" she asked.

"Seeking answers to questions."

"So am I."

"No doubt, but I'm the one doing the asking."

"Lance, put away the gun." She was amazed at the calmness with which she spoke.

He lowered the weapon.

". . . So, how did you know about the gun?"

"I just did."

"*How*, Zoe?"

"That night I unlocked your darkroom, I looked in the glove compartment of your car."

"Why didn't you confront me then? Surely the gun must have frightened you."

"Lance, there is a rattlesnake in our bathroom, and right now that frightens me a whole lot more."

"It's harmless so long as we keep the door closed."

"And how long is that going to be?"

"I'm not sure."

"Lance, get rid of it now! Will you please do that?"

"I'm the one asking the questions, remember?"

"I'm not on a witness stand."

"Ah, but you are." He bent down to her, his arms like bars on either side of her, the cold sapphire stare replacing the nozzle of the gun. "The note taped to the wall indicated you've had other communications."

"I didn't read it." She tried to rise, to go for the note. But he pushed her back against the pillows. The gun once again was close to her face.

"Don't move, Zoe."

"It's my note!"

"I quote: 'You ignored my warnings. I would like my money returned. Have your husband get in touch with me immediately.' "

She closed her eyes, ignored the gun. So Martin Fletcher had instructed her, after all, to have Lance call; and when he had asked, ". . . the snake got to you, didn't it?" he had been referring not to the coil of rubber she'd thrown into the garbage but to a reptile live and ready to strike. She opened her eyes and saw draperies embroidered with violets. How had this bright and lovely room become filled with such hate? There was so much to deal with, to sort out in her mind.

She turned to stare, over the gun, at her husband.

"He means business, doesn't he?" She spoke coolly, the voice in her head directing her.

"Who?"

"You know who."

"As a matter of fact, I don't."

"Then you must be blackmailing more than one person."

"What're you talking about?"

"If you'll get that thing out of my face, I'll tell you."

He tossed the weapon beyond her to the other side, his side, of the bed. "Talk."

"How many are you blackmailing?"

"That's not talking, Zoe."

"How many?"

"I am not above striking a woman."

"Lance, how many and why? Why anybody? What you're doing is — slime! It's worse. It's —"

He hit her then. Her head slammed back against the bedpost. "Now, what's going on?"

"Nothing!"

He raised his hand.

"No! Please!" She shielded her face with her arm. He pulled the arm away. The resisting dam crumbled.

"All right! All right! About two weeks ago he left a note —"

"Who left a note?"

She hesitated.

The hand was raised again.

"Martin Fletcher. It was unsigned and on my car in a parking lot warning me that you'd better stop whatever you're doing. You're blackmailing him, aren't you?"

"Go on."

She touched her broken lips. The cool, hard voice had returned, pouring balm, directing her. "And then — there were phone calls with no one speaking. A lot of them. And a toy snake streaked with fingernail polish. It came in the mail. And now — the live one."

"Why didn't you come to me?"

She shook her head.

"Instead you had to play Sherlock Holmes, didn't you? . . . Well, didn't you? . . . *Answer me!*"

"Yes!"

". . . Whom have you told?"

"No one." She thought of her father.

"Who knows, Zoe?"

"No one! I swear it." She held her breath, praying that he would accept the lie, that he wouldn't hit her again.

"Very well . . . ask your questions." He sat in a chair across from her.

This unexpected tactic threw her off balance. Again she listened for the voice in her head.

"What has Martin Fletcher done that would make you want to blackmail him?"

"Blackmail is your word, not mine. Fletcher and I are involved in business negotiations; and he's decided to welsh. It's as simple as that."

"What kind of negotiations?"

"Oil investments I wanted to surprise you with."

She fought against becoming confused.

"Why do you have that gun?"

"For an obvious reason. Look at the notes, the snake. Fletcher's crazy."

"Frightened!"

"Since we can't seem to agree on that subject . . . next question."

She groped for direction.

"What's your association with — Victor Solomon?"

"Victor Solomon?" He laughed. "The man's a board member."

"Yes, but are you blackmailing him, too?"

"Zoe, where do you get these absurd notions?"

"Observation."

"Then look again. Victor's an honorable gentleman and a friend. He'd never welsh on a business deal. Next question."

". . . Where were you tonight?"

"I felt nauseated and came home."

A chink had opened. She could press harder now. Lance had done something tonight which might trip him up.

"What about the phone call you said was from Nelson Biggs?"

"What did you tell our august host?"

"It's my turn to ask questions."

"Only because I choose to let you. What did you tell Charles Stanton about my leaving?"

She shrugged. The voice in her head again was helping her. "Just that you left."

"That's all?"

"That's all."

"OK . . . Time's up."

"Not quite! What *did* you do tonight?"

"I told you, I was sick and came home."

"I don't believe you . . . And I don't think the police would either."

"You're threatening me, Zoe?" His eyebrows were raised.

"Definitely!"

"I see." He leaned forward, his hands came down on his knees. "All right. Maybe they wouldn't believe me. So let me throw your inquisitive, and somewhat foolhardy, nature a bone. Potentially I could be in trouble. But I'm not going to be. However . . ." He paused as if for emphasis. "Part of my staying out of trouble depends on you. You are to speak to no one about any of this. You are to continue as though none of this has happened, as though —"

"That's impossible!"

"It's possible." He smiled. "And practical. Let me spell it out for you. If you do one thing — one thing, Zoe — to upset my apple cart, I won't hurt you, not seriously — you are my wife —"

"God!"

"But most certainly I will not hesitate to do irreparable damage to your father."

"You wouldn't dare!"

"Try me."

Their stares deadlocked.

"I mean it." He had spoken softly yet distinctly.

Her eyes searched his face.

"I believe you," she said and lowered her head.

"Good." He stood. "Now, your immediate instructions are to go to sleep and forget this happened."

Her head jerked up. She challenged him again. "You actually expect me to go to sleep with a gun in my bed, a man standing over me making threats about my father, and a snake in the bathroom? I'm not an idiot."

"On the contrary, you're one of the few women I know with above-average intelligence. Which is exactly why you'll follow instructions. Now, go to sleep."

She stood.

"Get back in bed."

"I'd like a nightgown, if you don't mind."

"I do mind."

"Well, that's unfortunate."

He hesitated then shrugged. "A nit-picking woman is a bore. And you have bored me for the last five years. Sleep in whatever you wish."

As she slipped the olive silk over her head, she fought rage and fear. If only she had listened to her father. Had his urging her to leave been only the night before? Since then she had virtually become a prisoner in her own house. If she sought help, Lance would harm her father. Long before he had struck her, the sapphire stare had told her he was capable of violence. She had simply been unwilling to recognize the unfathomable depths in this man, who was observing her now, coldly, as if she were no more than a store-window mannequin.

She got into bed.

He pulled the sheet about her shoulders then leaned to kiss her forehead. She was amazed and repulsed.

"Something you've never understood, Zoe," he said, towering again over her, "is that a few of us need wings to fly above the rest of you who would keep us groveling, like yourselves, in the dust of the earth."

"I never realized you were a poet." She turned on her side, away from him.

"That's what I mean. You crawl, like that snake in there, while I, in spite of you and your limited vision, am destined to soar."

She closed her eyes and thought of Icarus, the wax from his wings melting as he coursed toward the sun.

"Like Icarus," she couldn't help but say.

"Your comment only reinforces my point."

He placed the gun on his nightstand and crawled into bed beside her.

Lance Benson awoke before dawn. He made coffee, then sat waiting for the sound of the morning paper slamming against the front door. The sound came early. The headlines were pedestrian. The bodies had not been discovered.

Carrying coffee to his desk, he debated how he should alter his plans, which had been so exactingly conceived and recorded and had seemed so foolproof.

Going off duty at 5:00 A.M., T. D. Bass noticed that the Fleetwood Brougham was still parked in front of Apartment 88. He congratulated himself: "I had that one figured right. Her friend's making a night of it."

The shift had been more exciting than he'd anticipated. True, he'd had to generate the fireworks himself. During the thick of the rain, he'd ducked into Apartment 153, where a broad from Shreveport, Louisiana — no match for the looker in 88 but still not bad — was noted for being pretty free with her talents. He'd reasoned nothing would be doing during the downpour. And he'd been right. When he'd zipped up his pants and started on his rounds again, the place had been quiet as a tomb. The only item of interest had been a car pulling away from in front of 88. Maybe for a time there she'd had two of them on top of her. The lady traveled in highfalutin circles. He couldn't be sure, but he thought the car backing out had been a Continental. At any rate, the dude with the Fleetwood was lasting longer, or giving the orders, 'cause his car didn't look like it was going anywhere fast.

He got into his own twice-painted 1968 Mustang and yawned. Exactly twenty-six hours from now he would be back on duty in this shit-ass place. He flicked on his scanner to keep him awake driving home. Swiftly the scanner rotated. Crime was rampant in the streets. Somehow, he vowed, he would find a way to enter the

Houston police academy. Only as a full-fledged law-enforcement officer would he be able to realize his dream, which was simply to close his hands around the guts and the gore of the city and squeeze.

The illuminated hands of the clock pointed to five-thirty. Charles Stanton blinked sleep from his eyes. Pulling on his robe, he began a search through the upstairs rooms. When had she left the bed?

He descended the stairs quickly. Somewhere below she would be reading. She would glance up and explain brightly, "I couldn't sleep." The blood-caked scratch on his cheek mocked him. He would find her grieving before their son's portrait. Passing the flowers in the foyer, he contemplated calling Bonita to ask that she help Irene get hold of herself.

His son's eyes stared at him from the portrait in the living room. He went into the sun room. The wicker rocker was empty. He hurried away, through the dining room, on into the kitchen where she was no doubt sipping a pre-dawn cup of coffee. He switched on the lights. Water bugs scurried for cover.

Perhaps, he reasoned, she had gone into the guest room to sleep. Sometimes she did that. But the spread remained smooth on the bed where Churchill once slept.

He combed the rest of the downstairs: the library, his study, the game room, the powder room, the pantry, even the closets. He peered into the garage where both cars remained. He hurried outside. She was not in the garden. Nor was she swimming laps across a lighted pool or slamming tennis balls against a brick wall. He reentered the house to sit on the bottom step of the staircase. A cold dread inched up from the pit of his stomach through his tightening chest into the recesses of his logical mind. There was one room he had overlooked.

Slowly he returned to the guest room. He pushed open the door which led into the bathroom.

A slipper had fallen to the floor. He bent and slipped the white satin onto her bare, dangling foot. His combat years flashed before him. Pain cut deeper now than then. She was the equivalent of thousands dead, and more. Savagely he began jerking at the rope, blindly struggling to free his wife from that which he knew had already given her freedom.

✳    PART III

*Saturday morning, September 24 —*
*Friday afternoon, September 30*

SEVEN-THIRTY. She had overslept. Hazel Mabry rubbed sleep from her eyes and rushed to splash water into her puffy face. For days there had been no need to set the alarm, because her employer's predawn summons for tea and muffins had been alarm enough. Well, she would head straight for the kitchen, then on to his room with the tray which any minute now he would surely be wanting. Maybe with the hour being considerably later, he would accept a rose beside the linen napkin. She did like to pamper him, for there was hardly a better man alive, what with her husband having gone on to his reward some thirty years before.

Passing through the dining room, she admired the orchids floating in crystal. Today she'd have her hands full with last minute details for tonight's party honoring the mayor. Most likely her employer was sleeping later this morning to prepare for the evening. After all, he'd still been out last night when she'd gone to bed at eleven.

Sniffing the yellow rose she'd lifted from an arrangement in the foyer, she balanced the breakfast tray and knocked lightly on his door. When there was no answer after the third knock, she decided he was in the shower and entered the room to leave his tray. She would pull back the drapes and let in the day. Those were his instructions even when it was pitch-black outside.

"My word!" she exclaimed aloud. The bed was made. Never in twenty-eight years had she known Lowell Alfred Hook to make his own bed. She peered into the bathroom. No steam glazed over the shower door. Her employer was out and about. Most unusual. In fact, it was absolutely unheard-of! But who was she to question the comings and goings of a man who built empires as easily as her great-nephew erected castles out of blocks? It would be just like him to walk in ten minutes before his guests arrived. Hadn't he left everything, even the menu, to her supervision? And if she scolded — "I was worried about you" — he would probably chuckle and say, "Keeps you young; now lay out my clothes, and let's get on with this shindig."

She left the rose beside his bed, then carried the tray back to the kitchen where she promptly sat down and ate the buttered muffins while taking plastic rollers out of her hair.

She was so beautiful. And he had failed her again. But seeing Benson talking to her at the party last night had sent him straight to the bar. "I'm a man of my word," the bastard had said; but, hell, how good was a man's word when he was in the dirtiest of businesses? Besides, Victor Solomon was nobody's fool. If Lance Benson had set him up to the tune of one hundred thousand dollars, there were surely others he was blackmailing. And what if Benson tripped over his own feet on the way to the bank? How soon would it be before the police were standing on his and Roselyn's doorstep demanding to know the nature of his involvement with Lance Benson and Sandy whatever-her-name-was? He touched his wife's hair. She didn't move. They had screamed from opposite sides of their room last night until exhausted they had fallen into bed only to reach out for each other after he had promised, promised again, that he would stay away from the drinking. "But why? Why tonight?" she had cried once during their fight, and he had yelled back the lie, "Because I was thirsty!" Not "Because I was afraid — afraid one man may blow sky-high what we have now, what I have tenuously regained in spite of your determination to have a career." Watching his wife sleep, he assured himself that the career would be all right. He could handle her dashing around the city interviewing women who had made it in the sciences, which was her first assignment for the new magazine *The Tenth Muse*. He could even handle her flying off to California or New York seeking out other successful women to capture their profundities on paper. He could handle that if he knew, knew for sure, she would come back home. But he had to stay sober. He must find some other way to combat business pressures and to submerge his fear. If only Tuesday were here. He, Roselyn, and the children would be headed for Cozumel. He would aim the Baron straight through the clouds, leaving behind — at least for a time — the tensions of running a multimillion-dollar company and the disquieting feeling that Lance Benson would be apprehended by the law and that somehow he would be exposed.

Roselyn whimpered as though she were having a nightmare. He pulled her to him. Monday he wouldn't go in to the store. Instead he would check out the Baron, pack, then get to bed sober and early so that Tuesday morning he would be at his best for their trip.

Archie Moore had two jobs. The earnings he received as clerk for the Harris County morgue he shared with the IRS. The earnings he received as informant for Benny Harris, reporter for Houston's afternoon *Times* he kept. He worked hard at both jobs. Had Archie Moore been asked to give a one-word description of himself, he wouldn't have had to think twice. "Dependable," he would have said. Then he would have repeated for emphasis, "Dependable," for hadn't he remained single all these years so that he could live at home with an ailing mother whose primary contact with the outside world consisted of visits to the Medical Center to be hooked up to a dialysis machine? And who took her? Who paid for those visits by working his tail off at two jobs? Her firstborn, that was who, while his two sisters lived out their self-centered lives in Hot Springs, Arkansas, and Dayton, Ohio.

On Saturday morning, September twenty-fourth, Archie Moore — worn from the weight of all his "dependability," pallid from his sunless environment, and bitter from his realization that next Wednesday there would be only his mother to cheer him when he blew out forty candles — pursed his thin lips and reported to work over the phone on job number two. "Hey, Benny, get out of bed!" he whispered hoarsely. "They rolled in a live one, early this morning . . . No, no, nothing like that. It's clean. Suicide . . . Now wait just a minute. So it won't win you any prizes. The name on the big toe's worth something. Seems her husband's got some kind of title handed down direct from the queen of England!"

.   .   .

Without taking the time to shave what his mother affectionately called the "apricot fuzz" on his face, Raymond Reese dressed early; stuffed the fifty thousand dollars into a shoe box, which he then shoved to the back of his closet; and hastily scribbled his mother a note, explaining that for most of the day he would be in the public library researching period furniture. He reasoned that she wouldn't question his whereabouts, for design research had been a pursuit of his since college days.

After propping the note against the sugar bowl, he headed for breakfast at a House of Pancakes. The restaurant was directly across the street from a pay phone, which he eyed steadfastly while gulping five blintzes topped with a double order of cream cheese and strawberries.

Promptly at nine o'clock, he paid his bill then crossed the street to the phone — the same phone from which he had called Oram Balzer two days before.

"It's not necessary. You do your job; we'll do ours. But if you're that nervous you can check with me around nine Saturday morning at the shop," Balzer had finally agreed after Raymond had pled, "I have to know. I mean I *have to know,* to breathe easy, that your men got everything delivered safely. You know, without being apprehended." Even as he had spoken, Raymond had felt like someone else, an underworld figure in a late television movie. His hands clammy, his Adam's apple quivering, he had imagined Columbo leaning against a nearby building, an electronic device in his fountain pen recording the entire conversation.

He dialed the number of the Medici Shop.

Balzer was in.

"This is Raymond."

"Went fine."

"What?"

"They made it."

"You mean they *actually* made it?"

"What'd you expect?"

"Well, I don't know. You mean, they made it?"

"That's what I said. They made it. Now let's forget the whole thing, OK?"

"Absolutely."

"We each got what we wanted, right?"

"Yes sir. Thank you. You're right. Absolutely right."

Right, right, right! Raymond hung up the phone and leaned weakly, joyfully, against the side of the booth. There was still, however, more to be faced. The final payoff to Benson was scheduled for Wednesday; and before that would surely come the confrontation in the studio Monday morning, when his mother walked in the door and screamed, "We've been robbed!" Obviously he would have to put the approaching crises out of his mind. The best way to do that would actually be to go to the library. To hide behind books. To delve deep into the study of sixteenth-century Italian marriage coffers and German oak cupboards. There among the stacks he would postpone meeting his mother's eyes. He would avoid passing his own reflection in mirrors. He would stop thinking about his predicament. While pursuing scholarly research, he might even occasionally glance up to fantasize that it was Wednesday night, when all this would be behind him. Between now and then one bright moment offered reprieve: his Sunday brunch with Melissa Stebbins. At least that date was no fabrication.

When the phone rang, Martin Fletcher jumped. "I'll get it," he said to his wife, who was frying bacon for Saturday breakfast, which over the years had become somewhat elaborate. It had also become a time when they leisurely drank second cups of coffee, while sharing the morning paper and any personal problems that could be labeled, in Caroline's words, "Stumbling Blocks to Effective Living."

He picked up the phone.

"Fletcher, listen carefully."

Martin straightened.

Caroline turned from the stove. He mouthed, "It's for me." She nodded and flipped the bacon.

"See that Caroline goes to church tomorrow without you. I'll be coming to your house around eleven to return the money. That was some trick you pulled with the snake. I've got things covered with Zoe, but the game's over. In fact, you might say you've won . . . I've already destroyed the film. Now, do you understand? Eleven o'clock tomorrow."

"Yes. We're — uh, familiar with Conroe property. But we own land up near Austin and will be building there."

"Caroline's at your elbow, huh?"

"Yes."

"I take it you're confirming?"

"That's fine."

"I have to hand it to you. You're a bastard, but a smart one."

Martin Fletcher put down the phone. His hands were trembling. The long shot — getting at Benson through Zoe — had worked! He felt he was a boy again playing Flying Statues. Only this time he was never flung. High and hard over his head he spun his classmates. And though they landed in contorted positions, he was able quickly and deftly to guess exactly who or what they were.

"One of those salesmen for lake-front property," he said to his wife, who was placing the bacon on a platter.

"It's early for such a call, isn't it?"

"I guess he was getting a head start on the weekend. Smells good." He bent down to the bacon. "I'll tell you one thing, Mrs. Fletcher."

"And what is that, Mr. Fletcher?"

"This morning there's not a single Stumbling Block in my life."

"That's news," she said, cracking eggs. "You've been pretty glum lately."

"Caroline" — he thoughtfully chewed a piece of bacon — "that's only because men are sometimes as unpredictable as women."

"I'll accept that," she said, "as a cop-out. Now, Martin, please save the bacon for the eggs."

Lance Benson sat at his desk in his downstairs study. The conversation with Fletcher had gone exactly as he had hoped it would. He should get busy now. Begin preparing for the next few days.

But still he sat at his desk. His fingertips stroked the jeweled handle of the letter opener that he had purchased last month in Carmel. Last month. How long ago that seemed. So much had happened. Hook dead. And Sandra. If only she were alive, he would never again scold her for chewing gum. She could pop bubbles right in his face and he would laugh and threaten to turn her across his knee. What a fool he'd been to get rid of the girl who had loved him, the girl whom he could not love in return, but who had served him faithfully — that is, until the end when she had called him a murderer. That was not to be tolerated. It hadn't been tolerated. But, in a sense, Sandra had been right. She had accused him of murdering Hook, who would still be alive today raising libraries and research centers out of sawdust, had it not been for that single afternoon when he had been presented with Sandra Lowrey as a "gift." The old man had asked, "What's in this for you?" As it had turned out, nothing. Not one penny of Hook's millions would he be able to claim. Still, he must keep reminding himself that he had not murdered Hook. But Sandra? That death was another matter. Though hours before he had decided to let her live — to send her away to New York — he had nevertheless committed the very act he had decided against . . . And now she was dead. He was a murderer. His left eyelid twitched as he recalled that he had smothered her with the pillow he had once placed under the small of her back when they had made love.

Well, the murderer must proceed in order to emerge from the nightmare, to soar as he had sworn to Zoe he would.

He pushed the letter opener from him and studied the revised pages of his notepad. Today and tomorrow were crucial. Luckily, the bodies had not been discovered. At least not according to the morning's headlines. Still, the news could break at any time. He'd better collect his money from the lockbox. It was foolish not to have his assets available at a moment's notice. He cursed himself for not keeping an updated passport in a drawer, as the casual rich were accustomed to keeping. Should the police trace Sandra's death to him, there must be no record of his having recently applied for the passport which weeks ago he should have foreseen he might suddenly need.

Well, it was too late now. Another flaw in his supposedly infallible blueprint. But things had gone so smoothly up to now. How was he to have known?

This morning he also needed to purchase a steel hook. Fletcher was a weaker link than Sandra had ever been. Running around leaving notes on windshields and depositing snakes in showers, Martin Fletcher was likely at any moment to go completely off the deep end. And who knew what the results of that might be? The man could be his undoing. If he, Lance Benson, had murdered once, he could do so again. And this time there would be no emotional involvement.

He closed the notepad. He'd better hurry now to his darkroom. The concealed video equipment needed to be hauled down to his car. After leaving the bank, he'd bury the expensive set in a deserted landfill somewhere in the northwest.

There was something else he must do. Fletcher's and Hook's

tapes, along with the one Sandra had foolishly made, must be destroyed, and the red wig with its matching moustache as well. The salt-and-pepper wig he'd keep. As for the wig he'd left in Sandra's apartment, he would just have to gamble that she had actually thrown it away. Certainly, he couldn't risk returning to that place.

Unfortunately he'd have to get rid of his legal pad. He would miss his project scribblings, but the information was stamped indelibly on his brain.

The tapes which implicated Raymond Reese and Irene Stanton he would hide in his car. Raymond's final payment was due on Wednesday; Monday, soon after her husband left for his office, he would call Lady Stanton to inform her that she did not, after all, have ten days to deliver the money. She had forty-eight hours.

He stood. Vestiges of his project would be burned in his darkroom. Now, while Zoe was asleep. Zoe! He hadn't meant to involve her, but he'd had no choice. Thanks to Fletcher's damnable meddling, Zoe Harrington Benson knew far more than she should. He recalled how shrewd, though frightened, she had been last night. He admired that. Why, then, had he hit her? His fingers pressed against the twitching eyelid. God, what had he become? What was he? Where was the boy, with old Bailey tagging along, who ran fast into the spray of Lake Ontario? Where had that boy gone? He mustn't think like that. He mustn't think at all. He must act. When he walked out of the bank, no one must suspect that his briefcase contained close to two hundred thousand dollars.

He sat back down. For ten minutes he concentrated on a single image — a sea gull soaring upward. Up and up and up. He allowed no other image, no extraneous thought, to enter his mind. The hand left his face. The eyelid was still. He stood, composed. If someone were to guess the contents of his briefcase, what did it matter? The money belonged to him. He had earned it. Assuming there were no slip-ups, he was on his way, soaring, out of the nightmare.

"Stanton residence."

"May I speak to Lady Stanton, please?"

There was a pause. "Could I take a message?"

"Perhaps I could speak to her husband."

The answer came swiftly. "I'm sorry. He's unable to come to the phone."

"Then would you tell them both that Zoe Benson called simply to say how much she enjoyed the party last evening."

Again the pause. "We've met, Mrs. Benson. I'm Bonita Graves, the Stantons' neighbor. Charles wants close friends — and I'm aware that you are one — to know. Services will be held at Saint Michael's Episcopal Church, Monday morning at eleven . . . for Irene. She died unexpectedly late last night."

It was too much. She lighted a cigarette. Her stare went beyond the flame to the phone. God help her. Help Charles. Irene! How had she died? Bonita Graves had terminated the conversation before questions could be asked. There had only been time to say, "Tell Charles I'm here — if he needs me." And to think she had called — praying that he would answer, knowing that she was ready to accept the help he had offered earlier. No longer could she turn to her father. Charles was the person who could have helped her. Now it was she who must help Charles. But how could she? She was trapped here. Trapped by the scrawled note left on the breakfast table: "I'll be back shortly. Don't move. Keep in mind our discussion last night." As an extra precaution, he'd taken her car keys. He needn't have bothered. She would do nothing to endanger her father.

. . . Except maybe she could risk being gone for an hour. Risk calling a taxi to take her to Charles. But, once there, what would she find? A man inconsolable. His wife dead. Impossible. Could it have been a heart attack? Unlikely. The lady exercised daily on tennis courts and golf courses. She ate yogurt, sipped prune juice, and abhorred smoking. Could it have been cancer? But cancer didn't kill unexpectedly, did it? Feeding on healthy cells, cancer hung around for a while. How had she died? Why? At the party she had seemed strained. Perhaps later last night a snake had struck and killed her. No, the snake was still upstairs in her own house. Not in Irene Stanton's . . . She should go to the police. But what good would that do? They would probably arrest Martin Fletcher and lock him up, while Lance, smiling ever so slightly, the wrinkles crinkling outward from the sapphire eyes, would convince them that a raving maniac, rather than a desperately frightened man, was on their hands. Before it was over, the district attorney himself would apologize for the agony The Arch director had suffered at the hands of the psychopathic Fletcher. He might even suggest that Mrs. Benson seemed more than a little deranged. Sadly shaking his head, Lance would commit her. And then he might still go after her father. That would be his revenge.

If only she could bolt out of the house! But where? To whom? If only, to Charles. Together they could hold on tightly to sanity.

Captain Kermit Whalen, head of Homicide, ran the palm of his thick hand over his steel-gray hair as he studied the initial report filed by Patrol Officer Ron Griffin. Sipping coffee from a mug that proclaimed, "Damn I'm Good," he squinted and swiveled his chair to face the window overlooking Riesner Street. "It just goes to show you," he thought, "the rich are not immune." The newspapers would have a field day with this one. Here was a lady, high-society personified, who'd strung herself up but good. Had there been anything suspicious, he'd have put Dobson and Pritchard on it immediately. River Oaks deserved the best. But her husband, who was some kind of British nobility, had satisfactorily explained that the scratch on his face had occurred during a domestic quarrel. No, this was a file to be closed hastily. She'd been just another desperate slob wanting out of it all. "Yes sir, money doesn't guarantee you a damn thing," he said aloud. Sure, it helped — who couldn't use more? But he counted his blessings every time something like this came across his desk. So what if he had a wife who didn't raise his blood pressure in the bedroom? Between them they'd managed to produce five children. And she was a good woman who in thirty-five years of marriage had never been subject to moods. The only tip-off that she was feeling low was when she started humming tuneless little songs. As for the kids, they had turned out fine. The oldest was the only one to bust your britches with pride over, but the others were nothing to be ashamed of, not by a long shot. No, he had zero complaints in the family department. And in his work he'd done all right: getting a degree from the University of Houston night school; working his way steadily up through the ranks; treating his men right and, in return, knowing they liked and respected him. If only his old man, who'd walked the Market Street beat right up until the day he died back in the forties, could see him now sitting in his swivel chair looking out over Riesner like he owned it. All things considered, he wouldn't trade places with anyone. Certainly not with that fellow who had a nasty scratch on his face and a dead wife. Suicide was a bitch. He was thankful this one didn't require a detailed investigation. His staff was up to its eyeballs in work. And with a fresh rash of Saturday-night knifings not more than a few hours away, he felt like tipping his hat to the River Oaks lady, who had apparently known what she wanted and gone after it — cleanly and simply. No mess left around, not even the usual "I'm bailing out" note, her husband had said.

The taxi pulled into the circular drive. "Come back in an hour," Zoe requested, then walked quickly toward the house.

Bonita Graves, eyelids puffy in a composed face, opened the door.

"Thank you for coming. You were the only one he asked to see."

She followed the lady, with her sloped little dowager's hump, into the living room where the portrait of David Stanton was propped against a wall. Had this painting, the work of her hands, somehow caused Irene's death, she wondered. No, she mustn't think that. Hurriedly she opened the drapery. So what if this wasn't her home? Bonita had called her to help. She had come as fast as she could. She was here now. And there needed to be light in this room. Unable to look at the boy's eyes — his mother's eyes — she hid the portrait behind the sofa. Bonita Graves left her alone. She sat and waited for Charles.

She was accustomed to seeing him in a three-piece suit. Wearing khakis, a denim shirt, and tennis shoes, he looked boyish, too young to be bearing his age and the weight of his wife's death.

"Good of you to come." He avoided meeting her eyes.

"I wanted to."

"It was selfish of me to ask you. There's nothing you can do."

"I can be here."

". . . Yes."

Instinctively she stood. He hesitated, then came to her. For a long while she held him. There was no way she could tell him now — or ever — about Lance. And she couldn't go to the police because her silver-tongued husband would shred her slight evidence. But an idea had begun to crystalize. Bluffed force might ward off real force.

She held Charles closer. His tragedy minimized her fear.

Finally, he moved from her, over to a window.

"It's a nice day. She would have been out playing tennis." He turned from the window. "Did Bonita tell you how she died?"

"No." She spoke softly, as if the slightest sound would send him back upstairs where, Bonita had said, he had closeted himself since early morning.

"She hanged herself . . . I knew she was unhappy, but — Well, I shouldn't be troubling you." He smiled slightly. "If I remember correctly, you've got your own problem. And you've been extraordinarily self-contained."

"Please, don't worry about that. Charles, did she — did anything in particular upset her?"

"It wasn't the portrait, if that's what you're thinking. It was — I don't know." He breathed deeply. "Something else."

She straightened. Suddenly, without knowing, she knew.

"I need to ask — what's frightening you, Zoe?"

His question, aimed direct and on target, threw her off balance. She must choose her words carefully. She could be wrong. "Charles, maybe you need to talk about Irene."

"I *am* talking about Irene! Look, I have to know . . . Are you being blackmailed?"

So she wasn't wrong. Lance had something to do with Irene Stanton's death.

"No." She leaned forward, palms open to him. "I have nothing to be blackmailed about."

And then she waited for him to tell her more before she told him everything.

He ran his hand over his eyes. "Forgive me."

"There's nothing to forgive."

"Oh, but there is. That was a long-shot, and unwarranted. It's just I thought there might be some connection. Blackmailers often weave webs."

"Charles, Irene was — impeccable! I mean — how could she have been blackmailed?" She was asking the question as much of herself as of him.

He pulled an envelope from his pocket. His eyes searched her face.

"I trust you."

"You can," she said.

Irene's words lay on the coffee table between them.

Dearest Charles,

I am weak or I would not be leaving you with this problem. You may be blackmailed. Don't search for explanations behind that cryptic statement. I pray that he will decide not to approach you. If he remains silent, you must destroy this note and forget even the possibility of blackmail.

I won't give you his name, for I expect you'd turn "general" and seek him out. He is too crafty, even for you. If he does contact you, pay him. Preserve my name in order that you will not be destroyed.

The effort to be other than what I am has been exhausting. Forgive me. I love you. But you deserve better.

Irene

P.S. Had I long ago followed the dictate found in your beloved *Hamlet* — "to thine own self be true" — perhaps I would not now be writing this letter.

"Charles, this is hard and fast evidence. Against someone . . . You've got to go to the police."

"That's not what she wanted."

"But the blackmailer may be after you next." First her father; now possibly Charles. She felt wounded.

"Let him. That's what I want. I'm going to send Bonita home and start answering the phone myself. He won't know that Irene's dead. Not for a while. Maybe he'll try to contact her. Zoe, I've got to know what she was talking about. I can't go running to the police and end up reading in the paper about some monstrous secret my wife had. I have to find out firsthand. And if it's as bad as she seemed to have thought — if I have to pay off the bastard — I will." He stared into space, his eyelids narrowing. "Or maybe we can reach an agreement. I don't go to the police; he forgets whatever he knows about my wife." He laughed bitterly. "I've always prided myself on being an honorable man. How easily our illusions are shattered."

"Don't say that!"

"What? Don't speak the truth because it's painful?"

"The truth is you're thinking of her — of preserving your wife's honor." She recalled other words: "Lives, *lives* you understand — Caroline's — will be destroyed." Perhaps she herself should be showing more concern for her friend's preservation. The police would surely rip Martin Fletcher's secret from him, only to have it tossed, like confetti, into reporters' hands.

"You've hit upon part of the truth. But not all of it. I wonder how much of it is trying to save myself."

"I believe that's called self-preservation."

Unexpectedly he laughed. "It's too bad you can't be cloned and passed out to the rest of us. Lance is a fortunate man."

She wanted him to keep on laughing, talking. She didn't want to say what she had to say. To admit her own guilt. For the first time in days, she again felt dirty. Was her judgment so frail that she had married a man who had caused Irene Stanton's death? If only she had pushed Lance Benson on through Houston and beyond, out of their lives.

She spoke quickly. "Lance could be involved."

His head shot up. "*He's* being blackmailed? Whatever in God's name is going on?"

"No. I mean — the other."

The words came now. Tumbling out, falling over themselves, jigsaw bits and pieces.

He reached for her and held her until she became still and began again. "It's all right, it's all right," he said once, when her teeth started chattering. He held her closer.

When she was done, he knew as much as she.

". . . What could he have on Martin Fletcher?" he asked. "Victor — with his wild streak — I can understand. But Martin? And Irene?"

They sat in silence, each combing through memories for the slightest details of lives about which they apparently knew little.

Finally, he spoke. "Bonita was Irene's best friend, until they had some kind of falling out. Bonita would know. Somehow I've got to get her to tell me. Meanwhile, I don't want you back in that house. I'm taking you to your father's."

"No . . . I have to go back."

"He struck you; he pointed a gun at you; there's a snake in the shower! You can't go back, Zoe."

"If I don't, he'll do something to my father. I know he will."

"Then you leave me no choice. I'm going to the police. There'll be a search warrant for the darkroom, protection for you and your father —"

"And your name smeared over the papers."

"I can't help that." His jaw was set.

"And Irene's." She had made a dent. "And Caroline Fletcher's. Maybe I don't mind as much about hers. But Irene's — and yours, I mind a great deal. Besides," she lifted her chin, "I'm not afraid."

He touched a corner of her lips. "Well, I am."

"Charles, your first instinct was right. We've got to give it time. Until after the funeral. He may call here. And he won't hurt me. I mean, he's got some glorified notion that a man doesn't do — irreparable damage — to his wife. So I'm safe. We'll get enough proof, band together. We'll scare him into leaving us all alone. For good . . . Now, you're going to talk to Bonita. And I can talk to Martin . . . tell him we're on his side and —"

"No, leave Fletcher out of this. He's unstable."

"Then Victor Solomon." She was grasping at straws.

"Zoe, I don't think so. Solomon's a heavy drinker. Not discreet. No, this has to be handled by me."

"By *both* of us."

He smiled.

"Look, Lance is scared. Martin saw to that. Maybe we should thank him." He ignored her attempt at humor; she pressed on. "I just know we have to hold off. At least for forty-eight hours. I'll be fine."

"No." He stood. "I'm taking you to your father's and then I'm coming back here to wait. If he doesn't call before the news gets out, I'll do something else. What, I'm not sure."

"Charles, I honestly don't think —"

The knock startled them both. Bonita's entrance ended their argument.

"There's a taxi for you, Zoe."

"Thank you." She stood on tiptoe and kissed his cheek. Briefly she wondered about the long, ugly scratch that was there. "It'll be over soon," she whispered.

Turning to Bonita, she said, "See if you can persuade this man to get some rest. I'll call later."

She was gone before he could stop her.

·  ·  ·

"You haven't *done* anything wrong, Charles. You were a good husband. Believe me. It was just — Irene was not happy with herself. Now that's all I can say. Don't ask me any more questions, please." Bonita Graves hugged a sweater, though it was not cold, about her. She rubbed her arms and looked around the room as if for a means of escape. Why couldn't he let it rest? Why the questions? "What do you know? What did she tell you? What did I do wrong?" This wasn't like him. He had always been extremely self-contained. Sometimes she had thought that had he not been so controlled Irene might have found peace. No, that was impossible. It was the other. The other to which she must not become linked. She who was grieving, as much as he, for his wife, her former lover; she who felt raw nerves pushing against her skin; she who was about to marry a fine, respectable man whom she loved. She must keep quiet. But to see this dear man, her friend, torturing himself with guilt when he had done nothing wrong; to listen to his questions, his pleas; to have her own hurt pounding in her chest . . . She knotted her fist against her mouth.

"Bonita — not long before she died — she quoted *Hamlet:* 'to thine own self be true.' She said she hadn't done that. Now what did she mean?"

"I don't know, Charles. I honestly don't know. Zoe Benson's idea was excellent. You should get some rest."

She hurried to the door. She would leave. But he came over to her, stopped her, his eyes, hurt and bewildered, boring holes into her face. Why wouldn't he let her go? Why must the burden of guilt be passed to her?

"You know something, Bonita. Tell me. Please!"

"No!"

"I'm begging you!"

"Don't!"

"Begging you!"

"All right!" She put her fingers to his lips. "All right. Irene —" She fought for air; she pushed back tears. "Irene swore you never suspected. Because she was a good wife, she tried hard, she loved you, Charles, you were everything she wanted in a husband, you mustn't feel guilty, you mustn't —"

"Suspected *what?*"

"I'm sorry. I can't —"

"What?" He gripped her arms. "Tell me!"

"She was a lesbian. She had been for years. I'm sorry." He released her.

She cried now.

"Don't. Don't." Awkwardly, he patted her shoulder. "It's all right. It's all right, Bonita."

She nodded, struggling to regain her composure.

"Bonita?"

"What?" She tried to mask her apprehension.

"Thank you."

He let her go without asking her the question she had feared. And he never would, she knew. It was over. She was glad that she had told him. He could pick up the pieces of his life and go on — which was what she must do with her own life.

How could she use it most effectively? She crammed the sack into her purse as the taxi pulled away from Oshman's. "Hey, aren't you forgetting something?" the clerk had asked after she had paid and was walking toward the door.

"What?" She'd stopped, frozen.

"Shells!" He'd held up a box, so shiny red it looked as if it had burst into flame.

"Oh, those." She'd laughed. "I've got some at home."

The procedure had been quick and simple enough. But twice she'd glanced over her shoulder to see if Lance had tracked her down. What if he had come home, then left again, furious that she was gone?

"Could you hurry, please?"

The taxi driver wordlessly shifted gears.

She opened her purse and peered inside the sack. So she was now the not-so-proud owner of a .25 caliber Beretta. If all else failed, she would point the gun at Lance. As for bullets, they could stay in the store. No way could she kill, or even maim, another human being. But she could scare the hell out of him.

Winifred Reese bit into a plum and glanced at the Dutch canopy clock mounted in her foyer. Four-twenty. Raymond had been gone most of the day. True, he had left a note explaining his whereabouts. But after his fabrication about having a date with Melissa Stebbins yesterday evening, she couldn't be sure he was actually poring over books in the public library. She had, however, reached a conclusion: whatever her son's secret ventures, they were harm-less and, she hoped, educational. Perhaps he was visiting a pros-titute before broaching the subject of bed to Melissa. If that was the case, she was relieved. God only knew he needed the experi-ence. And how he acquired that experience was not the sort of thing a son would tell his mother, even if she was quite knowl-edgeable herself. Still, she intended to ask him why he had found it necessary to lie to a mother who was, above all else, under-standing and open-minded. She planned to adopt a light, almost nonchalant, manner in her interrogation. After all, she didn't want to alienate her only child.

Seated at her Hepplewhite desk, she began writing a letter to Florence Mitten, a suite-mate from college days, who had recently opened an antique shop in Jackson, Mississippi. She pictured Flor-ence, an Easterner by birth, flourishing amid magnolias, ornate samovars, and velvet sofas.

Midway through composing a lengthy paragraph about the joys of attending estate auctions, she looked up. The silver bell on the front door had tinkled. Raymond was home.

Carrying the afternoon paper and appearing a bit sheepish, he entered the room.

"The prodigal son returns."

He held out the paper, as if it were a peace offering.

"I had a fascinating day."

"A bit long, wasn't it?"

"No, time flew. Mother, I find myself becoming increasingly intrigued with Egyptian furnishings. Did you realize that in the Eighteenth Dynasty there was no such thing as a pillow? Ivory headrests were used and made according to individual measure-ments."

"That has a familiar ring to it, yes . . . Raymond?" She worked the rubber band off the paper.

"Yes, ma'am." She observed that he swallowed nervously, a habit he had acquired as a child soon after she had divorced his father.

"I've been meaning to ask you something." She opened the paper so that the question would appear to be of no great importance. "Why ever did you find it necessary . . ." She glanced down at the front page. "My God!"

"Mother, what's wrong?"

She was shaking her head in disbelief.

Leaning over her shoulder, Raymond Reese read with his mother on page one of the *Houston Times* that Irene Stanton had committed suicide.

Several times during the day Lawrence Harrington stared at his silent phone. Why didn't his daughter call? She had said that she would consider moving out this weekend, away from Lance Benson. He had put fresh flowers in her room, new towels on the bath racks, and extra coat hangers in the closet. But she hadn't come. Nor had he heard from her. He picked up the phone and dialed her number.

"No, Lawrence, I thought maybe she was with you."

"I haven't heard from her in a day or so."

"Didn't she see you Thursday night?"

"Yes, but —"

"Well, she's a big girl now."

"I'm sorry to have troubled you. I had thought perhaps the two of you would come for dinner this evening."

"Not tonight, thanks. Maybe next week. If you see Zoe, tell her to get on home, please."

The conversation was terminated. At least, his daughter had not been immobilized. She was out and about — perhaps shopping, visiting a friend, sketching a face. That was good. He would spend the remainder of the afternoon at the university. Research for his book was progressing nicely. His daughter was all right. She was simply working things out in her own way. He must give her time. But not too much time. After all, her confiding in him had been an unspoken plea for help, and he was determined not to fail her.

The phone was ringing as she entered the house. Quickly she went to it.

"Thank God you answered. I've been calling and calling."

"I'm sorry. The cab driver wasn't the swiftest."

". . . You got away before I could stop you."

"I had to."

"You're all right?"

"I'm fine."

"You're certain?"

"Charles, I'm fine."

"I take it he's away."

"Well, I'm not sure. I just walked in the door, but his car's here."

"Have you seen the afternoon paper?"

"Why?"

"The story's on the front page."

"You're not serious?"

"Just that she died — and how."

"But it's so soon!"

"There must have been a leak at the police station."

". . . Then we've got to keep Lance from finding out."

"It's no good, Zoe."

"I think it is."

"Look, I'm coming for you."

"No, let me think . . . We don't get the *Times*. Lance takes it at the office, so he doesn't even bother reading it on weekends. And tomorrow morning —"

"Zoe —"

"Tomorrow morning I'll get up early and hide the Sunday *Herald*. I'll say it didn't come."

"Zoe, for God's sakes, it'll be on the news."

"Then I'll keep him away from television. Charles, listen to me. He may try to contact Irene. That's what you said you wanted."

"I'll be there in twenty minutes."

"No! . . . We have to wait. Until Monday."

" . . . Stubborn, aren't you?"

"Only about things — and people — I believe in."

"It's too risky, Zoe."

"It's worth a try."

He sighed. "Well, since I can't force you to leave, apparently it's got to be Monday."

"After the funeral."

"You drive a hard bargain. But if he hasn't called by then, I'm confronting him myself or turning the note over to the police. You do understand that?"

"I understand."

"Monday, Zoe."

"Monday, Charles."

"I'm getting you out of there. And call every few hours. Or more. I expect that."

"I want that."

"Good, because, you see, I can be stubborn too about things — and people — I love."

She hesitated.

Charles had said he loved her. Maybe he loved her along with the whole mass of humanity, but he had told her what she needed to hear.

"I'm glad," she said simply. And then she asked, "Did you talk to Bonita?"

"Before she left."

"Well, what did she say?"

"Zoe, I can't go into it now. Can you understand that?"

"All right. I mean — yes, yes, of course. But it's that bad?"

"It's that bad."

"Then I promise you we'll keep it hidden."

"Only if we can, Zoe. There are other things more important."

When she hung up the phone, her thoughts delved back into the years she had known Irene Stanton. Lady Stanton. The mirror of perfection. That mirror broken. Shattered, as if Lance had struck a hammer across fragile glass. She ran her fingers through her hair and then she straightened as she listened for something, anything. The house was deathly quiet.

She got up and began walking through the silent rooms.

Rays of afternoon sun stretched thin fingers of brightness across the living room rug. She moved to the French doors and stiffened. How peaceful he looked! Stretched out on a rubber raft, arms behind his head, eyes closed to the sun, Lance floated on water. For an instant she fought an impulse to run diving into the pool, upsetting the raft, disrupting his tranquility as he had disrupted the lives of people who had befriended, trusted, and even loved him. She turned and hurried up the stairs. There wasn't much time, for she didn't know how long he would remain asleep on his raft. But she had to try.

Her fingers closed around the keys deep in the pocket of his slacks waiting there on the bed for him. She glanced out a window. He hadn't moved. Taking two steps at a time, she climbed to the third floor.

At the top of the stairs, she froze. The darkroom door was open. She was a fool whose husband mocked her now with this room which all but had a welcome mat before it. Slowly she went back down the stairs and returned the keys to his pocket.

There was nothing to do but wait and pray that Lance would try to contact Irene Stanton. No, there was something else she could do. Something she had sworn she would do. She must prevent Lance from learning of Irene's death. If she succeeded, he might walk into the trap Charles had set for him. At any rate, she had only to hold on until Monday. She took a deep breath. "Until Monday." Then she could leave.

In a nightstand drawer, she hid the gun beneath her Bible. The juxtaposition of the two startled her. She moved the Beretta to a cranny behind art-history paperbacks. Only to move it back beneath her Bible. The gun seemed to belong nowhere.

Combing her hair and running gloss over her lips, she studied her reflection. Coolly. Solemnly. And then she walked slowly out of her house and toward the pool.

She stood at the edge of the water. "Are you asleep or meditating?"

He squinted one eye. "You were supposed to stay here."

"I'm sorry."

"You mean, you're sorry you were caught."

"No, I'm sorry I left."

"I see . . . So, where have you been?"

"Thinking."

"That tells me what you were doing, not where you were doing it."

"I took a taxi to the park, and then I walked and thought and sat and thought some more."

"That's it?"

"That was it."

"Well, obviously I don't like your doing that, but this time I'll let it go."

"Lance, I needed to get out of here."

"I never said you didn't, but that's not what you were supposed to do . . . Well, I said we'd forget it, OK?"

"OK."

She knelt beside the pool.

"Lance?"

He rolled off the raft and swam over to her.

"I've been thinking . . ."

"Yes, that's what you said you'd been doing."

"I want to share whatever is bothering you."

He studied her face, then shook water out of his ears. "Do you really now?"

"Yes."

"Why?" His eyes had narrowed.

"Because I'm your wife."

"I thought you'd forgotten that." He laughed. The sound was clipped. "Have I ever told you, Zoe, that at times you remind me of my faithful old dog Bailey?"

"Only of your mother."

"You're more like Bailey." He swam away from her then back. "Well, you don't have to worry. It seems I've worked out my problem. I can even assure you there'll be no more ridiculous notes."

"How did you manage that?"

"Magic. Sheer magic. In fact, there's no problem at all. Whiff." He raised his hands. Water sprayed onto her skirt.

"Just like that?"

"Exactly. All you need to do is forget last night happened."

"Even the threat about my father?"

"Oh, you might keep that in the back of your mind. But, look, I'm sorry I struck you. And the snake'll be out of the shower tomorrow morning."

"Not before?"

"This is the lady, pressuring me, who wants to share my troubles?"

"Lance, that snake terrifies me."

"Be patient." He pulled himself up over the pool's ledge and sat beside her.

He lighted a cigarette. "Did you look in the music room?"

"Should I?"

"I brought the Betamax downstairs. I decided we might as well begin enjoying it together. I'll buy you another Christmas present. Something extravagant. How's that?"

"Lovely but unnecessary . . . Lance?"

"What?"

"Wouldn't it be nice if it could be like it was in the beginning?"

"Well, that was a long time ago. And life moves on."

"I know, but if we could just recapture at least some of what we lost. Maybe we could spend the rest of the weekend . . . trying."

"How would you suggest?"

"I'm not sure."

"I see."

"Maybe . . . tonight we could eat at one of our favorite restaurants. And afterward just go somewhere and dance. The two of us. Like we used to."

He stared at her through smoke. And then he smiled a long, slow smile.

"You are a mullet, Zoe," he said. "A real mullet."

He reached over and began unbuttoning her blouse. She watched his head go down to her breast. She closed her eyes and fought revulsion as he murmured, "Don't you appreciate secluded backyards?"

Mayor Theodore Beale eased his two hundred and fifty pounds into Lowell Hook's library chair and rubbed a hand across his forehead. He squinted over wire-rimmed glasses at Hazel Mabry.

"Let me get this straight," he said. "You mean, you haven't seen him since last night?"

"No, sir, not since he left — he said to go out for dinner — about seven-thirty. He gave Jason —that's his chauffeur —"

"Yeah, I know."

"— the night off. Not since then."

The mayor sat in silence.

"I kept thinking he'd come walking in here ten minutes before everybody else. But then the guests started arriving, and, well sir, they're all sitting out there —"

"Don't worry about them."

"It's *him* I'm worried about! I'm sorry, sir, it's just this isn't like Mr. Hook."

The mayor sipped his Perrier — diets were the devil, but his wife had said he needed to shed a few pounds before the election. Hell, he'd told her, he didn't know but what his roly-poly appearance didn't make him more lovable. "Nobody trusts fat people indefinitely," Eleanor had said, so he'd said, "On the off chance you're right, here goes," and he'd reached for the Diet Pepsi and cottage cheese.

"Could I see his calendar?"

Hesitantly, Hazel Mabry lifted the sacrosanct, tooled-leather book from her employer's desk.

He flipped through the gold-edged pages then stopped. "Interesting . . . he's got written here 'Rest' then 'Party for Ted — 8:00.' And for Friday, September twenty-third —" He glanced up. "Who's S.L.?"

"S.L. I don't know."

"Well, it seems he saw S.L. at eight o'clock Friday night." He noted that the appointment was printed in small, neat blocked letters. Beside the time, the word "Confirmed" had been scrawled more typically in Hook's style. "Confirmed" had two lines drawn beneath it followed by an exclamation point. Something special had happened Friday night. Something from which the man had not returned.

He stood. "I would suggest, Mrs. Mabry, you explain to the guests that Mr. Hook has been indefinitely detained and would like everyone to enjoy dinner without him."

"Yes, sir, but what are you going to do about Mr. Hook?"

"What am I going to do? Why, Mrs. Mabry, I'm going to find him."

After she had left, he shifted his glasses on his broad nose, slightly crooked from having been broken twice during UT football days, and picked up the phone. The police chief had better be available, because, if necessary, he would keep right on dialing straight up to the governor himself. Lowell Hook was going to be located and fast.

When his phone rang, Percy Harmon was at home drinking beer and watching the Astros beat the socks off the Mets.

He lowered the volume on his television set. The muscles in his jaw tensed as he listened.

"And, above all, Percy, keep Hook's name out of it, you hear? I want this to be discreet."

"Well, Mayor, then we're most likely talking about a hand-out bulletin."

"No, I want more than that. Let's do an APB."

"Sure, but it goes out everywhere."

"I'm aware of that. Now I want to know exactly how you're going to word it."

"Simple: HPD needs information on the location of a — here we'll put in a car description and his license number. Then we'll follow that up with, 'Do not apprehend but notify immediately Chief of Patrol Harvey Upson.' "

"Good. And you'll let me know as soon as it's located?"

"You got it."

"And, Percy, stress 'Do not apprehend.' We just want to track him down quietly. We don't want anybody embarrassed."

"I understand that; but something's fishy, isn't it?"

"Well, it's not like him to just disappear. Still, you never know, the old boy could be out playing poker with this S.L. person and he's just forgotten the time. OK, Percy, get it moving. And keep in touch."

"Yes, sir."

Mayor Ted Beale put down the phone. He thumped his fingers on the desk calendar. "S.L." Nothing felt right. His friend and strongest political backer wouldn't have missed this party unless something was drastically wrong.

He hiked up his pants and rejoined the guests. A hush fell over the room. Now what in the hell was he supposed to tell them? He guessed he'd reiterate, in his own inimitable style, what Hazel Mabry had said. They should all eat their quail or whatever fancy was being served — along with the quick-thawed, fried zucchini sticks invariably placed on Lowell Hook's most elegant tables — then go on home.

T. D. Bass stood in front of the Fleetwood Brougham and laughed. The car looked like it hadn't moved an inch since last night. The dude must be some kind of sex maniac if he wouldn't let the poor girl off her back long enough to take her out to dinner. Or maybe he was a cheapskate. With a car like this, he should be showing her some pretty fancy places.

Tapping his fingers on the hood, he debated. An unauthorized vehicle that had been on the property longer than eight hours was to be reported. But it seemed a shame. The Fleetwood gave the place class. He made his decision. The car stayed. But if it was still here when he came back on duty tomorrow night, he'd ring the doorbell of 88 and say, "Hey, buddy, either you move your rattletrap or it's getting *hauled off*." If there was no answer — if they couldn't stop long enough to be apprised of the situation — then he'd have no choice but to turn the license number in to Miss Reba, who ran a tight ship. She'd snort, "High-class buggy or no, this ain't no motel. It goes!"

He ran his index finger down the side of the car, then walked on, with a strut, and whistling. Tonight was going to be one long haul. He'd wanted to pick up batteries at U-Totem for his scanner, which had gone on the blink; but, running late, he'd had no time. He'd just have to dream up some fantasies of his own. His imagination got rolling. . . It was Saturday night and there was this big bust of a prostitution ring. He was right in there, single-handedly rescuing fifteen teenyboppers from the clutches of a pimp who was practically selling them into slavery. Naturally, a little blood had to be shed before the darlings could be freed, because the pimp, who was also dealing in heroin, had an army of karate-choppers surrounding him. Well, he, T. D. Bass, conquered all. Overnight he became a hero. And, damned if his picture wasn't spread all over page one of the newspaper. Having noted his clean-cut, upstanding appearance and his feats of bravery, the police chief immediately calls inviting — no, *begging* — him to enroll in the police academy. End of Fantasy One.

He guessed his imagination would hold him. Still, he missed his scanner. Right now he could be listening, and participating vicariously at least, in what was happening out there in the real world.

Lance smoked in the dark. Beside him Zoe slept curled in a tight little ball. He was reminded of Sandra. She had slept that way. Zoe usually sprawled on her stomach. This different position, he supposed, was simply another manifestation of her unpredictable behavior during an evening that had been strangely unsettling. Over dinner she'd listened wide-eyed to stories of his childhood which even now he could not understand why he'd told her. At least he'd had the good sense not to tell her about the twins.

When he'd finished the monologue, she'd said, "All these years you never took me home with you. I didn't completely realize, until now, that we come from such different places." Her hand had been on his knee. He had wanted to knock it off, to tell her to cut out the superiority crap; but he'd said nothing, realizing that in her own inept way she was trying to regain whatever she imagined had once been between them. They had made love three times during the course of the afternoon and night. Once he'd asked, "Tears, Zoe?" She'd answered, "No," but he had known she was lying. If he chose, she would stick by him all the way to wherever. That might not be bad. She was an excellent lover and a smart woman . . . but she had never understood him. Though tonight she had reawakened his interest, she would all too soon bore him again. If his new world held no place for a Sandra Lowrey, neither did it hold a place for a Zoe Benson.

Unfortunately much remained to be done before he could begin his more promising life. Tomorrow, the confrontation with Fletcher. Monday, the call to Irene Stanton. And Wednesday, the collections from both Irene and Raymond. He was tempted to shove the tape directly under Charles Stanton's nose. After all, his initial outline had listed as Objective Five: "To watch Sir Charles Ashton Stanton sweat." But, here at the end, he'd best hold off approaching Stanton unless it became expedient to do so.

His thoughts traveled over the long day, which had finally ended. This afternoon he'd pulled up to a newsstand and peered at the *Times* headline: "BOND ISSUE DEFEATED." And driven on. Hook and Sandra's banner was yet to come. Earlier he'd stopped by the library to learn more about rattlesnakes. He knew now exactly what to do with the reptile slithering around his shower stall. Once in the library he'd glanced up and thought he'd seen studious little asshole Reese seated at a table across the room. When he'd looked again whoever it had been was gone.

He should get some sleep, for he needed to be razor sharp tomorrow. But his thoughts trudged on. The briefcase filled with money was now safely locked in the trunk of his car. It also contained the tapes to be delivered to Irene and Reese, the gun, plastic gloves, and the wig he still needed. All other evidence had been buried or burned. While driving to the restaurant, he had leaned over and opened the glove compartment, ostensibly to reach for cigarettes but actually to show Zoe that nothing remained hidden there. She'd asked, "Where's the gun?" to which he'd replied "Gone" with a finality she hadn't questioned.

He mashed out his cigarette and slid down into the dark. Tension remained in his body. He rolled the sleeping Zoe onto her back and, with one deep thrust, penetrated her. She awoke, crying out. His climax came swiftly. He slid off her and slept.

.  .  .

She pulled her nightgown down over her hips and curved once again into the tight little ball. She had kept her husband from newspapers, televisions, and radios. He did not know that Irene Stanton was dead. But at what cost to herself? Once during dinner, and again during the foreign film he had wanted to see, she had gone to the restroom. Both times she had phoned Charles. "I'm all right. He doesn't know," she'd said. During the last call, he'd asked, "How are you managing to do this?" She had replied, "I know Lance." Well, she did and she didn't know him. Had they started out together as children running into cold water, sharing hopes and dreams, had she brushed the hair out of his eyes, assured him it didn't matter how he felt about his parents, they had each other — maybe things would have been different. But it hadn't happened that way. They had come together already shaped. They were each who and what they were. It had been too late. And now, she feared and abhorred him. He in turn had become weary of her. She recognized this last for what it was: an additional reality she had chosen to ignore. She bored him. But he disgusted her. And she disgusted herself. During these past hours, her body had responded to his. Though at first she had opened herself in loathing and in sadness for what was and was not, she had gradually become alive, attuned to him, until finally she had cried out in some deep, masochistic pain. Only when he had come at her just now, pinning her beneath him, had she physically recoiled. He had seemed an animal, wild and repulsive and selfish. Wide-eyed, she lay awake, recalling the words of the psalm that had comforted her in her childhood.

There were no surprises. At five o'clock Sunday morning the unauthorized Fleetwood was still occupying space. "This one's on the house," T. D. Bass announced to thin air. Then, fixing a dead-eye bead on the car, he said, "But come tonight, if you're not gone, I'm hauling your ass out of here!"

At 6:15 A.M. Zoe Benson shoved the Sunday *Herald* to the bottom of the garbage can. The paper carried on its front page the story of Irene Stanton's death. A paragraph listing her community activities stated that Lady Stanton had been a volunteer worker for The Arch Theatre on whose board her husband had served since 1970.

. . .

"I know, I know, I know. Look, Mayor, I *know*." Police Chief Percy Harmon shifted the phone from one ear to the other. "Yes, sir, if it doesn't turn up in the next twenty-four hours . . . all right, the next twelve hours, we'll do something else . . . No, I don't know what we'll do, but we'll do it. Only we'll have to be more open, you understand? Maybe even use spot announcements on TV. 'Have you seen this car?' That sort of thing . . . Don't get upset! It was just a suggestion . . . Good. Fine. Twenty-four hours. Thank you, sir. I'll lean harder on my men . . . For sure . . . I'll keep you posted."

He put down the phone and looked at his watch. Seven o'clock, Sunday morning. Lowell Hook had been missing for thirty-five hours. It didn't look good. You'd think his car, being the showpiece that it was, would have turned up someplace. But no! He felt like he was looking for a needle in a haystack. He rolled his eyes upward and longed for his boyhood days on a Kansas farm. Back then haystacks had been for fun, for sliding down to soft earth. Haystacks had not been torn apart, searched through for an infinitesimal nothing, which was what he was having to do now. And with all the help he had — 102 patrol units thrashing through hay — why, he wondered, was the haystack getting the better of him?

Spreading apple butter on his toast, Lawrence Harrington began reading his Sunday paper. Abruptly he shoved his breakfast aside. He stared out the window. The tablet of good and evil, which had formed in his mind after Zoe had brought Charles Stanton to visit, reappeared. Why, he wondered, did he see the tablet now after reading of Irene Stanton's death? He studied the article. Lance Benson was somehow connected to this suicide. He sensed it. Tomorrow he would attend the funeral and observe his son-in-law. If only for appearances' sake, Lance would be there. Impatiently he stood. He would have preferred logic to intuition. What he needed was one simple fact on which to peg his apprehension.

"You're sure you want me to go?" Caroline Fletcher stood beside the bed.

"Positive." He burrowed his head beneath a pillow. "I think I can sleep it off."

"But you felt so well yesterday."

"Must have been something I ate."

"Martin, we ate the same things."

"Don't worry. Go on to church. I just want to sleep."

"I'll come right home."

"Don't rush. I'll probably be asleep."

"Well . . . if you're sure."

"I'm sure." He burrowed deeper. She picked up her purse and left.

When she was halfway out the kitchen door, the phone rang.

It was Roselyn Solomon.

"Isn't it awful?"

"What?"

"Haven't you seen the paper?"

"No, Martin's not feeling well, and I've been in such a rush to get to church. What's awful?"

"Irene Stanton killed herself."

When the conversation was over, Caroline Fletcher stood very still. Her hand went to her breast. Only weeks before Irene had been consoling her. And now, unbelievably, her friend was dead. She bit her lip. Should she disturb her husband? Should she go on to church? The paper lay in its clear, yellow pouch on the doorstep. She wouldn't stop now to read what she had just heard. Church was where she wanted to be, was where she had to be. As for Martin, he needed his rest.

Dressed in blue jeans and a plaid shirt, his blond hair hidden beneath the salt-and-pepper wig, Lance Benson looked like an aging hippie as he strode through the woods in back of the Fletchers' town house. Brushing aside low-hanging branches, he congratulated himself on circumventing the guardhouse. He shifted the cage and hook from one gloved hand to the other and steeled himself for the mission ahead. Pushed to the back of his mind was his earlier dispute with Zoe who had become his scapegoat when he'd discovered the morning paper had not been delivered. He'd silently raged that he would have to wait to learn if the bodies had been discovered for, once he left his house, he would need to concentrate solely on Martin Fletcher. Not until afterward, when it was over, could he stop at a newsstand.

He stepped out of the woods into sunlight. Luck was with him. There were no Sunday joggers. Quickly he walked up the drive, past five or so town houses, and unlatched the gate leading to Martin's patio. "Well, what do you know," he said, looking down. Lying there at his feet, the unopened paper seemed an omen of success. The front door opened before he could ring the bell.

This was hardly her idea of fun. Stretched out on her sofa with a scanner balanced on her stomach, Molly Reidell settled down for what might well turn out to be a long day eroding into night. She'd planned to bicycle twelve miles, manicure her nails, and jog six blocks to her ex-husband's apartment, where they would fight for a while, go out for Chinese food, and probably end up in bed. That was how she had structured her free day. But ambition was riding herd over her plans. Here could be her opportunity to prove that the *Houston Herald*'s top reporter-photographer was indeed a twenty-eight-year-old woman named Molly Reidell. The bulletin blaring repeatedly over her scanner sounded bigger than big. When she'd called for additional information, the HPD data terminal had on its recording: "We are unauthorized to give out the information you request at this time." If only the Tax Assessor-Collector's office weren't closed on weekends. How she would love to know who owned that Fleetwood Brougham! The license number was coming through loud and clear over static. Well, all she needed to do was lie here and listen. When the car was located, she'd be ready to move.

The gun pointed at his throat. Martin Fletcher swallowed the capsule.

"I don't understand why you want me to sleep."

"I have my reasons."

"You don't seem to realize, Benson, I have the upper hand."

"How is that, Martin?"

"Well, I — I just do, that's all." He was perspiring. He wanted to leave the room. He wanted to run.

"Come over here, Martin."

"I thought I was supposed to sleep."

"It'll take a while for the pill to act. In the meantime, there's something I want you to type."

"Type?"

"You seem to enjoy typing notes, I've noticed. But this one —

which I'll dictate — will have a slightly different twist."

The gun motioned him to the typewriter.

" 'Dearest Caroline.' "

"You're not bringing her into this!"

"You should have thought of that before you began threatening my wife."

"Benson, I'll pay you the rest of the money. Just leave Caroline alone, please."

"Type. 'I am taking my own life . . .' "

Martin Fletcher tried to rise; the gun pushed him back into the chair.

"Type, Martin. '. . . with a capsule of Lightning.' "

Martin Fletcher paled. "Is that what I swallowed?"

"Ironic, isn't it? Your company's roach poison."

"My God!"

"Type. 'And as an extra measure to ensure that I'll get out of this world I find so distasteful —' "

"I can't."

"You can."

"Benson, get me to the hospital. I'll pay you double. Just take me, *please*."

" 'I have chosen to put additional poison into my system through the bite of a rattlesnake.' "

Martin Fletcher stared with bulged eyes straight ahead. His fingers refused to move on the keys.

"You're going to type or I'll blow your brains out *now*. I've allowed for that possibility. But think, Martin. Every minute you stay alive there's hope. You might even be able to kill me, overthrow your enemy, so to speak. *Type*."

His fingers moved on the keys.

" 'I've put it back in its cage so that you will not be harmed.' "

"You've thought of everything, haven't you?" There was defeat in his voice.

"I believe so, yes. Add this: 'I love you more than life itself, but pressures from your illness —' "

"I can't do that to her!"

" ' — pressures from your illness, my job, and what I suppose could be termed a mid-life crisis, make it impossible for me to go on.' " He picked up a pen from the desk. "Now sign it. . . . *Sign* it, Martin. At least, I let you tell her you loved her, something you obviously couldn't tell her while you were crawling into Sandra Lowrey's bed."

"You put me there!"

"With minimal effort."

"My God, what have I ever done to you?"

The question was ignored. "Now . . . type Caroline's name on this envelope and we'll place it beside you. Touching, don't you think?"

He tried to stop trembling; a hard knot was forming in his stomach.

"Seal it."

He put his head on the typewriter; sobs welled up from his throat, the knot was tightening.

"Seal it, Martin."

He licked the mucilage. His mouth was dry.

"Now put your fingers here and here and here."

"Benson, I'm not going to help you with this, I'm —"

The gun bore into his spine. He reached out. His fingers touched the snake hook's handle. If only he could wrench the tool and twist, turn, probe it into the bastard's guts, if only, if only . . . he weren't so weak.

"Stand up, Martin."

"I can't, please, I can't."

"Oh, I think you can." The gloved hands went under his arms and he was lifted from the chair only to be brought to his knees before the cage as if it were a shrine.

"Wherever I point press your fingers."

"I don't want to die!" The sobs, the trembling, were uncontrollable now.

Roughly Benson took his hands and bore his fingers hard against the cage. Bone would snap. Wood would splinter, crack open — a volcano splitting earth. The snake would devour his fingers!

"Holy Mary, Mother of God, make him stop!"

"Now, stretch out on the floor. On your back."

"It's not too late! Look, we can make a —"

He was shoved onto his back.

"Lance, I'm begging you, I'm begging —"

"No! You bend under pressure. Break. And I can't allow that."

"You can trust me. Listen, my God, you can trust me!"

"Sorry, Martin. It looks like you're just going to have to be a little man."

He watched, eyes rolling, as the lid slid open. With the hook clamped about its neck, the reptile was lifted into the air then aimed downward. He tried to edge away, but Benson's foot was a rock on his stomach. The knot had a life of its own now, growing larger, harder, filling up his stomach, cramping, shooting pain through his veins; the reptile edged closer, closer, until its tongue was against his neck. He closed his eyes and concentrated on life, on confessional, on the wings of a priest's robe covering him. He screamed. A man, he thought, should die in dignity, but dignity had deserted him. The snake was returned to its cage. The hook placed beside it. Benson sat across the room, watching. He turned his head from the cold, hard eyes.

On his way out the door, Lance Benson picked up the morning paper. Tucking it under his arm, he hurried back through the woods to his car, which was parked amid still machinery at a nearby construction site.

"Why are you doing this?"

"To get my mind off things."

She sketched rapidly. "Turn to the left . . . not so far. That's fine. You make a good subject."

"Flattery, Zoe, will get you about five more minutes of this, and no more," Lawrence Harrington said.

Unannounced he had appeared at her door; because, worrying, anxious to hear from her, he had finally left his own house and come here.

"When did you eat last?" he'd asked, noting her drawn appearance.

"I don't know. I guess — last night."

"We'll fix that." He had made tuna sandwiches.

They had sat at the kitchen table while she'd eaten in gulps. Without realizing it, she had been hungry, she'd said.

"And where is Lance now?" he'd wanted to know.

Her words had come in a rush: "He said he was going to kill it and dump it in a landfill. But I don't know. I thought maybe he'd take it to Martin. Probably it was stupid, but I tried to call there — only no one answered. I don't know where he is. I wanted to go with him, but he said no. He could be out buying a paper. I tried so hard to keep the news from him. But maybe I failed. Like I tried to keep all this from you, and I couldn't. I told you anyway."

"It's best you did," he'd reassured her.

"I don't know. I honestly don't know where he is. Maybe at the theatre."

After she'd eaten, they had searched through the house for a link, no matter how insignificant, that would connect Lance to Irene Stanton, or to Martin Fletcher, or, as Zoe — recalling Solomon's remark at the party — had suggested, "conceivably to Victor Solomon." They had found nothing.

They sat now in her studio, his head angled toward the light.

"I've been wanting to do your portrait for years."

"Let's go to the police," he said abruptly.

"I explained, we have to wait." She stopped sketching. "You understand, don't you?"

"I understand that your wanting to protect Charles Stanton's public esteem is admirable, but foolish."

"Would you do otherwise?"

She had trapped him. "I imagine . . ." He paused. ". . . Probably not." He resumed his pose. "Are you in love with him?"

"*Lance?*"

"No."

She sketched now in quick, sure strokes. ". . . I'm not sure. But I think, maybe so."

"He's much older than you."

"That wouldn't matter."

"No, I suppose not." He thought again of the tablet, his daughter's name suspended between the names of Lance Benson and Charles Stanton.

She closed the pad. "We'd better go. I'll follow you in my car. At least Lance and I have reached some kind of truce. He returned my car keys."

He carried her suitcases to his car. She had begun the move. The essentials she had packed were items that Lance wouldn't miss. When Monday came, she would leave for Saint Michael's Episcopal Church and not return. He wished tomorrow were here. His daughter would be away from this man who until now had seemed to wield a hypnotic power over her, and in a sense over him.

In a procession of two — her Toyota and his old Chrysler — they drove to Wood Park Funeral Home to pay their respects.

"I must talk to you." Charles led her aside.

She was glad she had hay fever today. Her sense of smell was dulled. Since her mother's death, she had hated the mingled odors of carnations and velvet in places with names like Wood Park, Peaceful Haven, and Fawn Meadows.

"What is it?" She touched his arm.

"I want to tell you now — the thing Irene had to hide."

"You don't have to tell me."

"No, please, I want to. You might even say I need to . . . My wife was a lesbian."

"Oh, Charles." She looked away. Her father was talking quietly to Victor Solomon. She turned again to stare into pained eyes and ask, though she knew the answer, "Are you sure?"

"Quite. And another thing. I checked her engagement book. She had lunch with Lance on Friday."

He wheeled his Continental out of the deserted construction site and drove to Memorial Park, where he parked under an elm and peeled off the gloves. For a time he rested his head on the steering wheel. Though he had felt all-powerful, all-knowing, as he watched Martin Fletcher writhe and beg — the begging had pleased him most — the taste of bile had come into his mouth and stayed while the feeling of omnipotence had deserted him. Sandra had been right. He was a murderer. But that was not what he had started out to be, was not what he was born to be. He had been forced to become what he was not. The killings were done. There would be no more.

He unfolded the morning paper. The bodies had not been discovered. Suddenly his stare became riveted by a headline near the bottom of the front page. What was this? Some kind of joke? It couldn't be! She couldn't have killed herself only hours before he had forced Martin Fletcher into what would appear to be a suicide. But there it was in print. Irene Stanton was dead. Two suicides, a murder, and a heart attack. Four people: all connected to The Arch. His eyelid twitched. What was he to do now? Approach Stanton himself? Today was Sunday. There was no way Stanton could gain access to his funds until Monday. And the funeral, the shit-ass funeral, was on Monday! The police would surely question him now. There were too many dead. He had to get out of the country, passport or not, as fast as he could. But how could he just yet? Didn't Reese owe him money? And without Stanton's thousands, his project was worth no more than a bucket of ashes.

Damnit! He needed his money. Now! How dare she? How dare the dumb butch with the high-flown title do this to him! He fought for composure. If only he were home. But where was home? Home was to have been someplace different. Someplace challenging. There was no home. And there never would be unless he kept his wits about him. He would return temporarily to the house he shared with Zoe. He would lock the door and go out to the pool. There, on his raft, he would once again reshape his plan. He would decide how best to confront Stanton. And, more important, he would come up with a viable means of escape.

He backed his car hurriedly from under the tree. The image of Peter Rabbit, caught in a briar patch, flashed before him. Once when he was six, and his mouth had been filled with blueberries stolen from what was to have been Saturday night's pie, his mother, her fat jowls shaking down into his face, had mocked, "Peter Rabbit. Just like Peter Rabbit. Caught. Greedy little Peter Rabbit. *Caught!*"

"I'm home," she called out, wondering if he was still asleep.

She hurried up the stairs only to find an empty bed, the sheets thrown back as if he had risen in haste. His bathrobe and pajamas were on a chair. "He's feeling better," she thought and went back down the stairs, a mild curiosity settling over her because he had not met her in the hall to kiss her and ask, "How was church?"

She'd planned to look for him in the sun room, but crossing the living room she noticed there in the library a black-screened box centered on the rug as if it were a centerpiece. Sunlight cast dust-flecked rays across the strange contraption. She thought she saw movement inside. "Martin," she said as she entered the room, "what on earth is —" The scream seemed to come from outside her body. It was someone else screaming. It was someone else rushing to the phone, someone whose fingers refused to dial. Finally, a voice she recognized as her own pled with the operator, "Get an ambulance, get the police! *Please*. My husband has been murdered." Later, when she had become calm, she was to wonder why she had requested an ambulance for Martin, who was obviously dead, and why, though she had read the note beside him, she had instinctively used the word "murdered."

Victor Solomon poured lemonade into paper cups. He handed a cup to Roselyn.

"Thank you."

Silently they leaned against the trunk of a tree. Across an expanse of lawn, their children tossed peanuts into a pond. Chad was jumping up and down, laughing. Rebecca began laughing, too. Holding hands, they ran over a bridge to fling more nuts into the water.

"The cranes must be hungry," Victor said.

"I guess."

She pulled a blade of grass beside the blanket they had spread on the ground.

They were both, he knew, thinking of the last hour.

"That's a somber place," she said.

"Name me a funeral home that isn't."

"I guess."

"You're full of guesses today."

She laughed. "I guess. But it makes you wonder . . ." She shifted to face him. "We have so much to be thankful for, I just hope —"

"What?"

"We don't mess it up."

"We won't." He gulped the last of his lemonade. "Look, they're moving on to the bears. Do bears like peanuts?"

"The whole world likes peanuts, crazy." She reached over and tickled his ribs.

"You're the one who's crazy." He removed her hands.

It was good between them now. But fragile. Why had Zoe Benson's father cornered him? "Is my son-in-law treating you well?" he'd asked.

"How do you mean?" He'd felt his guard go up.

"I understand he can be quite a taskmaster with his board members."

"Well, he's a past drinking buddy, so that keeps things in their proper perspective."

"Past?"

"I'm abstaining these days." He'd changed the subject.

He recalled that while he had talked to Harrington, Charles Stanton had drawn Zoe aside. Could it be that all of them — the dozen or so people who had spoken in hushed tones, surrounded him in that room — were trapped in Benson's blackmail?

Preposterous. But if that was true, certainly he was no longer trapped. He was free and clear. He had paid. Only suppose Benson were to miscalculate and end up in court? Then what? Witnesses would be subpoenaed.

"Where are you?" Roselyn waved her hand in front of his eyes.

He thought quickly. "Headed for Cozumel."

"Day after tomorrow!"

"You got it!" He stood, brushing blades of grass from his shirt. "What do you say we give them a hand with the hippos?"

"Good idea." She hopped up from the blanket. He was reminded of a child skipping rope. Impulsively he hugged her.

"Jesus!" Benny Harris hung up the phone, rubbed his freckled snub nose, and lowered his head over notes he'd scribbled while Archie Moore had rattled off the astounding news. Another scoop for tomorrow's edition, if the *Herald* didn't get there first. Was it his fault that the *Times* had the shortsightedness to be an afternoon paper? He did his job. He got the story. "The Kid" was what he'd been nicknamed soon after he'd arrived three years before from SMU's school of journalism; but lately a little respect, awe even — roughly translated: "The Kid has done it again" — was creeping into the old-timers' voices.

Securing an informant at the Harris County morgue was proving to be a worthwhile investment. Here, a mere thirty-two hours later, Archie Moore had delivered news of yet another prominent citizen's suicide. And this one offered drama. What a way to go! Swallowing roach poison, then sticking a rattlesnake to your jugular vein. You had to hand it to Fletcher — the man had guts.

He'd like to run a picture of the guy. Having been a company vice president, Fletcher just might be on file in the paper's morgue.

He visualized the headline. Now if he could inject flair into the article, using the angle that the man was no sissy — none of this sleeping pill stuff — he might land himself a front-page byline. "The Kid," they'd all say, "strikes again!"

·  ·  ·

Having canceled a fishing trip to Eagle Lake, Kermit Whalen had been in his office since early afternoon. He sipped coffee from his "Damn I'm Good" mug and listened to Police Chief Percy Harmon, who loomed over his desk.

Whalen put down his mug and explained his situation. "I just sent my top team out to Memorial."

"Well, get them back."

"Look, Chief, this is no small potatoes. Some executive with Powell Insecticides left a suicide note, but it doesn't exactly stack up that way. His wife, who's, incidentally, big in charity circles, swears he was murdered."

Percy Harmon pulled at his ear, rearranged three pencils on Whalen's desk, and cleared his throat. "I take it you've got Dobson and Pritchard on this one?"

"That's right."

"Contact them to swing back by Hook's place. *Now*. Have them check out his address book page by page, his correspondence, his bank statements. See if a name doesn't turn up to go with those two lousy initials."

"Fine, they can do that. But I don't want to take them off the Fletcher case unless I have to."

"Well, damnit, you may have to! I've got the mayor breathing down my neck." The police chief was silent. The homicide captain sipped his coffee. "OK . . . Have them work both."

"Yes, sir."

The senior officer started to leave. He stopped before a lithograph of Themis.

"That was a Christmas present from my oldest son."

"The lawyer?"

"He's had his shingle out for about a month now."

Harmon's finger traced the scales under glass. "You know, Whalen, it's the damndest thing."

"What?"

"This business we're in." He shook his head, as if to clear his thoughts. "Well, give your son my congratulations — and my con- dolences." Abruptly he left.

Kermit Whalen glanced up at the lithograph. The frame, he noticed, was crooked. "So it's a damnable business," he reflected. "Somebody's got to clean up the shit." He stared at the goddess of justice; her concrete eyes stared back.

·  ·  ·

Oh, she was such a lady! He sighed deeply. Melissa Stebbins had firm little breasts which reminded him of baseballs without insides. She'd been nothing like Sandra Lowrey, with her basketball tits and her deft fingers and swift hips, but this girl would do. Later he would tire of her or, horrors, she of him; but for the moment she was everything he wanted. Again he sighed. If only Scruffy Dawson could see him now!

"Was it OK?" Melissa reached for the little tray of bonbons she kept beside her bed.

"Delicious!" She popped a chocolate between his teeth. He chewed contentedly. To think that his mother, when she'd caught him in his lie, hadn't been angry. She'd somehow concluded that he'd been with a prostitute the night he'd looted the studio. "Well, some good, solid experience with a kindhearted whore never hurt anyone," had been her only comment. Amazing. Maybe the day Benson had threatened to sell the tape to a porno company, he should have bluffed, "Go ahead! It's not going to shock anybody, least of all my mother." What a woman! Maybe even now — before Monday, when she would surely shriek, "We've been robbed!" — he should confess. Conceivably she would have a solution to his problem. She was after all the most intelligent woman he knew. For years she had pushed him toward sensible girls. If only he'd listened. Today had been incredible: brunch at the Warwick then a tour of Bluebonnet Hill, where Melissa had told him that once as a child she'd eaten in the great dining hall seated at Lowell Hook's right, because, the host had announced to the other guests, "Young ladies occasionally deserve to be pampered."

Enthralled, he'd listened and observed her little baseballs move up and down beneath her blouse. They'd walked through the estate gardens until unexpectedly she'd announced, "There's a mocha torte in my refrigerator." They'd gone immediately to her apartment, where the furniture was white and gold and the walls leading to her bedroom were lined with framed snapshots of Melissa skiing, Melissa debuting, Melissa graduating, Melissa boarding the *QE II*, Melissa, Melissa, Melissa. Instead of a mirror over her bed, there was pale yellow voile, through which he'd looked up to the ceiling while his fingers reached down to the soft tufted mound. This afternoon had made him man enough to consider telling Benson to fuck off and forget the fifty thousand dollars hidden now in his closet. Should he muster the courage to do that, he would then place the entire stack of bills at his mother's feet and beg for her forgiveness.

"Who's Lance Benson?" Detective Clyde Pritchard looked up from the address book in which he had located a name to match two initials in the desk calendar. For Wednesday, September twenty-first, Hook had written himself a note: "Call L.B.!" On only one other page were there initials and an exclamation point: Friday, September twenty-third — "8:00 — S.L. — Confirmed!" The address book did not identify S.L. But L.B. and Lance Benson fit together like handcuffs locked around wrists.
"That's the theatre director," Hazel Mabry said.
"Of The Arch?" Detective Dobby Dobson stopped searching through correspondence.
"Yes, sir. Mr. Hook is a board member."

As the elevator began its descent from Hook's thirty-sixth floor penthouse, the two detectives spoke at once.
"Go ahead." Pritchard deferred. He recognized Dobson, though a year younger than he, as the senior partner and the one with the sharpest mental processes. He considered himself better on foot-work.
"Wasn't Fletcher a board member of that theatre?"
"His wife still is."
They stepped into the lobby. Dobson stopped and unwrapped a peppermint. He was trying to give up smoking. Thoughtfully, he sucked on the candy.
"Pritch, you know the Stanton suicide that made the front page this morning?"
"What about it?"
"Her husband's on that same board."

Blocks of the crossword puzzle were filled with proper and improper nouns. Most of the spaces, however, were blank except for penciled-in question marks. Detective Dewitt Dobson sat at his desk, a half-eaten hamburger and two empty Coke cans beside him. A circle of light from a student lamp shone on the puzzle he had constructed. With each new case, he applied his crossword-puzzle technique, rearranging and adding words until a pattern formed. He stared at the words in the blocks: Ornade, cage/hook, note, Thompson, Arch. A case could be made for either suicide or murder. He'd scrutinized the preliminary lab and autopsy reports. Pritch had tracked down the source of the snake. And now this Hook thing, which might or might not be connected to Fletcher's death, had developed. There were too many missing pieces for the puzzle to be solved overnight. He glanced at his watch. It was late. He was going home. Home was not exactly a haven these days since Melanie had taken their son and left six weeks before saying, "I love you, Dobby, but I can't take anymore. You get too involved. You're just not here, you *know?* You're never here even when you're here." He shoved the puzzle to the back of a drawer. To-morrow he would visit The Arch. For months Pritch and he had worked primarily on inner-city knifings and nobody had much cared, except Whalen. He always cared. Now, suddenly, an im-portant man was missing — just when they'd been assigned the Fletcher case, which was going to be a tough investigation — and the police chief on up to the mayor, he understood, were screaming for results. Did the higher-ups think there was any less urgency in dealing with crime among the people living where fire hydrants were scarce and rats gnawed at kids' toes? He tossed the remains of his supper into the wastepaper basket and switched off the lamp. The phone rang. Wearily he answered.

Hours after she had discovered her husband's body and the police had come and gone, Caroline Fletcher opened the front door to reach down in the dark for the morning paper. She flicked on the outside light and peered behind shrubbery. The paper was gone. "Such an insignificant thing," she thought, but she called the police department and asked for Dewitt Dobson, one of the homicide detectives who had been in her home earlier. Detective Dobson had looked at her with heavy, sad eyes as if he could see beyond facts to pain.

"It's a small thing," she told him, "but I mentioned earlier that the note didn't sound in the least like something my husband would have written, and now the paper is gone from our patio. Someone was here, I know it."

"You're sure it's not in the house?"

"Positive."

"That's interesting . . . Does anyone in your family take Ornade, Mrs. Fletcher?"

"Ornade?"

"It's a medication for allergies."

"No."

"The capsule your husband swallowed contains trace elements of Ornade."

"What would that mean?"

"Whoever poured the poison into the capsule first had to empty out the medicine . . . There's something else. The snake cage and the hook. They're clean."

"I'm sorry?"

"No fingerprints — except for those of your husband. But I will say his prints on the hook are at a rather strange angle."

"Then someone was here."

"We don't know that. Though if that's the case, he or she is what — on the whole — I would call a clever amateur."

"Detective Dobson, for Martin to have done this himself makes no sense!"

"Nothing makes sense, Mrs. Fletcher. But it will. Now, if you can think of anything else, anything at all, that might be helpful, no matter how slight, we would be most appreciative. I'll be out to see you first thing in the morning."

"Of course," she said. "I'll be here. My son just drove in from Austin. And my daughter, Justine — she's on a plane from Rome. I'll be here. Thank you." Dimly she was aware that she was babbling as if he were a trusted friend. But he was the one who would find out who had done this terrible thing. He would be her savior. No, that was too extreme. She clutched her prayer book and held on to the serenity she had discovered during her illness.

"There's one other thing."

"Yes?"

"The photograph you gave us of your husband?"

She held more tightly to the prayer book.

"A Mr. Frazer Thompson has identified Mr. Fletcher as the person who purchased the snake from him on Friday."

"I can't believe that."

"I'm sorry. It was a simple, straightforward location of evidence. And verification. Through your husband's company. Mr. Thompson traps reptiles for the research laboratory."

"But someone was here. You do believe that, don't you?"

"As a possibility, definitely. We'll keep at it."

. . .

T. D. Bass's scanner, equipped with new batteries, was blaring bulletins as he walked purposefully toward Carrousel Square's office. He had no alternative: Miss Reba was getting a call. For five minutes he'd rung the doorbell of 88, but no one inside had paid any attention. Disregarding the law was what they were doing. The broad knew the rules. It would serve them right, when they finally put on their clothes and walked outside, to discover that the Fleetwood had disappeared.

Halfway to his destination, he stopped and turned up the scanner's volume. He stood in the middle of the street. Listening.

"Christ Almighty!" he blurted, then ran the remaining three blocks to the office.

Police Sergeant Justin Graham observed that the security guard's hands were shaking as he inserted the manager's master key into the lock.

Apartment 88 was pitch black.

"Thank you," he said to T. D. Bass. "Now if you'll wait outside. There may be questions later."

"Yes, sir. I'll be right here. You're sure you don't want me in there? I know the floor plans of these places like the nose on my face."

"No, son, you've been a real help." The sergeant and his two patrol officers stepped inside.

After covering his hand with a handkerchief, Sergeant Graham flicked on the overhead light. The living room was empty.

He led the way to the bedroom. Politely he knocked on the door. "Proceed inside the apartment, but handle whatever's there with kid gloves," the police chief himself had ordered, emphasizing, "and radio me the minute you find out what's going on."

He knocked a second time. Again there was silence. As though on cue, the three men reached for their guns. Sergeant Graham opened the door. Brightness flooded the room.

"Holy Jesus!" The younger patrol officer, assigned to duty only two weeks before, peered between the older men.

"Don't touch a thing," Graham cautioned.

The younger man moved to the bed and stood, staring down. "Holy Jesus," he repeated.

Sergeant Graham unhooked his radio from his belt. "101 to 406. I mean, 406 to 101." He was visibly shaken.

The response to his signaling was instantaneous.

"101 to 406. Go ahead."

"Sir, we have a DOA–Suspected Homicide at this location. Two of them. Caucasian male, I'd say in his seventies; Caucasian female, early to mid-twenties."

"406, clear. I'll be there as fast as possible. Radio Homicide. Request Captain Whalen, Detectives Dobson and Pritchard get there immediately."

"Yes, sir. Anything else?"

"Stay put. I'm on my way."

Police Chief Percy Harmon placed one succinct call before he bolted out the door.

"You think we can keep something like this quiet?" he asked the mayor, then without waiting for his reply he informed him: "Not in a million years."

"Well, Percy." The mayor sighed. His order for discretion had disintegrated. Visualizing his political boat being rocked by a typhoon but recognizing his responsibility to his constituents, he said, "You're doing what you have to do."

"I'm glad we see eye-to-eye. After all," the police chief reminded the mayor, who needed no reminding, "from all indications — Lowell Hook's past the point of being embarrassed."

Sirens splintered the sounds of Houston's nightlife, lights whirled dragon-fire red into the crowded streets, as units sped toward Carrousel Square. Inside a ground-floor apartment was a DOA–Suspected Homicide. "Be advised there are two bodies," the dispatcher had forewarned.

Later, when the corpses were rolled out, their stiffness shrouded in zippered blue plastic, Molly Reidell of the *Houston Herald* was there poised on the curb, her adrenalin flowing, her dark curls flying, her Olympia clicking wildly.

During the night, Lance Benson dreamed of Sandra Lowrey. She danced a wild, fierce dance, a serpent dagger between her teeth, its ruby eye spilling blood into her mouth. He awoke drenched in perspiration and crept downstairs. He touched the letter opener, stroked its jewels. Trembling, he returned to bed and slept with the silver serpent beneath his pillow.

Zoe Benson awoke as her husband eased back into bed. He placed something beneath his pillow. Was it the gun, she wondered. Somehow she felt more secure knowing that her own gun, though unloaded, was close at hand. Perhaps she could slip it out of the nightstand. No, that was too risky. She concentrated on remaining still as she lay waiting for light to filter into the room. Then it would be Monday, when she could leave, not to return to this house until Lance had moved out — for good.

Gradually her thoughts focused on the day just ended. It had been a disquieting Sunday, filled with revelations: Irene a lesbian; Charles unsuspecting; Lance and Irene's lunch on Friday only hours before Irene had killed herself; Victor Solomon's evasive answers to her father's seemingly harmless questions. And then there had been the trauma of spending the major portion of the day alone in the house with Lance.

When he had returned from disposing of the snake — how had he done that? — he had come up behind her and kissed the back of her neck. Startled, she had instinctively recoiled.

"It's only your husband."

"I'm sorry. I was deep in this book."

Glancing at the Rembrandt biography, he'd commented, "I can imagine."

"So what did you do with the snake?"

"Exactly what I told you I was going to do — got rid of it. Here." He'd tossed a newspaper onto her lap. "Page one should overshadow Rembrandt."

He'd watched her face as she read the account of Irene Stanton's death.

"I take it you didn't know about this?"

"No, no." She had read on, her thoughts going beyond the article, which she had seen and hidden early that morning.

"You're sure?"

"Of course I'm sure! Lance, this is *terrible*."

"Yes, isn't it. Well, first thing tomorrow order flowers. I'm going for a swim."

The realization that she had failed to keep the news from him had sickened her. She had felt she was a failure. That she should leave. But logic had stopped her. If only Lance would pick up the phone and now threaten Charles, she'd reasoned, the noose might still drop swiftly and securely around her husband's neck. Confronted with Charles's strength and Irene's note, he himself would become so terrified of exposure that he would not dare harm either her father or anyone else. The blackmailing would stop. One phone call — but the call must be made by Lance — could accomplish that without floodlights having to pierce into the darkest corners of people's lives. Yes, for a while longer, she'd decided, she would stay.

While Lance floated on his raft, she had called Charles. "I'm staying, even though he knows. If things continue normally, he'll be more likely to go ahead with the blackmail . . . Only now the call will be directly to you."

"I don't like it."

"We can't give up now."

Reluctantly he had agreed.

Throughout the remainder of the day and long into the evening, Lance had stayed close to her side. As often as she could, she had moved to other rooms, away from him, hoping against hope that he would call Charles. That hadn't happened. With a single ring, Charles would have signaled to her approximately thirty minutes later that Lance's call — and therein, his indictment — had come.

Not once had the phone rung.

The charade had slowly degenerated into a farce. Her frayed nerves had almost defeated her will. She had become withdrawn, silent. "Sullen," Lance had said accusingly as she placed a light supper before him, then left the table.

Still, Lance might have called just now when he had gotten out of bed. And Charles would not dare signal at such an outrageous hour.

. . . Or, perhaps, Lance had gone downstairs to sit alone, thinking, reevaluating. Maybe even deciding to give up this madness. That was wishful thinking. Tomorrow, before they left for the church, she must give him the opportunity he would need to make the call.

She drew the sheet more closely about her. Her eyes remained open, unblinking.

. . . Tomorrow. Irene's funeral. Her death seemed unreal. But it had happened. Now they could only try, as she had requested, to preserve her name. At least, after the funeral, the pressures would change. A new strategy might have to be devised. . . . Regardless, Charles would deal with the blackmailing. And she could return to the home of her childhood. There she would gain courage. If necessary, she would stand ten feet tall between Lance and her father. She could do that — protect her only living parent to whom she had told everything except the most crucial thing: he did not know that threats were aimed at him. Indeed he thought her primary concern was for Charles.

"Are you in love with him?" he had asked.

"I'm not sure," she had answered. But was she sure? She knew only that she would lay down her life not only for her father but also for Charles.

Lance moaned in his sleep. He turned restlessly. She pushed farther away from him and waited for morning.

Sir Charles Stanton's suitcase was packed. Because he could not sleep, he had folded his clothes into the bag at two-thirty in the morning. The effort was premature, for he would not be flying to London until Tuesday night. Irene was to be buried in Burnham Cemetery between their son and her father.

Before he boarded the plane he must face the funeral, less than nine hours away, and afterward, if he had not heard from Benson, he must either contact him or go to the police. Either way, Zoe and her father needed protection. At least tomorrow she would leave that house where she had stayed longer than she should. And for what? So far it had come to nothing. He should never have given in to her persuasions.

He sat on the edge of the bed, his shoulders slumped. If only he could take Zoe with him. To England. If only, if only . . . Irene had chosen to live. With whom — how many faceless, countless women — had she made love? How had Lance Benson discovered that she was a lesbian? He had difficulty with the word, with the images that crowded into his brain. Why had she not told him, explained, why the lie all these years? Why had he not suspected? How much of her depression had been not because of their son's death but because of their marriage, which from the start must have been flawed? There were too many unanswerable questions.

He shook his head. For years he had prided himself on living an ordered, principled life. Black was black; white was white. And yet all along black and white had intermittently merged to form a third color. He had been blind to gray. He considered himself a fool; a general who commanded an army of shadows; a man who buried his emotions beneath layers of propriety. He would have to become as a child taking his first step, a child accepting his need to be held, a child plunging his fingers into marmalade, tasting and smearing. When the pain — that first raw emotion to erupt inside him — had subsided, he would learn to rely more on feelings. The mind and the heart would blend. When all this was behind him, he would hold Zoe and tell her what he felt.

"Kinky," Dobby Dobson said as he stared up at the mirror.

No one heard his succinct assessment, for he was alone. He'd finally gotten to bed around three, but two hours later he'd awakened with his mind circling the deaths of Martin Fletcher, Lowell Hook, and Sandra Lowrey. Irene Stanton's suicide lay in the periphery of his thoughts. All four people had died within the span of a few days. And all had had connections with The Arch. Although it was too early to visit the theatre, he could return to the girl's apartment.

Driving through the deserted streets of predawn Houston, he'd drunk from a thermos of coffee and dredged up memories of Lowell Hook, who had been the single largest contributor to the policemen's pension fund. The man was no murderer. Besides, the autopsies had proven that. Hook had died approximately fifty minutes before Sandra Lowrey. His heart hadn't withstood what must have been one hell of a climax. But the girl's death was another matter. Lowrey had been murdered. And not by Hook.

As he'd reentered the girl's apartment, the smell of death filled his nostrils. It was always the same. A dank, musty scent coming from his imagination — his insides recoiling — rather than from a place itself.

He turned now from the girl's bed. So, she had been into mirrors. Or maybe that had been the old man's thing.

Walking through the tiny apartment, he wished the bodies had been discovered earlier. Even one blurred fingerprint remaining on a lamp shade or an ashtray would have given them something to go on. He opened the refrigerator, closed it. What was he looking for? He didn't know. Something. Something to substantiate their one circumstantial clue.

Last night Pritchard had discovered a man's jet-black wig. As if hidden, it had been behind boxes on a closet shelf. A single blond hair, caught in the wig's lining, had since been classified as belonging to a Caucasian male. Stamped inside the wig were the words: "Property of The Arch." That place again. Everything went back to it. "S.L." — the initials in Hook's calendar belonged to Sandra Lowrey, deceased actress of The Arch. "L.B.," the only other initials in the calendar, belonged — though perhaps coincidentally — to Lance Benson, The Arch director. What, he suddenly wondered, was the color of Benson's hair? Preposterous! His mind was playing tricks on him. Still, in this business nothing could be ignored.

He returned to the mirror. It was an intriguing contraption. He stood on the bed and studied its construction. Why the squares? Certainly one solid sheet would have been less expensive and the reflection of what was going on below clearer. Perhaps the lady desired distortion. His eyes scanned the individual squares: each was meticulously glued to a board. Undoubtedly the mirror had been custom-made. But why were thick steel hooks securing the board to the canopy frame? Those hooks would support a hell of a lot more weight than a mirrored board.

He stretched out on the bed and looked up. Perhaps from this vantage point he would see something he had missed. His eyes roamed back and forth as he scrutinized the mirror. Suddenly he sat up. There, where two squares joined, was an opening that had been deliberately cut out. The nozzle of a gun, or something larger, could aim straight through the rounded hole.

He dragged a chair over to the bed. Lifting the canopy, he stared at the back side of the board. It reminded him of an empty loading dock. He dropped the canopy to the floor and peered again at the board. Distinct patterns were outlined in dust. Probably boxes had been stored here and recently removed. Or maybe they weren't boxes at all, but pieces of equipment. Machinery. He examined the hole cut straight through the board. His finger traced dust. "Well, I'll be damned. Video!" he exclaimed and headed for the phone.

"Hey, Pritch, wake up!"
"I am awake."
"Couldn't sleep, huh?"

"You kidding? I was dead to the world. I'm the guy, remember, who drove out to West Columbia?"

"That's life."

"Yeah, but this is the second call I've gotten in the last ten minutes. The first one being —"

"Save it."

"Not even if I told you it was our eager-beaver security guard who, if you can believe it, started off the conversation by asking if I'd help him get into the police academy?"

"At this hour?"

"That's what I said. But I told him I'd see what I could do. Anyway, seems he forgot to give us a vital piece of information."

"Like what?"

"Miss Lowrey had another visitor on Friday night. Bass's not absolutely sure, but he thinks a Lincoln Continental, either dark gray or black, pulled out of a space in front of her apartment around eleven o'clock. Interesting, no?"

"You're damn right it's interesting."

"Any ideas?"

"I'm not sure. But I want you to check out every single glass cutter in the city of Houston."

"Christ! What's that got to do with anything?"

"I'll tell you later. But if we get started, by the time we compile a list, it'll be —"

"Daybreak."

"Exactly. I'll meet you at the station in twenty minutes."

"Make it thirty."

"Twenty-five."

Because it would take him only fifteen minutes to reach the station from Sandra Lowrey's apartment, Dobby Dobson decided to continue his search. For something. Something else. He picked up the worn teddy bear, which lay on its stomach as though it had been flung across the room. Funny, he thought, a worldly girl like that still needing a relic from her childhood. He wondered if she'd slept with the one-eyed bear when she was alone, when there was no Lowell Hook or somebody else in bed with her while a video camera recorded their movements. As surely as he was standing here, the girl had been involved in blackmail. But Sandra Lowrey probably didn't have the smarts to conceive such a scam. She must have had a partner. A man. A man whom she had double-crossed or who wanted her out of the picture. The force with which she had been killed indicated that a man had murdered her. Heavy video equipment, loaded onto the board and later removed, again indicated masculine strength. Perhaps that brawn, plus the brains for masterminding blackmail, belonged to a blond-haired man who drove a Lincoln Continental and who possessed connections with the powerful and influential of this city. A man who was a clever amateur.

. . . Had Martin Fletcher ever been in Sandra Lowrey's bed? It was a thought.

He placed the tattered little bear on its stomach, exactly as he had found it. If a fight had taken place, perhaps a shred of evidence lay not far from where the bear had been flung. The broken stem of a man's watch. A thread of torn clothing. Such minutiae had once led him straight to the murderer. That one had been a clever amateur. Well, it looked like he was up against another one.

Crouched on one knee, he ran his hands over plush carpeting. Slowly. Nothing. Three minutes left. He'd better leave.

As he stood, the sole of his right shoe crunched down on something soft. He lifted his foot. A white powdery substance spotted the rug. The crushed capsule clung to the sole of his shoe. Carefully he removed it. The something else may have been found. He left to meet Pritchard at the station.

"My God!"

Lance Benson glanced up from his scrambled eggs. She had seen the morning headline. Before dawn he had crept out of bed and read that the bodies had been discovered. The account had pleased him, because it looked as though the police were going along with the theory that the old man had killed his mistress, then died of a heart attack. Refolding the paper into its plastic bag, he'd decided to leave it on the porch.

He went quickly now around to his wife's side of the table.

"Good Lord!" He reread the article.

She said nothing.

He watched as she stared out the window, her hand to her mouth. His wife was sitting there, connecting. He felt it as he observed her body stiffen.

She turned her head. Her eyes met his.

"We'll close the theatre, of course, for a day of respect. The old man practically founded the place."

"You seem so calm." She was scrutinizing him. That he didn't like.

"Well, what can I do about it? Apparently, while Irene Stanton was going nuts, Lowell Hook was leading a double life."

"What about the girl? If I'm not mistaken, you cared for her."

"Good grief, Zoe, that again? Look, I'm shocked. I'm outraged. I'll even get around to grief when all this melodrama —"

"Gore."

"All right, gore, sinks in. But I'm not going to fall apart. And neither are you. Our worlds will go on — set back, yes. Hell, I've just lost the theatre's most substantial contributor, but I'll recover and The Arch will not go under."

"That's what concerns you?"

"That's what had better concern me!"

He took his plate to the sink.

"You weren't surprised, were you?" She had spoken softly to his back.

He poured a second cup of coffee. "You know, Zoe, you're schizophrenic. Saturday you're fucking my brains out; acting like a bitch on Sunday; and now — you're accusing me." He faced her. "Of what?"

She sipped tomato juice.

". . . Does your silence imply retraction?"

She placed the glass on the table.

"I see . . . We're playing games. Well, if you are accusing me of — whatever — you know what I'll do?"

"Tell me." She looked up. Her stare was becoming a match for his.

As if drawing a gun, cocking its hammer, he spoke slowly, emphasizing each word. "I will kick you like I used to kick old Bailey."

"Or kill me? Like you killed — well, I don't know who, but —"

"Zoe, the police accept that the man had a heart attack after he'd murdered his mistress. Now why won't you?"

"Because I know it happened on the same night you left the party."

So . . . they were down to bare bones. Skeletal truths.

"Repeat that, please."

"You heard me."

"Yes, though I'm going to pretend I didn't. In fact, I'm going to forget this entire conversation. And I would strongly suggest you do the same. Have I made myself clear?"

"Explicitly," she said and left the room.

Lance Benson kicked the refrigerator and swore. He had been deluding himself. He was not above suspicion. His own wife had all but called him a murderer just now. It was only a matter of time before others would be accusing him. For more than an hour yesterday he had floated on his raft, but he still had not formulated a plan for hastily leaving the country. If he was smart, he would get in his car and head for Mexico. He would forget appearances, forget that the police had apparently bought the idea of Hook's killing Sandra, forget, forget. By now Martin Fletcher's death had been reported. That news would be in tomorrow's papers. Suddenly there were too many dead who had had connections with The Arch. With him! He had to get away. But how? And when? More than ever he needed Stanton's money. Perhaps he should call him now. He debated, his fingers drumming on the kitchen counter. It was best to wait. A call — or a visit — after the funeral would be more effective. The priest extolling Irene's virtues would heighten Stanton's vulnerability. There was one payment, however, he could demand immediately. So what if it was a mere fifty thousand dollars? He needed as much cash as he could lay his hands on.

"Will you answer that, Raymond?" Dressed in black so that she could go directly from work to Irene Stanton's funeral, Winifred Reese hurried to her car. She couldn't believe it. First Irene, and now Lowell and some actress. Lately just opening the paper was like entering a morgue. She shuddered and backed her Mercedes out of the garage.

She tapped the horn. What was taking him so long? If he didn't hurry, he'd have to drive his own car. No, that would be silly. After all, they were attending the same funeral. She switched off the motor and prayed that Raymond's extended phone conversation would result in good news. That, she sighed, would be a relief. Still, she kept glancing at her watch until finally, like a general in command, she pressed down on the horn — this time long and insistently.

"Certainly, Mother." Raymond Reese hurried to answer the phone.

He stiffened as he listened to new instructions on the other end of the line. Then he squared his shoulders. Over the bobbing in his throat, he spoke.

"Listen, Lance, I'm glad you called. As a matter of fact, I was about to call you." He gulped, surprised at the swagger in his voice. But he felt he had become a man. Melissa Stebbins was crazy about him; his mother had practically applauded when she'd assumed he had visited a whore; and now here the bastard was apparently sweating over the morning headlines. Lowell Hook must have been tagged for Benson's blackmail. Only something had gone wrong.

Briefly he'd mourned the death of Sandra Lowrey. After all, she had taken away his virginity, thereby opening a whole new world to him. And she had called his anatomy magnificent. So what if it had been a lie? In that instant — sprawled in her outrageous bed — he had felt he was ten million Scruffy Dawsons rolled into one. He was grateful.

Now, miracle of miracles, the bastard was in trouble. Why else would he be trying to move the payment date from Wednesday to today? And of all the risky places for the transaction to occur! Lance Benson was running scared.

"Well, Raymond, that's interesting that you were about to call me. What did you have in mind?"

The man's coolness unnerved him. Still, he plunged ahead as he imagined a Scruffy Dawson might have done.

"To suggest we meet today."

"What a coincidence."

"Not exactly, because you see —" He paused.

"You don't have the money?"

The concern in Benson's voice gave him additional courage. "Yes, but —"

"Then bring it! And I'll turn over your somewhat disgusting film."

"No, wait —"

"You wait! The parking lot immediately after the funeral."

"Lance, don't hang up!"

"There's nothing more to discuss."

The bastard had had the final say.

Raymond Reese sank to a chair, his hand rubbed the velvet upholstery. He had to think. He heard the Mercedes's horn blaring outside. "Shut up!" he yelled, then bit his lip in guilt and remorse. His mother had every right to be impatient. They needed to open the studio. How foolish he had been to think he could keep the money and still obtain the film. "I'm going to the police," he'd planned to threaten. He imagined now Benson's brittle laugh, his demeaning words, "And expose yourself, Raymond? Come now, we're in this together." That's exactly how the bastard would have responded. The swine! But the frightening thing was that Benson would have been right. Any exposure would incriminate them both. Whatever was he to do? In less than twenty minutes he and his mother were to enter a studio stripped of some of its most valuable antiques. Actually he was in deeper trouble than Benson. He — not Benson — had stolen his mother's heirlooms. And Hook — not Benson — had killed Sandra, then died from a heart attack. But grand old Mr. Hook a murderer? It didn't make sense. He shook his head, his hand rubbed the velvet. It was more than he could handle. His mother was blowing the horn again. This time she meant business. Suddenly his hand became still. He blinked, as if seeing a revelation. He knew what he must do. It was what he should have done in the beginning. He jerked up from the chair.

Running out the door and toward the car, he began shouting frantically, almost joyously, "I'm coming, Mother. Believe me, I'm coming!"

There was no duplicate tape, was there? That had been their agreement. And he himself had erased the original. Victor Solomon's hands shook as he attempted to knot his tie. Fear ricocheted around the lining of his stomach. Irene Stanton dead. Now Hook and the girl. Christ! He needed a drink. In fact, that was his sole reason for going to the store this morning. One scotch in the solitude of his office should tide him over the next twenty-four hours. Tomorrow, early, they would be on their way to Cozumel.

"Here let me." His wife looped the silk into the Windsor knot he preferred. "You're so *nervous*. It's horrible, but there's absolutely nothing we can do except pay our respects. I mean, not even able to tie your own tie. Honestly." She kissed his cheek.

The gesture irritated him. He moved from her.

"Look, Victor, maybe we shouldn't go to Cozumel."

"No!"

"Just a suggestion." She lighted a cigarette. "But maybe we should put off the trip until after Lowell's funeral." She snapped her lighter shut.

"Like you said, there's nothing we can do except pay our respects. Which we'll do tonight. This afternoon I'll check out the Baron."

"Victor, don't go."

"We're *going* to Cozumel." He knew that was not what she had meant.

"I accept that. I *want* that. I'm talking about don't go in to the store. You're upset. Besides, you'll just have to turn right around to get to Irene's funeral on time."

"I'll be there."

She inhaled. He looked away. "Victor, you had planned to take the day off. So why suddenly are you dead set on going to work?"

She knew. Eighteen years of marriage and she knew. He hated her; he hated himself.

Impatiently he jerked off the tie. "All right, I won't!" He stomped out of the room. He would show her; he would show himself. Flipping on the news, he slouched in a chair and stared at a man who looked like a bullfrog. The heavy jowls shook as the thick lips announced a rise in interest rates.

"Victor?" She knelt in front of the bullfrog.

"You're blocking my view."

She leaned closer. He could smell the scent of her hair rinsed last night in lemon juice. "I know what you're feeling."

"You don't know anything."

"I know that, too . . . I love you."

Tears stung his eyes. The fear subsided. "Thank you," he said and pulled her onto his lap as the newscaster with the unfortunate face began chronicling the philanthropic contributions of the late Lowell Hook.

. . . .

Clyde Pritchard drove deep into the northwest. At least he had help. Whalen had assigned two men to assist him in checking out Houston's glass cutters.

"But just for today," the homicide captain had warned.

"Appreciate it, sir." He had breathed more easily.

It had been a job narrowing the list of companies down to those which not only cut custom mirrors but which also, as Dobby had specified, offered either through their names or their advertisements or both, a touch of class, that something extra. Unfortunately no less than twenty-seven companies seemed to promise that something extra.

"Start by checking out the obscure ones — the not so well-known," had been Dobby's suggestion as his finger pointed to the name Master Glazier. "I like the sound of it."

"You like the sound of it." He'd gulped the last of his Jack-in-the-Box egg sandwich.

"Because I'll tell you something, Pritch . . ."

"Please do."

"That mirror is a masterful job. The steel hooks even have felt pads so the frame won't get scarred. Fine, fine detail."

"Yeah, but would you look where the guy's located — the other side of the world! I'll bet you like the sound of that, too."

"It's a damn probable location. Hidden. After all, we're not dealing with somebody who ordered a mirror for his dining-room wall."

"Good point." He'd wadded the sandwich wrapper into a ball and aimed it at the wastepaper basket. "Bingo."

Dobby had ignored his expertise. "Hey, Pritch?"

"Yeah?"

"Go there first, OK?"

He turned now off the highway onto a gravel road. Swearing, he steered his car over ruts. After six miles of tedious driving, he suddenly saw what he was looking for. Set back from the road was an old barn. Over its sagging doors hung a sign proclaiming in florid gold letters, MASTER GLAZIER — GUY PAXTON LUDDEN.

Raymond Reese was having difficulty inserting the key into the lock, but he was thankful his mother insisted all personnel enter through the main entrance. "That way," she'd explained more than once, "if anything needs rearranging, one of us is sure to notice." He steadied his hand and tried again. The front door opened.

Luckily neither the secretary nor the sales assistant had arrived.

Driving to the studio, he had planned exactly how he would dump the sordid mess into his mother's lap. First she must assume a robbery had taken place and then he would confess. Breathing heavily, he felt like a runner rounding mountain curves; but he knew his course was right. He should have turned to her long ago. It seemed so obvious now.

He stepped inside. "All's clear," he joked weakly. Then he switched on the overhead lights and waited.

Her reaction took a full second.

"Good God!"

She tore from empty space to empty space. "The Tudor armchair, the Florentine mantel, the Ōkyō screen, the — Raymond, call the police!" She sank into a chair.

Her hands fluttered like nervous little birds. He took them in his own. He felt the repentant sinner come before a sacred shrine. But he also felt the strong, powerful son. For a moment the only reality was that his tiny, pudgy mother was terrified. He would take care of her.

"Mother, it's all right."

"How can you say it's all right? Look!" Her hands flew out from the cage of his grasp. She paced the floor. "What happened to the burglar alarm? The bars —" She stopped in mid-pacing. "Raymond, call the police. *Now!*"

His Adam's apple lumped. Reality demanded confession. He straightened his narrow shoulders and plunged.

"Mother . . . I sold everything that's missing."

"You did *what?* Raymond, what are you saying?"

"I received fifty thousand dollars, cash."

"Fifty thousand dollars. That doesn't begin — Raymond, what on earth are you talking about?"

"Mother, I — Mother, I'm sorry. Listen!"

"I'm listening. You can be damn sure I'm listening!"

His mother was angry, angrier than he had ever imagined. Veins throbbed in her neck. Her lips curled. She would disown him; she would banish him from her sight. What was reality? Certainly not this. His ordered exposition deserted him. In its place came tears —

tears resembling those of his boyhood when no one, except Scruffy Dawson, would play with him; when there had been no valentines; when he was a failure at any sport he attempted. Such were the tears which coursed down his cheeks.

Sobbing, gulping, he told his mother honestly, straightforwardly — omitting nothing — what had happened.

When he had finished, her mouth formed into a round, horrified "Oh."

Then fiercely, unexpectedly, she cradled his head against her shoulder. She stroked his hair. "What you've been through — alone," she crooned.

"Yes, yes." This was what he needed, had hoped for. This was reality: his mother singing him a lullaby. "Yes, Mother. I'm sorry. I am so sorry."

Her tears mixed with his. "It's all right, it's all right, son. Mother will fix it."

Abruptly she changed. His cheeks locked between her hands. He felt her granite strength. Her eyes bored holes into his. The holes filled up with hope.

"Now, Raymond, we've got to outwit him. We have to *think*."

"Yes, ma'am."

"*I* have to think."

The front door opened.

"Beginning now." She whirled to greet her assistant. Raymond was reminded of a spinning top. "Good morning, Henri. Did you have a nice weekend?"

"Simply divine." The eyes rolled heavenward.

"Grand. Now, Henri, don't be alarmed." She spoke briskly. "Raymond and I cleaned house on Saturday. We decided it was time to take in another auction. Right, Raymond?"

"Right, Mother." He smiled broadly. For the first time in his life, he fancied a rainbow arched over his horizon.


"It's for you." Lance Benson's secretary handed the phone to Detective Dobson. Filing correspondence, she pretended not to listen. Not that eavesdropping was turning up any clues to help her figure out what was going on around here. All he was saying was "Yeah" and "Uh-huh." This was more than she had bargained for. She loved her job, but the murder of that gorgeous actress — and by seemingly sweet old Mr. Hook, who had been her favorite board member — would be giving her nightmares for months. A woman wasn't safe these days. Especially one who was attractive, which she considered herself to be. Hadn't her boss commented that she, Suzanne Porter, was a dead-ringer for a young Ali MacGraw?

"No kidding!"

She looked up. He turned his back to her. Smart ass. Still, he was kinda cute with his sandy hair and droopy eyelids. He couldn't be a day over thirty. And sharp! She could tell from his questions. If only Lance were here, he'd give the perfect answers. All she could do was answer openly and honestly. Her boss would expect that of her. His reasoning would be that the sooner the case was closed, the sooner the scandal could be forgotten. But what questions! Like: "How well did Mr. Benson know Sandra Lowrey?"

"She was one of the actresses, so he knew her quite well," she'd answered.

But he had persisted. "Did you see them together often?"

She had squirmed over that one. "Just when she came to the office."

"Frequently?"

What was he getting at, she wondered. An affair between the two of them? If that was so, it was no more than she herself had suspected. But what would that have to do with Sandra's and Mr. Hook's deaths?

"Frequently?" He'd had to repeat the question.

"Well . . . yes."

"More often or less often than the other actresses and actors?"

"Maybe . . . more often."

"More? Or less?"

"More." She'd wanted to throw a paperweight at him.

Finally, he'd gotten off that subject and asked for printed information about The Arch. "Any material you have would be appreciated." She'd given him a ton of brochures.

He was off the phone.

"So you say your boss will be in after the Stanton funeral?"

"I said I *expect* him then."

"Would that be around one?"

"Possibly."

"I see." He picked up the paperweight she had contemplated throwing. "Would you tell him I was here, and that I'll be back?"

"Certainly." She flashed her best Ali MacGraw smile. After all, the man was just doing his duty. And he was polite. "I'm sure Mr. Benson will be much more helpful than I've been."

"No, you did just fine."

"I did?"

"You did. And I thank you."

That was sweet of him to be so reassuring. Suddenly she wished he would wait for Lance. Disappointed, she watched him leave. At the doorway, he turned.

"By the way, what kind of car does your boss drive?"

"Gorgeous!" she said, flashing the smile again. "It's a Lincoln Continental."

Detective Dobby Dobson sat in his car in The Arch parking lot and rubbed a finger across an eyelid. He sighed. A nice lady was about to be hurt. The call from the lab just now confirmed his suspicion: the deaths were connected. The capsule found in Sandra Lowrey's apartment was identical to the one Martin Fletcher had swallowed. Both bore Ornade traces; both had been packed with the roach killer Lightning.

The possibility of her husband committing suicide was abhorrent to Caroline Fletcher. She preferred murder. But would she prefer a murder that was the result of her husband having slept with some young actress? His job wasn't getting any easier. The messes people made of their lives. The tragedies which began as diversions. Fletcher probably picked Lowrey up — or rather she picked him up — and, whammo, he fell right into her video trap. But was it hers? She was as dead as Fletcher.

He flipped through the material that Suzanne Porter had given him. It had to be there somewhere. Abruptly he stopped. On the front page of last summer's gala program was the photograph. Above striking blue eyes was undeniably blond hair.

He rubbed his eyelid again. Circumstantial — all circumstantial evidence, but all pointing to The Arch director. A man who appeared to have everything. Then why? If he was the blackmailer, what was his motive? Perhaps, surrounded by wealthy patrons, he craved more of the pie. Would greed have pushed his button, egged on a respected, intelligent — possibly brilliant — man to deal in blackmail?

He started his car. He wouldn't interrupt a funeral. The Arch director, who probably considered himself safe from the law, wasn't going anywhere. Benson could be seen later. But Caroline Fletcher was expecting him. It was too bad that such a lovely — and somewhat regal — lady, who reminded him of the Good Fairy in a school play he had attended as a child, would have to be asked some pretty disturbing questions.

"Sugar? Cream?" Caroline Fletcher touched the silver creamer, her hand poised to pour.

"No, thank you. This is fine. Just fine." He shifted in his chair, cleared his throat.

"Detective Dobson, I feel as though you want to ask me something, and whatever it is makes you uncomfortable."

"You're a perceptive lady, Mrs. Fletcher."

"I try to be. I'm not always." She waited.

"How aware were you of your husband's activities outside your home?"

"Two days ago I would have said extremely aware. We were — close. Now I can't say that. You tell me he purchased a rattlesnake. I find that preposterous." She paused. "I know he was a punctual man. He left for work promptly at twenty to eight; he arrived home at six-fifteen. There were exceptions, of course. And the evenings . . . we spent together."

Through half-closed eyelids, he studied her. Her serenity was apparent. "How well did your husband know Sandra Lowrey?"

"The actress? Not at all. I still can't believe that. I can't —" She stopped. "Excuse me. My husband didn't know Sandra Lowrey. We saw her in performances at The Arch, that was all. Why?"

"Routine check."

"Surely you don't think there's some connection between —"

"Mrs. Fletcher, how well did your husband know Lance Benson?"

"He was a close friend."

He stirred his coffee. "Did they ever get together — say, after work for a drink, that sort of thing?"

"No, they weren't friends like that. I told you Martin was punctual about coming home. We had our martinis together before dinner. Over the years we've spent evenings socially with Lance and his wife."

"What's Mrs. Benson like?"

"Remarkable. She's a wonderful friend. When I was in the hospital this summer, she came quite often and —" She stopped.

"Go on."

"Well, I just remembered a funny thing. One night Lance stopped by alone and I remember he thought that Martin should get away from the hospital for a while. Martin protested, but I insisted that he and Lance go out for a drink — which was what Lance had suggested."

He straightened. "When was this?"

"July — I can tell you exactly — let's see, it was the third night I was there. July third. That was it."

"After their drinks, did your husband return to the hospital?"

"I was sedated for the night. *Why?*"

He stared into large gray eyes. Leaning forward, he spoke softly. "Trust me. Mrs. Fletcher, I don't think your husband committed suicide."

Her eyes never left his. Slowly she nodded.

"Now . . . I need to know everything about your husband's financial situation."

"We're comfortable."

"I meant specifics. Bank deposits and withdrawals, stock certificates, records of negotiations."

". . . Martin keeps — kept his financial records in a special file. She stood. "My husband was an orderly man."

". . . Mrs. Fletcher?"

She turned at the doorway. Sunlight caught her braided hair.

"Would you think it terribly corny and inappropriate if I told you that you remind me of the Good Fairy?"

Her laugh, high and tinkling, came quickly. "I would be complimented; and I would tell you, Detective Dobson, that in the midst of all this — loss — I feel I've found a friend who doesn't think I'm crazy to insist that Martin would never take his own life."

She went into the library, only to return and place at Dobby Dobson's feet a small, black, metal filing box.

"Yeah, I remember that mirror." Guy Luden scratched graying hair matted at the open neck of his shirt. The short, barrel-chested man squinted an eye at Pritchard. "I figured something funny was going on."

"How's that?"

"Well, it's the first mirror I've ever had the law after." He chuckled.

"We got the mirror, Mr. Luden. What we want to know is who ordered it."

"I can tell you it wasn't the girl. And it wasn't the old man. That's some story, huh? You could have knocked me over with a feather when I read about it. 'Cause I knew right off that address rang a bell. That apartment's exactly where I delivered the mirror and installed it. Right over her bed."

Clyde Pritchard picked up a small square of emerald glass. He placed it back on the worktable. "So if Sandra Lowrey didn't order the mirror —"

"I never saw her."

"And it wasn't Lowell Hook."

"Not that I know of."

"Who did, Mr. Luden?"

"Tall blond fellow, never took off his sunshades, never gave me a phone number — I remember that. And I can tell you without looking the name up — it was a Mr. Black. 'Cause at the time I thought that's not the man's real name, not the way he's acting. Even paying cash, which is unusual these days."

"Do you recall what kind of car he drove?"

Luden squinted at barn rafters. "Big. A big car, maybe gray. Charcoal gray. American made."

"What if I got you a photograph or a drawing of the man?"

"I'd recognize him. That is, if we circled dark glasses over the eyes. I mean, he never took those things off — not the day he ordered the mirror, not the day I installed it. And he didn't talk much. But he knew exactly what he wanted, especially that hole cut round and placed where you wouldn't notice. That was my big tip-off. And I'll tell you something else."

"What's that?" Pritchard smiled. He liked the old man — his talkativeness.

"The wife and me are God-fearing people, good Lutherans, and anything — anything at all — I can do to help, just ask."

"I'll want a positive identification."

"For sure if you put those shades on him."

"We'll do that. I appreciate your cooperation."

"No problem." Luden waved his hand as if swatting at a fly.

"And if you ever need any stained-glass windows over at that police station, just let me know."

"I'll keep it in mind. The place could use some class."

"And some religion." Luden laughed at his own joke.

Clyde Pritchard got in his car and steeled himself for the return trip. Even if his tires shredded on the gutted road, the glass cutter's information would be worth the sacrifice.

The police officer was gone. The children were upstairs in their rooms. Intermittently they would come down into the library to be with her only to withdraw again into their separate cubicles of grief.

He had taken Martin's filing box into the kitchen to sit at the breakfast table, where she and Martin had spent so many hours over second, and sometimes third, cups of coffee. There Detective Dobson had sat, coffee at his elbow, as he pored through financial records about which she had seldom given a thought. "Don't worry your pretty head about the business end of things," Martin had remarked once years ago, and, relieved, she had busied herself with other concerns.

He had finally appeared in the doorway. His eyes penetrating, his hands holding papers.

"Were you aware, Mrs. Fletcher, that over the past two months your husband had sold a significant number of his company's shares and borrowed against his life insurance?"

"No." She had spoken barely above a whisper. "But if the evidence is there —"

"It is."

"I see."

"The money went somewhere. I'll find out where," he had promised.

He had promised. She closed her eyes. Her hand touched her chest as she prayed for additional strength. God had promised. How good was His promise?

Swiftly and lovingly she'd made the funeral arrangements. The afternoon paper was to read, "Services to be held Tuesday, 2:00 P.M." Though she would have preferred a morning service, she had deferred to Lowell Hook's age and position. Two funerals tomorrow. And, today, another one which she had chosen not to attend. How could she? Nor had she been able to call her friends about her own loss. Alone and with her children, she grieved. Alone, she contemplated. She must help prove that Martin had been murdered. But why? Why should she help prove anything? Why was she grief-stricken? Her husband had not been the person she had thought. He must have done something very wrong to have brought murder upon himself and unspeakable pain to his wife and children. She swallowed bitterness. And fear. She thought of her son and daughter, who overnight had become a young man and a young woman. A young woman. There was another young woman — murdered only hours before Martin. A young woman who, Detective Dobson had implied, had somehow known Martin.

An image rose before her: soft summer air stirring Japanese lanterns on a theatre balcony. "I'll be right back," she'd assured her husband, then escaped into the ladies' lounge to sit and absorb what she had been told that afternoon. The breast might be removed. Sliced from her body. She had thought of a saber dance. The door had been pushed open. It was Sandra Lowrey, come to smear color over her lips, to flaunt unwittingly mounds of healthy flesh. The girl's presence had unnerved her. She had fled from all that youthfulness. From what had seemed to be the girl's immortality.

But Sandra Lowrey was dead. And Lowell. Lowell, who would never have harmed a fly, much less that beautiful girl. Poor Lowell, apparently needing, even at a venerable age, the warmth of another body against his own. Sandra, Lowell, Martin, Irene. Detective Dobson had asked about them all. Lance was the only living person about whom he had questions. And Zoe. "What's she like?" he had wanted to know, but solely because she was Lance's wife. It was Zoe to whom she had fled the night of the gala. Away from Sandra, to Zoe. If there were one friend she would wish to have with her now, that friend would be Zoe. But what if Zoe Benson's husband was responsible for Martin's death?

That couldn't be. She sank to the floor. She felt bound by a chain of deaths. The deaths were linked. All but Irene's. Why not hers, also? Detective Dobson had asked only fleeting questions about that death. She must phone and urge him to talk to Charles. Folding her hands, she breathed deeply, evenly. Her daughter called from upstairs.

"Just a minute," she answered. She remained kneeling. Finally, she stood. God and His promise were intact. It was she who had momentarily weakened. She hurried upstairs to Justine, who had discovered a faded snapshot of her father — both children balanced on his knees — and begun to cry.

Five minutes away from their house, Zoe Benson launched her misguided strategy.

"After the funeral, I'll be riding home with my father for lunch."

"Absolutely not!" Lance practically slammed on the brakes.

And she knew she had lost.

Still she pressed on.

"Lance, I have *promised* my father. He's counting on it. And if I back out now, he's going to think something strange is going on."

"Let him." His jaw was set.

She shifted to face him. He looked straight ahead.

"Why are you doing this?"

"I have my reasons."

"*Please,* be sensible!" She was not above begging.

He said nothing.

She tried logic.

"Look, I'm not going to *do* anything. And we can't stay glued together forever. Like . . . Siamese twins."

He turned abruptly and stared. The cobalt eyes beaming hatred. And something else. For only a moment and then it was gone. Had it been fear?

He spoke solemnly, as if pledging vows.

"I can assure you, Zoe, that will never happen."

For a time they rode in silence.

The car shot through a yellow light. He eased his foot on the accelerator then glanced at her, the tone of his voice now light, the words tossed off like kites into air. "Cheer up. In a few days you can do whatever you wish."

"Meaning?"

"Just what I said."

She tried to decipher his ambiguity. Hope stirred. Was it possible that Lance intended to walk out of her life? Of his own accord? "In a few days," he'd said. What until then? . . . She could not return to that house.

"Fine." She looked out the window at shops on San Felipe. "But today I'm having lunch with my father."

He slowed for a child, wobbling on a bicycle at the street's edge, then sighed as if her protests exhausted him.

"I suppose I should tell you . . . the gun is tucked in my belt."

So Lance and I and the gun are a threesome again, she thought, as she struggled to appear unintimidated.

"Am I supposed to be surprised?"

"Not really. But what may surprise you is that I wouldn't hesitate to use it."

"Go ahead." She shrugged while muscles tensed. "I'm still going home with my father."

"After I shoot him?" He wheeled his car into the church parking lot. ". . . Which I could do with no one knowing who'd done the damage. You see, Zoe, the gun has a silencer."

A cross of white roses lay centered on the closed casket. Charles Stanton stared, not blinking, at the cross. He sat erect, ears strained to the priest's words. The text was from I Samuel — "I am a woman of a sorrowful spirit: I have drunk neither wine nor strong drink, but have poured out my soul before the Lord." Was that what Irene had done? Why had she not confided in her own husband? He would have tried to make things right for her. He would have set her free to live a life more natural to her. He would have confronted her blackmailer and discreetly, swiftly, put an end to his threats. It was too late now. He recalled the Bensons' supper party. Irene had spent almost the entire evening with Sandra Lowrey. Afterward she had seemed radiantly alive. Why not? She had made a conquest. The pieces were fitting together. He glanced across the aisle. Bonita Graves was crying softly. He felt sunken to his eyeballs in pain. Earlier he had searched for Zoe. Seeing her seated between her husband and her father, he had wanted her here with him. There was no one — no child, no parent — beside him. The priest was pronouncing: "The handmaiden has found grace in the Lord's sight." Were such statements platitudes or profundities? He bowed his head. Too late on this earth for Irene. For Lowell Hook and Sandra Lowrey. But perhaps there were others for whom it was not too late. Irene's note was in his wallet. He knew what he must do.

Personally, she intended to be cremated. Winifred Reese listened with one ear to the eulogy. The priest wasn't saying nearly enough fine things about Irene. But then he had never played tennis or golf with her. What a sportswoman she had been! Fair play had been her middle name, even if competitiveness had been her surname. She patted Raymond's arm. Though grieved, she couldn't concentrate on the service. Her thoughts kept sailing out the thick-hinged doors and on into the parking lot.

Roselyn Solomon found the Christian religion's emphasis on the hereafter disconcerting. With her head tilted toward the priest cockpitted in his pulpit, his arms poised as if for flight, she pressed closer to her husband. The physical contact gave her reassurance. Her hand slipped into the pocket of his jacket. She would burrow her fist there while imagining the good, full decades ahead. Her fingers closed around plastic. For a moment she was puzzled, and then she felt the prongs. Combs. There were combs in her husband's pocket. The kind used to sweep thick hair away from a woman's face. Such combs she never wore. Victor turned and smiled at her. He focused again on the priest.

Drawing her hand from his pocket, she held onto the combs. She saw that they were studded with chips of colored glass. She slipped them into her purse. And then she thought, "My husband carries the combs of a whore in his pocket."

The priest was an idiot. He was extolling the virtues of a woman he had scarcely known. She had been Lady Stanton, who had sat in his congregation and swelled his coffers. He had never known Irene Stanton, the lesbian. What a farce! Lance Benson shifted in the pew. His eye caught his father-in-law's. Why did the old man keep staring at him? What did he know? Harrington looked away. Had Zoe not been wedged between them, he would have asked the professor what he found so fascinating that he couldn't keep his eyes where they belonged. Well, soon he would be rid of the old fool. And of the young fool. Seated across the aisle, Raymond Reese had obviously followed instructions. A bulging envelope rested on his knees. The exchange of envelope and cassette should go smoothly. It was regrettable that Charles Stanton wasn't stupid, like Raymond. Contacting Stanton could only mean pitting wit against wit. But he had no choice. He needed Stanton's money. At least the royal asshole would not be at his best. But then, neither would he. For one thing, Zoe kept compounding his problems.

His wife was fast becoming a far greater millstone than he'd ever thought possible. The more quickly he shook himself free of her, the better. Why did the old man keep staring at him?

He squinted up at stained glass then down at the coffin. Irene Stanton had been another fool. But she was not to be pitied, for she had elected the coward's way out. Never would he choose death over life. Indeed, he intended to live life to its fullest. Under some other banner. In some other country. How to get there was the question.

Zoe Benson stared at Charles Stanton's bowed head. She would never reach him, touch him. She was still trapped in the enemy camp.

And it was her own fault!

She had made a tactical error.

Far better to have kept quiet until the service was over. Once outside the church, she could have held tight to her father and walked confidently through the crowd to his car. Though Lance would have been outraged, he probably wouldn't have caused a scene.

But now, forewarned, he had given warning. And she did not view that warning as bluff.

Pressing closer to her father, she tried to concentrate. The effort was futile — the eulogy too dry; the fear too great. She glanced around the sanctuary. So many familiar faces . . . but where were the Fletchers? Something was wrong. Very wrong. Caroline would have been here. What if her friend were in trouble as well? She would call her as soon as she was home again. Home! It was not to be, after all, that place where her bags were waiting beside the white iron bed of her childhood. Home was still some other place where the windows might as well be shadowed with bars.

Throughout the service, Lawrence Harrington kept glancing at his son-in-law. Arms crossed, his body angled away from his wife, Benson seemed remarkably composed. Once, he shifted his position and their eyes met. War was silently declared.

Unquestionably the time had come to act even if doing so displeased his daughter. Slipping into the pew beside him, she had whispered, "Don't ask questions. I can't go home with you."

He gazed, unseeing, at the twelve-foot teakwood cross which

dominated the chancel. He prayed for an oracle to thunder down his son-in-law's transgressions. He could then scoop his daughter up in his arms and leave Benson to the hands of a vengeful god. He was aware that his fantasy sprang from years of immersion in Greek mythology. There would be no oracle. There would be no vengeful god. Instead, he must rely upon his own ingenuity. To ensure his daughter's safety, he must quickly establish her husband's guilt. For that he needed help. He calculated. If he wasn't mistaken, the police station was no more than ten or twelve blocks from the church.

Chords of Bach swelled and filled the sanctuary. The congregation rose. Irene Stanton had been properly eulogized. Harrington observed that Lance held fast to Zoe's arm as they pushed out into sunlight.

Victor Solomon opened the car door for his wife. When he came around to the driver's side, he saw there on the seat a woman's combs, their chips of colored glass like prisms reflecting brightness.

He picked them up, then slid behind the wheel. For a moment he had to think, to sort through memories, and then he knew.

"Whose?"

"I've forgotten." He shoved the combs into his pocket.

"You carry them for luck?"

He shifted to face her. "Christ, Roselyn, couldn't you have waited until we got home?"

Her lips trembled. "No. No! Because I put my hand in your pocket — back there in the church — for some kind of security, some kind of — and that's what I found. Oh, Victor." She turned away.

They sat in silence. Somehow he must convince her that the combs were remnants from his past. They had nothing to do with the present or the future. But did they? The combs had belonged to Sandra Lowrey. For weeks unaware, he had been carrying the combs of the murdered girl in his pocket.

"Roselyn?" She didn't answer. He looked out the window. Near the edge of the parking lot was a plastic container. Printed neatly on its side were the words "Place Trash Here."

He got out of the car.

"Where're you going?"

He dropped the combs down among empty Coke cans and food-stained wrappers then quickly returned to the car.

They would not move from this place until she accepted the fact that those combs meant no more to him than the garbage into which they had been tossed.

"Give me the envelope, Raymond, and get in the car."

"Wait in the car, Zoe. If you have the urge to do otherwise, remember what I told you."

Winifred Reese and Lance Benson pushed toward each other through the throng of mourners. Most were hurrying to their cars, postponed engagements already crowding into their schedules. Some few walked slowly; others stood in clusters, their faces long and somber.

Among those walking slowly was Amanda Stebbins. She was thinking about Lowell Hook. She wanted to be at home, alone, asking into stillness, "Why? Why *him?*" But she spoke of the one just eulogized. "Isn't it a shame that Irene has to be buried in England?" Her remark was addressed to a frail, stooped lady who wore a black-veiled hat from another era.

"Oh, I don't know," answered her veiled companion. "Her little boy's buried there. And, thank goodness, we don't have to drive out to some cemetery. These Episcopal services last *forever.*"

The two dowagers passed Winifred Reese and Lance Benson, who stood facing each other now, squarely, solidly, in the church parking lot. Winifred smiled warmly; Lance nodded curtly. The women walked on.

Lance spoke softly to the short, pudgy dynamo who had parked herself like a Mack truck directly in front of him.

"Well, Winifred, this is a surprise. I assume you're Raymond's courier."

"And spokesman."

"May I have the envelope, please?"

"Lance, neither of us is very good at this. You sound like you're about to announce an Academy Award.

"Just give me the envelope." He glanced in the direction of his car. At least that was going according to plan: Zoe would be unable to witness the exchange. But he wished he'd had the foresight to shift the gun from his belt to his pocket. Something was obviously amiss here.

"You're nervous?"

"Impatient. The envelope, Winifred."

"The cassette, Lance."

"Of course." He laughed. "No wonder the delay. You don't trust me." He pulled a small white box from his pocket. "After I check the contents of that envelope, you'll have your cassette."

"I want a simultaneous exchange."

"That's out of the question."

"Don't be silly!" She fairly snorted. Several people turned to stare. "You have more to lose."

His voice dropped to a lower register. "You obviously haven't seen what's inside this box."

"I don't care what's inside that box. Raymond can stand the scandal. You can't."

"You're bluffing."

"Lance, you know me well enough to know that, if I have to, I'll blow the whistle. Loud. Now give me the cassette."

He hesitated. His free hand went into his pocket. He held the cloth stiff, as though camouflaging a gun. "I have a bullet aimed at your navel."

Her face reddened. "You'll miss your target. It's buried in mounds of flesh."

His left eyelid twitched. "I'd forgotten what a cool one you are."

"Just gutsy."

"Whatever! This has gone on long enough."

"No, Lance. I enjoy seeing you squirm like my poor son's been doing for weeks. The girl, I understand, is the same one found with Lowell."

He held out the box. The exchange was made.

Winifred Reese walked toward her car. She stopped briefly to chat with Barbara and Forrest Wesley.

Lance Benson opened the envelope. He peered inside at paper bills, the kind he had played with as a child, shaping green stacks into castles, lining moats with worthless counterfeit.

He had been outsmarted. Emasculated. And by a kid! A sniveling kid whose mother was notorious for her battle-ax guts. Her guts stronger, more sinewy than his own. Maybe he should have drawn the gun and actually fired at the fat-assed bitch. But what would that have accomplished? One more dead? That he couldn't handle. Besides, contrary to what he'd told Zoe, the gun had no silencer. The shot would have reverberated clear across Houston. And he would have landed in jail. Or . . . worse.

He felt like tossing the counterfeit bills up to the steeple, then standing back, watching them fall, observing people scramble to scoop up nothing. Nonsense! These snobs had too much inherited wealth to be fazed by a sky raining money. He began walking toward his car. If he didn't want a noose to drop around his neck, he'd better get out of here. Out of this town. This country! Fast, faster, he walked.

Abruptly he stopped to avoid a bronze Mercedes pulling out of a parking space. Roselyn waved; Victor stared straight ahead. Suddenly an idea spun wildly, like a meteor, through his head. He stepped in front of the car. The brakes screeched.

"Damnit, Lance, you want to get killed!"

"Sorry, ole buddy." He was perspiring. "I've got to talk to you."

Roselyn leaned over. "Lance, is something wrong?"

He ignored her, then thought better of it. "No, I just need a word with this husband of yours." He focused his stare, wavering but still commanding, on Victor.

"Excuse us, Roselyn." Victor switched off the ignition and got out of the car. When they were beyond his wife's hearing, he muttered, "That was insane."

"On the contrary." Again he lied. "I kept the duplicate."

Victor Solomon stopped walking, "You son of a bitch."

"Calm down and listen. You're to meet me in three hours at Renard's." The French bar, dark and out of the way, where he had taken Martin Fletcher, was the first place that had come to mind.

"And if I don't?"

"You will."

"You never stop, do you?"

"Eventually."

"Look, Benson, if it's more money you want, forget it. I couldn't come up with another dime without raising suspicions."

"It's not money."

"Then what're we talking about?"

"Just be at Renard's. If I'm late, wait. I'll be there."

.   .   .

"What was that all about?" Roselyn asked as he slid behind the wheel.

"You know Lance. Something about fund-raising." Victor Solomon started the car. All along he had known, had felt it in his gut. The duplicate had not been erased. Why had he rejected the knowing? Tenuously he held on to what suddenly seemed to be his salvation. Three hours from now, seated in Renard's, he could order a drink.

Lawrence Harrington stood quickly when Charles Stanton entered the waiting room. Each wanted to ask the other, "Why are you here?" Each knew the answer without asking.

Harrington spoke first. "You shouldn't have to be here, not with what you're going through."

"It's all right . . . Isn't Zoe supposed to be with you?"

"Yes, but it didn't work out that way."

"Well, where is she?"

"With Lance."

"Good God!"

"The police chief's at lunch. I'm not sure how long the wait will be. If it's much longer —"

"Let's not wait." Stanton turned to the receptionist. "I believe the head of homicide would do just as well."

Frazer Thompson, his legs propped on a porch railing, stared at the ten-year-old photograph of Martin Fletcher, minus his moustache. He let out a long, low whistle. No wonder that detective had driven all the way to West Columbia to find out if Fletcher had been the one who bought that rattler. Right off something must have looked fishy. A man putting a snake to his own jugular vein! But that was what Fletcher had done. Here it was, plain as day in the *Houston Times*. It was a good thing he'd picked up the paper when he'd made a delivery into the city. Otherwise he'd never have known. Not that his knowing changed anything.

Thompson cut a plug of tobacco and chewed. He felt bad. Why'd he been in such a hurry to trap the five-footer for somebody who was going to do such a crazy thing? He spat. A brown tobacco stream arched over the railing. But how was he to have known? Hadn't he warned Fletcher to keep the cage locked tight as a drum? As Alcatraz, for Pete's sakes! That was probably just what the man had wanted to hear. He'd carried off a snake whose venom would make him deader than a doornail. And scheming! The fellow had said he'd vaguely heard of Powell Insecticides when all along he'd been one of the company's big shots. Hell, he should have trapped him a coral. That critter would have finished the job in half the time. And, for sure, he wouldn't have needed that roach-killer the paper said he'd swallowed.

Thompson stood. He was going fishing. Maybe that'd get his mind off the darn fool thing Martin Fletcher had done and his own part in it.

Driving home from the funeral with his wife beside him, Lance Benson swung by a newsstand.

The early-afternoon edition of the *Houston Times* was off the press. He scanned the front-page headlines. Fletcher's death wasn't there. Why should it be? The man was a nobody compared to Hook. He forced himself not to read further. When he was parked in his own garage, he would comb each page.

Zoe reached for the paper he'd clamped beneath his leg.

"Leave it alone!"

"What're you hiding now?"

"Just keep quiet."

She didn't argue.

Except for that exchange, they rode in silence. And then they were home. He opened the paper to search for what he knew was there.

. . . Martin Fletcher's suicide was reported on the front page of the second section. The melodramatic account had earned a byline for somebody named Benny Harris.

"Here. You might as well read this." He tossed the paper to Zoe.

She read quickly. "No! No, no." She was crying.

"Zoe, Fletcher was obviously more disturbed than we'd realized."

"You killed him!" She got out of the car and began running. Before she reached the street, he stopped her.

"Come on inside. I'm not going to hurt you."

"Look what you've done! Look —"

"I'm not going to hurt you, Zoe."

Holding her arm tightly, he led her into the house.

.    ✳    .

Lawrence Harrington declined the coffee which the homicide captain offered him. He wished Stanton were seated beside him. Together perhaps they could convince the official that Lance Benson should be taken into custody. But he'd had to respect Stanton's request: "Dr. Harrington, go ahead — and get Zoe some kind of protection. I know that's what you're here for, and so am I. Though — if you'll forgive me — what I have to say is private."

He sat alone, now, before law and order. But all was not lost. Awaiting his turn, Stanton stood just outside the door. Surely their stories would coincide. Benson could be locked up by nightfall. And the more pressing concern was for Zoe's immediate safety.

"I'm sorry the police chief isn't in, but he's a busy man." Kermit Whalen eased his large frame into the swivel chair behind his desk.

He noted the captain's "Damn I'm Good" mug. He liked that. The mug indicated confidence and with confidence often went decisive action.

"Now, what can we do for you, sir?"

"I would like protection for my daughter."

"Why is that?"

"I feel strongly," he paused, "that her husband is going to harm her."

"Well, Dr. Harrington, maybe your daughter and her husband are just having a family spat. Between the two of them. It happens all the time."

"No."

Whalen drank from his mug. "Dr. Harrington, this is the homicide division. We go in after the fact, not before."

"That's a pity, isn't it?"

Whalen reddened. "Look, what makes you think your daughter's in serious enough trouble for you to come here?"

"Her husband is blackmailing someone. She's discovered that, and he knows it . . . I suspect there may be others."

Whalen straightened. "What's your son-in-law's name?"

"Lance Benson."

"The theatre director?"

"That's correct."

"And this person Mr. Benson is supposedly blackmailing?"

He hesitated. "The man has a fine family. I don't like bringing him into this unnecessarily."

"For God's sakes, Harrington, you've got my attention! . . . Excuse me, sir. But I can't help you without facts."

"His name is Martin Fletcher."

Whalen switched on his intercom. "Cynthia, get Detective Dobson in here."

Lawrence Harrington stared at the captain's mug and waited.

The captain leaned forward, steel gray eyebrows raised in a broad face. "I take it you haven't read today's *Times?*"

"No. Should I?"

"It would have updated your information. Martin Fletcher has been dead since yesterday morning."

"Fletcher? . . . How?"

"We're not sure."

The intercom buzzed. "Yeah, Cynthia?"

"Detective Dobson is out, sir."

"OK. . . . Contact the dispatcher to radio him back in." He switched off the intercom. "Dr. Harrington, are you willing to put what you've just told me on record? And anything else you might know about this?"

"If it would help."

"It would."

"Then of course."

"Good! . . . Now you mentioned there were others your son-in-law may be blackmailing. Again, sir, I'll need names."

He shifted in his chair. The gears had been set in motion. There was no turning back. "While I don't have concrete evidence," he said, "I suspect the late Lowell Hook. And, possibly . . . Victor Solomon."

Damn! Stanton should be at home by now. He let the phone ring long and insistently before he hung up.

Zoe sat on the kitchen counter, staring as though mesmerized at the coffeepot perking the strong dark chicory he'd instructed her to make. The brew was specifically to sharpen his thinking.

Without looking at him, she asked "He's not at home, is he?"

"Who's not at home, Zoe?"

"Whoever." She shrugged.

"Obviously if I'm making the call right in front of you, I'm not being secretive. So why are you?"

She looked at him then, but there was flatness — defeat, perhaps — in her voice. "Charles Stanton."

"Why him?"

"Why not?"

He let it go. How she had deduced fully three-fourths of his project he would never know and at this point he hardly cared.

The coffee was ready.

"Pour me a cup."

She got down from the counter and poured.

"You're not having any?"

She shook her head.

"Well, at least you're being somewhat cooperative."

"Do I have a choice?"

"Not really."

"That's what I thought."

She handed him a familiar mug. Miniature thespians, dressed in Elizabethan costumes, were hand painted on bright red china. The mug was from a set of six she'd given to him one Father's Day. His finger traced a tiny, plumed hat. He was remembering. Annoyed by the gift, he had raised his objection: "No child, no present." She had replied, "No child, at least a present." This was a woman who was incapable of understanding him.

"Come on!" With a flick of his hand, much as he had used to signal to Bailey, he indicated she was to follow, pronto, up the stairs.

He led her into their bedroom.

As he jammed clothes into open suitcases, he occasionally glanced at her. She sat on the edge of the bed, smoking a cigarette, staring out a window. Her shoulders were slumped, her chin propped in a palm. She reminded him of Rodin's *The Thinker*.

It was a bit unsettling to know he'd had to knock his own wife into such submissiveness.

When they'd entered the house, she had marched directly to the phone. His hand had closed over hers.

"What do you think you're doing?"

"Calling Caroline!" She'd all but screamed.

"To tell her what?"

"That I'm so sorry, that — oh, Lance, get your fucking hand away!"

And he'd slapped her. His palm print remained on her cheek. He hadn't meant to do that; but she had, once again, pushed him too far. Well, soon she could live freely, telling anybody anything she wished. He would be gone. Her freedom would be his parting gift.

He stopped packing long enough to dial Stanton's number again. Zoe looked up.

Still no answer. He slammed down the phone. He'd thought he'd allowed enough time to contact the bastard and direct him forcibly to his savings, to Irene's jewels, to whatever would quickly yield money. Another miscalculation! If he couldn't reach Stanton in the next thirty minutes, he would drive to River Oaks and park in his driveway. He would wait there for Stanton just as Solomon would wait at Renard's for him. He dialed again. Where in the hell was Stanton? Surely not prostrate over the lesbian's coffin.

"I want to ask you something." Zoe shifted her position on the bed. Cross-legged, her dark skirt fanned out about her, her gray eyes large in her small face, she looked like a child. A waif.

"You look like a waif."

"You look like a madman. Look at you! Throwing suits into bags, slamming down phones, hitting your wife, murdering — you *are* a madman."

So, The Thinker had come to life.

"What was the question?" He tossed a cashmere cardigan on top of his shirts. He could have owned dozens of cashmeres had he been able to get his hands on Hook's millions. But not now. Damn, where was Stanton?

"Nothing . . . yes, something. What made you become this — other person I don't even remotely know?"

He stuffed socks into side pockets. "Let me explain something to you. I've always been the same person. As long as I can re-member, I've searched for a way to get what I wanted, what I didn't have, what I deserve. It's you who thought I was somebody else. So you see, my dear, it has been a case of mistaken identity."

"God!" She mashed out her cigarette.

"I will grant you one thing, Zoe. I haven't lost my mind, but I have misjudged. Everything that could have gone wrong just about has. I wouldn't do this again."

"Do what?"

He spoke more to himself than to her. "I would have found some other way — some foolproof way. I wouldn't have had a partner, brought anyone into my scheme. Next time —"

"Next time!"

"Next time." He closed the final suitcase. As he lined it up beside the other two, he pondered what he'd just said. "Next time." Perhaps he'd chosen those words for their shock value. . . . Or had that phrase been a Freudian slip? His left eyelid quivered. He didn't know. Regardless. "This time" had to be gotten through before there could be, or not be, a "next time."

Zoe had begun watching his every move. She reminded him of a cat poised to pounce.

She spoke softly. A cat walking on velvet. ". . . Your partner was Sandra Lowrey, wasn't it? Wasn't it, Lance?" He chose not to answer.

"I knew it. Since our party — I've known. Well, it's not really important, is it? I mean, she's dead."

"Time to go, Zoe."

"Where?"

"Upstairs."

She straightened. "We *are* upstairs."

"All the way up."

She drew back as if expecting another blow. Still she resisted. "Come on, Zoe!" He grabbed at her elbow.

She held up both hands.

"All right, I'm coming!" She leaned down.

"What do you think you're doing?"

"Getting a fresh pack of cigarettes." She opened her nightstand drawer.

He let her. That seemed little enough to permit.

But then she pulled from beneath her Bible —

"What the hell!"

He reached out; she sidestepped.

"Now, if you will hand over your gun." Her voice was level, but he noticed she gripped the small weapon as if to steady trembling.

He debated. Then he raised both arms over his head and thought fleetingly, nonsensically, "Cary Grant in Hitchcock. That gentleman has been known to win by bluffing."

He would out-bluff Zoe's bluff.

"Go ahead."

"Lance, just do what I said."

"Pull the trigger, Zoe. Go on, shoot, shoot, shoot!"

She lowered the gun so that it was level with his chest. And then she cocked the hammer.

She meant business!

He switched tactics to bear down with his mightiest weapon — his directorial skill. "All right, Zoe, all right. Don't shoot. Don't shoot. Goddamn it — don't shoot! Drop the gun!"

For an instant she wavered. In that instant he lunged. She fell back on the bed, the gun flew from her hand.

He bent to pick it up. Straightening, he smiled.

"A toy one would have served just as well, don't you think?"

He tossed the empty weapon to her. It landed on her breast. She cried out; he jerked her up by the arm.

His own gun, drawn from his belt, directed her. Its metal against her spine.

On the stairs she turned to face the gun and him. He saw fear — and possibly sadness — in her eyes. Those soft gray eyes. They had been the first thing he'd noticed about her.

"Where will you go?" she asked.

"Do I detect concern?"

"No, but — There's something I need to know . . . You never really loved me, did you?"

He looked away, then back at her. She had asked an honest question. He would try to give an honest answer.

"Yes . . . I think I did. I think so. But, Zoe, you have never understood me. And that has made all the difference."

He ushered her into the darkroom. She cried, "Don't do this! *Please*," as he locked the door.

"That's him! That's Mr. Black. Don't even need to draw sunshades on him." Guy Luden slapped his knee. He was seated at the kitchen table, where Clyde Pritchard had found him eating a late lunch.

Folding The Arch brochure into his pocket, the detective braced himself for another trip over the gravel road. "I'll be in touch," he said, then thanked Mrs. Luden who'd insisted that "a man of the law, helping keep this country safe for God-fearing Christians," should be served hot biscuits and honey for all his trouble.

"And maybe this'll teach you, Mr. Luden" — she addressed her husband formally — "to stick to what you know."

"Which is?" Luden cocked an eye at his wife.

"Serving the Lord and not the devil."

"Amen!" Pritchard agreed, enjoying the couple's exchange.

"As for you, Mr. Pritchard," said Celia Luden, an expansive smile on her ruddy face, "you can come back any time for more of my biscuits and honey."

So she had left a note, after all. And what a note! Kermit Whalen studied the barely legible script. He had figured her wrong. Irene Stanton was not just another bored society matron wanting out of it all. The woman was running scared because somebody knew something about her which even she had trouble facing.

"Any idea what this was about?" He looked across his desk at Sir Charles Stanton.

"I'd rather not go into it."

"You may have to."

"I understand that, and I will if — and only *if* — I have to."

"I see." Whalen fingered the note. Although coming here had taken guts, the gentleman — war hero or not — needed to be reprimanded.

"Why'd you wait so long to bring this to our attention?"

"Captain Whalen, if your wife had written you that note, what would you have done?"

Whalen rubbed a palm across his face. The man had hit home. He wouldn't press the withholding-evidence issue. "Probably exactly what you did," he said.

Stanton visibly relaxed.

"Now, you say she had lunch on Friday with Benson, but you don't know why or what went on."

"I've told you my suspicions. And, as I mentioned, she was noticeably upset that evening at the dinner party. After Benson left, she seemed more at ease but still pretty miserable."

"He left the party?"

"Shortly after the first course was served."

"What time was that?"

"Oh, it must have been — I'm not sure. Everything was running a bit late. Somewhere around nine, I'd say."

"What reason did he give?"

"He didn't. His wife simply said he had to leave."

"Did he get a phone call, or what?"

"I honestly don't know."

"Well, we can check with the staff on duty that night."

The homicide captain made another trip to the coffee urn. He was thinking. Lowell Hook died at approximately nine o'clock that same evening. Sandra Lowrey died approximately fifty minutes later. During the pocket of time between Hook's heart attack and Lowrey's murder, where was Lance Benson?

Walking back to his desk, he slowly stirred his coffee. Suppose Lowrey had called Benson to tell him to get over to her place fast? The theory was farfetched but possible. The intercom buzzed.

"Yeah, Cynthia?"

"Detective Dobson is here."

"That was quick."

"He was already on his way back in."

"Excellent. Ask him to wait outside."

He sank into his swivel chair. This was turning out to be quite a day. "Look, Stanton — Sir Charles —"

"The first is fine."

"Yes, well, Sir Charles —" He felt awkward each time he said the fancy title, but from what he'd read in the newspapers the man had earned it. "The detective outside is the one I mentioned earlier. He's the best. The best I've got, and I'd like to bring him in here. He's been working on this case. Well, not your wife's case, there is no case, at least there hasn't been until now."

". . . I would expect his confidentiality — the same as yours."

"You'll have it. And if it's possible — considering what Dr. Harrington has told us and your wife's death being unquestionably a —"

"Suicide."

"I can say — taking these things into consideration — that we may — I'm not promising, but we may — be able to get your man and leave your wife's name out of it."

"Thank you. We — I would be grateful. But, regardless, I want Benson stopped."

"Good! Then I'd like to set up telephone surveillance on your phone and monitor all incoming calls. In case he tries to contact you. That'd make for some pretty solid evidence, which would hold up a lot better than all this circumstantial stuff we've got."

"I would agree."

"And another thing . . . I may have to ask you to postpone your trip."

Stanton hesitated. "You understand — there's a burial involved. And her mother over there is quite elderly."

"I can appreciate that."

"Yes, well, my main concern is that Zoe Benson has protection."

"We'll see to that."

"See to it? I thought you'd taken care of that while her father was here!"

"Sir Charles, we're only human beings! These things take time. The man's no dummy. We have to move carefully. And *legally*. Now, for starters, let's get Dobson in here."

Stanton glanced at the lithograph of Themis that hung on the wall. "You're an intelligent man, Captain Whalen. I can see that. And one who knows his business. But, for God's sakes, get on with it!"

Kermit Whalen switched on his intercom. "Cynthia, tell Detective Dobson to come in, please."

Raymond Reese and his mother sat at his worktable eating croissants, filled with egg salad and bacon bits, which Henri had brought back from the little French deli across the street.

Winifred thoughtfully dabbed at the corners of her mouth with a paper napkin. Raymond gulped Perrier.

"You know, Raymond, I have no desire to see it." She unzipped her purse and handed him the cassette. "I suggest you get rid of the thing."

"Yes, ma'am." He bent his head to his croissant.

"Son, have you learned anything from this?"

"That you're the most brilliant woman who ever lived!"

"Fiddlesticks!" Her ringed fingers spread into the air, then clenched into tight little fists. "That was not what you were supposed to have learned."

"I learned . . ." He searched for the right answer. "Oh, Mother, what I learned was — so help me God, never to get myself into a situation like that again."

"Well, obviously, not if you can avoid it. But I'll tell you what I wanted you to learn. Honesty and decency and fearlessness. You've got to stand up to the big bad wolves of the world. Or they'll gobble you up. Surely you've learned that." She unwrapped a square of amaretto cheesecake.

"I have. I think I have."

"Know it, Raymond! Listen, you're lucky. Even if you never get back a single penny of the money you've already paid him, you're still lucky. And don't you forget it. As for this place —" She glanced into the showroom. "We'll take the fifty thousand dollars and look for bargains. Bargains, Raymond, because we'll have to, but if you've learned, if you've become a man — a man, Raymond — even if you're just on your *way* to becoming that — then some good will have come of this." She pushed her cheesecake toward him. "Here, I'm not as hungry as I thought I was."

"I'm not either." He looked down at his unfinished croissant.

"I've never known you to refuse food."

"Mother?"

"Yes?"

"I'm so ashamed."

"Why, son, you needn't be. You've come through this just fine. You've got scars, but you won the battle. You won the battle, Raymond! Now *win the war*. And, for heaven's sake, don't give up eating. You're skin and bones as it is."

"I guess you're right."

"I know I'm right."

"Yes, ma'am." He smiled and bit into the cheesecake.

Erasing question marks and penciling words into the blocks of his crossword puzzle, Dobby Dobson waited for his partner to return from the northwest. He hoped Pritchard would bring back news that Benson's photograph could just as readily be that of Mr. Black, the mysterious customer who had ordered the custom mirror.

Angling his puzzle up to light, Dobson felt like a doctor examining an X ray. He stared at a single block. The name "Marrs" filled the tiny square.

He pressed his thumbs against his eyelids. This was getting to be an exhausting investigation. He'd left Whalen winding up the conversation with Stanton and driven to Stanton's club. From there, he'd been directed to the maitre d's home.

Off duty, Roland Marrs had stopped washing his 1939 Packard long enough to verify that yes, Mr. Benson had received a call from a woman shortly after nine o'clock the evening of the Stanton party. To the question "Did the woman sound agitated?" he'd answered, "Not that I recollect." Regardless, Benson had definitely taken a call from a woman shortly before he left the party.

The phone rang. "Damn!" he said and answered.

"This is Caroline Fletcher. I hate to bother you, but —"

"It's no bother." He pushed aside the puzzle.

"Well, I've been thinking — perhaps you should talk to Irene Stanton's husband."

"Why is that?"

"Because . . . Irene was involved with The Arch. They all were."

"That makes sense. I'll do that. And Mrs. Fletcher?"

"Yes."

"Thank you."

He put down the phone. He had been tempted to tell her that only a short while ago Sir Charles Stanton, as well as Lance Benson's father-in-law, had voluntarily walked into the station and the results of those illuminating visits would help solve her husband's murder. It had been Harrington's statement that suggested a motive. Apparently, midway through making payments, Fletcher had done an about-face and started blackmailing the blackmailer. If that was the case, Caroline Fletcher was going to have to hold on tight to whatever it was that lay, like granite, beneath her calm exterior.

Again he concentrated on his puzzle. He circled three blocks. Three items: Ornade, video, Lightning. They were only circumstantial clues. But he'd be willing to bet that a bottle filled with Ornade capsules, a VCR, and a can of the insecticide could be found in Benson's house. Legally, there was no way he could search the premises. But he could question the man concerning his whereabouts on Friday evening and Sunday morning.

Clyde Pritchard walked in the door.

"It's about time."

"You ever try making that trip?"

"No thank you."

"I always knew you were the brains of this outfit."

"You get what you were after?"

"Right on the money."

"Don't sit down."

"I just got here!"

"Look, Pritch, we gotta move!"

"He hasn't come in. And he hasn't called." Suzanne Porter looked from Detective Dobson to Detective Pritchard. She spoke pointedly to Dobson. "But you're welcome to wait."

"No thanks. Could he be at home?"

"Well . . ." She pursed her lips as if she were thinking. "I'm not sure. Do you want me to call?"

"No, we'll come back later."

"You're sure?"

"Sure." Dobson dropped a peppermint onto her desk.

Watching them leave, she unwrapped the candy and popped it into her mouth.

Why didn't she stop that infernal pounding? Quickly he loaded his luggage into his car. When he reentered the house, the noise was louder. She had taken a heavy object, probably a chair, and was striking it against the door. He tried to ignore the sound. Surely she would stop when she realized how futile her efforts were. He walked through the downstairs. For a moment he paused in front of the French doors and stared out at the pool he had built lovingly with his bare hands. Then he hurried on into the library, to his desk, and dialed Stanton's number.

He let the phone ring. Still no answer. What if he drove to Stanton's house but the bastard didn't return home for hours? He couldn't wait. From across an entire ocean, he would contact Charles Stanton and order him to deposit the money in a Swiss bank account. It was not impossible.

As he hung up the phone, he glanced out the window directly into the eyes of a man coming up the front walk. There were two of them. Men he had never seen before, men who knew now that he was home. Zoe's incessant banging suddenly sounded like thunder rolling throughout the house, striking at the foundation. The doorbell rang. Taking three steps at a time, he rushed up the stairs into the bedroom, where he threw on a sweater to hide the gun; then on he rushed to unlock the darkroom.

He was right. It was a chair she had been hitting against the door.

"There are some men outside. When I let them in, you're to sit beside me and verify whatever I say." He propelled them both down the stairs. The doorbell was ringing. "And, for God's sake, pull yourself together."

"Pull myself together!"

"You heard me!"

They had reached the first floor.

"Keep in mind I won't hesitate to use the gun."

"Of course not."

He opened the door.

"Mr. Benson?" The man whose eyes he had met spoke. "I'm Detective Dobson and this is Detective Pritchard. We're with the Houston police homicide division." He held out an identification card. "Sir, we'd like to ask you a few questions."

"I assume this concerns the unfortunate deaths of Mr. Hook and Miss Lowrey?"

"Yes, sir." The other detective had found his tongue.

"Well, I won't be much help, I'm afraid. But come in . . . Zoe, Detectives Dobson and Pritchard. My wife, gentlemen."

"May I offer you coffee?" Fleetingly he admired her breeding, her grace under fire.

"No, thank you, Mrs. Benson." The one named Dobson was clearly the leader.

"But it's already made." Now why was she pressing when she knew he wasn't about to let her leave his side?

"Well, then — yes, thank you. Black."

Damn!

The sidekick echoed: "Black."

She slipped away quickly with a cheery little "This won't take long."

Conniving bitch!

As he led the two men into the living room, he fought an impulse to cover his trembling eyelid.

"Well, let's be seated, shall we?" He gestured to chairs. He himself sat on the sofa. A large coffee table separated him now from the enemy.

His eyelid became still.

"So . . ." He crossed his arms. "What can I do for you?"

"Mr. Benson?" Dobson again. "Sir, where were you last Friday evening?"

"That's hardly the type of question I had anticipated. But we were at a dinner party for the late Irene Stanton. I wasn't feeling well and I attended only because Lady Stanton had been a close friend for years. At any rate, when I became increasingly ill — nauseated, actually — I decided to come home to bed. My wife can verify that, of course. Except I'll have to go for her. Perhaps help with the coffee."

He was up and into the kitchen before they could react, one way or another, to his leaving the room.

She was placing the Father's Day mugs on a tray.

"Is this in slow motion?" he asked and poured the coffee himself.

Disregarding the tray, he picked up two of the mugs, then ordered, "Bring ours and get in there fast."

Wearing a smile usually reserved for top-echelon patrons, he rejoined the detectives.

"Well, gentlemen, drink up. But, I warn you, it's strong."

"The blacker the better!" The sidekick — Pritchard, was it? — took a deep swallow. "Delicious."

"Yes, chicory is rather like ambrosia, I always say."

Zoe, ever the proper little hostess, was handing out napkins. Amazing. She hadn't brought out the linen.

"Your saucers," she joked.

The two men accepted their paper napkins and laughed.

"Now, you were saying, Detective Dobson?"

"Oh, since we've got your wife here, let's bring her into this . . . Mrs. Benson, the night of the Stanton party did you return home with your husband? That is when he left — because of illness, was it, Mr. Benson?"

"Yes. And no she didn't. But I hardly think that's germane."

"What time did you arrive home, Mrs. Benson?"

"About — well, it was after twelve. Closer to one. Twelve forty-five, probably."

"And your husband was here?"

". . . Yes."

Why did the bitch hesitate?

"I was in bed, asleep. Right, Zoe?"

"Yes."

"Well, I guess that settles that. Excellent coffee." Dobson took a long sip. "Sir, we understand that while you were still at the party you received a call around nine o'clock from a woman."

The bastard had done his homework.

"Was it a woman? That's interesting. When I reached the phone, there was no one on the line. You've at least solved part of the mystery."

Dobson laughed. "I'm glad we could help you out — even if it's only up to a point."

Zoe sat immobile, a lump of salt.

"Anything you'd like to add, dear?"

"No."

What a hindrance! But he'd had to put a stop to her infernal pounding.

Pritchard cleared his throat. "Mr. Benson, moving on to another date . . . yesterday morning, Sunday, September twenty-fifth. We'd like to know your whereabouts then." The sidekick did not have the finesse of his leader.

"Why that date?"

"It ties in."

"I see . . . Well, my wife and I were together; mostly here; out and about some."

"Could you be more specific?" Dobson leaned forward.

This had gone far enough.

He stared unblinkingly into the detective's eyes.

"Yes, but I don't care to. Because, frankly, I find your questions insulting. I'll answer, but only with my lawyer present. That is my prerogative, am I not correct?" He stood. "Now if you'll excuse us, my wife and I have just returned from a funeral."

Dobson rose quickly. "Sir, please consider this a routine interview. We're asking the same questions of a number of people associated with your theatre."

"I understand, but I'll stick by my decision."

He went to the front door and opened it.

From behind a curtain, he watched the two men walk to their car. The innocuous white Plymouth hardly broadcast what they were. Well, he had outwitted them. Temporarily. But why had he been questioned concerning his whereabouts on the morning Fletcher had supposedly committed suicide? They knew more than they were letting on. They would be back. And if he weren't here, the bloodhounds would sniff out his hiding place. He might have to forego his dream of eventually getting to Switzerland. Instead, he'd be forced to live out his days in a country which did not have an extradition agreement with the United States. But where would that be? And how was he going to gain entrance into any country other than some backward place whose only admittance requirement was the show of a driver's license or birth certificate? Shit! Why hadn't he gotten a passport? Perhaps stupidity — a trait he abhorred — had become his own predominant characteristic.

He had better calm down and take one step at a time. At least he knew where he was headed now. Once there, he would hide. Assume a new identity. He would rest, devise a plan and, above all, recoup the clear, brilliant thinking which, for years, had been his trademark.

He turned from the window and observed his wife. She sat straight in a straight-backed chair.

"You were a fine help."

"What did you expect?"

"More than I got. Now get back upstairs."

"No, I won't do that." Her hands — the knuckles white, he noticed — gripped the arms of the chair.

He tried reasoning. "Zoe, your old man'll come looking for you before too long. You'll be all right. So do as I say."

"You just go to hell!"

He pulled the gun from his belt. For emphasis he cocked the hammer.

"Go ahead, use it!" Her eyes, no longer soft, bored into his.

"Look, I don't want to do that."

"Then don't! But I'm not going back up there. Not ever again!"

"Zoe, I don't want to hurt you."

"You've said that before."

"I meant it."

"I'm not moving!"

"Oh yes, you are!" He jerked her up from the chair. "Now, move!"

"No!" With her free hand, she began hitting his chest.

He carried her up the stairs. But she refused to stay still in his arms.

"Lance, they'll get you! They'll find you and they'll get you. They'll lock you up. They'll . . ." She kept twisting and turning. He wanted to hit her, to knock her unconscious. Damnit! Why wouldn't she stay still? And she was heavy! She was like Sandra.

Like Sandra. Thank God, he had reached the landing. A few more steps and he would be there. He carried her thrashing — a wild woman, like Sandra, like Sandra — into the darkroom.

"Lance, don't do this! Don't."

He dropped her — a sack of flour, a dead weight — on the floor. But she didn't stay where she was supposed to, she reached for his foot, and jerked. God, he was falling, falling. Not down the stairs, at least. At least, to the floor. His head hit the banister. The flat, harsh sound of the gunshot pierced his eardrums. It must have pierced hers, too, for she screamed. Slowly he raised himself on one elbow.

A bright red spot was on her temple. She was still. Like Sandra. He crawled over to her and felt her pulse, then he stumbled to the phone. Trembling he dialed zero. He thought of nonsensical things: blood would stain antique silk, the blouse had belonged to her mother; good thinking to have a phone in the hallway, good thinking, good thinking. What had he been thinking of when he released that safety? She mustn't die! She couldn't. "Operator, send an ambulance immediately to 11809 Memorial. There's been an accident . . . That's right. Up on the third floor. The door will be unlocked. Get them here fast!"

He looked at her one final time. Blood was gushing now into her hair. For some inexplicable reason, he thought of the Red Sea. He shook his head. It wouldn't be like it had been with Sandra. Not Zoe like Sandra. But both of them had tried to stop him. To control him. They — *she* shouldn't have done that. Why had she done that? He tore down the stairs and out of the house. There was no time. No time at all now. Not even time to contact Stanton. He had to get away, out of the country. If she lived, she would talk. But she had to live! He hadn't meant to kill her. The gun had gone off. It had been in his hand. He hadn't meant — he had to get to the bar, Victor would be there. Victor was his only hope. He hadn't meant any of this. What was happening to his life? He would like to start over. From the day of his birth and move forward. Things would be different. He backed his car out of the driveway. When he was a mile away from his house, he imagined the high shrill sound of sirens, a swirling red orb blinding him.

Charles Stanton drove from the police station to Sunset Boulevard. Harrington would be expecting him. Together they were to drive to the Bensons' house. Since making that agreement, however, another plan had formed in his head.

The professor was waiting on his front porch. "Let's go," he said.

Stanton hesitated. "Sir, you may not like this, but I think I should do this alone."

"I appreciate that, Charles, but she is my daughter."

"We may be exaggerating the seriousness of the situation."

"I hope so, but let's find out."

"Dr. Harrington, just hear what I'm suggesting. Do you own a tape recorder?"

"I do. Why?"

"If I were to go alone, your son-in-law, I believe, might say things to me he probably wouldn't say in front of you — perhaps even incriminate himself."

The old man stared beyond an elm tree shading his lawn.

"Wait here," he said, then disappeared inside his house, only to return almost immediately with the recorder.

"There's a tape in it you can erase. It's got useless notes on it. I don't like staying behind. You know that. It makes me feel — ancient and inadequate."

"That's non —"

"No, don't protest. I'm staying . . . Well, here it is." He held out the recorder. "But I suspect the damn thing's too big for what you have in mind."

Stanton threw up his hands.

"That shows my thinking . . . Well, I'll swing by a store and pick up something pocket-size."

Halfway to his car, he stopped and returned to the porch.

"Dr. Harrington," he said, "I want you to know — I don't intend to leave without her."

Victor Solomon nursed his second scotch. The first he had gulped down. The bartender had impassively poured the second, then resumed stacking glasses on a long shelf behind the bar. Business was slow. No wonder. At this hour most respectable men were hunched over desks. What then was he doing slouched in some dark bar, waiting to dance to whatever tune a blackmailer played? He answered his own question. He was here because the blackmailer — the scum — had welshed. The duplicate had not been erased. His hand tightened around the glass. He took a long sip. The scotch warmed his insides. This was his best friend. Maybe his only friend. The only friend who never asked questions. Never demanded, only gave. Fuck Roselyn for throwing those combs at him. Roselyn, stone-faced, granite woman. Lips tight, legs tight. Fuck her. Ordering him to get home in time to pay their respects to the old man before dinner. So what were they going to do? Eat lamb chops after staring down at a dead man who was past caring if they paid their respects or not? Roselyn didn't know it, but he — not Hook — could have been lying in that funeral home. Hadn't Hook died in Sandra Lowrey's bed? For sure, Lance Benson's deft hand had closed around them all. He glanced at his watch. The bastard was late. It would serve him right to be met by an empty bar stool. But how could he leave? He was next in line for whatever Benson had in mind. He had said it wasn't money he wanted. What then? Solomon finished off the drink and ordered a third.

With one hand Dewitt Dobson steered the white Plymouth out of the Bensons' driveway; with the other he tossed a crumpled paper napkin to his partner.

"Look what came with my coffee."

Clyde Pritchard smoothed out the napkin and let out a long, low whistle.

"Holy shit," he said.

"Holy shit, is right."

Dobson drove slowly up Memorial. Suddenly he wheeled into a cul-de-sac. The car swerved around the circle then out again onto Memorial.

"We're going back," he said.

"After the bastard practically threw us out of his house?"

"Oh, we're not setting foot in his yard. We're just going to park where we'll have a good view of that driveway."

"For what?"

"I'm not sure for what. But we'll wait and see."

"Well, we'd better radio in."

"Good thinking."

"Sure it's good thinking. And, unless Whalen's got some other idea, I'm thinking Victor Solomon, since Harrington said he might be one of the ones Benson was putting the screws on."

"Pritch, we've got a lady in distress. Now since we can't go barging back in there, we've got to do something else."

"That's exactly what I'm suggesting! Get enough on the guy so we *can* barge in."

". . . If we could just figure a way to get her out, on her own. Maybe with a phone call. Fake some emergency."

"You think Benson's going to let her go near a phone? 'Don't let him out of your sight. He has a gun. Dangerous!' she said. I mean, come on, Dobby. She knows too much. And look at the kind of questions we were asking him."

"I said *if* we could . . . Pritch, did you notice the way his eyelid twitched?"

"No, I was too busy watching his wife sitting there scared shit-less." Clyde Pritchard looked down at the napkin. "But, you mean to tell me, that little thing actually passed this right under his nose?"

"Right under his nose." Dobson parked on a curve.

"Hey, you want to get us killed?"

"I'll take my chances."

"*Your* chances?"

"Look, this is a ringside seat for that driveway. Without being noticed. And the way *I'm* thinking is, if a man's running scared, he doesn't hole up in his house. He's got to move, do something to change his situation. And in this case, I'd say do something fast."

"Well, if he does move — and we'd better hope he moves alone — "

"I think he will."

"OK, that's when we go back in, get her out, and get her story!"

"No. Because if we do that he'll get away."

"Rest your case," Pritchard said.

"Good." Dobson grinned. "Now, let's radio in."

"Sounds on target. I'll get Mrs. Benson covered. You two stick with the suspect," the captain had ordered.

The homicide detectives were silent now as they waited.

Sliding down in his seat, Clyde Pritchard lighted a cigarette. Sitting erect, Dewitt Dobson unwrapped a peppermint.

The cigarette had been smoked to the length of a fingertip, the

peppermint sucked wafer-thin, when suddenly the Continental came
zooming out of the driveway.

"There he goes and alone," Dobson said under his breath as he
switched on the ignition.

"Yeah, but the wrong way!" Pritchard all but yelled.

"No problem." Dobson spun the Plymouth around. The ma-
neuver brought an oncoming Mercury to a screeching halt. A man
lowered his window and thrust a finger into the air.

Three cars were between them and the charcoal gray Continental.

"That's good. We'll keep it that way." Dobson checked his rearview mirror. Traffic was slow and heavy.

"Say, you don't suppose he's headed for The Arch?"

"No way."

"Well, wherever he's going, he's in a hurry to get there!"

"That's for sure." Dobson downshifted and passed one of the
cars. "Damn!" He pulled over to the shoulder. An ambulance, its
siren blaring, roared past from the opposite direction. The Continental never slowed.

"Dobby, we're going to lose him!"

"The hell we are!" He pressed down on the accelerator and
passed another car.

A crawling Volkswagon and a pickup, which had rammed its
way through the traffic, separated them from the speeding Continental.

Lance Benson had crossed under the freeway and entered that
strip of Memorial Drive which curves through the park, before he
noticed the white Plymouth weaving in and out of the traffic behind
him. His hands tightened on the wheel. His left eyelid flickered.
He was already late for his meeting with Solomon. How in the
hell was he going to shake those damned detectives?

The Continental leaped forward. The Plymouth gathered speed.
He was reminded of the game Simon Says. As a child, he had
always won. Simon says do this, Simon says do that. Simon says,
"Get lost." The Continental shot like a bullet through the park.

Glancing in his rearview mirror, he watched the Plymouth pass
a Volks. The pickup that remained between them edged over to
the middle of the road.

The Continental, the pickup — its driver bullying, blocking would-be overtakers — and the Plymouth coursed down Memorial, on to Shepherd. On, on. He prayed there were no radar traps. The Continental streaked through a yellow light. The pickup, brakes screeching, stopped for the light turning red. A solid bracket, formed by the pickup and cars in the left lane, had trapped the Plymouth.

He breathed more easily. Over a sweep of rising concrete, he veered down a sidestreet from which branched a network of spider-thin roads lined with tenements. "Prime commercial property," Lowell Hook had once remarked. "But I'll buy up the land before I'll let some bastard bulldoze houses out from under people." How strange that he should seek refuge in an area that Hook had so zealously protected.

He eased out into the main flow of traffic. The Plymouth was nowhere in sight. He picked up speed, for he was still ten minutes away from Renard's, sunk deep in the inner city.

He flicked on the radio. The music was country and western. "Would you hold it against me, if I said that you had a beautiful body?" He changed stations. He was good and ready to get out of this red-necked country.

Finally, Renard's! He swung his Continental into a space beside Victor Solomon's Mercedes. Changing his mind, he backed out and steered into an alley which snaked between the tiny bar and a dry-cleaning establishment. At the end of the alley on a brick wall were the faded, paint-dripped words, TOW-AWAY ZONE. He had no quarrel with the warning. After transferring his luggage into Victor's car, he would have no need for the Continental. Let it be hauled off to a junkyard and buried under rusted fenders. The detectives would have to dirty their hands to unearth something that would ultimately yield nothing.

He walked through the alley. All along he had known that Victor would wait. After all, he was Victor's leader. Poor Victor. With the exception of running an inherited store, he had probably never experienced the exhilaration of being Simon, commanding others to do this, do that, watching the less adroit drop like flies. Drop like Sandra. Like Zoe. He mustn't think of that now. The ambulance — he had seen it — had come for her. She was safe, she was alive — blood transfusing into her veins, the bullet scooped out. He must concentrate on being Simon. That was a nice, powerful feeling. He *was* Simon. Hadn't he lost the detectives? And Victor was waiting. He was almost — not quite, but almost — home free.

He pushed open the door. Blinking through darkness, he saw him hunched over the bar. He had forgotten. Victor Solomon was not noted for stopping at one drink. Christ, how many had he had?

A clever amateur had outmaneuvered him. Dewitt Dobson pulled over to a filling station, slammed out of the car, drank from a water cooler, and simmered down.

"OK," he said. "Don't say anything. Just let me think."

"I wouldn't think of it." Clyde Pritchard grinned. "But I might make a suggestion."

"What?" Dobson scowled.

"See if Whalen won't issue a bulletin and get the car located. The guy's headed for someplace specific. Probably in this area. So let's find out where he went. That's all." Pritchard shrugged. "Go back to your thinking."

". . . All right, let's do that." Dobson got back in the car.

"Then why don't we —" Pritchard lighted a cigarette.

"Another suggestion?"

"Check up on Zoe Benson."

"OK."

"And after that —"

"*Another* suggestion?"

"Check out Victor Solomon."

"OK to that, too." Dobson snapped on his safety belt. "Provided Benson's still on the loose. The damned amateur!"

"But clever," Pritchard reminded him.

Later he was to reflect on the timing. It had been that kind of timing authors avoid writing into their stories, for it is too coincidental, too nearly perfect. But he had observed such synchronism in life. He had heard of it. Childhood friends — separated by an ocean for thirty-two years — standing unexpectedly one day beside each other in front of the Parthenon. And during the war, a British soldier walking into a deserted house in Freiburg and seeing on a bureau a snapshot of himself, the house having belonged to his nanny who had left England years before to return to her native Germany. Such timing was possible.

There had been no such timing during those early-morning hours when Irene had hanged herself. Why had he not awakened, wanting a glass of orange juice or a bowl of cereal, which was seldom but sometimes his inclination? Had he gone downstairs at the precise moment she had looped the rope over the door, he could have stopped her. He would have taken her hand, led her back upstairs. They would have talked. She would be alive.

But there had been more nearly that perfect timing when he had rounded the curve on Memorial and seen the ambulance pulling out of the Bensons' driveway. Instinctively he had known that Zoe, not Lance, was inside. Never losing sight of the flashing red light, he had followed the speeding vehicle. He had been there when it stopped at the hospital's emergency entrance. He had been there when the doctor emerged from the operating room and looked for someone to whom he might explain, offer reassurances.

"She's a lucky woman," the surgeon had said. "All it required was a good cleaning out. She'll have a nasty headache, and her ears may ring for a while. Possibly her vision will be blurred, because, along with the scalp wound, she's suffered a slight concussion. But all that's temporary. We'll run a few tests, of course. And I'm going to recommend that she remain hospitalized for three or four days. Not just because of the tests. But because she's upset enough that she needs the rest."

"That sounds like excellent advice," he'd said.

When she regained consciousness, he had been there, remorseful because he had not shielded her, grateful because she was alive.

"Charles?" She tried to rise. Her head fell back on the pillow. Her hand went to her temple. To the shaved scalp, the bandage. "What?" And then, as if remembering, she grabbed his hands, her eyes wide. "Where is he?"

"We don't know. The police are outside. Later, you can talk to them."

"No, I want to now!"

"Not now, Zoe."

The door was pushed open.

"I need to check your vital signs, Mrs. Benson." The nurse spoke with a crisp Jamaican accent. Deftly she slid the thermometer into the mouth, wrapped the gray band around the arm. She recorded her findings. "There." She adjusted the covers and left.

"Zoe, you should sleep."

"No." Again she attempted to get up. "Oh . . . my head."

"That's why you must keep still."

". . . I thought you had gone to England."

"That was to have been on Tuesday."

"It is Tuesday."

"It's Monday, Zoe."

"You have to go."

"I will . . . when you're all right."

"But I think —"

"Zoe, you've got to —"

"My father? Where's my father?"

"I've called him. He's on his way here."

"He'll be so worried. Don't let him worry. Don't —" She squinted. "You're so . . . blurred."

"The doctor said that would clear up."

"Charles, we've got to find him. He had his bags packed. He's leaving. He —"

"Rest, Zoe. Please."

The door opened.

"Mrs. Benson, I want you to relax. Can you do that?" The doctor leaned over her bed.

"I can. I think so." She closed her eyes, tears rolled down her cheeks.

"Zoe, that may make your vision worse."

"I know. I know. But I can't help it. I want — I don't know what I want."

The doctor led him into the corridor.

"There's nothing more you can do here."

"Thank you, doctor. But I prefer to stay."

"I think it's best if you go home. What she needs now is —" They both turned.

She held onto the IV stand she had pulled with her to the door of her room. "I want to talk to the police."

"You're a difficult patient, Mrs. Benson."

"Please."

The doctor scowled. ". . . For a few minutes. That's all."

"Thank you." She managed a smile.

"Well, sir" — the doctor shook his head — "if you'll escort this lady back to her bed —"

As he guided her across the room, he was aware of how small she was.

"Charles, I have to see them. I have to tell them what I know. I have to. You understand, don't you?"

"You drive a hard bargain, Zoe." He leaned down and kissed her forehead. "But, yes, I suppose I do."

"You're not going to get away with this. I'll have to file a flight plan, fuel up the tanks —"

"Just keep driving." He shoved the gun deeper into Solomon's side. His own action sickened him. This time, at least, he did not have the hammer cocked. Well, he couldn't worry about feeling like some underworld character in a James Cagney movie. He had a far more serious concern.

"Here, finish this." He handed Solomon the Styrofoam cup which he'd had the bartender fill with steaming black coffee.

Solomon gulped the coffee. "You're crazy, Benson."

"And you, Solomon, are drunk."

"You're right. Too damned drunk to get you off the runway."

"Just keep drinking that coffee and you'll do fine." Craning his neck, he peered through the windshield. "Would you look, Victor! We've got perfect weather for flying."

"No comment." Solomon belched.

They rode in silence.

"How much farther?"

"Jogging distance."

Three miles later, Victor Solomon switched on his left turn signal. The Mercedes passed under an arch. Over their heads, blazed in steel, were the words Stuart Reins Memorial Airport.

"Go straight to the hangar."

Solomon handed him the empty cup and did as he was told. "Tell me something, Benson. How'd you get this harebrained idea?"

"Actually the idea is brilliant. As you will see . . . Pull in there." When the car was parked alongside a corrugated tin building, he motioned with the gun: "Now, get out. And you can forget the flight plan."

"Like hell you say!"

"Whatever. But, Victor, you're not filing one."

. . .

The search was on. They could bring him in now. A bulletin had been issued notifying patrol units to be on the lookout for a charcoal gray Lincoln Continental, license plate number 606-LMB. To cover all bases, Whalen had stationed men at airports, and even at bus terminals, though if Benson were traveling anywhere, he would probably go first-class or not at all. On the other hand, he couldn't afford to be choosy. The man was running scared. His wife was lying in a hospital bed as a result of a shot he'd fired. He'd be more alarmed if he knew what she'd told them. She'd even disproved his alibi. Zoe Benson was willing to testify that she had not been with her husband on the morning Fletcher had died. Christ! Evidence was falling like manna into Dewitt Dobson's lap, but he couldn't scoop it up fast enough, or shape it into something whole, cohesive. The evidence *was* manna. Unwieldy dough.

"Why so quiet?"

"Looking for the house, Pritch."

Dobson drove slowly down Beacon Street. Houston, he reflected, was a city of borrowed names. His wife — his estranged wife — had come from Boston and pointed that fact out to him.

He felt he was fighting time. Never enough time to do a job thoroughly, to close in on the clever ones. Never enough time to have a decent personal life, to make a marriage work not only for him but also for her.

"That's it." He stared at the Georgian house, its hedged walk pointing like an arrow to a tall, heavy door.

Pritchard whistled. "How the rich do live! And not even working if they don't feel like it."

"Yeah." He knew that his partner was referring to the useless trip they'd made to Solomon's store. "Mr. Solomon's taking the day off and doesn't want to be disturbed," the model-thin blond had told them in no uncertain terms.

"Well, Pritch" — he glanced at his watch — "it's a little late — what with the delays."

"You're complaining? So we had to wait around the hospital. When they finally let us in there, look at all she had to say."

"It's not that."

"What then?"

". . . Thank God it was only a scalp wound."

"Like I told you, we did all we could. *What* we could."

"I guess." He shook his head as if to clear his thoughts. "OK. Let's go in and see if this guy can hammer the nail in the coffin."

They got out of the car.

"Dobson." Pritchard stood squarely in front of him. "We've got good things going now on this case. Solid stuff. But ever since we lost Benson's tail, you've been a real pain. You wanta explain that one?"

"Yeah. I've got a hunch . . . The man's going to get away."

"Where to?"

"I don't know where to. It's just a hunch."

Roselyn Solomon paced the polished floors of her house. Twice she stopped at Victor's desk and contemplated opening drawers, searching until she found some shred of evidence to confirm what the detectives had implied. What had they implied? She wasn't sure. But it had been something absurd! They had repeatedly asked questions about her husband's association with Lance Benson.

Mashing out a half-smoked cigarette, she listened to Chad and Rebecca in the next room. They were arguing over which was meaner, a tiger or a bear. What on earth? Where was Victor? He was to have been here by five. It was past six. The baby-sitter would be coming soon. Victor knew, *knew,* they were to go to the funeral home before dinner. She lighted another cigarette. That place! Even Martin there now. Like Irene, he had killed himself, the paper said. What was going on? And where was Victor? Had he seen the paper? They should be at the funeral home. Caroline would be there needing friends. Who would be there needing comfort because Lowell was dead? She didn't know. But she wanted to offer sympathy. Not empathy. She couldn't imagine such loss in her own life. Even her parents, both in their seventies — one slightly deaf, the other arthritic — were still alive. No one who touched the core of her being had died. No one ever. What had the detectives wanted? She had told them that her husband was at the airport, checking out their plane for a trip. And one of the men had had the nerve to suggest that Victor might have to be interviewed before they left tomorrow. Interviewed? Could those men stop them from leaving? She — *they* had to get away, immediately, before something happened. She stopped her pacing. That was the fear, wasn't it? She was afraid something would happen to Victor. It wasn't important that he might have done something wrong, might be in some kind of trouble. The important thing was that Victor be safe.

She would give him one more hour. That was all the waiting she could endure. Then, if he hadn't returned home, she would drive to the airport. Surely she would find him there. And she would ask him why in the hell it was taking so long to check out a plane!

Her children on either side of her, Caroline Fletcher knelt before the open casket. He appeared serene, years erased from his face. She was reminded of how he had looked as a young man — a boy, actually — courting her . . . Marrying her. Looking back, she realized now how young they both had been when they'd left Philadelphia to seek their place away from the familiar. But had they stayed in that brownstoned security would Martin be alive today? It was an empty question, for that was not what they had done.

They had come to Houston and from that first day — their pencils running down the want ads in search of an apartment — they had loved the city. For almost thirty years it had been their home. And until now, until the last few months, the years — the city — had blessed them. She stared at her husband. She wanted to touch him. Instead, she squeezed her children's hands and stood. She nodded to the funeral director, who waited in back of the chapel. "You may close it now," she said.

Her head held high, the French braids tightly plaited as if to anchor her skull to her neck, she walked into the reception area. Martin had possessed few, but steadfast, friends. Those few would have read that awful newspaper story and, unable to stay away until the service tomorrow, they would be bringing their grief and disbelief here this evening. She would comfort them. Her own comfort resided in her faith, her children, and a young detective who was somewhere at this very moment seeking the truth — the facts behind her husband's death.

Though Hazel Mabry had not worn the black taffeta, its white lace collar yellowed with age, since her husband's death thirty years before, she had somehow managed, after letting out the seams, to zipper her body into the dress.

Now, squeezed into her mothballed finery, she watched the

parade pass by. Amanda Stebbins, holding tightly to her granddaughter, was crying openly. "So many loved him," the housekeeper thought, keeping a stiff upper lip as Mr. Hook would have
expected her to do. What a shame that she, his employee, should
be the one standing here. He'd had three brothers. Two had been
killed in World War One; the third had died of pneumonia in
those days before penicillin. And not one of the brothers had left
so much as a single heir among them.

She straightened her collar. The mayor had arrived. It didn't
matter that Mr. Hook had died in some hussy's bed. He was still
respected. As for his killing that girl, she didn't believe it for one
second. From the looks of things, nobody else did either. Including
the police, who'd asked her about fifty thousand questions.

She would invite the mayor to stand beside her. She didn't feel
she alone should be representing Mr. Hook. But, oh, she had loved
him! Tomorrow, with a spray of his favorite orchids on his casket,
she would put him to rest in fine fashion. If only he could come
to his own funeral! He'd compliment her on the affair like he'd
always done after she'd organized one of his more elaborate dinner
parties.

In a few weeks she would close his penthouse and go to live
with her niece, who had called and told her that was exactly what
she should do. There could never be another Mr. Hook. Besides,
if by some miracle another such employer existed, she was too old
to go looking for him.

The plane taxied onto the runway. The black coffee had helped,
but not enough. A drunk was his pilot. He deserved better. But
Victor Solomon remained his only hope of escape.

In spite of the churning in his stomach, the twitch in his eyelid,
he fought to appear calm. For he had decided. By the sheer force
of his presence, he, Lance Benson, would guide his drunken pilot
over the Gulf and down into Mexico.

Victor Solomon had passed V-1. There was no turning back.
The Baron lifted into the air.

Benson stretched, then placed the gun on his knee; his fingers
stroked the nozzle. Victor was reminded of a man caressing a
woman's breast. Involuntarily he trembled. If only he, like the
bastard, were relaxed, bloodless. If only he could think! The sky

was clear, but fog enveloped his brain. He reduced power and headed south.

Never before had he piloted with so much as a single scotch under his belt. Never before had he taken off for Mexico without first filling his auxiliary tanks. His passenger, who obviously knew just enough about flying to be a menace, had decreed: "The mains are almost full. That's enough."

But, at least, a flight plan had been filed. "Look, Benson," he'd argued, "when you talk about flying over the Gulf, you're talking about international waters."

"Well, fly low and get under radar!"

"Fifty feet off the water?"

". . . All right, Solomon, file your plan!"

"Where to?"

"Make it Cozumel."

"Cozumel?"

"Cozumel."

Beside him, Benson kept stroking the gun. He was smiling.

"Victor, isn't it a happy coincidence for me that you happen to be a pilot? And an excellent one."

"Not under these conditions."

"Sorry, they're the best I could arrange. Your charming wife mentioned that you're making the very same trip tomorrow. Think of this as a trial run. You'll be back home tonight, and in the morning on your way again." He lighted a cigarette. "Of course, this isn't exactly a trial run."

"What do you mean?"

"We're not flying all the way into Cozumel. We'll veer west and somewhere along the coast — you're going to find a deserted airstrip."

"How in the hell am I going to do that?"

"Look at the sky. Clear as a bell! We'll fly low and spot one."

"You're crazy!"

"Victor, you're not approaching this venture with the proper attitude. I repeat, somewhere along the coast — near one of the fishing villages — we'll find one."

"You're thinking of the other side — near Baja."

"No. But, if you prefer, we could always extend our trip."

"Not on this fuel."

"That's exactly why you'll go where I'm telling you."

"And, I'm telling you, there's nothing on that peninsula except jungles and Mayan ruins! . . . Besides, I've got to think about refueling."

Benson flicked a cigarette ash. "Simple. Drop me off, then fly on in to Cozumel."

"Look, by the time I find you an airstrip —"

"Which I'm confident you'll do."

"—land, take off — I'm not going to have the fuel to get to Cozumel!"

"Victor, let's not make mountains out of molehills."

"You're not listening to me! What about refueling? I'll need octane! What about me?" He realized he was shouting. His hands were sweating. Christ! He could hardly concentrate on keeping his wings level, much less landing in the middle of some jungle or along a rocky coastline. What if he overshot? "What about me?" He couldn't stop the shouting. The demanding.

Benson touched his arm.

He jumped.

"Victor, calm down." His words were like oil sliding toward him. He would drown in the thickness. "I'm your friend. Some of my board members —"

"*Your* board members?"

"My board members have fished on the Yucatán. I know that. Now they had to land somewhere. We'll find an airstrip. Near a village. Then we'll go from there. Believe me, refueling is a minor problem. Consider my rusty Spanish. That's *my* minor problem. Both of our problems, Victor, are trivia that can be overcome. I promise you."

For a moment, listening, he felt he was a child again. A child who had misbehaved and was being forgiven. Soothed. He was grateful. Grateful to the bastard? He must be losing his mind. What if he surprised them both and, like some crazy kamikaze, nosedived the Baron straight into the ground?

He stared at his instrument panel. Nothing made sense. He struggled for inner control as the plane coursed like a kite through the sky.

Looking downward, Benson exclaimed, "Marvelous! We're over the Gulf."

.   .   .

At 8:05 P.M. a patrol unit assigned to the Montrose area spotted the Continental parked in an alley between Renard's Bar and a Pilgrim Dry Cleaners.

"That's it!" Officer Patton exclaimed. She was ecstatic. After only a month in this district, she had unearthed the car that the dispatcher had repeatedly described over the past two hours.

Her partner, hardened by ten years on the force, commented, "Could be." He double-checked the license-plate number. Only then did he radio in that the car, which appeared to be abandoned, had been located.

"Yeah, he was in here." The bartender, who was exactly three minutes away from going off duty, handed The Arch brochure back to Pritchard. "But he didn't stay long. He ordered coffee to go, then left with another guy who'd been in here for a while."

"What'd the other one look like?"

"Dark hair, medium height. Early forties, I'd say. Good-looking guy. Never said a word, just sat at the bar ordering scotch like it was about to be rationed. The way he kept looking at his watch, I figured he was waiting for somebody."

"You overhear any of the conversation?"

"Listen, detective, I learned a long time ago to keep my eyes and my ears closed unless somebody's speaking directly to me. But they weren't chummy, that's for sure. I remember the one who'd been waiting said, 'It's about time you showed up, you bastard.' The other one never raised his voice, except to order coffee. Right after that, they left."

"Together?"

"Yep, together."

The Baron's hangar slot was empty. Roselyn Solomon ran the length of road, of grassy lawn, to the two-story stucco building. There was an eerie quiet inside the private terminal. She and the old man, reading *AOPA*, had the place to themselves.

"Excuse me." She was out of breath. "I need information about my husband Victor Solomon. His car's outside, but his plane is gone."

The man closed his magazine. "He hasn't been in here, Mrs. Solomon, not since I came on duty at seven."

"Would you check with the control tower, please?"

"Yes ma'am, I can do that." He punched in a number on his phone. ". . . Hey, Jim. Jess here. You fellows notice Mr. Solomon going up today?"

She leaned over his desk. "It probably would have been this afternoon." Then she waited. She stared down at the magazine and wondered vaguely if reading its pages and watching other people lift into air was the closest the old man ever came to visiting foreign places.

He put down the phone. "Mr. Solomon took off around four-thirty, heading south."

"Are you sure?"

"That's what they told me."

"I can't believe it. I mean, where would he be going?"

"You might call the FSS. Just in case he filed a flight plan."

"But . . . why would he do that?"

The old man rubbed his stubbled chin. "Ma'am, your guess is probably a whole lot better than mine."

She had turned from the airport onto the highway before she realized she was driving in darkness. Quickly she flicked on her headlights. Her concentration centered on her husband. Over the years he had caused her anguish, most of it having to do with his drinking and other women. Never once, however, had he taken off in his plane without calling her. Never! Then why had he done this bizarre thing? And why today when tomorrow they were flying to Cozumel? Was he alone? What was his destination? Lights of a strip shopping center shone up ahead. She thought of lights illuminating a runway. Had he already landed someplace miles from here? Was he still in the air? Perhaps lost! Where was he at this moment? And why? "Your guess is probably a whole lot better than mine," the old man had said. Well, he was wrong. Her only clue — and it was more a suspicion — was that her husband's disappearance was somehow connected to the detectives' questions.

She pulled into the shopping strip and searched in her purse until she found a quarter. For a time she sat staring dumbly at the coin. Confusion and anger and fear churned inside her. The emotions whirled as stubs in a lottery bin. She tried to slow their spinning. The detectives suddenly seemed like old and dear friends. Though she couldn't recall either their names or their faces, they were the police. That was their one memorable, and now redeeming, feature. If only they would help — find out where he was, notify the Civil Air Patrol, do something, anything, everything! If only they would bring back her husband, she would become a lifetime supporter of a policeman's widow and his children. Why had she thought of that? Of someone's death. She stopped thinking and rushed to the phone. The police — the experts — would take over the guesswork. She was no better at it than the old man.

"I can't do it!"

"Of course you can."

"I'm telling you, I can't!"

"Just do it, Victor! Now we've been back and forth over this goddamn peninsula for over an hour, and I've finally spotted what I've known all along was down there. So land!"

"It's a fucking beach! Look at it! Nothing!"

"It's near Progreso. Fuel, Victor. Think of fuel."

"I'm thinking about staying alive."

"Then you'd better get us down fast!"

"If you'd let me fill the auxs! If we'd taken the time —"

"We won't *need* the auxs if you'll do what I tell you!"

"I *can't*, damnit!"

Benson pointed the gun at him. "Tell me, Victor, what would Roselyn think of finding her husband with a bullet up his ass?"

"You're not serious!"

"About as serious as when I killed Sandra Lowrey and Martin Fletcher."

"Fletcher?"

"Don't look so shocked."

"You killed Martin? *And* the girl?"

"Only because I was forced to. Similar to the way you're forcing me now. I'm telling you this because I know you, Victor. You won't go to the police. I've got the duplicate tape. Besides, you're not the type to stick your neck out. And, what's more important, I'm telling you so you'll know I'm quite serious. If I have to, I'll land the plane myself."

"You're insane!"

"Just land the plane."

He prepared for landing. As the plane descended to the beach, he suddenly threw power to the engines and climbed back into the air.

"What the hell!"

"There's a goddamn tree!"

"Victor, you're a gutless wonder."

"Look, Benson, we've got an eroded beach down there with a fallen tree smack in the middle of it. Now, if we're going to crash, it's not going to be straight into some jungle!" He was trembling, but his jaw was set.

"Amazing. Truly a gutless wonder."

"Maybe so, but I'm also the pilot."

The plane was again over the Gulf.

Benson put down the gun. "Well . . . since you seem to be sobering up, what do you suggest?"

"I don't know. My fuel's too low for Cozumel . . . Maybe Mérida."

"I've already told you, we're not landing at a public airport!"

"All right! But the air patrol will be out looking before long."

"That's because you filed that flight plan!"

"I had to!"

"Go ahead, Victor. Land. Wherever you wish. But if anything goes wrong, rest assured, every skin-flick theatre in the country is going to be showing the great Victor Solomon —"

"Look, I'm doing the best I can!"

"That's better. I appreciate a man's best efforts."

The silence was a relief.

Victor supposed his passenger was plotting again. Benson as a blackmailer was hard enough to believe. But Benson a murderer? The first time he'd seen him, the bastard had been speaking quietly to actors on a rehearsal stage. How strange that the man could direct others so effortlessly yet screw up his own life so miserably.

He studied the sky. Night was setting in. But his head was clearing. Benson's confession and the aborted landing had sobered him. He would fly his plane in to Mérida and take his chances that things would go smoothly. And if they didn't? He would face Roselyn's wrath, public disgrace — anything rather than die attempting to land on some postage-stamp beach with a jungle to the sides and back ot it.

Benson cleared his throat. "I've changed my mind. We'll land on another strip of beach."

"Benson, if you think I'm going to —" He stopped in mid-sentence. The engine was sputtering. He looked down at the gauges. The Baron had abruptly lost fuel pressure. Quickly he threw on the boost pumps.

"What's going on?"

"Can't you see!" He jerked at the lever. By switching tanks, he could utilize what little gas there was in the auxs.

"You'd better do something!"

"I am!" The engines were not responding. Frantically he began cross-feeding out of the auxiliaries.

The plane was going down. Acting out of reflex, he switched on the emergency frequency. No one would hear. He knew that.

Benson's hand closed over his. "No! Just set it down easy, Victor. Easy. We're not far out."

"What're you talking about? We're a good five miles out!"

"Easy."

"Damn! You've got ice water in your veins. We're going down!" He studied the roll of the waves. He had to think fast, talk fast. "OK, we're going to ditch." He had to keep his head, keep the gears retracted, the flaps lowered. "Get the life jackets, the raft."

"Where?"

"In back, you fool!" The bastard was useless — a hindrance. But he couldn't worry about that now. He tried to fly into the wind. From twelve hundred feet, the Baron was descending. Lower! Lower, still. It was going down! He wedged open the door with his shoe.

"What're you doing?"

"Just do what I'm doing. Open your goddamn door! Wedge it. We'll have about one minute when it hits."

"For what?" Benson was clutching his briefcase. "For what?"

The plane skipped over the water. In vain he attempted to keep the nose up. Just before the plane hit the water a second time, Victor Solomon bit into his tongue and tasted blood. He heard Benson beside him crying "God!" With the force of hitting a brick wall, the plane went straight into the swells.

A mountain covered him. Its stone weight pressed into his chest. He fought for oxygen; water rushed into his lungs. He thrust through pain — the pain in his chest. Through dark cold. He tried to crack open the crust of stone, of water smothering him, hurting his chest. He struggled against waves effortlessly, relentlessly, sucking him deeper. He spun, shoved, propelled himself free to the surface, his mouth open as he gasped for air.

He was on top of the mountain. His arms flailed, his fingers closed around fabric which slid away. Again, he strained, stretched toward the cushion ripped from the plane's interior. Waves hurled him forward. The cushion was his! This time he held tightly to his minuscule support. The waves, pushing inland, flung him up, under, over, as if he were no more than a fleck of foam.

Blood stained the water. He clung to his makeshift raft and prayed.

It was night when the little fishing boat headed back into Progreso. And in the pitch blackness, the boat's bow struck metal. One of the men raised his hand. "*Oye!*" he shouted. He could have sworn that he heard a human cry above the sound of the waves. His flashlight beamed over the water.

Zoe Benson awoke before dawn. "Who's there?" she asked into the shadowed hospital room. She switched on the light. She was alone. But she had felt someone had been standing over her bed. She must have been dreaming. She lay still and watched the slow, steady rise and fall of her chest. Strange that she had awakened startled but not afraid, for it had been Lance's presence she had felt in the room. She squinted at her clothes folded neatly on a chair. Her vision had cleared. Only a dull headache and a persistent ringing in her ears remained.

Vaguely she recalled that yesterday she had cried out, "I want — I don't know what I want." Now in the predawn hours, when the world seemed balanced on the edge of some deep, mysterious reservoir, she could think. She knew what she wanted. She wanted to put the past behind her. She had done what she could. The police would find him. She wanted to survive the present. Somehow she would find the strength to do that. When she walked past Lance Benson in a courtroom, she would turn her head. Never again did she intend to look directly into those eyes. She would move quickly to the witness stand and then on beyond into a future which she hoped would hold no threats or lies or brutalities. At least none in her own home. Perhaps that much she could ensure, for she knew what she wanted. She wanted a future filled with love and goodness. A future which involved painting until she had used up all her time on this earth. But she also wanted a future in which she never again closed her eyes to ugliness in the midst of beauty, to want in the midst of plenty, to another person's pain. And she wanted a future that conceivably included Charles.

At 5:30 A.M. Roselyn Solomon was permitted to enter the room. *"No más se puede quedar un ratito,"* she had been told. She stood beside her husband's bed.

A phone call had brought her here. The heavily accented voice at the other end of a bad connection had sent her rushing out of her house and onto the first plane she could charter to Progreso. During the flight she had sat erect, fingers locked, legs uncrossed, feet close together and pointed straight in front of her, as she willed Victor to live — to withstand the concussion, the broken ribs, the far more serious injuries; to withstand the trauma of being in the water until the fishermen, coming in late, weighed down with their catch, had discovered him and lifted him over the side of their little boat.

"Live, Victor," she whispered, pressing his hand. If only he would respond, she would get down on her hands and knees and kiss the feet of her husband's rescuers.

"You're strong, Victor. Strong," she insisted. She felt as if she were urging a runner over the finish line. "Strong. Strong," she repeated. Her words seemed a sham. He reminded her of one of Chad's toy soldiers wrapped in gauze. " 'Cause he's wounded and I've got to fix him," her son had explained, not a trace of a smile on his tiny face, as he tightened the gauze.

She bent over her husband. "Be strong, Victor. You *are* strong." She refused to give up. "Look, you've made it this far! Now you've got to keep on being strong!"

He was so still. Suddenly, she was angry.

"Damnit, Victor, we need you! Chad and Rebecca and I *need* you. So, you've *got* to be strong. For all of us!"

She sat, waiting, beside his bed. His hand moved in her own. For the first time since she had been told of the crash she cried.

Later he would explain what had happened. She — and unavoidably the police — would expect that of him. But for now all that mattered was that Victor Solomon, her husband, was going to live! Somehow she knew that.

. . .

Dobby Dobson sucked a peppermint and stared out a window in the waiting room. He finished the peppermint, then walked down the hospital corridor.

Whalen had decided there was no point in breaking the news to her during the night. "Let her sleep," he'd said. But it was morning now. Somebody had to tell her. And he had been appointed.

She was sitting up in bed, a breakfast tray in front of her.

"Good morning." The question was in her eyes.

"Mrs. Benson, I do have some news."

"You've found him." She pushed the tray away.

"We located his car . . . abandoned in an alley."

"Then he got away."

"Not exactly."

"I don't understand. I mean, you told me you were stationing men at airports, bus terminals —" She ran her fingers through her hair.

"Mrs. Benson, we have reason to believe your husband was involved in a plane crash."

"A plane crash?"

"A private plane. Victor Solomon's. It crashed in the Gulf. His flight plan indicated he was carrying a passenger. Now, Solomon's alive, and when he can talk, we expect him to verify that his passenger was your husband."

Her stare was direct, unblinking. "What happened to the passenger?"

"Some fishermen located Solomon not too long after the plane went down. The passenger hasn't been found . . . The search will continue."

"For how long?"

"A reasonable length of time. But it'll be thorough. They're using airplanes, helicopters, boats. The works."

"And if they don't find him?"

He paused. "Mrs. Benson, statistics regarding crashes of this type are not in our favor."

"I see."

She stared down at her hands.

"Look, do you want me to call someone to be with you?"

"That's not necessary."

"You're sure?"

"I'm sure." She held out her hand. "Thank you. Coming here couldn't have been easy. You'll let me know when he's found?"

"The first thing. But, in a situation like this, sometimes — well, the Gulf is a big place."

"You're saying he may never be found?"

"Unfortunately, that's where we stand."

Lawrence Harrington pulled weeds from beneath his gardenia bushes. He stopped, arched his back — stiff from bending — and squinted at the afternoon sun. Wiping dirt from his hands, he sank into a lawn chair and gazed at his backyard. Mimosas and willows shaded his small plot of earth. A brick walk curved around phlox-covered mounds. Honeysuckle climbed trellises. Perhaps he would hang a hammock here. For Zoe. When she was a child, he'd roped an old tire from the branch of a willow. She'd swung contentedly for hours, the soles of her sandals scuffing a hollow into the grass. What had he done with the tire? He couldn't remember. The years had hidden the memory. He wished that a hammock could be waiting for Zoe when he brought her home from the hospital.

He supposed he'd been some help to her this morning, but she'd seemed withdrawn. "We'll just have to wait," she'd said, then added, "And wait and wait." He'd suggested that she try to get on with her life while waiting. And she'd asked, bewilderment on her face, "How can I? What if I *never* know?"

"Then you'll have to live with that," he'd said.

"I know. I know." She'd hugged her arms to her as if she were cold.

"And it will still be a fine, good life, Zoe, you'll see."

The only time she'd brightened was when he repeated his earlier suggestion that they take a trip to Greece. "There's a vast amount of research to do for my book, and you'd be a tremendous help."

"I'd like that." She'd smiled and reached for his hand. "Could we go soon?"

"Soon," he'd promised, then left because she had wanted to be alone.

"Maybe I'll even sleep," she'd said.

So he had come home to work in his garden. The simple task helped him over the hump of his own waiting. Ridding his yard of weeds, he had tried not to think about the fate of his son-in-law. He felt guilty wishing him dead.

He stood to empty his wheelbarrow, filled with clover and dandelions, into a trash can. He must keep occupied. He must try again to help Zoe in yet another small, and perhaps insignificant, way. Near the university was a garden shop which might have a hammock. And, if not, he would search until he found one. He would also stop by a travel agency to ask for brochures on Greece.

The hammock, hung between two trees, and the brochures would be waiting for his daughter.

Caroline Fletcher stared at the stained-glass window depicting Moses molding brass into a serpent. She thought of the rattlesnake she had discovered in her home, its mark on her husband's throat. She looked to the priest. Relief was not there. These past two days she had begun wondering if she had been wrong to insist that Martin leave his Catholicism to join her in a Protestantism which back then had held so little meaning for her and even less for him. All these years her husband had abstained from eating meat on Fridays. "A stupid habit from childhood. After all, even the church has given that up." he'd said sheepishly as she had prepared one of those meatless meals. Their Friday dinners, numbering into the hundreds now, had been her sole concession to the fact that Martin had ever been anything other than an Episcopalian. How pious she had been! How wrong. She lowered her head and listened to the words of her priest — not Martin's priest — never his. Not really.

She longed to enter the pulpit herself and announce that at this very moment her husband would be seated behind his desk had he not been murdered. The priest's eulogy was implying that Martin had taken his own life. That she and the children were not to feel guilty was implicit in his message. But she mustn't blame him. How could he know? She would hold her head high, ignore the misguided words, and wait. Soon the priest *and* the world — at least her world — would know. Soon she would understand. Hadn't Detective Dobson called only hours before to say that news was breaking, that the pieces of the puzzle were fitting together? "Just be patient. You'll only have to wait a little longer," he'd said. So . . . she waited.

But for what was she waiting? Perhaps, after her vigil had ended, there would be even greater shame, greater hurt than there was now when people shook their heads and murmured, "If only we'd realized how unhappy he was. Maybe we could have done something." Still, she mustn't blame them, just as she mustn't blame the priest. They were trying to help, these people surrounding her.

But why was the church so empty? Perhaps Martin had lost out to Irene and Lowell. Those who stayed away were probably exhausted from attending other funerals. Certainly the ones who mattered were here. Relatives had come from as far away as Philadelphia and Calgary. She hoped the two from Calgary would leave quickly. Last night, at midnight, the children had driven to the airport to meet them. When she'd heard the car pull into the garage, she had rushed to the door. Then, startled, she had wanted to run upstairs, out of the house — away. She had not been prepared for what she saw.

It had been seven years since Martin and she had flown to Calgary for a week's visit. Those seven years had etched almost identical lines into the identical twins' faces. Marvin remained the mirror image of Martin.

At the doorway, her husband's twin had folded her into his arms. She had looked beyond to his wife. "The sweater girl," Martin had labeled her. Again she had felt pain as she recalled her husband's fascination with breasts. Penny reminded her of an older, worn Sandra Lowrey — that vibrant girl, that child, whose death was surely connected to Martin's death.

Yes, the exposed truth would bring deeper shame. More pain. She must be prepared. In her religion there was a scripture: "The truth shall make you free." After Marvin and his wife left, she would give away her husband's possessions — his suits, his books, his golf clubs. Everything. Then she would begin a new life. Perhaps for a time she would live in India. But never again would she coerce anyone into accepting her beliefs. Conversely, she would learn from the beliefs of others. India! How strange — and intriguing — to picture herself there. It was possible. She was not too old to begin again. After all, wasn't life a series of beginnings?

Late Wednesday afternoon, as a Texas sunset shot streaks of pink through a cloudless sky, a 1970 Ford station wagon, covered with dust, pulled into a parking space in front of the Harris County morgue. A tall strip of man and a short, stout woman got out of the wagon. She pulled at her cotton dress then stuffed a handkerchief into her straw purse. The man buttoned his seersucker suit.

"I guess this is it," he said.

"I reckon it is," she said.

He took her elbow, and they walked up the gray steps into the building.

Inside they were directed to a clerk who sat, with his head bowed, at a metal desk.

They stood before the clerk. The man cleared his throat.

Archie Moore, thinking there were better things to be doing than working on his fortieth birthday, looked up from the desk and frowned.

"Excuse me." The man's manner was apologetic. "But we're from The Good Shepherd Orphanage. I'm the Reverend Harmon Stevens and this is Miss Lela Traylor. We've come for the body of Miss Sandra Lowrey.

Moore glanced from one to the other. "I see." Sensing something more should be said, he added, ". . . I imagine she was a real pretty girl."

"And a good one." Lela Traylor spoke through needle-thin lips.

"Raised right!" The Reverend Stevens intoned as if he were pronouncing a benediction.

"Well . . . she's down that hall." Moore jerked his thumb. He watched until they were out of sight — the man and the woman who had traveled over a hundred miles from east Texas into Houston to take back one of their own.

On Thursday evening Dewitt Dobson stood in the doorway of Zoe Benson's hospital room.

"Mrs. Benson, they've given up the search."

". . . Without finding him."

"The coast guard did everything they could. I'm sorry. And, well, I think you should know, this afternoon Victor Solomon confirmed that his passenger was your husband. When he's able, he'll make a statement and probably —"

"He'll have answers?"

"I would imagine so."

"Then the case will be closed?"

"If the answers are what we're anticipating . . . yes."

She nodded. "But he could still be alive?"

"That would be a miracle."

"And what is your definition of a miracle, Detective Dobson?"

He looked down at the tips of his shoes. "That's a tough question to answer. But I'd say — a miracle would be the impossible happening."

"You're that certain he's dead?"

"Certain enough to term it a miracle if he's alive."

"I see." She looked down at her hands.

"Mrs. Benson, I wish there was something I could do, or at least say."

"No, you've done what you could . . . And thank you."

As he left her room, she turned to stare out the window, the blinds half-closed to the night.

What had he done wrong? He wanted to be with her, but since Tuesday morning she had refused to see him. Her father had suggested that he be patient, that in time she would ask for him. "She wants to be alone until she hears if he's alive or dead," Harrington had said. Well, Zoe had heard. He had just spoken again to her father, who had confirmed what he himself had surmised about three hours ago when the police had discontinued monitoring his calls.

Charles Stanton poured a brandy, then left it untouched. He considered going to the hospital. He looked at his watch. It was past ten. She was probably sleeping. He should have left for England tonight. He should take the first plane out tomorrow. He'd received Whalen's clearance for the trip. The dead — his wife — had to be buried. Perhaps after placing Irene to rest beside their son, he would be granted some semblance of peace. But what of Zoe? Without the finality of burying him herself, would she be able to accept that her husband was dead? His grave unmarked in the Gulf, Lance Benson would never again threaten her or those whom she loved. She must allow herself to believe that.

If only she would reach out to him or let him reach out to her! What was she thinking? Why had she closed herself off from him? He must talk to her — listen to her — touch her. Only then could he leave.

Dobby Dobson carried a beer and a sandwich — bologna and cheese between slices of rye, spread thick with mustard — into his living room. He stretched out on the sofa and ate slowly. He sipped his beer. He had thought little about food during the long day which was only now ending. The house's emptiness was almost a relief. Had Melanie not left him, she would have met him at the door, fixed his sandwich, then sat with him while he ate, but she would also have complained that though he was home his thoughts were someplace else. She would have been right. He felt he was out in the Gulf. It was close to midnight. The water would be dark.

He finished his sandwich. Though bone tired, he was wide awake. He should get up, do something, anything. Pack a bag. Tomorrow he was flying to Mérida. At least he wouldn't be headed into the wilderness. In the late afternoon, Solomon had been helicoptered the twenty-three miles from Progreso to Mérida's more modern hospital.

He remained on the sofa, the empty beer can balanced on his chest. He placed the can on the floor and reached into his pocket for a peppermint. His hunch had been right. Benson had gotten away. But one could hardly call death an escape. At any rate, the books would soon close on Lowrey's and Fletcher's murders. Solomon's statement would do the closing. He was as sure of it as he was of being alone in this house. The statement might even provide answers to why Irene Stanton had killed herself. On that one, however, he wouldn't place bets. Still, the deaths had to be related. Stanton, Hook, Lowrey, Fletcher — four people who had been closely associated with The Arch Theatre, with Lance Benson. All dead. And the bastard had gotten away. But, no, Benson was dead! Why did he have to keep reminding himself of that? Maybe because after he'd left Zoe Benson, staring through her hospital blinds, there had been other news. A briefcase, ripped open and empty, had washed ashore. Perhaps that bit of information was what had him so on edge, his thoughts racing over a worn track. Had the briefcase come from the crashed plane? To whom did it belong? Where was its owner? Had he also been washed ashore? If so, could he have dragged himself deep into the Yucatán? There were villages there. Help there.

He sat up, hunched his shoulders. His imagination was running wild. The real world had no place for such fantasies. He had been truthful when he'd told Zoe Benson that if her husband was alive he would term it a miracle. But Solomon was alive. Wasn't that a miracle? Who was to say that two miracles couldn't happen in the span of a day? In the span of a moment? And who was to say to whom miracles were to be meted out? Hell, he could never put a lock on the case until Lance Benson's body lay, positively identified, in a morgue.

"It's going to rain," Zoe Benson thought. Only when she felt the first drops of water would she go inside. She laid aside her sketchpad and closed her eyes. A slight wind swayed the hammock.

Why couldn't she stay like this forever? The wind and the sounds in her father's garden soothed her. She felt protected. Fears and uncertainties could not find her here. Or could they? The coming rain reminded her of other water. Whether Lance had survived or died, he had gone down in water. That must have been a frightening thing. She mourned for him. She mourned for herself. Not to know. To go on and on being Mrs. Lance Benson. The thought was unbearable. And yet she did not wish him dead. For his sake. Not for hers. Everything was so confused. She had wanted him locked up, away from her. Away from those she loved. She had wanted the quickest divorce possible. She had wanted . . . Charles. How long was it — seven years, was it, before a person could be declared legally dead? Was she to go on being Mrs. Lance Benson for seven years? And then what? Suddenly, legally, was she to become Lance Benson's widow? Was she that now? What was she? She didn't know. She was her father's daughter, that she knew. She was . . . what else? An artist. She was still that. Certainly she was no one's mother. Who was she? Why didn't the rain come?

"It's going to rain."

She avoided his eyes. "That's what I was thinking."

"But maybe not for a while . . . The wind's nice."

"Yes, it's been so hot . . . I thought you had left for England."

"Tomorrow . . . I tried calling you, but it seems somebody took the phone off the hook."

"Ever since the news broke . . . there've been so many calls."

"Well, people — your friends — are concerned."

He sat on the edge of the hammock.

"Charles, both of us may be too much for this."

"Let's chance it."

". . . All right."

"How do you feel?"

"My ears aren't ringing, and my vision is fine, my head is fine. I'm" — she looked away — "not so fine."

"You will be."

"You sound like my father."

"You told me that once before, remember?"

She nodded.

"And you also told me that was a compliment."

"It was."

"So if your ears aren't ringing, and you've done this remarkable sketch —" He held up the pad. "I could walk into the garden on this page — so why aren't you fine?"

"You can ask *that?*"

"Certainly, because you've been through a lot, but the worst is over. Now there's mainly the healing."

"I told you, my head is fine!"

"That's not what we're talking about!"

"I know." She fingered the hammock's fringe. "We're talking about what's inside my head."

"Share that with me."

"You wouldn't understand."

"Then help me, Zoe, to understand."

"It's just — well, for one thing, I don't know who I am."

"Look at me." He took her hands. "Look at me, Zoe."

She raised her eyes.

"You're you. Nothing can change that."

"But it does! If I have to wait seven years —"

"For what?"

"To be free of him."

"What're you talking about?"

"He could be alive."

"He's not!"

"How do you know! And even if he's not, I have to wait seven years for him to be declared legally dead."

"If you're talking about dividing community property, you may be right. But if you're talking about other things — divorce, a new life. Zoe, one does not have to wait seven years for those things."

"Oh."

"For an intelligent woman, you are sadly lacking in legal knowledge." He lifted her chin. "Now, tell me something." He smiled. "Who are you?"

She was silent.

"Tell me."

"Charles . . . you make me feel ridiculous."

"Come on, Zoe, humor me."

"All right! . . . I'm me."

"Yes, you! And if he is alive — which I seriously doubt — he can't hurt you. Not ever again."

"I want to believe that."

"Believe it!"

"I can't!"

"You will."

Her eyes searched his face. She touched the lines about his eyes.

"That's better." He pulled her to him. His chin rested on the top of her head. He stroked her hair. "So why wouldn't you see me?"

"Because I thought I'd be a burden."

"A burden? Zoe, listen to me. We won't forget. Not in seven years, not in twenty. It hasn't been pretty — what's happened in both of our lives. That's the burden. Remembering. Never you."

"Never?"

"Never," he repeated.

He held her face between his hands. She smiled. Slowly, deeply, he kissed her.

He had gone inside to talk with her father, because she had wanted to be alone. "For a little while," she'd said.

She looked at her sketch of the garden; she pushed the ground with the tip of her sandal. The hammock rocked gently. A drop of rain fell on her hand. A cloud moved, thick and heavy, across the sky. The rain would be coming soon. She should hurry now, on into the house. But for a few minutes more, she needed to stay here to say something, to think something. Her lips moved. "Wherever, whatever, Lance." The words had no meaning. She tried again. "If you're still out there, somewhere, alive — change! You can. You didn't leave me to bleed to death. You called the ambulance. But don't ever let me know you're alive. Let's just live separately — peaceably. Maybe we can, I don't know, but maybe we can."

She felt the impossible idealist. But, somehow, looking up into the dark sky, saying those words, made her feel better.

The rain came suddenly. She held her head low and ran. Once, glancing up, she saw that Charles held the door open for her.

✿    PART IV

Hunucmá, Mexico